Who Drew the Short Straw?

Sam Sumac

First published 2024
by Rowanvale Books Ltd
The Gate
Keppoch Street
Roath
Cardiff
CF24 3JW
www.rowanvalebooks.com

A CIP catalogue record for this book is available from the British Library.
ISBN: 978-1-83584-041-2
ePub ISBN: 978-1-83584-042-9

Who Drew the Short Straw?

OR

Phallically Insecure Men Can Be Such Dicks

by

Sam Sumac

This book is dedicated to the memory of Carolus Linnaeus, the father of taxonomy. If it weren't for his discovery of binomial nomenclature, only God knows where we'd be.

"Slavery is also as ancient as war, and war as human nature."
François-Marie Arouet

"What's the name of this?"
"Little Village. A little village, motherfucker, a little village!"
"There isn't a mother fuckin' thing there about a village, you son of a bitch! Nothin' in the song has got anything to do with a village!"
"Well, a small town!"
"I know what a village is!"
"Well all right, goddamn it! You know, you don't need no title! You name it after I get through with it, son-of-a-bitch! You name it what you wanna. You name it your mammy if ya wanna!"
Exchange between Leonard Chess and bluesman Sonny Boy Williamson II during a 1957 outtake of a recording session of the song "Little Village."

"If we do not know the names of things, the knowledge of them is lost, too."
Carolus Linnaeus

A Note from the Sam Sumac Association

We are extremely excited to have this complete transcription of Sam Sumac's novel *Who Drew the Short Straw?* ready for publication. Although the story is clearly written in the usual/ unusual style of Sam Sumac, there are many features of it which have us entirely captivated. As a staffer recently described it, "This book is like watching Erich Brenn spin plates and bowls on *The Ed Sullivan Show.*"

Now, even we had to look this reference up, but the description is more than apt. Certainly Sam Sumac is spinning multiple pieces of crockery at the same time in this one.

We continue – on a daily basis – to learn things about Sam Sumac. Many times, admittedly, we generate more questions about him than we discover answers, but that is the nature of this author and his works. One thing we can say with some authority: Sam Sumac was someone who was prone to preoccupations. Whether it was idioms, blues music, names, politicians, the apocalypse, aliens, or the Kennedys, his stories are rife with details that don't always make sense but were clearly very important to him.

Some might say these were his obsessions, but we reject the negative connotation of this term and use "preoccupations"

instead. Just one look at his quotation page for this novel –
an extremely important piece of the puzzle that is this book
– and it is clear what was preoccupying the author when he
wrote this tale.

Human history is chock-full of both the importance and
the dangers of naming things, but to Sam Sumac, this concept appears to have been paramount to him for grasping
the direction of the journey our species has been on since
its inception. We'll never know if he ever used the expression
"calling a fig a fig and a trough a trough," but we have to assume that he did...and that he would of added the scientific
name of a fig (*Ficus carica*) when he did.

Enjoy!

That's a Recipe for Disaster, Julia Childs!

Needless to say, the middle-aged Midwesterner who'd become convinced that his wiener was not of adequate size did not singularly cause the enslavement of the human species.

Rather, like a strand of hemp (*Cannabis sativa*), this man's story is twisted and woven together with those of a rather eclectic mix of personalities – a trio of feuding psychic mediums, a rogue billionaire who dreamed of owning everything in sight, an Indiana town desperate to become relevant again, one alien species who'd grown too complacent and unemotional, another alien species who was too power-hungry and angry, and yet another alien species who had a secret plan – to form a stout hawser that tethered humanity to what some would say was its predestined fate.

That being said, there really isn't an entirely good-hearted main hero or a wholly evil villain in any of this. The events leading up to the rather apocalyptic outcome here are actually the result of a collective effort by a host of highly flawed individuals – earthly, spiritual, and alien – who, perhaps all exhibiting a healthy portion of burgoo stew of those villainous and heroic qualities of their true inner natures, either allowed themselves to be manipulated or sought to be the big puppet-master in the sky and do the manipulating. Yet it would be plainly unfair to attempt to label any of us with a single moniker of good or bad, since we all seem to reside in the outlier circle of some perverse, fucked-up Venn diagram that makes up this story.

No one could have foreseen this all happening the way it did.

Well, that's not true. There were at least three of us who believed that we had the ability to know how things were going to turn out. I cannot speak for the other two individuals at this particular moment, but I'd imagine that they're each as completely flummoxed, humbled, and embarrassed as I in regards to our utter and epic failure in this whole matter. Even though we thought that we could view and predict the potential events of the future enough to know what was going to happen here in the present, we were fooling ourselves. In the end, we found out right quick that we really couldn't see jack shit.

But how could *anyone* have predicted all of this happening, really? Sure, perhaps some of us should've been able to perceive that the malaise of a middle-aged man from Indiana might become a kind of spiritual lightning rod that attracted the psychic energy of the age-old cycle that my colleagues and I were in the midst of undertaking. But since the three of us were blinded by the personal conflict we were engaged in, we were unable to recognize the fact that we might become the vehicle that carried this world to the present catastrophic situation. As always, life remains a perpetual act of too little, too late.

To put it another way, when Morton Richardson, the fifty-something-year-old insurance president from Vincennes,

Indiana, began to feel inadequate in the penile department, the ugliness of his discontent was just like a drop of blood that falls into the ocean and attracts sharks from miles away. His psychic-emotional angst – obviously the result of a midlife crisis of some sort – was dispersed out into the ether, and this attracted any predators circling around in the mystical Fourth Dimension to come near. Meanwhile, far away in the outer reaches of the Universe, this activity alerted an alien species that the time had come to enact their plan. Sadly, the resulting Rube Goldberg machine caused the downfall of the human species.

As one unusual alien said to me just before imprisoning me, "The bottom line is this, earthling: you simpletons lost sight of everything while you willingly and enthusiastically handed control over to your over-inflated egos. Then, you inserted a gigantic stick of TNT up your anuses, let its fuse be lit by powerful influences from outside your own galaxy, and everything ended up blowing up in your faces."

While I can forgive the creature for mixing up his metaphors – making a reference to assholes and faces in the same cautionary oration – it's as clear as day that my psychic sisters and I were way out of our league. We were playing a game on a three-dimensional chessboard which we thought we understood, but truthfully, we didn't have the faintest clue as to what we were doing. Not all the blame is ours, but some most definitely is. As psychic mediums, we'd been around long enough to know better. We'd already witnessed so much of the muckraking, shit-slinging, and murderous qualities of human history on this planet over the centuries that we really should have seen the writing on the wall. But we didn't.

The alien *was* certainly correct in his assessment that this whole ordeal could have been prevented. At every single step of the way, throughout its twisted and asinine progression, someone – anyone – could have pumped the brakes and put an end to this whole awful shindig. I know that I look back with 20/20 hindsight and see more instances than I care to count when I, myself, could have come to my senses and averted the disaster at the end. I have no excuse for why I didn't. Perhaps it was the thrill of the chase that blinded me or, as the alien pointed out, maybe my over-inflated ego got the best of me. Whatever justifications or rationalizations I throw out there, the fact is that I did nothing but help guide the residents of this planet down into the proverbial meat grinder.

I guess it's time for me to introduce myself. My birth name is Morgen an Spyrys. I was born during what the Earth historians describe as the Bronze Age. Through means that will be explained in depth during the rendering of this tale, I've been involved in a ridiculous strife-filled game with two other prophetesses, Pythia and Haggur, which has spanned the globe and the centuries. Before my aforementioned imprisonment by the alien, I thought that our little triad of participants was the only troupe of actors on the stage. However, now that I can see *everything* – on this planet and in the far reaches of the Universe – I understand that we were actually the pawns in a game being played by someone other than us.

Before I start telling you the whole story, let me add that I transferred my soul into the body of a young American man by the name of Harvey Ferguson on St. Brigid's Day in London, England. I'd done my research about Mr. Ferguson and I knew that he was the assistant to the richest and most power-ful man on the planet, and that made him the perfect target. He was in town to negotiate for his boss to buy Stonehenge, and I snuck up on him at Julius Caesar Taylor's molly-house and incapacitated him with a squash racket before taking over full control of his body. Using him, I was then able to get next to Buchanan Sanderborn, not only a billionaire with an obsession about owning Stonehenge and the monument's related artifacts, but a man who had so much money that the owners of the golden dagger I was desperately seeking could name their price.

The following tale, including its disastrous ending, is a tapestry I made up from bits of fabric from the past, the present, and the future, not to mention from here on Earth and from out there in the limitlessness of space. I think, in the end, it creates an image about the universality of the worst qualities that sentient beings seem to possess. That there is an endless repetition to the acts of stupidity in the panels is just a testament to life's proclivity for the inane throughout the galaxies.

Once upon a time...

Spill the Beans, Jack Spriggins!

Morton Richardson, the fifty-seven-year-old president of the Wheatfield Insurance Company, slowly made his way back to the darkened den of the Dennison household during the waning moments of the latest social mixer of the Vincennes business community. As he navigated through the hanging curtains of the party decorations of comic memorabilia, which were to inspire humor and make everyone laugh during this celebration of the sixty-sixth birthday of Vincennes' own native son, Red Skelton, he found a certain level of comfort in the irony that he was experiencing firsthand.

After all, his current mission was to amble casually past all this hilarity to get close enough to hear his wife Eve's confession, which would break his heart and make him cry. The acceptance of this somewhat cruel juxtaposition did not bring much brevity to his gait. Instead he looked more like he was laboring to walk with weighted deep-sea-diver boots on his feet.

As highly respected members of the "First City in Indiana" community, Morton and Eve knew exactly what to expect from these overly frequent gatherings. Everything that happened at these events was scripted, and the end result was always the same. It was a night to see and be seen, and although the Richardsons dreamed of somehow being able to avoid these parties altogether, they both accepted they had a specific role to play – even if those roles were quite different for each of them.

From the moment he stepped inside the suburban home that hosted the party, Morton understood that he was going to be beset by people seeking his opinion, trying to sell him something, or asking him for a favor. He had to endure the schmoozing, the thinly-veiled lobbying, and even the overt begging, all as if he enjoyed it. He was supposed to mingle with all the guests, shake hands and reconnect with the other business owners, and lend himself to anyone who needed to catch his ear, all the while smiling, nodding, and dispensing rationed optimistic responses to everything thrown at him, no matter how inane it all sounded.

One other thing that Morton had started noticing about these get-togethers was the fact that no one had anything new to say. Because their little world of Vincennes was so self-contained and self-centered, the usual bitching and complaining about one another or about the issues of their small city took the place of any meaningful dialogue. Even those people who had been lucky enough to travel to the big urban centers of Chicago or Indianapolis recently really had nothing new to share. They resorted to retelling the same stories about life in the outside world. They either went on and on about the unlimited opportunities and superiorities of those far-off places or they bemoaned how much more crime and filth there was there than in their beloved Vincennes.

Morton wasn't even sure what constituted juicy fresh topics to talk about anymore, but he found himself starving for some kind of intellectual stimulation as he watched the people he was conversing with move their lips like the mouths of goldfish (*Carassius auratus)* in an aquarium. His only defense was to sink deep within himself and try to ride out these ridiculous nights of banality.

Eve, on the other hand, had developed her own strategy for surviving these all-too-predictable soirees. Her role was to show up with her husband, be instantly judged upon her appearance and how happy she and her husband seemed as a couple, and then be virtually ignored the rest of the night. So, once the usual throng of supplicants had gathered around her husband to get his attention, she quietly slipped away unannounced to find the other bored wives – her co-conspirators – and head to a quiet corner of the house to blatantly gossip while they drank, safely away from the main arena of the mutual male economic masturbation that was going on in the rest of the house.

As soon as the party seemed to be starting to run out of gas, Eve and her cohorts started playing what amounted to an adult version of Truth or Dare. In the darkened confines of their relatively secluded setting they'd let their alcohol-loosened tongues wag and tell all, talking about taboo topics that none of them would ever address when they were sober and the lights were on. Some of the most shocking, most intimate secrets of the social circle were shared openly in these moments, and only the retrieval by their spouses at the end of the night stopped their continuing exchange of this confidential information.

Morton had discovered these secret tell-alls by accident one night at a gathering celebrating the Battle of Tippecanoe. As he was about to call back to Eve in her secluded back room with her cronies to tell her it was time for them to leave, he'd overheard her tell a snippet of one lurid detail about herself. He'd frozen in place and listened intently to what was being said. His curiosity had been too piqued to stop himself, and he'd stood there, soaking it all in.

Before he could be discovered eavesdropping so blatantly, he had eventually called out to her and pretended that he'd just arrived. But he made a conscious decision to repeat the same maneuver at each following gathering in the future so he could hear more.

Morton was not proud of his behavior during the following months, but he had, indeed, followed through with his plan to listen in to his wife's admissions at the end of each of these Vincennes social gatherings. To make matters worse, like some kind of drug addict, each time he'd undertaken one of these embarrassing spying missions and heard a valuable tidbit from his wife, it only increased his interest in doing it all over again. Unfortunately for Morton, he'd begun to discern a distinct pattern to Eve's confessions, and he developed a hunger to hear the next clue she would disclose. And while each one of these pieces of a rather depressing puzzle was a continued source of sadness for him, the completion of the whole picture became so important to him that he was willing to endure any kind of emotional crash that came afterwards.

At this particular Red Skelton birthday gathering at the Dennisons, Morton had watched calmly as Eve departed from his side and ventured into the shadows of the group, but he'd kept her in his line of sight. Like some kind of a self-adjusting SATCOM system, his body had unconsciously turned and pivoted to keep a visual on his wife. By this time he'd become highly skilled in continuing his cocktail conversations while, at the same time, adeptly monitoring her movements as well. He was well aware that his behavior might appear overtly controlling, or even creepy, but he'd become so dependent upon arriving at the secret gathering in the den at the precise time for the final big reveal, he really couldn't help himself.

As the first wave of partygoers began to leave and the others seemed to realize that their evening was ending, Morton proceeded in the direction of the women's clandestine gathering in the den. He'd worked his way through the thinning party crowd, hopping from one conversational lily pad (*Nymphaea odorata*) to the next like a crawfish frog (*Rana areolata*), to get to the doorway of the room in question. Here he hovered, just out of sight, but within earshot of the naughtiness originating from within. This part of the routine of Morton and Eve's party attendance had become as highly choreographed and practiced a performance as Arseny Mikhaylovich Avraamov's *Symphony of Factory Sirens*.

As he took up his position and started listening, the hushed tones of the darkened room were shattered by Nancy Tannenbaum's raucous laughter that was more akin to the barking of a sea lion (*Zalophus californianus*) at a marine show. These abrasive guffaws crashed the serenity of the others' conspiratorial whispers in the small space enough to make Morton flinch in discomfort. This burst of gruff mirth was followed up by her gravelly voice talking far too loudly.

"Oh, my goodness, there's just no way, Sarah – no way! You'd never let Terence have sex with you in the no-no hole! I'm terribly sorry, old girl, but I know you're making all of this stuff up now."

The rebukes and shushes which responded were like the gusts of wind during a winter blizzard, and Morton had to lean in a little more to hear what followed. Having been properly chastised, Nancy Tannenbaum remained silent for a moment or two, but when she resumed her pointed verbal assault once more in an inept attempt at talking quietly, she sounded more like a razor being drawn down a leather strop.

"Aw, come on now! Let's cut the BS tonight, ladies, shall we? We all know that you're out-and-out lying, Sarah. Most definitely, without a doubt. No one here would *ever* admit to ever having had sex down there...back there...right?"

It was obvious from the throat clearing and the sound of tired and melted ice cubes rattling down the inside of empty highball glasses toward their pursed lips that there was an unspoken admission that the disagreeable woman's comment and question had brought them to the very edge of their inebriated zone of safety. Admitting to having had public sex in their car in the parking lot of the A & P, or of doing it, ever, twice in one night, or fantasizing about a torrid affair with Phil Donahue, those were all appropriate things to voice in a public situation such as this. Admitting to engaging in anal intercourse was most certainly not.

Morton then heard his own Eve's voice cut through the greasy silence with her calm confidence.

"One of my ex-boyfriends, Carlos Adams, wanted to do me down there, but he was *so* big, I was worried that he'd rip me wide open."

To Morton Richardson the following cacophony of titters and snickers and muted cackles from the other women in the den sounded like threatening hailstones hitting the windshield. He looked straight up at the white ceiling as if he could see through all the wood, plaster, roofing tiles, and clouds and spy the moon shining up there in the Indiana nighttime sky, and he clenched his jaws tightly together. While his wife's overly honest disclosure had blown up the logjam that Nancy Tannenbaum had created with her insensitive challenge to the group – which was now resuming its usual track of talking about the sexual happiness they all were experiencing these days with their current spouses and the benign acts of spontaneity they all supposedly engaged in during their normal copulatory moments – Eve's announcement had hurt Morton more than he could currently acknowledge.

In fact, he now resembled a patient who'd just received a dire cancer diagnosis. He was somewhat grateful to receive the truth, but he was also utterly devastated by the starkness of the prognosis.

He stood there in the hallway like a boxer who had just been hurt and dazed, and he struggled to figure out what to do next. He had no other recourse than to call out his wife's name and declare that he was ready to leave. His announcement silenced the group and then caused them to offer the usual salutations and send-offs to Eve, who came out of the den with a quickened step towards her husband.

On their drive home, Eve Richardson could sense that her husband was being unusually quiet, as if he were suddenly burdened by a great weight upon his shoulders which was crushing the air out of his lungs. She was well aware of how much of a toll these stupid social gatherings took on him, but tonight Morton seemed more troubled than usual. He needed to focus on driving safely because of a recently developing struggle with diminishing night vision, but Eve could tell that his demeanor was due to something more than his growing frustration over that.

She chose to wrongly assume that someone at the party – other than herself – had caused him some distress, and she sought to help him shed some of his discontent with a jolt of humor.

"Whoof, did you see Mayor Gandy? Boy, he really needs to let go of some weight, don't you think? They're gonna have to start rolling that man into rooms like a tractor tire soon."

Morton chuckled at his wife's comment. She wasn't wrong. The mayor looked more and more like a walking, talking globe, and it was getting harder to take the man seriously. When he'd first run for the mayoral office, he'd been one of the most hardworking and successful corn farmers in the entire Wabash Valley, and he had been a large but fit man. The years of sitting behind a desk and his pursuit of a hedonistic political lifestyle during his long, unchallenged tenure as city mayor had led him down a more unhealthy and potentially gluttonous path, one which had resulted in an ever-expanding girth. No longer resembling his younger self in any way, shape, or form, the very public and noticeable downfall of Mayor Gandy was yet another indication that Vincennes was slipping further and further into the abyss of irrelevance. The demise of his once proud community was already a growing belief of Morton Richardson's, and it greatly depressed him further.

Although Eve's question in the front seat had just provided him a needed reprieve from the mental tempest that had resulted from his overhearing another one of his wife's hurtful reveals, this moment was short-lived and fleeting. In the silence that followed, he began to dwell once again on the implications of the latest detail she'd chosen to share with her secret group. This particular one had been like a capstone, cementing the whole unpleasant picture together in a shatterproof image for him, and it wasn't a pretty picture to look at, that's for sure. Spousal honesty was not at issue here. Morton and Eve had been entirely transparent with each other in regards to their former lovers. They both knew all the names of each other's exes, the intimate details about their failed prior relationships, and even the sadness resulting from the breakups. There was a strong belief that honesty was the best policy in regards to their lives before getting married to one another. Because of this, there was little to no information withheld, nor any jealousy in regards to this whole matter. So Eve's sharing to the group about her former partners was not the most hurtful aspect to Morton.

No, his pain was self-inflicted.

He'd been helpless to stop himself from becoming like some kind of card shark counting cards at these social gatherings as he tallied each of Eve's secret disclosures about an ex-boyfriend and about the man's big dick. He hated himself, but he was putting each one into some kind of a mental Rolodex that he was compiling in his case against this growing group of over-endowed wrongdoers who threatened him. With this final addition of Carlos Adams, the entire roster of his wife's prior sexual partners had been publicly described at these cocktail parties as having a larger than normal penis. To add salt to the wound, Morton's name was never mentioned in these conversations...not once. He was no longer able to avoid drawing a most painful conclusion. His wife thought he had a small penis.

He certainly couldn't ask her about any of this. He'd been snooping around private conversations and he'd unscrupulously heard things she obviously had never intended to tell him, so there was no way to casually bring this up with her that didn't itself indict him. Plus, he'd already been dealing with feelings of inadequacy from his aging process of late, so the perceived allegations of his lacking manhood fit too well into the narrative he was constructing for himself. None of this, of course, could be shared with his wife. So, unable to address the pain of her references to her ex-lovers, and what they meant to him, he decided to vent his feelings in another way.

"Do you think that I'm a failure, Eve?"

Eve Richardson gasped audibly. Her husband's question was shocking. He was the president of the Wheatfield Insurance Company, one of the soundest companies in the entire Vincennes area, and he usually carried around an innate sense of self-confidence that exuded as warmly from him as a heat lamp. While he was too nice a person to be described as an "alpha male," he was one of the top dogs (*Canis lupus familiaris*) in the insular business world of Vincennes, Indiana. He didn't express this status with the usual arrogance of other businessmen; he just walked around with a pretty rock-solid aplomb that those near him found comforting. Asking if she thought that he was a failure was...well, in her mind it was almost unthinkable for him to do.

"Good god, Morton, why would you ask such a *ridiculous* question?"

"Well, I've been feeling like I'm missing the mark these days."

"That's absolutely preposterous! You're a pillar of the community. Think about it. You are liked by most, envied by many, and deeply respected by all around you. That's the best any businessman can wish for living in a small town like Vincennes. And Morton, you have a devoted wife and children who cherish you. No signs point to anything but an amazing, incredible success, if you ask me."

"I just don't feel like I measure up anymore."

Being completely ignorant that her husband had been either hearing her party divulgences or tallying them into evidence against himself, Eve did not know that this was about as close as Morton was going to get to the real issue. If she had known any of this, she could have soothed his hurt feelings at this point and averted the future disaster. Instead, she just chocked it up to his struggles with getting older, a more frequent source of some of his irrational rantings recently. She shook her head fiercely and placed her hand gently on her husband's knee.

"Oh, Morton, you're an ethical, yet motivated business leader, an eminent fixture of the community, a faithful and caring husband, a sweet and loving father, a consistent church-goer, a true dyed-in-the-wool, red, white, and blue American. There are not many who can measure up to *you*."

"Do you love me, Eve?"

"Oh, how can you ask that, Morton Richardson? I love you so, so much."

"But are you happy...with me?"

Still unaware that they were having an invisible conversation about a penis comparison between her husband and her ex-lovers, Eve had been put, unwittingly, into an unwinnable position by this last question. If she answered too quickly, her husband was going to take this as an insincere response. But if she hesitated in the least, that would be an indication that she had to think about it too much, and that would have much greater implications.

Truthfully, Eve Richardson was distracted at the moment. The absurd social gatherings were atrocious overall, but her secret chit-chats in the darkened dens with her cohorts were so full of unbridled steamy and sexy topics, and the alcohol flowed so freely, they just got her juices flowing. Her mind had already been flashing with the images and dirty thoughts about what she wanted to do with her husband once they got home. For this reason, and this reason alone, she hesitated just a little too long.

"Of course, darling."

This should have been the end of it, but it wasn't. Eve's soothing words came just a nanosecond too late for them to be the balm needed on Morton's penile wounds, and he was sent tumbling downhill in the start of an emotional avalanche that was to jumpstart this whole destructive tale.

That's Quite an Erection You've Got There, Nimrod!

Safely ensconced in his private office in the basement of his lavish new NYC skyscraper, billionaire Buchanan Sanderborn sighed melodiously as he looked at his recently purchased framed watercolor, *Stonehenge* by Joseph Mallord William Turner. He'd secretly negotiated the piece away from an English museum for an absolutely insane amount of money. The eccentric and unfathomably wealthy man had been able to get his hands on the one painting he wanted *and* the Wiltshire cultural institution had gained an absurd financial infusion that would fuel its survival for generations.

To save face, the museum had claimed that the infamous and iconic British cultural piece of heritage had been stolen during a daring break-in by some overly brave thieves. This, of course, had been staged for insurance purposes, which were likely to result in further financial gain. So, for all involved, except the British people, perhaps, it was a real win-win situation.

Sanderborn always got emotional whenever he looked at this particular painting. The artist had captured the mystical powers of the mysterious place by using a series of earth tones and some flashes of stark blue to create a visual looking glass. He could not stop staring at the painting. The symbolism of the flock of sheep milling around the ancient stones – some of which were on the ground, either sleeping or dead...it was hard to tell – was an irrefutable truth that Turner seemed to be forcing upon the viewer. This was only amplified by the skillfully painted tumultuous sky of sandstorm-like clouds and the speck of blue on the sleeping shepherd – or was he dead, too? It *really* was hard to discern.

Truthfully, Buchanan Sanderborn felt too connected to the image to worry about what was actually happening in it. As soon as he'd seen the painting, he'd desired it so much that he was willing to consider illegal means of getting it. Now it was here, hanging in his office, and he had to admit that he felt a tad more complete with it so close to him.

The intercom on his desk suddenly came to life. "Excuse me, Mr. Sanderborn, but I need to speak with you. May I please enter?"

The voice belonged to none other than his assistant, Harvey Ferguson. This young man wore many hats within the Sanderborn Corporation, but the title of personal *consigliere* to the head honcho was probably the most accurate way to describe his role. As the billionaire's number two, he was allowed to be closer to the man than any other human being. Harvey worked hard to make his boss comfortable, confident, and happy. He listened to him and advised him in subtle ways, but mostly he did whatever was asked of him. Although his sexual preference was nothing the two ever talked about, Harvey understood that he was to act like the eunuch, the gelding, the oxen in the office – at least in a professional sense. He was the one person who was supposed to be free enough of ambition or self-drive to be a non-threatening presence for his all-powerful employer, and he relished the chance to perfect this role.

"Of course, Harvey. If you don't mind, could you please rustle up two cups of Earl Grey tea for us to enjoy during your morning briefing?"

"I have them in my hand, sir."

Buchanan Sanderborn spun in his rare presidential Matteo Grassi office armchair designed by Tito Agnoli and he looked at the windowless walls of his office, each adorned with a priceless piece of art. He crossed his arms contentedly behind his head, leaned back in the chair and beamed a big smile...to no one. This world that Buchanan Sanderborn had created for himself was damn near to perfection!

Although there were throngs of detractors who did not understand his desire to put his executive office in the basement of his new building, Sanderborn himself knew why he did, and that's all that mattered. Unlike most captains of industry, who wanted to overlook all that they possessed, he longed for a secure space that no one would want to visit. Instead of an aerie of a peregrine falcon (*Falco peregrinus*), the man sought the subterranean sett of an American badger (*Taxidea taxus*). He felt safer that way.

If he was being honest with himself, Sanderborn would have to admit that he'd always accomplished most of the more impressive aspects of his career whenever he was less visible, hidden as it were, and almost unnoticed. By being active in the background – and out of sight, out of mind – he had been like a Torreya trap-door spider (*Cyclocosmia torreya*) ready to jump out and pounce when most people had least expected him to do so. He had the same hopes for his office in the bowels of the engineering marvel that was his newest building, which, according to most, was his *magnum opus*.

The Edificio de Erik Weisz *was* unique – as in, it was something that had never been attempted before, and it was likely never to be duplicated again...ever. The Spanish language-inspired title that used Harry Houdini's birth name was only the first unusual feature that the building presented to the world. Buchanan Sanderborn had set out to design and construct the very first, what he had coined "peek-a-boo structure." So he found the christening with the name of perhaps the greatest escape artist to be extremely appropriate – actually, this silly inside joke still made him laugh aloud whenever he thought about it. If there was anyone who could disappear and then make a splashy entrance, it was definitely Harry Houdini, *nee* Erik Weisz.

For most of the world, this whole endeavor had started off seeming quite normal. All the usual city officials, inspectors, and zoning board members involved in the planning, permitting, and licensing of the new building in Manhattan were all well-compensated. With their hands out, their palms ready to be greased, they had all been, at first, quite happy to accept Sanderborn's more-than-generous initial payouts. Then, in further quiet acts of backroom lubrications, larger and larger economic incentives were dispensed, with the obvious caveat that everyone who received one was supposed to turn a complete blind eye toward the project. With their pockets literally bulging, NYC officials were content to do just that. However, over time the complete secrecy that Sanderborn himself demanded soon began to trouble even them.

To the casual observer, nothing was occurring to indicate that a skyscraper was being built on the piece of prime

Manhattan real estate that Sanderborn had purchased. The entire acreage of the site was fenced off, per usual, but other than a startlingly magnificent golden pyramid having been erected to cover the entire site, nothing else seemed to be taking place. Yet, day after day, vast armies of workers went in and out at all hours, endless fleets of dump trucks entered empty and returned to the streets full of rocks and debris, fully loaded semis drove into the pyramid and exited empty, and there was a continuous cacophony of sounds typical to the raising of a skyscraper heard morning, noon, and night. However, other than the presence of the golden pyramid, nothing at all seemed to change.

As the years passed without any seeming progress, the trite New York City business world buzzed with the belief that the Sanderborn Corporation had bitten off more than it could chew. Some started the rumor that the company must be swimming in too much debt to actually start construction. There was a consensus that the entire project was soon going to get foreclosed upon, and many a developer rubbed their hands together and drooled a little over the chance to swoop in and get a prime Manhattan site for next to nothing. There was also a silent reveling that this demigod of industry, Buchanan Sanderborn, was finally going to get the comeuppance that they'd all been praying for all these years.

It goes without saying, these bloodthirsty critics and rivals could not have been more wrong...about everything.

With the sudden announcement that the Edificio de Erik Weisz was completed, there was a lot of head-scratching. There was still no building standing on the site, just the typical post-no-bills green construction fencing around the same old golden pyramid. Yet, a highly marketed announcement indicated that there was to be some kind of opening of a new building. The entire business community of Manhattan couldn't help but become abuzz with confused excitement, and the streets around the construction site suddenly teemed with seas of onlookers who jostled and pushed to be the first to see what was going to happen next.

On the day of the building's unveiling, the fencing was taken down and the gleaming golden pyramid shone in the springtime sun like a tribute to mammon. There was no noise from the massive crowd gathered there, rather just a stunned silence. This was finally followed by a quiet chorus of titters and snickers, which was probably similar to the initial response from when the sheet fell off of the painting *Crossing the Line* by American painter Barnett Newman when he unveiled his blue work for the first time. There were a lot of people who could be heard saying, "Um...is that it?"

Then the most miraculous thing happened. The building slowly began to lift up out of the ground...revealing another story! Then another. To say that this awed everyone in attendance would be a gross understatement. Some would later say that it was akin to watching the head of a giant and dangerous serpent come emerging out of a hole in the ground. And, like a bunch of those natives in old Tarzan movies, more than a few of the onlookers that day were so spooked they took off running in fright down the sidewalks, screaming and yelling out nothing but unintelligible gibberish.

Turns out, the entire Edificio de Erik Weisz had been constructed underground. The structure had been complete, but wholly unseen. Not only that, the massive building could be raised or lowered, as need be. Miraculously, Sanderborn's engineers had managed to design an immensely powerful hydraulic system capable of slowly elevating or lowering the half-a-billion-ton building by using an intricate cog system with massive locking pins to securely keep the building in a desired position. Such an engineering marvel had never been attempted, nor successfully completed.

It soon became clear that absolutely no expense had been spared during the building's construction. Estimates of the final project costs usually were so high that they were more than the combined military budgets of the southeastern countries of Laos, Cambodia, and Burma. But none of that mattered now that the world was aware of the building's unique construction. Simultaneously, around the globe, the collective mouths of architects, engineers, and city planners opened, and stayed open, in pure shock.

That's not to say the structure didn't have some immediate and challenging qualities to it. Since no one knew for sure how tall it was – and Sanderborn wasn't telling anyone – the final location of any office space rented from the Sanderborn Corporation in the new building was a crap-shoot. One day, such a location might be on the ground floor, but the next day the edifice might get raised up and that same office now was on the tenth floor. Since each story had on it a front door and a lobby containing elevators and stairs, people were able to enter and travel up or down to the other visible floors, no matter how much of the building was "up" at the moment. However, the prospective tenants had to be aware and comfortable with the fact that their space's elevation was likely to change, and this would have untold implications in many of their undertakings. That being said, there was a huge initial rush to get any rentable spaces – which cost an ungodly amount of money – because, no matter what, everyone wanted to be inside the most incredible structure in the world.

Some other quirks of the trendsetting skyscraper were harder to live with. The elevator button panels had no floor numbers on it, since such information would be misleading and cause a sense of confusion whenever the building was raised or lowered. So, instead of numbers, tiny screens with the individual company names were situated next to the seemingly endless rows of elevator buttons, and the print of these was so small that most passengers needed a hand-held magnifying glass to read them. Also, to keep random people from wandering onto the empty floors underground and risk stumbling upon Buchanan Sanderborn's private office in the basement, the elevator did not allow riders to travel to any floors currently underground without a special clearance code, and no one but Harvey Ferguson was given that outright. The rest had to go through an extensive application and screening process, and most were turned away.

Not all were fans. The city government of New York City, for instance, struggled with how they could assess the property value of the corresponding structure when most of it could be hidden underground. A five story building, a ten story building, and a hundred story building all have different taxable brackets, yet the Edificio de Erik Weisz could be all of those heights, more or less. City officials took Buchanan Sanderborn to court to demand to know exactly how many stories comprised his revolutionary building, but the judge in the case agreed that any potential space that did not affect the infrastructure of the city, nor its skyline, was not essentially public information. Plus, Sanderborn's attorneys invoked the tricky national security element, implying that the building could serve as some sort of refuge or bunker if NYC was ever attacked, and they won all challenges with this slippery interpretation of such law.

Again, Buchanan Sanderborn was unconcerned with any of this. Good or bad press really did not matter to him. He now had an automated living space, a personal gym, and a library built around his office, and he lived and worked in the peacefulness and security of this underground lair. Plainly put, he was as happy as a member of the class *Insecta* in a rug. Sun lamps provided him the necessary amount of sunlight, and he rarely left the confines of his protective spaces unless it was entirely necessary. Other than a few trusted secretaries, only Harvey Ferguson was given daily access to the man.

Sanderborn smiled now as he heard his assistant ring the bell to enter his office.

"Ah, Harvey. Come in, come in."

"Here you are, sir. Your tea is just as you like it."

"Oh good. I'm sure it will be perfect. Well, well, what's on the agenda for today?"

"Uh, I have the Prime Minister of Great Britain on the line, like you requested, sir."

"That's most excellent. I'll talk to ol' Maggie after I finish my tea. It will be good to finally get some answers, huh?"

Harvey fidgeted noticeably with the placement of his tea cup on Buchanan Sanderborn's vast wooden desk. As he did this, he looked just like a black-capped chickadee (*Poecile atricapillus*) fluffing itself up against the chill.

"Well, sir, she's been on the line for quite some time. It might be important to converse with her first. I mean, she might be a bit bothered for being on hold as long as she's been."

Sanderborn looked gratefully upon his right-hand man and nodded his consent about this matter. He was always so impressed at how the young man was more adept at dealing with the likes of politicians and world leaders than he was.

"Quite right. Okay, here we go."

He pushed one of the clear plastic buttons on the red phone on his desk and began talking without any introduction or explanation or apology. "So, Maggie, have you had any time to consider my offer?"

There was an audible inhalation similar to the breath that a snake in the *Pituophis* genus – especially the northern pine snake (*Pituophis melanoleucus*) – might make when it forces air over the small flap of cartilage in its windpipe to create its characteristically deafening hiss. The veteran politician British Prime Minister had not, in fact, issued a serpentine sound, but rather a polite – if not stilted – breath before responding to the question.

"I most certainly have, Mr. Sanderborn. I am sad to say that my final answer to your inquiry is the same as the one I initially expressed to you in the strongest of terms during the original issuance of the question. No, you may not buy Stonehenge."

"And why not?"

Flustered by his insistence, she answered tersely. "As I stated before, Mr. Sanderborn, Stonehenge is a cultural landmark of the British people, not some kind of a commodity bought and sold to the highest bidder."

"McCulloch bought the London Bridge."

Another strong inhalation, another stifled reptilian hiss.

"Yes, he did, Mr. Sanderborn. But that was a different situation...entirely."

"He wrote you a check for about two and a half million dollars. I know, because I helped finance him, Maggie. I don't see how there's any difference between that transaction and the one I am proposing."

"Mr. McCulloch came along when an out-of-date bridge across the Thames was being considered for replacement. He bought something that was going to be torn down anyways, and then he rebuilt it in the state of Arizona at one of his developments. That hardly compares to the buying, digging up, and transporting of the ancient and irreplaceable legendary stone circle from British soil to have it be reassembled in America. The London Bridge was a historic relic that found a new home. What you are proposing is buying a piece – an integral piece, actually – of English heritage, Mr. Sanderborn. And that is not something I am ever going to let happen."

Sanderborn looked over at his Turner painting and sighed.

"I'll double my original offer, Maggie."

"Oh my giddy aunt, Mr. Sanderborn. It doesn't make any difference how much cash you throw at me. I cannot, and will not, even begin to bargain for this priceless piece of human history. It is not for sale...now or ever. Why do you Americans always think that money can buy anything?"

"Perhaps we should ask the British people, Maggie. After all, with much of your economy in the tank these days, don't you think they'd celebrate you as an economic hero to be able to give them some financial relief? I'd say that they would thank you from the bottom of their collective hearts, quite honestly, for giving them a piece of the chunk o' change I'm offering for Stonehenge. I mean, how many of them even go out to see the place anymore? Most would be a helluva lot more appreciative of an influx of some much-needed economic relief, don't you think?"

"No, Mr. Sanderborn, I don't think that...not at all! Now, you have kept me from my duties for long enough today. Thank you for your kind offer, but good day, sir."

The click and the resulting static on the line was the definitive end of the conversation. Harvey looked over at Sanderborn with a worried expression on his face. His boss was never turned down, and he wasn't sure what the man's reaction to this rejection was going to be.

"Ah, Harvey, I think she's wavering a bit there."

"Really, sir?"

"Oh, of course. I definitively heard some hesitation in her voice. Truthfully, I think a couple more phone calls and she'll cave. I'm pretty sure that we can start planning on where to put it. I mean, we own plenty of properties in all fifty states to put the monument in, so we might be spoilt for choice."

Harvey Ferguson found himself in the unenviable place of disagreeing with one of the richest and most powerful men on the Earth, and he grimaced and cleared his throat – the specific tell he'd unconsciously developed for whenever he had to utter something potentially unpopular and even dissenting to his boss.

"I think you need to enact my Plan B, sir."

Sanderborn looked over at his assistant and furrowed his brows. There wasn't any anger in his expression, only an annoyance that would season with time into a warming acceptance to the straight-forward truth that the humble younger man had just pointed out. Sanderborn rarely got irked with Harvey, but he did not always like what he had to say. However, over the years that they'd worked together, a comfortable and kind system of operating had developed between the two of them.

"Your Plan B? You think that the old limey battle-axe isn't going to give in, huh?"

"I do not, sir."

"No matter how hard I try?"

"I think you could try a hundred more times and she wouldn't agree to sell Stonehenge to you, sir."

"And you don't think it's worth the trouble of digging all the ground out from under her feet with some backroom deals, huh? I've been quietly paving the way through some secret conversations with a few sympathetic Labour MPs, not to mention approaching some individuals with ties to the Irish Republican Army to see if – with much-needed funding for them – they'd be up for something impressively clandestine."

Harvey shook his head as he answered, "I don't think it's worth all that trouble, sir. And I don't think you can fake another heist."

Sanderborn nodded and then smiled at his assistant. "Damn, you're a smart cracker, Harvey. I'm lucky to have someone like you in my counsel. You know what? I think you deserve a raise."

"You gave me one last month, sir. Perhaps you should wait until my next performance evaluation."

"Poppycock! You're worth every penny, Harvey. Enact your Plan B...immediately. Get in touch right away with our team of rock carvers and get them started on making an exact replica of Stonehenge."

"Yes, sir."

"We will still need to figure out where to put it when it's finished, but we'll cross that bridge when we get there.

Anywhere is good enough, I'd expect. It doesn't *really* matter where."

In this case, Buchanan Sanderborn could not have been more wrong, and Harvey Ferguson knew it. He just needed a smooth way to broach the subject with his boss.

Way to Throw Caution to the Wind, Dorothy Gale!

At this very same moment, on the other side of the Universe, in his cubicle at the Ministry of Spatial Events in the Mkultran capital city of Glaxopolis, Xandrus sighed contently after the wave of bliss from his cranial remediation washed over him and removed all traces of the negative emotions he'd just begun to feel. He looked back at the screen he was assigned to watch, and he saw even more evidence of the brutal violence from the Gherrardian invasion of the Mkultran colony on the small planet of Noosbit. It was now hard to see the carnage clearly, thanks to the amount of magenta Mkultran blood splashed onto the camera lens filming the scene, but he could discern enough to know that truly horrific things were taking place there.

Luckily for Xandrus, the pangs had been removed from any kind of reaction he'd had after having seen the unthinkable maelstrom being unleashed upon the innocent citizens of the colony. In fact, the sanguinary coloration on the screen reminded Xandrus of a beautiful pink-purple sunset on Kukulkan, his favorite vacation spot in the galaxy. So, instead of looking at the atrocious images with a sense of understandable outrage, dread, and even nausea, he imagined himself being at the beach and having smooth, sun-protective cream sensuously rubbed all over his body.

While he was physically incapable of feeling anything about the ferocity of the Gherrardian attack, the fact that those ruthless invaders were still on their way toward him and his planet could not be entirely denied. It was no understatement to say that as soon as they had sated themselves with their bloodbath on Noosbit, these vicious invaders were one step closer to launching an imminent invasion of Mkultra, and that was going to threaten the very existence of Xandrus and his whole species. Instead of either being pissed off enough to prepare to make a final stand, or scared shitless enough to run for the hills, Xandrus performed the most characteristic of Mkultran gestures. He shrugged his shoulders. And then he went back to gazing dreamily at the screen once again.

Mkultra is a planet in the Ewa star system. The exact location of this star system is beyond the scope of most average earthlings' comprehension. That may seem rude to put it that way, but if an attempt was to be made to describe the pathway to get from Planet Earth to Mkultra, after the first few familiar terms or names, these directions would sound more like a Vietnamese newscaster trying to explain to a typical English speaker how the national volleyball team had fared in the last Summer Olympic Games. Let it suffice to say, Mkultra is really, really far away.

The only way to successfully get from there to here is through a series of wormholes which condense the very expanse of interstellar space into some manageable and travelable bites.

However, in terms of planetary conditions, Earth and Mkultra could be identical twins who were split up at birth. The atmosphere and geology of the two planets are so similar, one could replace the other for a day or two and get away with it. To take the analogy one step further, one could donate a kidney to the other without any issue...if planets possessed kidneys, that is.

Not only are the planets so eerily that similar, but the modern-day inhabitants of both planets could be doppelgangers of one another as well. Except that a Mkultran has a third nostril and a giant cephalopod-looking creature sitting atop his head, one might not be able to pick one out of an Indianapolis police lineup, especially if he were wearing some kind of head covering. Certainly, there are far more differences between the two species internally, but short of cutting them open on a coroner's table, it'd be rather hard to tell one apart from the other without a closer examination.

Regardless of all this, the Mkultrans are a fascinating species with a very colorful past. During their modern existence, they've become known around the vast reaches of space as being a powerful, cerebral, peaceful, and very contented species. Their skill in using wormholes to navigate effortlessly through space has truly set them apart from any other race in the Universe. Their knowledge about these interstellar travel routes through these celestial anomalies is so complete – and confidential – that they've been frequently accused of having a monopoly on it all. Because of this, the more covetous species around them usually call them the "wormhole surfers," and even though the usage of this nickname was meant to be insulting, most Mkultrans really don't give a shit about what anybody says or thinks about them these days.

Ironically, it was this intimate knowledge of wormholes that made the Mkultrans the target of the Gherrardians in the first place. These bellicose and single-minded creatures became hell-bent on slaughtering the Mkultrans to get their hands on the keys to the car. After all, they figured that if they could gain complete control of these uber-secret time-space passageways, they'd be able to punch their own ticket. And, to be frank, since it would only be a matter of time before the Gherrardians massacred the Mkultrans and stole their knowledge about wormholes, pretty soon they were going to be the ones calling all the shots, they thought...in the whole known Universe.

To understand why the Mkultrans presently have no future, it is important to go back to their very beginnings. Mkultra had then been an unnamed planet with overly abundant natural resources. All of its life forms were flourishing because conditions could not have been more perfect. The weather was ideal for sustaining growing populations. There was more than enough viable space and food for all to live on, or under, the ground, in the seas, and in the sky. The place was the epitome of somewhere quite comfortable. There was such a plenitude, there was no need for the life forms of the planet to compete too vigorously against one another. The entire ecosystem was so perfectly balanced, no species had a pressing need to fight to be at the top of the food chain. As a result, the place was an Eden, a real haven of pure contentment.

But this all changed when a powerful meteor shower bombarded the planet and did a number on everything. After the dust from this cataclysmic event had cleared, those ideal conditions from before were suddenly gone, and a much more caustic and challenging situation was left in their stead. The harmoniousness had been instantly erased, and survival for any living creature on the planet had become tenuous, at best. All life forms had been immediately thrown into the ring to compete for their tiny piece of the pie. Overnight, the place had become a dog-eat-dog world, if those creatures in the *Canis* genus had lived on Mkultra, that is.

One species, an organized society of peaceful human-oid-looking bipedal creatures who called themselves the Gottliebians, were put into a terrible quandary by all these changes. For generations immemorial, they'd had it so good that they were more akin to what an earthling might call gentlemen farmers. However, after the meteor shower, and their planet's environment flipping upside down so drastically, there was no way they could survive as purely peaceful agriculturalists anymore. Instead, they were forced to become ruthless hunters and gatherers.

Luckily for the Gottliebians, they were wired to be a strong species with impressive critical thinking skills. They had already engineered some impressive farming technology, but now, facing starvation and extinction in their more sterile world, they had to give up on farming and turn their strongest attributes into ones that allowed them to kill enough prey to eat. And they succeeded.

In a relatively short time they became one of the apex surviving species of the planet. They had been forced into the changing room of life by that meteor shower, and they slipped out of their earlier casual outfit of being peaceful providers and into their new uniform of single-minded consumers.

This transition might have happened more quickly, but it hadn't been without its complications for the Gottliebians.

They'd been a structured population full of self-contented and self-reflective individuals before the meteors rained down, but forced to adapt to even attempt to survive, they'd become a horde of overly emotional and aggressive creatures preoccupied with taking all the now-limited resources of the stricken planet for themselves. When it came to being victorious in this big new game of survival, these new versions of the Gottliebians were in it to win it – at all costs.

Thanks to the radically changed climatic conditions, the other species on the planet faced similar challenges for their survival. Not many of them were able to make the necessary changes, and mass extinctions happened left and right. The Milbrookians were another example, though, of becoming lucky survivors. These eight-legged creatures, which remarkably resembled Earth's common octopuses (*Octopus vulgaris*) – except that they were scaled, terrain-based life forms – were able to switch from their vanishing food sources to being able to get sustenance from an energy field that emanated from a specific type of magnetic ore found in one region of the planet. While the limited quantities of these geological deposits meant that the Milbrookians were restrained to an extremely narrow area of inhabitation, with their perilously low population, they survived when many others didn't.

It should be noted that the Milbrookians truly counted their blessings when they'd been able to switch nutritional sources to avoid a mass extinction. The moral of the story which they took away from their experience was that whenever a species is truly confronted with starvation, they should consider sucking on rocks as a viable option.

Unfortunately for the Milbrookians, they lived in the same area as the Gottliebians, and soon they became their prey. By sitting out in the open while they soaked up their energetic nourishment from the rocks, the Milbrookians became easy pickings for these aggressive Gottliebian hunters. To make matters worse, the Gottliebians thought that the Milbrookians tasted just like the flesh of the Nokoko Nut, the much-loved staple of the Gottliebian diet before dust clouds from the meteor strike wiped out these beloved trees. With their tastiness and with the ease of hunting them, the Gottliebians began to feast on the lowly Milbrookians with reckless abandon.

What happened next is still, to this very day, hotly debated. According to the Gottliebian legends, a lone hunter, Chyggan, out on a routine hunting expedition, was about to spear a Milbrookian by the name of Oxus. But instead of killing the creature, Chyggan allegedly grabbed his prey and held the scaly creature safely away from him as he stared intently into its eyes. Lore has it that, once their gazes met, there was an immediate connection between these two creatures. For some still unexplained reason, Chyggan placed Oxus atop of his head like a helmet or snuggly hat.

Regardless of the reason for Chyggan's act, the incredible results of this pairing were almost immediate. As the talons on the ends of the Milbrookian's eight legs bored through Chyggan's skull and provided an excruciating experience for the Gottliebian, both of these creatures instantly understood that their union was going to be something very special...and they were not wrong, not in the least.

It must be pointed out that, at the time, Chyggan had no way of knowing that the Milbrookian wasn't burrowing into his skull to savor his brain as a light, afternoon snack, suddenly far preferable to the ingestion of mere and tasteless magnetic ore. In fact, it's hard to think of another such instance in all of intergalactic history when an individual allowed such a painful operation to happen on the pure basis of faith in a former enemy. If nothing else, Chyggan was one trusting SOB!

However, once the two creatures were officially merged, the Milbrookian began to convert the emotion of the Gottliebian host's brain into a pure and potent food source. In the process of feeding on these tasty brainwaves, the resulting emotional waste products of the Milbrookian then became a highly nutritious meal for the Gottliebian. In the wink of an eye, neither Chyggan nor Oxus felt hungry anymore.

Their symbiotic relationship not only fed one another, it now released the two of them from the prime limiting factor on their damaged planet. By becoming each other's food source, they both had assured the other of continued survival.

This all, of course, would've been incredibly positive in its own right, but there was yet another benefit. As Oxus ate all of Chyggan's overbearing emotional feelings, there was a sudden, new, and startling mental clarity within the Gottliebian that allowed him to shrug off the yoke of his over-emotional nature and think on a level that was, up to this point, unheard of for the species. This newly formed, unified entity of combined Gottliebian and Milbrookian spirit understood that it was now poised to become a vastly intellectual and uniquely impressive species.

Oxus and Chyggan somehow settled on a new shared name and they decided to call themselves a Mkultran. Together, they had formed a composite organism that had the ability to thrive in places with very little natural resources and use their superior mental ability to do some very great things...on their own damaged planet – the now so-named Mkultra – and far, far beyond it!

Birds of a Feather Flock Together, John James Audubon!

Having Hunter Cooper as a friend was like owning a copperhead (*Agkistrodon contortrix*) as a pet. Sure, it might look like any other snake, but it's extremely dangerous. Actually, it could be fatal. Unless one's an expert on how to handle a poisonous serpent like this, it's probably best to keep one's distance from a copperhead. There were many times that Morton Richardson wished that he'd kept his distance from this odd little man and had not entered into a relationship so fraught with danger.

To most, Hunter Cooper was a complete crackpot. He had an absurd sounding name, was a perfect twin to the author Truman Capote, and was renowned for having a consistently slippery grasp on reality. Assumed to be a homosexual, most locals were derisive of the Lilliputian man and wary of his acidic tongue and tempestuous mood swings. Because of this, the members of the tight social circle of Vincennes gave Hunter Cooper an extremely wide berth and kept him at arm's length at all times, which meant they had imposed what amounted to a social embargo on him after they'd relegated him to being an outlier. As an untouchable, Hunter

Cooper then swam uninterestedly around them, lurking in the dark orbits just outside their world, and he was content to do this. He had no desire to get into their spotlights. He liked being hidden in plain sight, as it were.

Morton Richardson had never had the luxury of shunning Hunter Cooper. From the very moment that the two had met on their first day at the Washington Elementary School, the dwarfish and flamboyant little boy had taken a shine to the taller and handsome star pupil, and the two of them were somehow united into a duo that no one could put asunder, no matter how much they tried. While Morton's cooler friends could not fathom how he could stand the vicious verbal lashings, the confounding emotional about-faces, and the seeming insanity any friend of "that little faggot" had to endure, Morton knew that the relationship somehow provided both members with something that they needed. That being said, Morton was well aware that, to preserve his own sanity, it was advisable to keep interactions with Hunter Cooper to a minimum. While the colorful character provided Morton with something that his life was lacking, Hunter also consistently threatened to take him down with the ship, and Morton strove to keep that from happening.

Unable to look past their own prejudices about Hunter Cooper, no other citizens of Vincennes allowed themselves to see that, beyond his obvious faults, the little, absurd man could, and would, listen to any intimate disclosures from others and never be surprised, shocked, or offended by them. He would, of course, judge the hell out of them, but his judgments were usually spot-on, even if they were delivered in his usual caustic renderings.

More importantly to Morton, Hunter could think outside the box, thanks to his nature of being so loosely tethered to reality. He was able to imagine a whole host of solutions to any problem without getting bogged down by the quagmire of sensibility or being confined by the rules of socially accepted norms...or even by scientific facts.

Morton invited his friend, from time to time, to have a cup of coffee with him at the George Rogers Clark Memorial, where they could privately chat with one another in their own think tank, far from the judging and scornful eyes of the mainstream Vincennes social members, and they could confide in one another, in the safety of a public place.

Two days after the impactful Red Skelton's birthday cocktail party at the Dennisons' – another event that Hunter Cooper was once again openly excluded from, even though he owned a local business, albeit one struggling to survive, and so should have received an invitation – the two men sat at one of the memorial's benches with their tall, white Styrofoam cups of coffee in their hands. They looked around them as they both let their drinks cool enough to sip them. The multi-shaded tones of the leaves of the park's many trees and the monumental manicured lawn provided a big wash of green hues as the background color to their rendezvous.

"Did you hear about the gigantic flash in the sky over by the farmland of that asshole Egan Zumquist on Saturday night?" Hunter began.

Even all these years later, it still unnerved Morton whenever Hunter Cooper spoke. He so resembled and sounded like the author of *In Cold Blood* that hearing him start a conversation was more than a little shocking. The childlike, shrill, and high-pitched voice that came out of his mouth always made Morton do a double-take to make sure the infamous American novelist, screenwriter, playwright, and actor was not sitting next to him. As he did this now, he saw that it was indeed Hunter Cooper there, and that he was wearing one of his infamously colorful suits, with a woolen scarf wrapped around his neck and a stately fedora above shading his thick-framed glasses. The man was so short that his tiny feet didn't reach the ground from the bench they were sitting on, and he swung them with the wild energy of an impetuous child on a set of swings.

"Uh, no, I didn't..."

"Well, everyone's talking about it. I'm going to go over there and poke around for the source of the event after our little chat...if you want to come along. It'll be fun...and maybe we'll find something of some extreme value, hm?"

"I'm working this afternoon, Hunter. But, no, I didn't hear about it. I was at that stupid and boring gathering to cele-brate Red Skelton at the Dennisons' the other night."

Morton was always quite sensitive whenever he was forced to tell Hunter Cooper about another community busi-ness owner event that he hadn't been invited to, but he knew that the little man was always aware of it already whenever such a snub had happened, and he'd developed a very, very thick skin in regards to the matter over the years.

"I heard the mushroom puffed pastry bites that night tasted like Sarah Dennison had used her finger to scoop out their filling from the rectum of their house tabby."

"Well, I couldn't say anything about that, Hunter. I didn't get a chance to eat..."

"...any. And I heard that poor Nancy Tannenbaum looked like she had taken too many Quaaludes with her glasses of vodka. Perhaps she was preparing for whatever that beluga" (*Delphinapterus leucas*) "Mayor Gandy was going to extract from her in the laundry room later on in the night. You know his motto, 'ride 'em hard and put 'em away wet.'"

"Again, I wouldn't know anything about any of that, Hunter. I was there purely to mingle. Eve and I came straight home without tasting the mushroom puff pastry bites or seeing any interaction between the mayor and..."

"...Nancy Tannenbaum, the sow. And don't you dare play dumb with me, Morty-baby. You and I both know that I can tell whenever you're lying. You have...certain tells."

Morton knew he did, but he wasn't presenting any of them now and he wasn't lying about the stupid party and its participants. Instead, he was pondering whether to include Hunter in his most recent discovery about Eve. They'd discussed other confidential information about Morton and Eve's marriage before, but Morton had neither shared the revelations about Eve's former lovers nor admitted anything about his secret tabulations because he hadn't felt comfortable doing so.

He was extremely surprised now to hear himself say, "You remember how I've mentioned how I've had to extract Eve from those silly adolescent gatherings..."

"At those cocktail parties? Of course. You've expressed how horrendous having to do so has made you feel before."

Hunter Cooper had several particular mannerisms that made it challenging to talk with him. He constantly rubbed his right eye and the bridge of his nose like he had a loose eyelash bothering him. When his hands weren't up in his face, they were clasped together almost in prayer, giving him a sanctimonious posture that was most off-putting. The way he talked with his eyes either closed or focused down on the ground made it hard to tell to whom he was speaking. And his tendency to quickly blurt out the ends of the sentences of those talking with him or to correct them with unneeded details – not to mention calling Morton Richardson "Morty-baby" – made all conversations with Hunter feel more like they were a contact sport.

"What I haven't told you, Hunter, is that I have been listening to their conversations each time. I've been..."

"...eavesdropping. Oh, Morty-baby, that's a dangerous game to play. Take it from me, an expert on the matter, we aren't meant to hear *everything*. What hurtful truths have you been forced to listen to?"

"Eve has disclosed that some of her ex-boyfriends might have been more endowed than most. Over the last few weeks, she's mentioned three or four or..."

"All of them? She said that all of them were big...bigger...than normal? Oh, my goodness, that's really, really bad."

"There's more. She hasn't..."

"...even mentioned you at all, has she, Morty-baby?"

Morton closed his eyes tightly, breathed in, and then breathed out, trying to calm himself. He hated how quickly Hunter had read between the lines and had issued a reply without any needed or expected sensitivity. He was always prone to hit the raw nerve at the center of every bull's eye.

"That's all true," Morton agreed.

"*Do* you have a micro-penis?"

Such an abrupt and inappropriate question was intended to catch his verbal sparring partner off-guard, but Morton was a seasoned foe. He quickly and firmly responded without showing that any emotional damage might have just occurred.

"No, Hunter. Of course I don't."

"I mean, how would you know, really? It's not like you've ever had a professional wing-wong assessment, have you? You know, I could, for the proper compensation, provide you with that service right now, right here."

"Uh, no, thank you, but definitely, no. I've been in enough locker rooms, Hunter, to know that I am normal. I'm neither over or under endowed. At the very least, I'm average...down there."

"Whenever you've been in these experiences, have the others around been aroused? I mean, the gift often gets bigger once you get it out of the wrapping paper. Am I right?"

"I am not going to talk about this anymore with you, Hunter. I do not have a small penis. I'm just hurt that my wife has been sharing with other people – strangers really – that she thinks that I might. There's no other conclusion to make, is there? Since she hasn't thought to mention me with all of her..."

"Big-dicked hot lovers?"

"This was a huge mistake. I should never have mentioned it to you."

"Ah, Morty-baby, I think when you're talking about what we're talking about here, it might be better to used descriptors like tiny or too small."

Here Hunter Cooper laughed his annoying Truman Capote-esque chuckle, complete with closed eyes and a smug grin on his face.

The snide facial expression punctuating Hunter's laugh set Morton off and he stood up abruptly, inhaled deeply, and began to stalk off.

"Has Eve complained about what you two do in the sack?

The shrillness and the brusqueness of these parting words were like a razor-sharp machete slicing the thin veneer of the Indiana summer day. The shock of Morton hearing them was quickly followed by his checking to see if there was anyone around them, but there wasn't, thank god. He stiffened dramatically as he said in the best impression of a shocked Mexican telenovela star, "Never."

"Has she ever seemed to avoid sex with you, Morty-baby? I mean, more than any normal spouse does?"

Hunter Cooper's questions were coming out so rapid-fire now, Morton had no choice but to resume his position on the bench next to his inquisitor to avoid the topic of the inquiries being released loudly into the air with too much uncontrollable freedom.

"No, of course not. She often initiates our times together."

"How many children do you have?"

"Two, Hunter. You know that."

"Was conception either time a challenge?"

"No, we started trying and it happened, both times. Why are you asking such ridiculous questions?"

"Oh, Morty-baby, am I hearing you correctly? Are you saying that your wife has been happy with you sexually *and* you have performed your biological function flawlessly?"

Morton was taken back by the impact of the answer that was forming in his mind, so he hesitated before responding. Instead, he started nodding his head like a red-bellied woodpecker (*Melanerpes carolinus*) working on a dead tulip tree (*Liriodendron tulipifera*).

"Yes, that *is* all true."

"Do you see what I'm getting at, Morty-baby? You've done your 'job' as a husband. So, you have nothing to regret or doubt. Eve acts satisfied and you've sired progeny. You've accomplished something in this world that all heterosexual males strive for in their lives. You're not a failure with a micro-penis, you are a success with a…"

"I do NOT have a micro-penis, Hunter!"

"'The lady doth protest too much, methinks.' Listen, Morty-baby, human beings are a lot of things, but throughout our existence, we've proved that we are mostly petty comparative creatures. The truth is, when push comes to shove, it's in our very nature to estimate, measure, and take note of each other's similarities and dissimilarities. Sometimes it's so ingrained in us that we do it without thinking about it. We just look over at someone else and say to ourselves, 'Gee, that person is really…' Insert any applicable adjective here."

"But how does that explanation help me feel any better, Hunter? In fact, what you just said triggers much more painful reactions from me. You're stating that my wife had no other choice than to judge me and my parts as being inferior from what's she's seen before, and that just makes it worse."

"Oh, Morty-baby, if you can name anyone who hasn't reviewed the size of the assets of their lovers at one time or another, I'd let you spank me, right here and now. Oh, please, God! Let it be that you can't name anyone. Please, try. Please try."

Hunter remained silent for half a moment.

"Eh, no? That's a pity. Anyway, Eve wasn't trying to emasculate you or make you feel badly, she was merely observing something and then saying it aloud. If there's something to indict the old gal for, it might be for sharing a private thought in public. But again, who amongst us hasn't been guilty of doing that, for god's sake?"

"Sure, that makes some sense. It just was hurtful hearing her say all those things. I'm feeling...vulnerable these days, Hunter."

His own shocking admission did not surprise Morton. He was accustomed to revealing more than he had expected to his odd friend.

Hunter Cooper took in a deep breath, and when he spoke again it was as if he were explaining the laws of thermodynamics to a toddler.

"Let's put it this way, shall we? Imagine Eve was describing the spoons in her silverware drawer. She probably would point out that the serving spoons are all bigger than the others, but she would also add that one cannot use a serving spoon when you are trying to eat a much-desired yogurt for breakfast. Now, you certainly wouldn't get your panties in a bunch about spoons if your wife made that kind of statement, would you, Morty-baby?"

"Probably not, Hunter. But these days, I am feeling more like an old antique, battered, useless coffee spoon myself."

"Ah, that's interesting. But I would like to delve deeper into the implications of you having a micro-penis."

"Fuck you, Hunter!"

We Got Off on the Wrong Foot, Dr. William Scholl!

Shaniqua Bishop knew she was finally getting close to finding what she'd been looking for as she drove on the road that surrounded the dense copse outside of Vincennes, Indiana, which was her target. She was certain that the old-timer at the gas station had been spot-on about the location of a grove of pawpaws (*Asimina triloba*) on the Bishop family ancestral land, but she was now realizing the overt dangers that would result from her trespassing on the current owner's property.

Egan Zumquist, the well-known local firebrand corn farmer who owned the land these days, had made his views on race relations entirely obvious. It didn't take a savant to figure out where he stood on the topic. The objectionable man had proudly hung a large hand-painted sign on the barbed wire fence between the dirt driveway leading up to his house and his cornfield that read "Black Man, Don't Let The Sun Set Upon You In These Here Parts."

Because the sign sat on private property, anyone who dared oppose the blatant hatred in the offensive banner was impotent to force the old racist coot to take it down. Thanks to a rather loose interpretation of the First Amendment by local governmental officials, owners of private property in and near areas around Vincennes were given complete freedom to say whatever they felt like on their own land. The last civil servant to even go near Mr. Zumquist's property to discuss the matter of the racist message submitted his repair bill for the buckshot lodged in his car's trunk to Mayor Gandy personally, and afterward a semi-official memo was circulated saying that any future challenges to Zumquist should be done through the mail...or not at all.

Shaniqua had seen the hand-painted sign as she'd driven past it to find the more remote dirt road that gave the best access to the woods, and she had clucked her tongue and wagged her head woefully even as the discriminatory message faded in her rearview mirror. Being a thirty-five-year-old black woman living in America, Shaniqua was no longer shocked by the sight of such public racist displays. She'd experienced enough racism personally in her own lifetime to understand just how pervasive it was from sea to shining sea, but she also understood that these types of threats – both open and inferred – were a part of a black person's everyday life. Because of this reality, she was no more deterred by the sign than if she were looking at a pretty sunrise or sunset.

However, as she quietly closed her car door and got ready to sneak into the woods, she did whisper to herself quietly, "Well, Mr. Zumquist, since I ain't no man and I aim to be off your land well before sundown, you're not gonna have any problems with me."

It should be noted here that, if she hadn't been so preoccupied with the ramifications of the thinly-veiled death threat posted by the ignorant corn farmer, Shaniqua would have noticed another car parked on this same dirt road. Up ahead, slightly concealed, was a sunshine yellow AMC Gremlin owned by none other than Hunter Cooper. As he had told Morton Richardson, he was investigating the source of the flash seen in the skies over Egan Zumquist's farm the previous Saturday night.

The reason Shaniqua was putting herself at such risk as this was to complete her graduate thesis. As a student in the African American Studies Program at Boston University, she'd stumbled upon the specific topic of her research in the most random of ways when her mother had sent her the ancient family recipe book. This venerable document, which had been handed down through the generations, contained a recipe that had instantly caught her eye. Pawpaw bread. The sound of the word "pawpaw" was so unfamiliar and so unusual, she went around saying it as if it were a forgotten biblical name. It tickled her tongue when she spoke it aloud.

Noah Landon, a fellow BU graduate student and close friend, had only further inflamed her interest when they'd met up in a coffee shop and she showed him the cookbook from her Indiana relatives. Shaniqua pointed out the specific recipe that had attracted her attention, and he had smiled knowingly at it. As a doctorate candidate in American Indian Studies, Noah knew all about pawpaws. He informed her that these native fruit-bearing plants had been a major food staple of the Native American tribes that had lived within the growing range of that specific plant. He went on to point out that, although most of the tribes of Indiana had been displaced to Oklahoma, handfuls of these people with the same aboriginal ancestry had remained, lived on the land, and nurtured their hidden groves of pawpaw trees.

Almost immediately, Shaniqua had come to the conclusion that this family cookbook recipe was an example of the connection between her African American heritage and the Native American population. She realized that this recipe for pawpaw bread might be her best chance to connect with the larger issue of the cross-cultural exchanges that might have happened between these two marginalized populations in Indiana, and throughout the United States. Such a topic was not one that had been washed out by too much graduate research or interest, and she was keen to get started on this new academic pathway as soon as possible to cut off any competition.

Before she could get too excited about this topic, however, she'd first needed to learn as much as she could about the mysterious pawpaw. So Shaniqua waded right up to her elbows in botanical texts. As a member of the *Annonaceae* family, also known as the custard apple family, pawpaw trees thrive only in the temperate woods of eastern North America – from southern Ontario in the north, eastern Nebraska and Kansas in the west, and northern Florida in the south.

The tree's edible fruits, she learned, physically resemble Ataulfo mangoes (*Mangifera indica*) and have a pale yellow flesh that has the taste of a custardy mix of banana (*Musa acuminata*), mango, and cantaloupe (*Cucumis melo cantalupensis*) when they ripen in late August or mid-September. Their delectability is the main reason that most people have sought the plant throughout the ages. Many of the largest eastern Native tribes – including the Osage, Sioux, Iroquois, and the Shawnees – savored them. But this delicacy had played a bigger role than just food. The Pawpaw Moon was named and celebrated during September by the Shawnees, while other important Native American place names translate to "The Pawpaw Eaters" and "Pawpaw Village."

This love of pawpaws was passed down to the colonizers of North America. As a matter of fact, Shaniqua discovered, chilled pawpaw fruits became the favorite dessert of both George Washington and Thomas Jefferson. Generations later, a small but highly dedicated number of modern-day Americans continued to hunt for these wild plants in the woods of the Midwest from mid-August through September in hopes of finding the ripe fruit of these elusive little trees. As a result, their locations were usually kept a closely guarded secret.

Having become somewhat of an expert on the plant and its fruit, Shaniqua returned her attention to the family cookbook that her mother had sent her. It was an ancient document filled with an amalgamation of recipes, most of which would fall into the category that people assigned to the "soul food" of rural populations of either white or black country folks. Because there'd been multiple owners and authors of the book throughout the years, the only way to attempt to discern the ages of the recipes was to look at the handwriting and examine the ink of the entries.

The most recent notes in the margins of the pawpaw bread recipe were clearly in her grandmother's script. This woman and her husband had been the last black tenant farmers on a piece of land outside of Vincennes, Indiana, so Shaniqua had decided to start her search there.

She knew finding the pawpaws was definitely not going to be easy. According to all the sources Shaniqua had read, these little trees usually hid in the shadowy recesses of the thickest woods, making them particularly challenging to locate.

As she now looked at the tangled and dense woodland in front of her, she knew she was going to have to climb through the thorny brambles and over the clumpy mud of creek beds to find her target grove. The flat, broad leaves of the pawpaw tree were not going to be easy to spot or identify, and she could pass right by her targets without ever knowing she'd missed them. However, she was determined not to stop until her search was successful, and she set off from her hidden parking spot with high hopes.

If you've ever walked through the western Indiana woods in summertime, then you're aware that, due to the fact that the cooler temperatures and lower humidity of fall aren't even a gleam in the eyes of Mother Nature in that region at that time, traipsing through ensnaring brambles in semi-tropical conditions can be extremely taxing, to say the least. And if you've ever been a black woman trespassing upon a racist asshole's land in direct opposition to an obvious sign of warning hanging on his driveway fence, then you know exactly how hard Shaniqua Bishop was breathing or how fast her heart was beating at that very moment. So, while she was sure the pawpaws were very, very close, she also imagined an agent of death probably was, too.

Like a recon soldier on point, Shaniqua carefully carried her cookbook in her arms like it was a piece of weaponry that could protect her. She stepped precisely and stopped at any semblance of a misplaced noise, and only once silence had fallen again would she resume moving as if she had coiled springs loaded into her calf and thigh muscles.

That's why she froze in place when the first strong gust of wind rustled the treetops as if an angry giant had been shaking them. She needed to pause to ascertain the threat level.

She looked all around her, but she did not look up. Some ancient, hateful, white corn farmer wasn't as likely to swoop down from the sky to nab her as he was to jump from behind a massive trunk of a nearby American beech tree (*Fagus grandifolia*) and brain her with a shovel. If she *had* looked up, however, she would have seen the rotten branch of the hickory tree (*Carya ovata*) right above her getting ready to crash down.

Because she didn't have any clairvoyant powers yet, she was completely unaware of what was going to befall her in the next moment. With the coast seeming to be all clear around her and with a set confidence that no sheet-wearing Ku Klux Klan moron was sneaking up behind her, she started to take one well-placed step over a rock to continue on her way.

The ensuing snapping and cracking sound of the branch above her was startling enough, though, to cause Shaniqua to finally glance up at the source of the noise, but the heavy wooden deadfall was already on its way down. Having a good look at it before it hit her, Shaniqua said to herself as she brought the cookbook up to protect her head, "Aw, damn. This is going to hurt like hell."

That was the last purely human thought Shaniqua Bishop was going to have for a very long time.

Now, it would be irresponsible to imply that the woman had been instantly transformed into a completely new entity, like the Mkultrans had been. But the very instant that the branch struck the cookbook, which then was slammed into Shaniqua's forehead and knocked her out, she was no longer just Shaniqua Bishop, black graduate student from Boston. She now shared her cranium with Pythia the Magnificent, an ancient time-traveling medium.

She knew none of that right at that very moment, of course. According to her, after she'd been knocked out cold from the blow, she experienced a dark calmness like a draping of a black velvet cape over her head. When she awoke, she was totally untroubled. This calmness struck her as unnatural, but it was reassuring to her not to feel any more worried about what had happened to her than someone who had just gone through a car wash.

The reason behind this serenity was that Pythia had already had a chance to have an in-depth conversation with her new host during the interim of her unconsciousness. In the process, all contexts of concern over being knocked out by a big branch and lying helpless in some woods that no one knew she was in were removed completely.

Once she regained consciousness, Shaniqua saw with clarity that she first needed only to remove the heavy branch from her body before making her way out of the woods to her car. She could already begin to sense her new part in the unfolding of the future, though, so there wasn't any need to be too concerned about her current situation or continuing the search for the pawpaws.

She became agitated by having to struggle to get the thick branch off of her, but Pythia reminded Shaniqua how – once one has the ability to tickle the low-hanging fruits of omniscience – one tends to not have panic attacks anymore. Such an honest recognition was calming to Shaniqua, and she turned immediately to giving a stronger shove to dislodge the branch. With this task completed and with her own self-assessment that she was mostly unharmed, she stood up, got her balance, and then started walking back to her car.

The shock of the incident – the falling branch, the concussion, and the possession by a spiritual medium – had now been replaced by Pythia with a newly given, all-important mission for Shaniqua to undertake. Pythia had retracted her psychic antennae, but she was now unfurling them and beginning to psychically pick up once again the current transmissions of all possible future lanes of fate.

Instantly, the possessing medium was aware that the all-important Bronze Age dagger was startlingly close-by, that her nemesis was getting ready to reappear and renew their antagonistic relationship, and that a certain local man was gearing up to enter the world onto the onramp to the freeway of doom.

There was a lot for Pythia – and her new body – to do to prep for all of this.

As Shaniqua confidently ambled toward her car, she nodded at the possessing spirit's explanation of her new role that she was to play in everything. She felt like she was hearing in the tone of Pythia's voice the songs of a New Orleans jazz band. Pythia kept whispering in her brain's ear the seductive message that, together, they were going to change the world. Surprisingly, the young black woman responded to this unusual message and to her radically new Pythia-given life-goal as if she'd just heard the best news ever.

It's Worth a Shot, Chuck Mawhinney!

The buzzer on Buchanan Sanderborn's desk sprang to life, followed by the tinned voice coming through the intercom. "Mr. Sanderborn, I have some interesting information. Can I share my findings with you some time, sir?"

"No time like the present, Harvey. Just bring in some cups of..."

"Tea, sir? I have them in my hands as we speak."

"Alrighty then, come in."

As he prepared to enter the luxurious office, Harvey rolled his eyes while he thought about how his billionaire boss was already far too predictable, and almost too easy to manipulate. He vigorously tapped the manila file onto the flat surface of his desk to settle the papers within, tucked it up under his armpit, grabbed the two cups of tea, and started walking toward the executive office door. He hit the automatic opening button with his hips and the heavy ornate wooden door slowly swung open, allowing him to stroll inside.

He proceeded directly to Mr. Sanderborn's desk and set one cup of tea down before taking up his regular place in the Eames Lounge Chair facing his boss. Harvey put his own cup onto the floor next to him and looked like he was ready to give his presentation.

Attempting to not appear too eager, Buchanan Sanderborn continued to read the article he'd been scanning before. He looked quite official doing this, but Harvey knew it was actually a comic book he was reading, one of his boss's guilty pleasures. Sanderborn put his index finger down onto one of the speech bubbles, and he glanced up to his assistant.

"What do you have to tell me, Harvey?"

"As requested, sir, I made a series of phone calls to talk with the most knowledgeable people around the globe about Stonehenge, and I've come up with some surprising results."

"Oh, I used to so love surprises, Harvey. When you get to this juncture in life you find that those moments that are truly capable of creating a sense of genuine surprise are very far and few between. Tell me, what have these so-called experts told you? Let's see if you can give me a bolt from the blue."

"Okay, how about this? I really think we need to go to Vincennes, Indiana, immediately, sir."

Sanderborn sat expressionless in his chair and seemed to be waiting for Harvey to acknowledge that he'd just uttered some kind of inside joke. When the young man returned the gaze with silence and no emotion, the billionaire snickered to himself.

"Well, okay, Harvey, I take it back. You've just surprised the *shit* out of me. Lemme get this straight. You think we need to go to the Midwest of the United States to learn about Stonehenge? I kind of assumed all of the leading authorities on that vaunted British Bronze Age landmark would reside in Britain, not here in America."

"That may be true, sir, but it appears that your persistence with the prime minister has landed you on the blacklist over there. As soon as I make any mention of your name, even in regard to our goal to learn more about Stonehenge, everyone clams right up and says that they'll call us back. Apparently, Mrs. Thatcher has put it out there that no one is to give us the time of day."

"Bloody limeys!" Sanderborn snarled.

"But not all is lost, sir. During my search I actually came across writings about an obscure antiquities professor from Vincennes University whose out-of-print book about Stonehenge might be very, very helpful in our quest. Not only that, but this same man was interviewed before his death, and he stated that the university possessed a very rare artifact attributed to Stonehenge, a Bronze Age dagger of extraordinary value."

"In Vincennes, Indiana?"

"Yes, sir."

"What's his name?"

"Carter Cooper, sir. According to his bio, he worked at the university for his entire academic life, retired a couple of decades ago, died shortly thereafter, and – except for a park bench outside the library dedicated to him – has been largely forgotten by the university and its staff."

"Hm, and why haven't I ever heard about this guy's research before?"

"Well, he was a little...unorthodox, I guess, sir."

"In what way, Harvey?"

"Well, sir, apparently he had some far-fetched theories and ideas."

"Like what, exactly?"

This question was thrown out there like the perfect lob of a softball pitch in a picnic-friendly match...tossed high enough and benignly enough to either inspire a home run or cause a scene of the greatest embarrassment possible in life.

"He thought Stonehenge was a beacon for aliens."

"Whoof! You're kidding."

"No, I'm afraid I'm not."

"So, he was a total quack, huh? Why in god's green Earth would you think that we need to go to some backwater Indiana town to take in the ramblings of a complete nut-ball, Harvey, when we could go down to Central Park, right now, and find someone who thinks that they're Carl Sagan?"

"Mr. Sanderborn, to get access to Professor Cooper's research I had to come at it from the proverbial backdoor. There are certain science fiction groups – admittedly in the fringes of regular society – who believe that this man was dead right about almost everything he wrote. Sure, they're conspiracy nuts, mostly, but I've reviewed some of their ramblings and I find them to be scientifically sound enough to yet be proposing some particularly interesting ideas."

"Like *what*?"

Harvey inhaled sharply. When you are the right-hand man of someone like Buchanan Sanderborn, your life becomes one big, endless Scottish sword dance as you tip-toe over some sharp and potentially perilous truths. Your movements have to be performed flawlessly, since if you make one mistake, you won't have a leg to stand on...literally. The imposing billionaire was no fool, nor someone who was prone to having the wool pulled over his eyes, so Harvey had found it important to make sure that he always mixed a good version of the truth and a palatable portion of fiction, all the while staying on the man's good side.

There was never a good time to risk summoning up his boss's more ireful qualities.

"Well, sir, for example, these people wrote that Cooper had thought that the proper arrangement of all of the main aspects of the monument was only half of the puzzle. The other half, according to his...uh, followers, was that there had originally been some kind of cabling strung around the stones. The author supposedly had theorized that both the stones and the copper cables would need to be properly installed for the beacon to work. He likened it to having all the electronic parts of a garage door opener's remote control connected and working properly. If any of the components are not hooked up right, then the whole thing won't work at all. That makes some sense, doesn't it, sir?"

Sanderborn took a hearty swig of his tea and then he sat very erect. He did not move for such a long time that he looked like a carved figurine, but Harvey knew better than to blurt out something that might break this fragile and static silence. He waited for his boss to do that.

"Are you implying that this nut-job equated the Stonehenge monument with a garage door opener?"

"Well, yes and no, sir. Most importantly, he seemed to make it clear that he believed that there were specific conditions that were needed to be met to make the monument function like it was supposed to by the original builders."

Sanderborn nodded, but then tilted his head.

"Why?"

"I dunno for sure, sir. Supposedly it's all in his book."

"And what about the dagger you spoke about, who owns it today?"

"The university there in Vincennes, sir."

"Hm, that *does* sound like an artifact that would make a good addition to my collection."

"That's what I was thinking, too, sir."

"Well, just run down and grab a copy of this lunatic's book at the Strand, my good Harvey. Maybe after we look at it, we'll get enough information to see if we need to go any further with things."

"I called there already, sir. They don't have any copies stocked, and their rare book section doesn't have a copy either."

"Huh, well then just jog down to the NY Public Library at Bryant Park and get us a copy."

"Can't do that either, sir."

"Why not?"

"They don't have it."

"Okay, Harvey, I've grown tired of chasing you on this one. *Where* does one get a copy of this mysterious book with all the answers?"

"I think there's only one copy left in the entire world, sir."

"And it's in Vincennes?"

"Yes sir, at the university. Supposedly it's in the same archival box as the ceremonial knife. As far as I can tell, no one has seen either item in nearly thirty years. Think about it, sir. We'd be the first in over a generation to shed some light on these two momentously important artifacts. Wouldn't that be something?"

Harvey found it very frustrating how difficult it was to get a rise from his boss. But now, with the last tidbit flung out in front of the man, he could tell that he was a little more than curious. Like a giant muskie (*Esox masquinongy*) trailing after a Creek Chub lure, Buchanan Sanderborn was about to swallow the whole thing, hook, line, and sinker.

"Huh, okay, Harvey, call me intrigued. Phone over to the airfield and have Captain Simmons fuel up the jet so we can head over there. I still have some more business to attend to here...namely helping that big dummy Vice President Ted Kennedy figure out if there's any way to purchase Newfoundland. Those Canucks are being pretty stubborn on the matter, but I think we can make it worth their while. Let me know what else you find out."

Harvey Ferguson stood up crisply and headed out of the office. He was accustomed to being sent on his way by his employer with a mere flick of a hand, but this time the young man had what some would call a shit-eating grin on his face as he left the office.

He couldn't help himself from thinking that the first domino had just fallen, and the rest of the snaking line of them were about to start tumbling down just as they were supposed to. His plan was starting to get some traction.

Come on, John Augustus Roebling, Bridge the Gap!

The new and unlikely partnership between Chyggan and Oxus was the first step in the formation of the new Mkultran species, but there were many more challenging obstacles to overcome before anything became permanent and official. Sure, those two individuals from two very different and antagonistic species had entered into a new and special union, which was an incredible accomplishment on its own, but they then needed to go back and convince their own kinds to do the same. And that feat would prove to require some hardcore convincing, some thoughtful negotiations, and some underhanded trickery.

When Chyggan returned to his people with Oxus attached to his head along with an armful of other Milbrookians willing to join into similar symbiotic relationships with their former enemies, the other Gottliebians were not initially receptive to wearing their food source atop their heads. Many not only felt that it looked far too ridiculous, but they feared that it was a ruse by the strange Milbrookian creatures to somehow gain control of them. They were even less thrilled when they heard it was a rather painful process having a Milbrookian insert its tentacle talons into their skulls. Instead of submitting to the idea, most grabbed their weapons, ready to put up an armed defense.

But Chyggan was a smart cookie. He quickly fabricated a sales pitch that included a white lie. He boasted that he now had greater than normal strength, a noticeable increase in his warrior skills, and a major up-tick in sexual potency... all because of the Milbrookian he was currently wearing on his head. Knowing that the Gottliebian species' Achilles' heel was their over-compensating eagerness to be the best at everything, he overtly exploited their natural susceptibility to this bogus claim. As he then watched them all scan him with a knowing expression that indicated that they'd heard and were thinking about the unspoken promise that he'd just given them, he was fairly certain of his success.

It was quite a gamble. Chyggan hoped that they would take him on his word and wouldn't want to test him directly. He had figured that, while he could probably out-fight and out-fuck most of his dimwitted peers, he wasn't one hundred percent sure that his claim was completely accurate. The truth was, he knew, he was bluffing. As he continued to return their powerful glares with an unflinching scowl and a statuesque show of confidence, the whole thing turned into a staring contest of sorts.

However, in the end, his understanding of the potential of his people's greatest weakness paid off. Their overly competitive nature meant that they wanted nothing more in this world – or the next – than to be the best. Many of them started to break ranks and knock the others out of the way to line up to be the first to wear a Milbrookian atop their head and become an improved specimen over what they were.

Once the agonizing attachment procedure was finished, most Gottliebian individuals with a newly merged Milbrookian experienced the same well-fed satisfaction and clarity that Chyggan had first had from the symbiosis. And almost instantly, they all began to benefit from an ability to plan and think without the clouding emotions that had previously so ensnared and debilitated them. Seeing the natural advantage this new union gave their fellow tribe members, eventually nearly all the remaining Gottliebians decided to merge with a Milbrookian.

The task of convincing the Milbrookians to join such an arrangement with the Gottliebians was a far, far easier sell for Oxus. He merely had to mention how, once they sank their talons into their host's skull, they'd all be completely safe from predation, never be hungry again, and be part of an exciting new experiment that was bound to pay out huge dividends. These simple creatures might never have been mistaken for the smartest beings around, but the decision to join into this merger was, literally, a no brainer for them.

Most of the Milbrookians lined up to hop aboard, and the formation of this formidable union was, without a doubt, a real game-changer for all involved.

When this mass uniting was over, the brutality and violence of the Gottliebians and the timidity and fearfulness of the Milbrookians all instantly vanished, then and there, and a singular, more cogitative, and highly innovative Mkultran race now stood proudly as an advanced replacement. The members of this newly formed species found themselves taking the first footsteps on their new path toward prosperity and success.

No longer encumbered by those qualities which had anchored them to mediocrity, the Mkultrans were free to spend their time thinking deep thoughts and sparking new ideas instead of either committing acts of violence or hiding in the shadows to avoid predation in the name of survival. They were now able to put all of their energies into striving for purely intellectual gains, learning everything there was to know and working tirelessly toward improving conditions on their battered planet.

The result was the rapid creation of a great Mkultran civilization. They began to dream up and invent new technology at an astounding rate, put it to good use, and quickly set about fixing all the problems facing them. Their small fort-like villages grew into organized towns and then into cities. As these population centers continued to fill up with throngs of contented inhabitants who wanted nothing more than to help their species attain its complete potential, their enhanced mental ability brought about at an accelerated rate more and more advancements in technology and scientific learning. In a metaphorical fortnight, they'd begun to address the global environmental issues that had altered things so dramatically after the meteor shower, and their scientists began to find remedies to many problems. Oh, things were definitely on the up and up for the Mkultrans.

That's not to say they didn't have some bumpy patches. With everyone involved getting rewarded by this new symbiotic physical union, and the new Mkultran civilization taking on such a meteoric rise, there'd been no need to question any of the details about the arrangement. After all, when things are going well, why ask why? It was far simpler to be satisfied with the successes than to nitpick or to find anything bad about it all. Simply put, all of the complaint boxes over the newly named planet of Mkultra were totally empty.

Because of this, most of the solutions to any arising problems had been solved organically and without structure or direction. Complex aspects of their new shared life cycles required some compromises and decisions, but these happened almost without anyone noticing them happening. Issues of life span, mating, and other intimate connection-points just resolved themselves without much intervention.

Being hermaphrodites, Milbrookians were able to mate whenever their Gottliebian hosts came together to copulate. And incredibly, the gestation periods of both species aligned perfectly, so a newly born Gottliebian was delivered at the same instant that a new Milbrookian hatched, and the resulting offspring pairings could happen while both infants were minutes old. Even though this might sound somewhat odd to earthlings, this process of starting a life-long union just after birth became as natural to the Mkultrans as the zipping up of the two sets of teeth on a zipper. This arrangement was now simply considered to be a tenet of their shared lives.

After many generations of this assumed reality, a doctor by the name of BZit proposed a radical experiment to test a theory. He wanted to conduct trials in which newborns fated to be paired were not allowed to merge. Since most assumed the result would merely be two individuals from their separate primordial ancestry – a pissed-off and emotionally stunted Gottliebian and a timid and weak Milbrookian – the doctor's research was chided as being a complete waste of time. Undaunted, Dr. BZit ignored these complaints and conducted his trial nevertheless.

What happened next stunned everyone. Both infants, left alone to their own devices, became sickly and died...almost instantly. When Dr. BZit performed autopsies on them, he was shocked to discover they'd each starved to death in a very quick amount of time. There was no other conclusion for him to make than that the two species had grown so entirely dependent upon one another that they were no longer capable of living apart.

The aftershocks of this discovery sped through the Mkultran population and shook the very pillars of their belief system. It was one thing to enter into a relationship and reap the benefits of the partnership, but it was a completely new ball of wax to discover that one's own survival rested completely upon another creature. Such a codependency made each player an equal member in the relationship, and that was very tough for the hardline philosophers with Gottliebian sympathies to accept. Suffice it to say, many found it a difficult pill to swallow.

But time heals all wounds. So, eventually, the Mkultran society got over this shared shudder in their unexpectedly fragile interconnectedness and accepted it as one of their fundamental truths. They then continued to charge forward as a united species, and they advanced at a truly breakneck speed until they became an advanced culture. By embracing their dramatically increased intellectual ability and their newfound freedom from emotions, the Mkultrans' thirst for the acquisition of knowledge was unquenchable. While many stayed on the home planet to maintain and improve the conditions of their own society there, others began to travel out into space to learn as much about the planets and stars of their own galaxy...and then beyond.

It was during one of their many ambitious missions into outer space that they discovered wormholes, and after putting their collective heads together and exhaustively studying them, they figured out how to use them. They set out to map each one and its corresponding conduit's destination. Within a very short time the Mkultrans became unparalleled space travelers. Their knowledge about the wormholes, their intellectual curiosity, and their high ethical codes combined to make them the quintessential galactic explorers as they searched for new worlds and new life forms almost purely for the sake of learning.

Perhaps the most impressive quality that the Mkultran explorers ever exhibited as they made their discoveries throughout space was their resolve in avoiding all temptations to interfere with these newly discovered worlds or to become an agent of change to the life forms that they came across there. The Mkultrans held themselves at the highest standard to be pure scientists, so they went through incredible lengths to make sure that they could glean all the gatherable information without making any direct and potentially damaging contact with the native species. The Mkultrans neither sought to impact, control, or dominate any of these other planets or organisms, and remarkably, their scientists were more prone than not to sit back and study them to learn as much as they could.

As a result, the information from each and every space mission was compiled for their purely academic understanding of the diversity of life in the Universe and stored on the immensely large computers on Mkultra. It would not be an understatement to say that their capital city had become a virtual Library of Alexandria.

And for the most part, the Mkultrans stuck to their mission of non-contact with a completely unerring determination. Only in two places did they make an itsy-bitsy mistake in this noble pursuit and stray a teensy bit from their proudly maintained abstinence of interference: Earth and Gherrardia. And in both cases, the Mkultrans actually became the main ingredient to a ruinous end for the species of each planet.

Sometimes You Really Have to Scrape the Bottom of the Barrel, Annie Edison Taylor!

Shaniqua Bishop and Pythia set about getting their bearings in Vincennes, Indiana.

Because she'd been so focused on finding the pawpaw groves on her ancestral land before being denied that accomplishment by the falling hickory branch and the subsequent possession by Pythia, Shaniqua hadn't really learned how to get around the small town. She'd purchased a map at the Exxon station upon her arrival, but she hadn't used it except to find her way to the woods on the old Bishop property. Now, in the safety of her motel room, Shaniqua's finger hovered over a host of unfamiliar modern landmarks while the medium within her also struggled mightily to find the information that she needed.

It was a true case of the blind leading the blind.

Pythia's confusion was understandable. After all, as soon as she'd been imprisoned in Shaniqua's family cookbook, she'd lost her ability to see...in the traditional sense. Her soul was entrapped within this paper book, which, obviously, lacked anything resembling eyes, so she wasn't able to visually obtain information. Instead, Pythia had had to rely on the energies and sensations from the outside world to filter in to her inside those recipe pages. At first, she could sense that her nemesis Morgen and the all-important dagger were close by, but then both got further and further away until she had finally lost all direct contact with them. She'd had to live with the merest wisps of knowing that the desired ceremonial knife was out there, somewhere, in the world, but the decades had passed with only the faintest of reassuring wavelengths reaching her.

Now, freed from the book and comfortably inside Shaniqua Bishop, she could feel its presence again...actually very near. And while she needed to guide her host to find it quickly, Pythia couldn't just explain the whole story of the dagger to Shaniqua. Such knowledge could overwhelm the young woman's mind. And to make matters worse, she couldn't force Shaniqua to just drive around in circles until the object was located, since having a black female graduate student do that in an Indiana town was liable to put her into the most negative of spotlights. No, Pythia had to come up with some other kind of a plan.

The main problem was that a lot had changed in the town of Vincennes during the last fifty years of her imprisonment within the cookbook. And, let's be frank, time hadn't been kind to the small town on the banks of the mighty Wabash River. The fifties, sixties, and early seventies were decades which saw the town shrivel up a little bit more with the passage of every year, until it actually could be referred to as a raisin of its former self. Anything that had been familiar to Pythia from her days as a walking, talking psychic medium with the traveling circus that had once visited Vincennes

– other than a few churches or a couple of renovated historic buildings – had been either demolished or replaced with something new.

Pythia needed Shaniqua to find something – anything – that was recognizable. So she encouraged her to head straight to the fairgrounds where she'd first been imprisoned all those many years ago. She hoped that going back to the scene of the crime might trigger her ability to pick up the trail of where the dagger had gone after it had been taken from her. However, a quick search of the trusty road map revealed that, in fact, the George Rogers Clark National Monument now sat on those very lands.

With more excitement than Shaniqua had so far experienced from her mental stowaway, Pythia energetically directed her to drive to the monument immediately to begin their mission.

Shaniqua parked her car in the visitors' parking lot and got out to have a look around. Immediately, she was impressed with the sheer size of the monument. At more than seven stories tall and nearly one hundred feet wide, the marble structure stood starkly on the riverfront land in front of her and towered over its surroundings. The metal placard outside the visitor center claimed that it was the largest Beaux-Arts style monument on an American battlefield outside of Washington, D.C., and it was clear that that statement certainly looked likely to be true.

Pythia guided Shaniqua to stroll around and help her locate anything familiar. With the whole place having undergone such a drastic facelift over the last five decades, this endeavor proved to be a big fat failure. The vegetative tessellation resulting from the precisely planted young sycamores

(*Platanus occidentalis*), sugar maples (*Acer saccharum*), little leaf lindens (*Tilia cordata*), dogwoods (*Cornus florida*), and Purple Prince Crabapple trees (*Malus* 'Purple Prince') and the meticulously mowed Kentucky bluegrass (*Poa pratensis*) created such a homogenized scene that nothing resulted for Pythia but bewilderment and confusion. In this type of featureless expanse there were no sparks of recollection and no clear trail to lead them in the right direction to the missing dagger.

Without any other options, Pythia prompted Shaniqua to take a ranger-led tour of the monument to see if that would bring them any closer to where they needed to be.

The ranger, Annie Bliss, was a big-boned, redheaded, and freckled woman who looked and acted like she had been in the military police before becoming a National Park Service tour guide. Shaniqua thought that the white woman had sneered at her because of her race, but Pythia reassured her that she'd noticed the ranger give the same response to each member of the small tour, regardless of their skin color, so her ill-humored behavior was not based on any prejudices Ranger Bliss might or might not have harbored. All told, Pythia pointed out, the ranger could just have a healthy case of xenophobia. Why a person who had a fear of strangers might want to become a park ranger and deal daily with nothing but strangers was a bigger topic that neither Pythia nor Shaniqua wanted to dwell on at the moment.

The terse tour guide led the half dozen people, including Shaniqua, into the vaulted rotunda and stopped in front of the seven-and-a-half-foot-tall bronze statue of George Rogers Clark. Here, she explained to the group how, during the late winter and early spring of 1779, Clark's men had surrounded the fort and tricked the British into thinking that they were part of a larger army. These American soldiers, who were nothing more than experienced woodsmen, had fired their long rifles so furiously that they convinced the redcoats that a massive force was outside the walls and meant business. Clark then ordered tunneling operations to commence, hoping to force the British into negotiating. Their leader, a Lt. Gov. Henry Hamilton, decided to meet with Clark at the nearby St. Francis Xavier Catholic Church, but they failed to agree upon acceptable terms and each commander had returned to his respective post.

At this point in the story, Ranger Bliss stopped and looked at everyone like she had a big, big announcement to share. With more enthusiasm than she'd been mustering before, she stretched her neck forward and addressed the group with what could be called a twinkle in her eye.

"This guy Hamilton was a potato-eater with a long sordid history in the British military. I bet it would surprise them Bermuda short-wearing, Rum Swizzle-drinking onionheads down there on that British island territory in the Atlantic that their very own capital city is named after this same Lt. Gov. Henry Hamilton and that he was someone who, during his military commandership of the infamous Fort Detroit several years before his exploits here in Vincennes, paid the natives for so many scalps from white settlers that he obtained the nickname of 'Hair Buyer.' Imagine that!"

The members of the tour merely shrugged their shoulders at this news. Ranger Bliss, clearly defeated by her lack of inciting any enthusiasm in them, went on to talking in such a passionless way that it seemed like she was reading cue cards.

After the ineffective peace attempt between Hamilton and Clark, an ill-timed Indian raiding party, sent by the British to attack American settlers along the nearby Ohio River, was defeated by the frontiersmen. Five of the captured warriors were brought to the fort and tomahawked to death in full view of the Englishmen. It was this horrific scene that had finally and fully convinced the lieutenant governor that these violent, psychopathic American madmen surrounding his fort were not men he wanted to keep dealing with. So, he graciously surrendered. The defeated British army marched out of Fort Sackville and laid down their muskets before their victors on February 25, 1779.

After recounting these historical tidbits, Ranger Bliss suddenly seemed slightly happier again and she opened her arms wide as she exclaimed, "In a funny twist, as an American flag was being raised above the captured fort and thirteen cannons were being discharged in celebration, an accident happened which severely burned several of the men, and many of them died later and were buried in the church cemetery adjacent to the fort."

The ragtag tour group glumly took in this last macabre bit of information, and their seemingly apathetic reaction to hearing it disappointed the ranger enough to make her somberly add, as the finale of her spiel, that George Roger Clark's brilliant military activities had eventually forced the British to cede to the United States a vast area of land west of the Appalachian Mountains, and that territory became the states of Ohio, Indiana, Illinois, Michigan, Wisconsin and the eastern portion of Minnesota.

As the tour members now dispersed to look at the seven giant murals painted on the walls of the great space,

Shaniqua moved closer to the disinterested park ranger and cleared her throat before speaking softly. "Excuse me, Ranger Bliss. Can I ask you a question?"

"Yes."

The acoustic signature of the ranger's reply did not have the customary appearance of a sine wave to it, but more closely resembled a horizontal line with a slope of zero. There was very little emotion, no inflection, and all the letters came out like air from a punctured tire.

"Well, I was wondering if you knew about the Great Fair of 1929? It was held right here on these grounds, and I...uh, didn't know if you could tell me anything about it."

"This monument was constructed between the years of 1931 and 1933 and was dedicated in 1936 by then United States President, Franklin Delano Roosevelt."

The response was as decisive as if Shaniqua had asked what two plus five equaled and Ranger Bliss had responded by saying seven. Such an answer invited no follow-up questions nor any further inquiries. The ranger even turned her body rudely away from Shaniqua and gazed at the quiet elderly couple from Kenmore, New York, who were taking in the first mural – entitled "Cahokia: Peace or War with the Indians" – to signify the culmination of that conversation.

Pythia encouraged Shaniqua to persist and even have the audacity to place her right hand on the shoulder of the park ranger now facing away from her. Clearly, Ranger Bliss did not want to continue this interaction, but by the way that she shrugged Shaniqua's touch off with such an aggressive twitch, it was also certain that a physical confrontation might now result from this infringement of her personal space.

"I'm sorry, Ranger Bliss," Shaniqua said, undeterred, "but I read those dates of construction and dedication in the visitor's center. I was really asking if you knew anything about the giant gathering that was held here in October 1929 to celebrate the purchasing of this land by the Memorial Commission for this monument."

"Never heard of it," Bliss responded unemotionally. Then, without warning, she turned her head and bellowed out, "Geraldine, have you heard of some stupid gathering here before they built this place?"

Shaniqua spun to look where the ranger was yelling and saw a spindly elderly woman who had been trailing unseen behind the group. As soon as the words of the question registered with her ears, her eyes opened wide as she proclaimed joyfully, "Indeed I do."

Ranger Bliss leaned out and stared intently at some teenagers who were standing too close to the artwork on the wall, and she was clearly evaluating whether she needed to kick their asses or not. Speaking out of the side of her mouth back toward Shaniqua, Ranger Bliss stated in a monotone, "Geraldine is our docent today. She's as old as dirt, so there's a good chance that she actually attended that fair that you're pestering me about. Why don't you waste *her* time with your questions? As for me, I got them punks in my sights. They think they can do graffiti with me standing right here? Whatta they, stupid?"

Shaniqua made her way over to the woman, who now looked ashamed that she'd ever answered the ranger's bellowing. Shaniqua politely asked her the question again. "Excuse me, ma'am, but what happened at that Great Fair?"

"Hmm, it sure seems like we need to work on Annie's people skills some more, doesn't it? She's a natural when it comes to cornering an adversary in an abandoned building and forcing their surrender or when she's tracking down some teenage vandals and scaring the pants off of them, but she can be a bit too brusque at times with our regular guests. I'll make a note and have someone in HR look into it."

The frail woman stopped speaking and carefully pulled her scarf more tightly around her neck as if the ranger's hearty outburst might have somehow just loosened it.

"As for the Great Fair of 1929," she continued, "I'm surprised you know about it, dear. Not many people have ever heard about the great, glorious gathering of entertainers, preachers, and musicians who assembled here to celebrate and to raise money for this monument. I'm told that the infamous evangelist Billy Sunday was even there. It was quite an event for the ages, but mostly it's been entirely forgotten these days."

A group of teenage boys suddenly sped past them with Ranger Bliss chasing right after on their heels, yelling out at the top of her lungs various curses and death threats involving their rectums and parts of her own anatomy. Shaniqua and Geraldine watched the disturbance go past and then headed out the door of the monument before resuming their discourse.

"Do you remember if anything unusual happened at that fair?"

"Well, when you bring together such diverse elements and throw a big carnival-like party, something unusual is bound to happen, isn't it, dear? But, oh yes, I most definitely recall that there was something quite memorable that occurred. From all accounts there seems to have been a violent attack on a psychic that caused a near riot of sideshow performers. Supposedly this brawl spread to an all-out fracas involving the paying customers. In the ensuing kerfuffle, a giant fire was started, people were knocked unconscious, someone died, there was extensive property damage, and many valuables went missing."

"Valuables missing? Like what, exactly?"

"I don't rightly know all the details, dear. But I did hear some rumblings about some authorities coming over from the university afterward to search through the ashes of the great fire to locate any relics that had survived the flames. From every account that I've read, they didn't find anything. After all of these years, any speculation and mystery have blown away with time."

Just then another tour member shouted out. "Omigosh, that ranger is beating the crap out of those kids out there!"

"Oh dear, I really should notify someone in the visitor center that Ranger Bliss is at it again. Good luck in your search, young lady. If I were you, I'd go over to the Department of the Antiquities at Vincennes University. If you are looking for anything old and mysterious, I'm sure there's a good chance that it might be in their storage space. I'd say it would be a good place to start, there."

Shaniqua stood rigid as a statue as she watched the elderly woman shuffle away, meekly intoning for Ranger Bliss to desist from the fisticuffs at once.

Almost on cue, the lost energy trail of the dagger began to ping, and then it grew in force. Pythia began to suffer from a throbbing headache and it too began to intensify.

Like a bloodhound picking up a scent, Shaniqua's own movements became frenzied and unfocused. Inside her head, a frantic Pythia was shouting out commands like an insane Captain Bligh to hurry up and find the dagger, which, she psychically screamed to Shaniqua, was very, very close. Never one to respond well to this type of antagonistic relationship, Shaniqua took a moment to advise Pythia that she needed to cool her jets and be a little more fucking patient.

Take It With a Pinch of Salt, Mr. Joy Morton!

As Morton Richardson watched Hunter Cooper fumbling with the keys to let them inside the decrepit building of the Knox County Poor Farm, he couldn't take his eyes off of the foolish-looking turban that the odd little man now wore atop his head. The combination of this unusual headwear and the man's appearance as an exact duplicate of Truman Capote made Hunter now resemble the world famous author portraying Johnny Carson's well-known psychic comedic character from his late night television show.

"Huh, Carnac the Magnificent, I thought you might be able to let us in with nothing but your mind."

Hunter turned around slowly and acknowledged his friend's slight by closing his eyes into tight slits and issuing a toad-like grunt for a laugh.

"Oh, Morty-baby, sometimes you can be a real dick...or should I say you can be a real little dick?"

Morton recoiled from the man's acerbic jab, and he began to seriously have even more second thoughts about being around him at all. In spite of a host of his own internal warning signals, Morton had accepted Hunter's invitation to meet to discuss the matter of obtaining insurance to cover Hunter Cooper's new purchase. Now he mightily regretted his decision.

"I'm sorry, Morty-baby, that you don't appreciate my fashion sense. You, like all the simpletons of Vincennes, are what we would call fashion-challenged. This is the rage in Paris...France. Plus, I felt like my head was getting cold these days, so I wanted to cover it."

He slowly turned his body and once again started working the keys. After a few more futile attempts, he placed his small hands onto his childlike hips and looked up at the roof like he was inspecting it.

"Goddamn it, the realtor told me that one of these keys would open the lock on this door. He never said that there'd be *so* many choices."

"Well, Hunter, if we can't make it inside today, perhaps we can discuss the matter of getting insurance for this place at another time, huh?"

"Don't be ridiculous, Morty-baby. You need to be inside this glorious building when you hear my plans for this great space."

Morton looked up at the heavy brick pediment with a large circle of bricks surrounding what resembled a stone tablet in the middle. Then he stared at the skinny barred windows, and he shivered. The disheveled structure had been built almost a hundred years prior and had housed the county's poor and potentially insane for upwards of seventy years. But after some serious charges were brought up about inhumane treatment of the patients, the whole institution had been moved to a much more modern campus. This building and several others had sat abandoned for as long as anyone could remember. Inspecting it now, Morton had to wonder why anyone in their right mind would buy it.

"Ah, there's the winner, winner, chicken dinner!" Hunter said.

The creepiness of Hunter's exaltation was a stark reminder that the man was not in his right mind – and neither was Morton, if he was still volunteering to go inside alone with him.

"Let's not dawdle, Morty-baby. We need to get inside so you can envision what I have in mind."

"Uh, I'm not entirely sure why that's necessary, Hunter. I mean, if we're only talking about getting insurance for this old building, we could do that in the comforts of my office. That is what we're talking about today, right?"

The little man seemed to deflate with having to explain himself again. He sighed dramatically and sounded as if he were prepared to address Congress on a matter of the utmost national importance.

"You need to come inside so you can try to picture the incredible institutional entity that I am going to grow within these stout walls. I know you tightwads in the insurance industry only deal in the absolutes of life and death, stroking your actuarial statistics like they're your little flaccid phalluses, but Morty-baby, today I want you to assess the *full future potential* of this place, not just itemize the obvious conditions of its present-day squalor. I want you to look deep into the future and put a price on that. Do you think you're up for that?"

Before he could answer, Hunter spun and walked inside. Morton looked at the empty door space in front of him and hesitated. This was the point of no return, but when it was clear there was no way to avoid having to enter the building and talk about Hunter's ridiculous dreams, he stepped over the threshold and went in.

All abandoned buildings share similar qualities of their decline. True, some of the evidence of damage, neglect or even angry vandalism from their inactivity may vary in terms of severity, but all such spaces reek of specific aromas and sensations from sitting lifeless too long. For a man like Hunter Cooper, the discovery of such a space usually provoked strong feelings of unlimited opportunity. For Morton Richardson, it evoked nothing more than the desire to tear the whole building down and start anew. Their differing reactions were apparent on their faces. One looked like he'd just stepped into a pile of dog shit, while the other displayed an expression of joyous rapture of seeing something marvelous for the first time.

"Well, Morty-baby, welcome to the future headquarters of the new and improved Vincennes Medical Society."

Morton groaned quietly. Having already had the displeasure of being forced to listen to Hunter wax on nostalgically about the tumultuous Cooper family history and the criminally cruel treatment of his long-ago ancestor, Harper Cooper, by this antiquarian medical society far too many times, he'd heard, *ad nauseam*, all about the long litany of failed attempts to revive the Vincennes Medical Society. Undeterred by any sane thoughts, Hunter and the previous generations of his Cooper relatives had undertaken some kind of resurrection of the VMS dozens of times in the last one hundred years in order to right the apparent wrongs perpetrated upon their long-dead relative.

Vincennes had been the location of the first medical society in all of Indiana. This organization – the aforementioned

Vincennes Medical Society – had been formed in 1817 by a dozen and a half delegates who were elected to a board to help maintain medical standards in the new state. For nearly the next thirty years, the VMS had operated independently in the Wabash Valley until the Indiana State Medical Association was founded. The ISMA's first act was to incorporate all of the widespread local chapters into one centrally based organization in the new capital city of Indianapolis. This transition had been an effort to increase efficiency, but it was also used as a thinly veiled excuse to purge some of the failing founding members.

Dr. Harper Cooper, as it turned out, had indeed been one such member of the VMS who found himself on the outside looking in when the ISMA. centralized everything. However, this wasn't entirely because of a culling issue or even of a matter of him perhaps being too elderly to function as a board member anymore. According to organizational documents and logs, the reason for this decision was that the man was viewed as being absolutely insane.

The severity of the language used to describe the elder medical officer's growing oddness was so stark that certain members of the Cooper family had actually plotted to steal those documents and burn them in a brush fire. When it came to their specific heredity, most people of Vincennes did not refer to there being a Cooper family tree. Rather they spoke about the poison ivy vine of that genealogy.

"Oh, Hunter, not *another* attempt to revive the Vincennes Medical Society?"

"Now, Morty-baby, you know precisely *why* I have to do this. The people of this stupid backwater town all laugh at me and my family, but dammit, when you take a look...a fresh look...at my great-great-great-great-great-grandfather's writings, you can see that he wasn't a lunatic, he was a great thinker and a progressive intellectual. Actually, he was ahead of his time. People treat him as a mistake, but he was the beginning of a long line of superior brains."

Morton brought his left wrist up and made a spasmodic motion to free his watch from the cuffs of his shirt and coat so he could look at it. He had other places to be. He didn't want to get into a debate about any of this with Hunter right now. He just wanted to give the man a quote on how much this fire hazard was going to cost to insure and then get on with his day. However, Morton felt helpless to resist an attempt to appeal to Hunter's rational side once more.

"Dr. Harper Cooper wrote about witchcraft, Hunter. He wrote about aliens from outer space, psychic possessions, magic, pagan ceremonies, and the occult. He was probably as crazy as a Betsy Bug." (*Odontotaenius disjunctus*). "He was cast out of the Indiana State Medical Association because he had been found out as an unsound mind in an unsound person."

"Oh, Morty-baby, I could take you by the hand and walk you to my house right now to show you all of his personal writings that we've archived, and you'd see just how his brilliant ideas fit into the known reaches of the modern universe. The man was an intellectual pioneer, for god's sake! He was just *misunderstood*...as all Cooper family members have been over the years."

Hunter Cooper had played Terry Malloy in the Lincoln High School 1956 performance of *On the Waterfront*, and although the play had been one of the most memorable flops in school history due to the shortness in stature and the shrillness in voice of its leading man, the levels of passion he'd brought to the role had never been questioned. Now, as Morton watched the diminutive man's chest heave under his vest and sport coat from this last emotional outburst, he had to admire the depth of Hunter Cooper's commitment to everything he undertook, no matter how guaranteed of failure it all might be.

"Okay, Hunter, what do you see as the main purpose of this building, once you renovate it?"

"Well, I thought it was obvious, Morty-baby. As the new headquarters of the Vincennes Medical Society, it's going to be a tribute to all of Harper Cooper's innovative ideas and to the accomplishments of the entire Cooper family. Therefore, it will be part museum, part think tank, part laboratory, part medical facilities...part entertainment venue."

"Ah, so you are trying to create some kind of a tourist attraction to get people to visit Vincennes now, are we? Where's the waterslide going to go?"

Hunter put his hands back on his hips and tilted his body in such a manner to strike a completely sassy pose of defiance.

"You know what, Morty-baby? I asked you to come here to give me an insurance quote for my future business venture, not to be yet another dunderheaded critic to all of my endeavors."

"Okay, okay, Hunter. I apologize. I was just trying to ascertain why you'd think anyone would want to see your family's junk in this rundown building. I'm being practical here. I'm not trying to be insulting."

Hunter's eyes narrowed and Morton readied himself to receive another one of his odd friend's notorious outbursts, but the little man opened his eyes up wide and put his hands together like he was about to engage in an act of supplication.

"I've got the perfect example of the absolute brilliance of the Cooper family that I want the visitors to this museum to understand, Morty-baby. Hold onto your hat, this is gonna rock your world! My grandfather, Carter Cooper, gave an envelope to my mother the day after I was born. On the outside of this was written my name and the instructions to only open it on July 11th of my fifty-seventh year. It specifically stated this, and so my family carefully made sure that they took care of this important document until I was mature enough to take it myself and keep it safe. And for the last forty years, Morty-baby, I did just that. So, you can imagine how insanely excited I was when the date came up a couple of weeks ago. After a lifetime of waiting, I was finally going to read what was inside the envelope. I was going to hear my grandfather's sagely words."

Morton was attempting to remain skeptical, but even he had to admit that he was being sucked in by Hunter's tale enough to want to know what was going to happen next.

"Did you open it, Hunter?"

"Oh, Morty-baby, I sure did!"

"And what did it say?"

"It said 'Find the Bronze Age leather pouch in my things.'"

"That's all?"

"Well, yes, Morty-baby, but that's not the end of the story. I went into the basement of my house and located the object he had commanded me to find. I had never seen it before. It was wrapped up in a bundle of fragile notebook paper, and this was written on it: 'Go out into the backyard and push the button. It's time to call in the cavalry.'"

"What the hell does that mean, Hunter?"

"I don't rightly know, Morty-baby, but I did what it asked. I opened the leather pouch, which literally turned to dust in my hands, and uncovered a perfect metallic sphere that had a noticeable olive drab colored button on it. There was the tiny stencil of an artichoke" (*Cynara cardunculus var. scolymus*) "on it."

"An artichoke?"

"Yep. Anyway, I took this sphere to the backyard and I pushed the button with the artichoke on it."

"What happened?"

"A blast of blinding white light came out of it and shot up into the sky."

"That's it?"

"Well, it was a pretty impressive sight, I can tell you that, Morty-baby."

"What happened next?"

"Nothing. I pushed the button again, but nothing came out of it. I tried a couple of times more, but that must have been a once-in-a-lifetime event. But, you see, this is exactly what I'm talking about when I say there are things about my family that I want to display here in this museum. An exhibit with my grandfather's letter, the note around the object, the pile of dust from the ancient pouch, and the mysterious metal orb – well, that would leave the visitors to this museum with goosebumps, don't you think, Morty-baby?"

"You want to show off examples of written gibberish from your dead grandfather, some dust that could have come from a vacuum cleaner, and what amounts to a cheap Radio Shack flashlight that doesn't work anymore? Are you absolutely sure that the Met in New York City wouldn't be interested enough to buy this stuff from you for millions of dollars?"

"Oh, good, Morty-baby, sarcasm. That's what I expected from you. I just knew you wouldn't get what I'm trying to show you today. You're too *small* of a man to..."

"Okay, okay, Hunter. I'm sorry. You don't have to get mean. Why don't you walk me through the building – if it's safe to do so – and show me where you're planning on locating these treasures from your family? That way I can get a good idea of how much insurance you're going to need for this project."

"I forgive you, Morty-baby. Now...take my hand."

"Um, I'm not sure that's required, Hunter. Maybe we can walk together through this place and you can just outline what you have planned for it so far. That'll give me a good enough idea on how I will need to proceed to give you a quote."

Most of this tour went the way Morton had imagined it going. As the two men sauntered through the rooms full of water damage from burst pipes, mounds of desiccated human feces from various squatters who had lived in the abandoned building, crudely insulting graffiti on the walls, and the occasional holes in the floor, Hunter had babbled on about the displays he envisioned for each space. Most of the time he sounded like a tour guide from a Believe It or Not! museum high on a hallucinogenic mushroom trip.

Because of this, Morton wasn't able to completely grasp all of the ludicrous words coming out of his host's mouth. Instead, as his eyes landed on the uncountable issues presented by the woefully poor condition of the building, he kept uttering the necessary, "Oh, yes, I see. Uh-huh, that's grand."

But when they came to what must have been a central dining hall, Morton stopped in his tracks and really began listening to Hunter Cooper. Whereas the other rooms had all been described by the new owner as being filled with what sounded like a hoarder's collection of purposeless items from the Cooper family storage unit, Hunter's startling declaration here was that this vast space was to be the site of only *one* single artifact. This bold announcement caught Morton's attention as his queer friend began to describe it.

With a voice dripping with an almost pornographic amount of lust, Hunter introduced the idea of the object that his grandfather Carter Cooper had brilliantly studied, but he never named the specific article outright. Instead, he coyly teased the story by elaborately describing its venerated placement in the center of this large open room for all the visitors to see, and then only hinted at the splendor it was going to instantly create for everyone entering the grand space. When he abruptly stopped talking, the two men stood staring silently for a moment or two at the spot he was still pointing toward in the middle of the room.

"But, Hunter, what is *it*?"

The little man libidinously bit his lower lip and rocked on his heels. Clearly, he was aroused by his friend's curiosity, and he gazed at him for too long with what almost looked like a seductive leer. When he leaned in to speak in understated tones and tell his secret, Hunter appeared as if he were preparing his hands for an inappropriate groping of Morton, but instead they hovered just off of him as if he were using some magnetic levitation technology straight out of a *Popular Mechanics* magazine.

"I can't tell you *everything* today, Morty-baby. You'll have to wait – just like the rest of the world – to see the artifact when it is finally exhibited in this divine space."

Now that the moment of an inadvertent touching was over, Morton attempted to assuage his burgeoning personal interest and resume the visit in a more purely professional manner.

"Well, Hunter, I'd say that since I'm attempting to place values onto the spaces and items of the future Museum of the Vincennes Medical Society, I should have *some* idea about the monetary value of this great artifact."

"Oh, it's priceless, believe you me! My grandfather first came into possession of this special piece during the Great Depression, studied it while he was a professor at the university, and even wrote about it in his book about Stonehenge. The little peons at the vaunted University of Vincennes recognized the power of the artifact and the brilliance of my grandfather, and so they reacted like the scared sheep that most academics are. They took this piece and his book and buried them deep in their archives. They sought to imprison the knowledge, Morty-baby! But my grandfather took the item back in, let's just say, a less-than-legal way when he retired. Still, there's no doubt that it belonged to my grandfather and that it now belongs to me. And when the whole world sees it displayed again, they'll understand that the Cooper family has been on the right track all along. They will certainly see that as clear as day!"

"But, Hunter, what is *it*?"

Hunter Cooper snorted derisively and shook his finger at him.

"I'm not sure that you're *man* enough to hear what I have to say, Morty-baby."

Morton pushed his head, neck, and chest back and, for just a split instant, looked more like a fer-de-lance (*Bothrops asper*) ready to strike.

"Careful there, Hunter Cooper. I've been patient with your nasty digs against me, but I am losing my patience."

Seemingly unfazed by Morton's aggressive response, the short man continued on like he hadn't just been threatened. Once again, the short fellow leaned in close, looking like he was going to speak directly into his friend's diaphragm.

"All I will say today, Morty-baby, is that it is a gorgeous ceremonial knife from ancient times. It has gems all over it, and it's magical in nature. Now, no more. My lips are sealed about it. I shan't talk about it anymore until it is out in the sunlight for all to pay admittance to see in its full grandeur. Now, let's continue. You need to see the rest of the place."

Hunter started to walk forward and continue his tour, but he stopped short, turned, and looked at Morton.

"You know, I brought you here to share my vision with you. It's so much clearer to me than it's ever been, Morty-baby. I can see it *so* precisely. My thoughts are all calmed down and I can envision the future of this place without any interference. Can't you?"

Morton looked around and didn't see how anything could eclipse the squalor and decay of the old building. He shrugged his shoulders like he'd just heard a joke he didn't get.

"Ah, well, it doesn't really matter if you cannot now, Morty-baby. You will, you most certainly will, very shortly. But for now, I expect an answer from you and your company soon about how much the insurance for my dream is going to cost me. I'm a very busy man. As a matter of fact, I have a session at Nang Yak's House of Thai Massage scheduled in a little more than a half an hour from now. So I can't dilly dally here with you all day."

You're the Best Thing Since Sliced Bread, Otto Rohwedder!

As the G-1159 Gulfstream II, code-named *Pegasus*, banked above the lush agricultural fields of western Indiana and flew over the shimmering Army-green waters of the Wabash River, Harvey Ferguson looked outside his window and smiled at the familiar territory down below.

He then turned his gaze back onto his boss, Buchanan Sanderborn, and looked closely at the man. Away from his underground fortress of an office, the older man looked positively radiant with the excitement of traveling somewhere to learn more about Stonehenge.

When the two men made eye contact, Harvey decided to address him.

"In terms of the itinerary for our trip, sir, I did start to make plans over the phone for this visit to Vincennes, but... uh, apparently you'd already made contact with most of the people I was calling. Nonetheless, after we land, a driver will pick us up and take us straight to the university to start researching the dagger and to take a look at the book in their collection. After that, we will check into our motel and set up camp for as long as we need."

Sanderborn nodded wordlessly back.

Harvey's boss had been oddly quiet throughout the flight from New York. He hadn't seemed troubled or unhappy, but he appeared just to be savoring the quiet time. Harvey enjoyed having the opportunity to fly over the country in such a contemplative tranquility, and he had been able to go over everything he was hatching in the peace and quiet of the flight.

As the plane approached the Lawrenceville-Vincennes International Airport, Harvey noticed how the two long main runways formed an immense arrowhead pointing due northeast, and he was shocked to see such an unexpected amount of activity on the ground. The small regional airport seemed to be swarming with cars, vans, and what appeared at first glance to be a marching band.

When he turned to face his boss again, his facial features were etched with a great sense of uncertainty.

"It appears that there's some excitement out there about our arrival," Harvey said.

"Hm, probably because I bought the airport yesterday."

"You did what, sir?"

"I bought the airport. If Vincennes is going to play as important a role as you made it sound, we need to have the ability to come and go as frequently and as easily as if we owned the place. So I've begun to turn that goal into a fact."

Harvey's role as chief advisor did not mean that he was directly involved in all of the billionaire's financial actions and deals, but he was a little startled at such a big and surprising reveal. Working for a man with such unlimited means had taught Harvey to never underestimate him, but this news caused him an inkling of uneasiness.

The jet touched down and taxied to the end of the runway. Outside his cabin window, Harvey spied a fleet of huge earthmovers and bulldozers parked next to a row of massive dump trucks. Construction workers seemed to be preparing these mighty machines for an as-yet-to-be-started project, and there was diesel smoke belching from their exhaust pipes as they idled expectantly.

The plane made its way around a tight corner between two runways and started heading toward a huge hangar next to a large circular building. As soon as it came to a complete stop, airport personnel – more closely resembling a NASCAR pit crew – descended upon the aircraft, effectively appearing as if they were getting ready to change the tires, fuel it up, and get it back onto the racetrack as quickly as humanly possible.

Behind them a large audience of people and a high school marching band had taken up position to greet the occupants of the plane as they disembarked.

When the main cabin door was opened, the twangy sounds of Johnny Cash's hit song, "If It Wasn't for the Wabash River," drifted inside. Sanderborn and Harvey came down the steps to face the small crowd now applauding so noisily that the band musicians had to play louder to keep from being drowned out.

When the song was done, the band went silent. A train whistle could be heard off in the distance as two men came forward and introduced themselves as Mayor Walter Willard of Lawrenceville, Illinois, and Mayor Paul Gandy of Vincennes, Indiana. They each presented Buchanan Sanderborn with a large brass key to their cities as they effusively thanked him for his support of the entire Wabash Valley region. When it was clear that no one was going to talk any more at this moment, the band began playing another Johnny Cash song, "Wabash Cannonball."

Members from the entire business community of both Lawrenceville and Vincennes were in attendance in this crowd. Morton Richardson was there, as was Hunter Cooper. Actually, other than the unusual appearance of the dwarfish lookalike of Truman Capote in their midst, the gathering at the airport had the feel of one of their local business social mixers – except that it was being held outdoors. The agents of commerce were more focused on what the famous billionaire from New York City had to tell them than on what they had been commenting to each other, but they all took notice of one another and gave the knowing compensatory nods of recognition that established their nonverbal pecking order.

When the band's second, rather painful-to-listen-to rendition had ended, Sanderborn paused for a second and then began speaking loudly to the crowd. "My assistant Harvey Ferguson and I are very happy to be in this beautiful area on this fine Hoosier day, and we're overjoyed to tell you the good news that this entire airport facility is going to receive a complete overhaul. We're going to update the whole place, including a necessary lengthening of the runway and a modernization of the Mid-American Air Center so it can resume its role as an international aviation terminal. I've spoken to my buddy Bob Love, and he has promised me that Allegheny Airlines will renew passenger service to this area once the work is completed. It will only be a matter of time before there's a healthy stream of trade and tourism flowing through this region once more. Now, if you'll excuse us, Harvey and I need to complete some important tasks in Vincennes. Thank you all for coming out today and giving us such a memorable greeting."

With that and after some vigorous handshakes, Harvey and Sanderborn made their way toward a waiting limousine that had parked next to the band. The two men moved quickly through the applauding crowd to get into the car. Several of the "pit crew" members now carried the arriving dignitaries' suitcases and placed these into the trunk efficiently and then stepped back to allow the vehicle to depart.

As it sped away, the sweeping notes of Hoagy Carmichael's iconic classic "Can't Get Indiana off My Mind" bounded from the band in a fading serenade.

"Take us right to the Kum Back Inn, Jerry," Sanderson said to the driver. "I want to unpack and change before we head over to the university."

"You got it, boss."

Clearly Harvey was thrown off slightly by the familiarity between Sanderborn and the driver...as well as their change in plans. "So, what do you have on tap for us, sir?" Harvey asked without trying to sound too shocked.

Sanderborn looked over at his assistant with a confused look, and then his eyes brightened with realization. He swept his hands dramatically as if he was revealing the interior of the new limousine.

"Ah, quite right, Harvey. I haven't included you in all of the most recent developments about this trip, have I? Driving us today is none other than Jerry Moniz, the former owner of the Vincennes Taxi Company. I bought his company yesterday and formed the new Wabash Valley Limo & Taxi Service. Jerry was gracious enough to stay on and run it for me."

The driver turned his head and spoke toward the rear chamber. "Quite the opposite, Mr. Sanderborn. You gave me top dollar for my crappy little cab company and put me in a position to make some serious dough driving for a much higher crusted crowd."

"So, the rest of the new limos arrived as planned, Jerry?"

"Yes, sir, the whole fleet is ready to go. Twelve new Cadillac Fleetwood Limousines arrived late last night from Chicago, and gosh darn, they're real beauties. Those new Checker Marathon taxicabs came down from Kalamazoo yesterday, too. I'm tellin' ya, overnight we've become one of the most top-flight transportation companies of the whole Midwest. Thanks to you, Mr. Sanderborn."

"Pshaw. We're all going to play our own roles in bringing Vincennes back into the limelight again, Jerry. Now, excuse me, but I need to confer with my assistant."

"Yes, boss."

At this, the glass and metal divider between the driver and the riders of the limo rose up and sealed up the compartment in which Harvey and Sanderborn sat.

The billionaire looked at his assistant and smiled at him. It wasn't an entirely kind facial expression, but more like the one a great chess player shows his opponent when they know the match is already over, even if their opponent doesn't know it quite yet.

"Oh yes, Harvey, I've been on a bit of a spending spree lately in Vincennes. The pompous fool from Lawrenceville thinks I'm going to bring my resources to his town too, but if it weren't for the airport being a shared facility between the two cities, I wouldn't have thought to reach out to him. But I'm sure that any benefits from my investment in Vincennes will have a positive influence on that ridiculously dinky Illinois town, too. The two cities have developed quite a symbiotic relationship over the years."

"What else have you purchased, sir?"

"Apart from the airport and this limousine company, I also currently own a motel, a parcel of industrial land in the downtown area, and a former garage building. We're headed to the motel right now. It has the regrettable name of the Kum Back Inn, and we need to put the spurs to the employees to start the much needed improvements that will turn that roach motel into a five star inn – something worthy of the visitors who are going to start flooding this town."

"So, sir, it appears that you've developed a keen interest in Vincennes, and this goes beyond just doing Stonehenge research. Is that true?"

"Quite right, Harvey, thanks to you. You've been pushing so hard for us to come here, I must admit that I was off-put by this a bit. Such blind enthusiasm usually causes me to become a little hesitant, so I started to research the area on my own. It didn't take me long to see the inherent value of the place. You see, Vincennes not only has a prime, central geographical location in this country of ours, but it's also a surprisingly affordable place due to its long-term depressed economic nature. Like my dear old dad used to say, 'When times are tough, nothing is sacred – people will practically give away everything they own just to survive.'"

Sanderborn shook his head for a moment and muttered something Harvey could not hear. He grunted and started to address his assistant again.

"My old man was a bit of an a-hole, Harvey, but he was generally correct with his business sense. If he were here today I'm guessing that he'd call me a complete ass if I passed up this kind of opportunity."

"But we're still going to look into the dagger and the book about Stonehenge at the university, right, sir?"

"Of course, of course. That plan hasn't changed. One cannot really purchase a university, per se, so I've made a very, very generous contribution to the University of Vincennes. School officials have been very keen to show their appreciation, and that includes free access to their antiquities collection. However, when I made inquiries about the dagger and the book, I was informed of a quite startling fact."

"Oh, really? What's that, sir?"

"Well, the book about Stonehenge is still there, but the sacred dagger has somehow inexplicably gone missing. Obviously, the staff are beside themselves with embarrassment over this matter – which they really should be – but apparently when they retrieved the box in which the two items were stored, which hadn't been opened in decades, it only contained the book. Someone has made off with the dagger, I guess."

Harvey sat up straighter in his seat as if he had a cramp in his lower back, and he stared hard at his boss.

"Well, it can't be far, sir. I can feel it. It's got to be close by."

"That's good, Harvey. But I'm more interested in the book. Once we're done settling in, we can light a fire under the butts of the employees at the Kum Back Inn and get things rolling there. *Then* we'll head over to the university and put our eyes on the book. Whether we figure out the location of the knife isn't really that important to me at this point. Learning everything we can about Stonehenge is the real priority, isn't it?"

In spite of receiving all this somewhat unsettling news and startling revelations, Harvey Ferguson now appeared composed and calm. He looked outside the window of the speeding limo and then turned back to nod at his boss.

As his head slowly turned back to look out at the scenery going past, he said, so softly as to not be heard, "That's what you think, dumbass."

That Show Really Bombed, Dr. Robert Oppenheimer!

The Mkultrans first visited the Earth about forty-five hundred years ago. During their exploration of a mostly lifeless galaxy that orbited a medium-sized sun, they came to the rather stunning discovery that there were actually signs of life on the third planet. Not trusting their long-ranged sensors fully, they set about to take a closer look at it.

As with all of their scientific missions, the Mkultran scientists were careful to vet the place thoroughly to ensure that they didn't barge into a sensitive situation and disrupt the natural flow of development with their presence. They orbited their ship above the planet and, using a hodgepodge of drones and sensors, scanned everything there, from pole to pole.

Initially, the similarity of the physical conditions between this planet and their home world was utterly shocking to them. They were further amazed when their investigations revealed that a cornucopia of life, albeit primitive, existed down there. But the real head-blower was when they saw that the planet's current apex creature closely resembled the Mkultrans. These seasoned scientists tested this discovery and retested it, trying to dispel their utter amazement of apparently looking at carbon copies of themselves. When there were no other explanations, these scholarly creatures decided it was time for an even closer study of these two-legged, two-nostrilled primitive beings.

The Mkultran scientific team opted to land their ship in a remote woodland setting in the northern hemisphere of the planet inhabited with a moderate population nearby. Cloaking their ship, they descended silently and then vanished right into the scenery. The plan was to watch from a safe distance without alerting the creatures, so as soon as the landing gear had gently nestled into the soil of the land, they commenced their reconnaissance.

As luck would have it, they had chosen to set up what amounted to a hunting blind right next to the first version of Stonehenge. And while the alien scientists were impressed with the rudimentary skills required to build up mounds and moats with an opening facing a precisely positioned heel stone – not to mention the placement of fifty-six timbers and stones into a perfect circle – the cute little construction project showed promise, but seemed to lack the sophistication that these advanced space explorers would have expected. They hoped to see if their further observation of these creatures explained why they hadn't attempted to build a more impressive structure.

When the hunters and gathers of the nearby village came closer one day to the yet-undetected landing site, the Mkultran scientists nearly all jumped out of their skins with shock at just how much these individuals resembled and sounded like their own species. It truly was like watching reflections of themselves in a mirror, and because of their amazement, the Mkultrans lost their objectivity.

Such an event had never happened before in all of the Mkultran space explorations. During their exhaustive studies of planets in galaxies far and wide, the scientists had kept an impermeable barrier between themselves and their subjects. Since all of the life forms that had been encountered up to this point were so wholly different from them, they'd had no problem keeping their feelings and their subjects separate. Now, however, as they found themselves staring at life forms who were indistinguishable from them, they struggled to keep it together.

Looking at these individuals, who appeared to be some kind of kissing cousins, these usually reliable and objective Mkultran scientists began to formulate some uncharacteristically crazy theories. Even the slightest possibility that these creatures might represent some kind of lost tribe of the now defunct Gottliebians caused several of these respected scholars to start postulating implausible hypotheses aloud. Most of the others then started to drink the Kool-Aid, and they swooned over the fact that they'd just stumbled onto a truly staggering discovery of mind-blowing proportions for their entire species.

Regrettably, their unchecked excitement caused them to throw their usual scientific practices to the wind, and the decision was made to directly engage with this new species to examine possible long-lost historical connections between them and the Mkultran ancestors.

Such a fundamental and catastrophic straying from their guiding space exploration principle of "no contact" could almost be forgiven. After all, seeing creatures who were identical to them in every way – in thought, word, and deed – had amped up an uncontainable level of childlike excitement within these Mkultran scientists, and that itself was somewhat adorable. They actually believed that they were going to hop out of their technologically advanced spaceship and engage these primitive creatures on this faraway planet as if they were catching up with long lost relatives at a family reunion.

However, that's not how things went down. It would be fair to say that the initial contact between the Mkultrans and the earthlings did not go well. Almost instantly, the alien scientists came to the stark and somewhat painful realization that these beings who they were introducing themselves to were actually not much more than barely clothed members of the family *Cercopithecidae* running around like they owned the place. What the highly intelligent Mkultran academics failed to understand was that these creatures were simply mentally incapable of comprehending the sudden appearance of highly advanced space travelers.

To put it another way, the Mkultran scientists' sudden materializing outside the village was similar to a stripper jumping out of a cake for these country bumpkin locals. The reaction of the people of Stonehenge to the event was akin to what a community of chimpanzees (*Pan troglodytes*) would do if fireworks were suddenly set off in their jungle.

A handful of them instantly shit themselves, and many others were so blinded by panic that when the entire lot cut and ran, they trampled their own young in the flight to get away. And, of course, some of the alpha males turned to make a feeble defense against the intruders, which was filled with silly acts of overt aggression and obvious bluffing behavior.

The Mkultrans were very disappointed. They'd had some unrealistic expectations, and the pathetic reactions they were now witnessing certainly did not fit those. Truthfully, they were less than impressed with these people. If these were in fact long-lost cousins of theirs, they now suddenly wanted to disown the whole bunch of them and get on their way.

It was at this moment that a local holy woman stepped forward and righted things. This elderly shaman, who went by the name of Haggur, had used her divinations to not only predict the space explorers' arrival, but had come to grips with the fact that there were other life forms out there in the stars. In contrast to her simian-like peers, having the Mkultrans standing there in front of her did not surprise her the least bit. As she watched the embarrassing reaction from the panicked villagers in dismay, she swam against the human current fleeing the scene to get close enough to fix things with the visitors.

Haggur quickly apologized for the shocking behavior of the other locals and started a dialogue with the alien scientists. Their speaking the same language certainly helped – one other ability the multilingual Mkultran scientists had – and soon they were able to talk in depth about things. It did not take the Mkultrans long to come to the conclusion that, while most of her species were a bunch of moronic fools, this Haggur was something special.

She implored the Mkultrans to play to the audience in front of them. Since her kind only behaved well when they were most fearful, she suggested that the aliens should pretend to be visiting gods who were imposing their divine wills upon their subjects. Sadly, the Mkultran scientists decided to wholly discount her sage advice and stay their own course instead.

That turned out to be a big mistake. If they *had* pretended to be some kind of deities who had popped in to subjugate all who they had encountered there, they would've appealed to the more primitive aspects of these simpletons and found a way to control the situation. Instead, because the Mkultrans continued to act like they were in the middle of some kind of incredible interstellar reunion, these crude Bronze Age humans immediately began to show their true primitive colors. Some plotted how to kill the visitors off so they could take their really cool stuff, some sought to use their bodies to seduce them to get what they wanted that way, and some came up with elaborate con-jobs to simply try to trick the aliens.

Haggur did her best to keep the peace, but even she knew that her hands were somewhat tied in the matter.

The Mkultrans clearly admired Haggur and enjoyed speaking with her, but they soon grew weary of having to deal with the others. These imbeciles were still clearly driven by only their most negative innate emotions and behaviors. There really was no other conclusion to come to – at least at this point in time of their evolution – than that these creatures were far too underdeveloped to stomach for very long. The wise woman was certainly far ahead of her brethren and sistren, so there was a glimmer of hope that the rest of her species might catch up to her and develop into something worthwhile...someday.

The Mkultran scientists, however, did not have the time to wait around for that to happen. They decided that the best course of action was to go away and let these dimwitted brutes do some growing up before they attempted another contact with them again.

Before taking off, the Mkultran scientists instructed Haggur that, if she saw any improvement in her species, she was to give them a call. She rightfully pointed out the lack of any means of communicating with them – even Haggur couldn't exactly make a collect call out into space and across the Universe – and so, after some deliberations, the aliens decided that they'd finally take Haggur's initial piece of advice and pretend to be gods, leaving their subjects on this planet with a present that would impress even the stupidest of them. By upgrading this sacred burial and religious site, they hoped that maybe they could instill some seeds for growth within the species and, in the process, also provide Haggur with a way to keep in touch.

They found the perfect type of stone not terribly far away, quarried it with their laser cutters, and then transported the cut pieces back to the site aboard gravity-defying levitation equipment. They carefully arranged these in a tight circle and started to put lintel stones atop them to make a very impressive new structure. The ease with which their newly identified cosmic guardians undertook this overly impressive endeavor wowed the humans into a moment of passive obedience that had heretofore been extremely rare for them.

While this monumental construction project was being closely supervised by most of the alien scientists, one Mkultran, who reeked vaguely of something far more sinister – a member of military intelligence or a spymaster, perhaps – got Haggur's attention and quietly suggested a clandestine meeting between the two of them in a nearby dense grove of trees. This individual directed the holy woman to bring to their secret rendezvous her cloak, made from the big pelt of a red deer (*Cervus elaphus*), a small leather spell pouch, and her ceremonial dagger.

Haggur brought all of these prescribed items, and the two disappeared from view within the dense undergrowth for over an hour.

When they came back out, Haggur, who was holding the carefully rolled deer hide in her arms and had the pouch and knife tightly hung from her belt, went directly to her dwelling.

The mysterious Mkultran then ambled silently over to join the rest of the scientists and instantly acted like he was busy with their operation. His absence hadn't been noticed by them, as their attention was still hyper-focused on the erecting of the stones for the new Stonehenge.

The aliens were not done when all the stones were in place. They took some special crystal specimens from their home world and, using a kind of sonic displacer, inserted these into the lintels that formed the tops of the outer sarsen stone circle. Then they wove delicate strands of copper thread along and across the stones to create a gigantic god's-eye-like craft project.

Once they were completely finished with their project, they called out to Haggur to come learn how the beacon worked. They explained to her how the planet's magnetic field would be channeled through the perfectly placed stones and the intricately interwoven copper cables and finally through the strategically set crystals to send a strong beam that would shoot out and head right to Mkultra. They showed her exactly how to send her message to them, and they promised her that they'd come back as quickly as they could as soon as she signaled that her people had advanced enough to act like grownups.

Haggur had not been entirely happy with the Mkultrans when they'd announced that they were leaving without her. She'd made several emotional pleas to go off with the Mkultran scientists, saying that the last thing that she wanted was to be left behind with this gaggle of dullards. However, after her secret cloak-and-dagger meeting with the mysterious Mkultran in the woods, she seemed more resigned to the fact that she was not going with the aliens. In fact, when the Mkultran scientists became overly apologetic about leaving her behind – just before they prepared for takeoff – she said that it was her cross to bear to stay and nudge these man-apes toward becoming civilized. Haggur seemed to know that she had no choice but to accept their decision; however, she did remind them that she was very, very hopeful that she'd be able to activate the beacon soon to get her out of this insipid cesspool.

Sadly, these Mkultran scientists were quite naïve. While they had traveled throughout countless star systems and en-countered many life forms along the way – none of which showed an iota of promise of ever adapting to amount to something – they were quite convinced that, given a little time, every population could develop the same grit and aplomb that the Mkultrans had and could better themselves. That they hadn't met another entity yet with the same forti-tude only enhanced their desire to keep looking. So, as ridic-ulous as it sounds, they thought it was only a matter of time before this wise woman was going to call to let them know that these inferior copies of themselves had caught up to their level of advancement. As soon as that happened, they'd beeline it back to have a mature conversation with them and a proper reunion.

With little fanfare, the aliens then said goodbye and blast-ed off.

As Haggur watched their ship ascending up into the at-mosphere with its plumes of smoke and fire, she knew she needed to come up with some whopper of a mythological story to cement the worship of the space gods and to further ensure that the beacon at Stonehenge gained a celestial notoriety and respect from the humans. She came up with a grand prophecy and said that the space visitors were shooting up to heaven to stay in the sky and watch their puny subjects down on the ground to make sure that they behaved. She figured such a warning would be enough to rein in the doltish people she served and get them back onto the straight and narrow.

Such a creative fabrication turned out to be a complete waste of time. Haggur's people stood around the new monument of stones with their mouths agape at the impressive sight of the alien craft roaring upwards, and then they took to quickly pilfering the pieces of the valuable metal cables the aliens had left behind. It turned out that someone had noticed how pretty the copper was, and others immediately set about to create decorative torcs with it. Before the Mkultran spacecraft was even out of sight, they'd made quick work of dismantling the beacon to create their new jewelry.

Haggur justifiably felt that the unique crystals on the stones were also now in danger from the destructive and irreverent mob, so she conjured a spell to dislodge them from their places and fuse them onto the most important ceremonial dagger she owned. While this amounted to her taking a ball-peen hammer to an already disconnected telephone line to the Mkultrans, she went through with it anyway and instantly created an artifact that was so deeply revered by the humans that they bowed down before her in a way that they hadn't ever done before.

Haggur hadn't, in fact, destroyed anything. Instead, she'd created a sacred and symbolic item that solidified her power with her people and also ended up sealing her fate in deciding the outcome for this world.

Later, after the stripping of the Stonehenge monument had run its course, Haggur took a moment to look at the blade of her knife in the safety of her dwelling. The shadowy alien had somehow etched the metal to leave behind some important directions for her, which she immediately set about to follow. She placed the rolled-up hide and the leather pouch carefully in a stone box she'd had made earlier for ceremonial purposes, and she went out alone and buried this in the very midst of Stonehenge in the light of the waning moon.

Being a witch, the older woman had an opal tear of happiness stream down one of her cheeks while a black tear of bitterness streamed down the other.

As for the Mkultran scientists, they excitedly set their ship on a direct course back to Mkultra to share the news of their discovery of a far-off planet that was inhabited by what appeared to be their kinsmen. Their return with this shocking news caused quite a stir, and it was all that everyone could talk about for a while. But eventually, the official logs of that specific mission were buried in the depths of the archives by the continuous cascade of reports from the other extensive interstellar research expeditions going on across the galaxies.

If the Stonehenge beacon had been set off within the next few years or even during the next decades, the aliens probably would have been intrigued enough to venture back for a quick second visit. But with each passing day, they soon lost interest. Eventually the Mkultrans' ability to care about anything withered away to a perilously low level, and they forgot all about the mysterious planet inhabited by their primitive cousins.

Of course, that was all going to change. When the beacon on Earth was eventually turned back on, it would come at the precisely perfect time to add fuel to a blaze that was already burning out of control on Mkultra. And while it's sad that it had to happen this way, the truth is it was actually fated to be like that. After all, if the Universe is really unfolding as it should, it's all a done deal.

All that's ever really in question is whether all of the on-lookers will see the future approaching them clearly or be blindsided by it.

Way to Dig Up the Past, Louis Leakey!

Returning to her room at the Kum Back Inn, Shaniqua found herself in the rather unusual situation of having to soothe the spiritual rider within her. Pythia was an absolute mess. Thoroughly frustrated with the failed search to find the sought-after dagger, which was so close she could just about feel it, and unable to dispel the swelling sense that something huge was about to happen, the psychic medium had the swirling, uncontrollable stress of someone searching for shelter after feeling the foreshocks of a great earthquake that was about to happen. And in a total shake-up of their individual roles, Shaniqua was now attempting to talk the entity within her off the ledge.

She calmly pointed out to Pythia that the intensity of the psychic pings currently emanating from the dagger only indicated the blade was most definitely in Vincennes. And although the city was the same acreage of Denali National Park, it would be a helluva lot easier to search for it there than in the remote Alaskan natural preserve. They'd find it, she told her psychic companion. All they had to do was keep looking.

Shaniqua's new soul-mate's response had been the immature retort of, "Duh."

Poor Pythia was in a tough spot. She was utterly consumed with the frantic desire to find the dagger, but if she attempted to make the young woman understand why, she'd be, in essence, condensing every single novel that the prolific writer Isaac Asimov had written into an all-too-brief Japanese *tanka*. Not only was such an effort beyond her current state of mind, she was also worried about the impact of such a condensed version of the past upon the brain of a humble graduate student.

There followed an awkward psychic silence between the two, which indicated that someone needed just to say something, anything. So, switching gears, Pythia used an analogy with the racist sign at the corn farmer's house as a way to explain her conundrum to Shaniqua. That hand-painted message, she said, simple in both its grammar and hateful meaning, actually contained a hidden number of levels to it, each with an overwhelming emotional pain to be processed. The impact of the generations of slavery and the resultant discrimination from it in the American experience was not something that could be easily explained, understood, digested, or shared. She hammered this point home with Shaniqua by saying that anyone who tackled trying to summarize that sign and its deeper significance into a singular sentence would come out as effectively as if they were stating repeatedly, "Yep, same o', same o'."

This all made a lot of sense to Shaniqua. She could see that the dagger held an unspeakable importance and power for Pythia and that the reason why she was sputtering and spitting in her efforts to explain it so far only indicated that there was a lot more to it all than a mere mortal could take in at one time.

Then, in a moment of true bravery, Shaniqua lied and said that she was ready to hear the truth of the matter.

Pythia was embarrassed to admit that she could not do so, even if she wanted to. After being imprisoned in the Bishop family cookbook and out of the game for fifty years, she was still struggling to get back into psychic shape to undertake this whole search. And that was part of the problem. She was having to take everything too slowly, and that was blindingly frustrating for her. She just wanted to act fast and get her goddamn hands on that dagger, but she wasn't ready to do so yet.

Shaniqua shared with Pythia the biggest piece of information that she'd inferred from the docent's report about the disturbance at the fairgrounds, which had obviously been the moment when the dagger had gone missing. If the University of Vincennes had any information for them about the sacred blade, then being a graduate student meant that Shaniqua had a legitimate reason to request access to such an object. All she needed to do was make some phone calls and see what transpired. Meanwhile, she said, Pythia just needed to stay even-keeled and not hit the panic button yet.

The way that Shaniqua and Pythia were assuaging each other's stress was a clear indication that they were gelling into a good team, and they set out to take the next logical step in acquiring the dagger.

However, it was at this very moment that a new sensation within Pythia began to grow like an oncoming migraine. From her millennia of experience with this phenomenon, she knew exactly what was happening. Calmly, she urged Shaniqua to walk over to the motel room door, open it, and take a look outside. She needed to get her eyes on the source of her currently building discomfort.

Looking out at the still and somewhat squalid scene outside their motel room, Shaniqua and Pythia were staring so hard that they seemed to be trying to view something discernible underneath the pavement or within the parked automobiles. But only the gentle cooing from a breeding pair of mourning doves (*Zenaida macroura*) up on the power lines and an occasional screech of a lone catbird (*Dumetella carolinensis*) in some nearby black walnut trees (*Juglans nigra*) provided evidence of any activity going on out there.

Shortly, however, a long and sleek black limousine smoothly slid like a shadow into the space under the portico of the front office and stopped. The driver got out and dramatically went to the rear passenger door and opened it. Out stepped a man who, to Shaniqua, looked exactly like the actor William Holden. He stopped for the briefest of moments to scan his surroundings. He seemed to be partly surveying what was in front of him and, at the same time, assessing his kingdom. Satisfied with what he was seeing, he tugged on the lapel of his expensive suit coat and strode toward the door of the motel's office.

The next person out of the limo was a younger man who was skinny in stature, and clearly the older man's personal assistant. He looked like he was feeling unwell. He, in fact, was moving in such a way as to indicate that he was about to throw up. He craned his neck to look around like he was searching for both a place to spew his guts and to find the source of *his* discomfort. When he saw Shaniqua standing in the open doorway of her motel room, their eyes met and locked onto one another.

The young man suddenly turned and vomited violently upon a battered Japanese yew (*Taxus cuspidata*) that was the

sole sentry outside the motel's main office door. His retching was powerful enough to bring him to his knees. Meanwhile, Pythia psychically shrieked at Shaniqua to make a dash
through the motel room and run posthaste to the toilet to
avoid making a horrible mess. The black woman took off and
navigated the distance in the nick of time.

When the horrendous dry retching had finally stopped,
Shaniqua rightfully demanded an explanation as to what the
hell had just happened. The psychic medium within her had
a blunt response. She had just gotten too close to her eternal
nemesis, Morgen an Spyrys, for the first time in a very long
time.

It was, in fact, the first time that Pythia and Morgen had
laid eyes on one another in fifty years.

It's Time to Forgive and Forget, Dr. Alois Alzheimer!

Two days after their meeting at the Knox County Poor Farm, Morton Richardson received a handwritten note from Hunter Cooper. When he saw the distinctive handwriting of the odd little man on the envelope sitting on his desk, he looked up at the white panels of the suspended ceiling of his office and uttered a silent prayer, hoping that whatever his friend Hunter had written wasn't going to lead to further embarrassment in the long run. He knew it was absolutely foolhardy to do this, but he couldn't help himself.

Inside, there was a note with the cryptic message: "I have *all* of the answers, Morty-baby, so swing by my house today promptly at three o'clock, Central Standard Time, and I will share everything with you."

Morton put it back onto his desk like the paper had suddenly turned to lead and weighed too much to hold. He looked back up at his ceiling and exhaled. His body spasmed suddenly as his hand hit the intercom to call his secretary, Nadine Gaynor.

"Good morning, Nadine. Could you tell me, am I free at three o'clock this afternoon?"

There was a slight hesitation on the other end as the woman checked her boss's planner. When she came back on, her voice was overly pleasant.

"Sorry, Mr. Richardson, but you have an appointment at three o'clock."

Morton smiled broadly and exhaled a massive sigh of relief. He now had a valid excuse to not meet with Hunter Cooper.

"Thank you, Nadine."

"Of course, sir. You have that appointment with Hunter Cooper, at his house, at three o'clock."

At first, Morton did not hear the specifics of Nadine's reply, and he was ready to hit the disconnect button on the intercom, but then his brain registered what she'd actually said, and he shook his whole body as he spun to get himself closer to the intercom, as if that would change her answer. With the awkward position of his body and the startled expression on his face, Morton looked like he'd just been juked out of his shoes by this sudden realization.

The ensuing silence caused Nadine enough discomfort to speak out of turn. "He made the appointment yesterday, Mr. Richardson, and he told me that you and he had already talked about it in great depth, and I only needed to remind you a few minutes beforehand. I'm sorry, sir, I thought you knew about it."

"No, that's fine, Nadine. I was just hoping I had something else that would get me out of having to meet again with Mr. Cooper, that's all."

"I'm sorry, sir. Should I call Mr. Cooper and tell him that something has come up in your schedule?"

"No, Nadine, it wouldn't make any difference. Some things in life just cannot be avoided."

As soon as he said that, Morton regretted it. Several years back Nadine's husband, Paul, had been cut in two by a northbound CSX freight train headed to Terre Haute. The man's shoelace had become entangled on a spike in the railroad crossing in the center of town, and he'd been run over before he could shed the tethering footwear. It had been this gruesome demise that had first introduced Nadine to the Wheatfield Insurance Company and to Morton Richardson. After witnessing how hard they had fought for her to get a proper settlement, she'd been bound and determined to work for the company and for the man. Now, Morton realized that if anyone was painfully aware that some things in life, especially death, could not be avoided, it would be Nadine Gaynor.

"Well, thank you, Nadine. Sorry to bother you."

He felt ridiculous apologizing to her for doing her job and signed off abruptly. Left alone to his thoughts, he looked over at the clock and counted the amount of time he had before heading over to Hunter's house. Time may fly when you're having fun, but it creeps along when you dread something, and Morton had to admit to himself that he dreaded this visit more than anything he could remember as of late.

At three o'clock, on the dot, Morton pushed the doorbell to the Cooper House, which languished in a hidden corner of the downtown area like an old horse (*Equus caballus*) that had gone off to die. After he heard the last resonance of the bells end, he stood back in hopes that maybe no one would answer the door. As he looked up at the building's giant pediment looming above him, he backed up until he was off the porch and away from any imminent threat of being crushed.

This Greek Revival house was built in the late 1830s by Harper Cooper, and at the time of its construction, it was one of the most prestigious mansions of the up-and-coming young town of Vincennes. With massive stone pillars worthy of an Egyptian temple holding up a third floor pediment that seemed too large for the house, there was something impressive, and somewhat harrowing, about the structure.

Time had not been kind to it. Not enough upkeep had been done to the building over the last century, and the old manse looked ready to collapse in on itself. The pillar and pediment combination that had formerly awed anyone coming to the front door now more resembled a huge deadfall trap than an architectural gable, so much so, in fact, that those infrequent visitors to the house nearly all did what Morton Richardson had done and stepped clear of the dangerous area to avoid becoming its prey.

The front door swung open, and there was Cooper Hunter standing in the doorway, gesturing at Morton with a flourish.

"Oh, Morty-baby, why are you standing all the way out there?"

"I didn't know if you were home, Hunter."

"Oh yes you did, silly. 'Why don't you come up sometime n' see me?'"

Morton slowly made his way up the front steps and across the porch towards the front door like he'd resigned himself to the fact that he had no choice in the matter. His movements were such that it seemed, as he plodded past Hunter Cooper, that he was made completely of cold molasses. To add to this mournful image, Morton muttered incoherently to himself as he entered the house.

Only when he was inside and the door was slammed behind him did Morton notice that Hunter was wearing a matching khaki shirt and pants combo with a green, yellow, red, and black crocheted rastacap on his head. He watched as the little man neatly performed an enthusiastic little *entrechat* to lead him into the drawing room. His eyes focusing on the back of Hunter's cap, Morton giggled at the idea of Truman Capote singing reggae music.

"What's so funny, Morty-baby?"

"I'm just imagining you breaking out into 'No Woman, No Cry,' Hunter."

Hunter brought his hands up to the sides of his knitted cap and smoothed it gently. His eyes narrowed, and Morton knew he was about to be the recipient of one of Hunter Cooper's infamous verbal flensings.

"Morton Richardson, I don't blame you for failing to recognize that this cap upon my head is a piece of multicultural fashion. You and all the rest of the backwater oafs of this ridiculously unimportant Podunk little shithole wouldn't know fashion even if it came up behind you, grasped your shoulders firmly with its hands, and whispered breathy, lustful sweet nothings into your ears as it got ready to thrust its hard, erect..."

"SO, what *did* you want to show me today, Hunter?"

The Lilliputian man seemed so startled by this verbal intrusion that his anger immediately dispersed. His eyes opened up wide and he bounced on his toes in excitement.

"Oh, Morty-baby! Get ready to have your mind...blown! I mean, I am going to...Blow. You. Away."

Relieved to have escaped the verbal lashing, Morton could only encourage Hunter by saying, "Well, show the way."

They entered the dusty, gloomy, and dark drawing room. Heavy blackout curtains succeeded in starving off all the sunlight attempting to make its way into the room from the outside, and dim light bulbs from several lamps replaced this solar brightness with an illuminance so fake that it seemed embalmed. Several ancient and decomposing examples of bird taxidermy were perched around the room, and they were molting so badly that they had piles of lost feathers gathered at the bases of their wooden stands.

Morton had had the displeasure of being in this horrible room more times than he felt like he deserved, and each visit to the morbid place set him on edge. The grossly mounted birds were bad, but the lone stuffed vermin in the corner was so atrocious, he felt himself now involuntarily moving away from it. He knew better than to even glance at it, but he was unable to stop himself from doing so. The poor red fox (*Vulpes vulpes*) had been positioned in such a way as to sit upright in its vintage metal, lawn furniture chair, and its crossed rear legs dangled casually while its front paws piously pushed together in a prayer-like supplication. The taxidermist had apparently wished to punish the creature for all eternity by posing it in such a humiliating way. The animal's eyes were opened as if it was perpetually surprised, and its mouth was in an insincere smile. In its corner, the fox sat like some kind of jester king on its throne surveying its ridiculous kingdom.

In his attempt to get away from this horrific entity, Morton found himself pushed up against a folding card table with a sheet over it. Relieved to not have to avoid the ever-present stare of the monstrous fox in the corner anymore, Morton was somewhat intrigued by the presence of something so new, so foreign, as a card table in this nightmarish and usually unchanging room.

"Hunter, what is this?"

"Ah, that's the surprise, Morty-baby."

"Well, let's get to seeing what this visit's all about, shall we?"

"We can't, Morty-baby, not yet. We're currently waiting on just one more guest, and..." Hunter looked down at his watch like he was trying to speed up time somehow. "I'd venture a guess that they're almost here by now."

Almost on cue, there was a tumult at the front door. This vicious bout of knocking was followed up by the doorknob being twisted in spastic convulsions. Hunter headed toward the ruckus, but he seemed to slow his usual quick gait as he made his way leisurely over to the door. By the time he finally reached it and started to undo the latch, the familiar feminine voice of Eve Richardson could be clearly heard yelling out something from the other side. Her speech was too oily with fear for a full comprehension of what she was saying.

Hunter stood back as soon as the door was unsecured, and made the elaborate gesture of a matador in a bullfight. The door sprung open with the dangerous velocity of a mousetrap and nearly came off its hinges from the force of the entry. Eve Richardson was the picture of pure disheveled agitation, and she rushed through the house and into the room with the sheet-covered card table like she was a knight storming a besieged castle. She caught sight of her husband and charged in his general direction, prepared to repel anyone who got in her way.

"What the FUCK is going on, Morton?"

This was only the second time he'd ever heard his wife use the f-word. The first time had been some years back when

Eve had been trying to retrieve a jar of her beloved Sechler's pickles from the shelves in the garage, and the glass container had slipped out of her hands and fallen and shattered upon the cold cement floor. Not only were the hard-to-get fermented cucumbers (*Cucumis sativus*) gone, but her pair of black patent ankle strapped shoes which she'd just received from the Sears & Roebuck catalogue was ruined. Thinking that she was alone in the space and furious at the accident, Eve had let the curse word thunder out of her mouth unchecked. Morton had been standing unnoticed behind his wife, and he'd backed up and spun around to let Eve fume and erupt in privacy.

Now, Morton was as dismayed to see his wife's frantic entry into Hunter Cooper's house as he was for the profanity she'd just uttered in public.

"Eve, what the hell are you doing here?"

"Saving your ass, Morton Richardson! I came as quick as I could."

"Saving me from what?"

Hunter Cooper now entered the room as if he had just announced the arrival of Princess Grace of Monaco.

"Oh, Eve, I'm so glad you were able to make it."

Eve looked at her husband, but his facial expression was clearly indicating that he had no idea as to what was going on, so she turned her gaze fully onto Hunter Cooper. Under the ridiculous Jamaican knit cap on his head, his face was set in a smug, self-congratulating smirk.

She gasped a few times to catch her breath before trying to speak again, but the creepy little man beat her to the punch.

"Now that you're here, Eve, we can begin to talk about why I've brought you two here today."

"You told me my husband was in imminent danger, you creepy little cocksucker! I drove straight over like some kind of a maniac so I could get here before you killed him."

"I *never* said I was going to kill Morton."

"You inferred it."

"Not even once, my dear Eve. I merely said that he was coming over here today at three and that I was very, very worried about him. Those are factual statements, my dear."

"But you mentioned that you had a plan to save Morton and you were going to keep trying, even if it killed you...and him."

Eve spun to look at her husband. Her eyes were terrifyingly fierce.

"Morton, what in the hell *is* going on here?"

"I'm in the damn dark as much as you, Eve."

"I had no idea that you two were such potty-mouths. If I had, I'd have suggested this little get together much, much sooner. I'm deeply impressed by the two of you...and mildly turned on."

"Well, I am neither, you little pervert. Spill it. Why are we here?"

Hunter gave Eve and Morton a sustained, loving look, and then he inhaled deeply and dramatically.

"Please sit. I have a lot to talk with you two about this afternoon."

"We're not staying unless you start explaining yourself, you little shit."

"Okay, okay, hold your horses, Eve. I've got a perfect trifecta of extraordinary revelations to share with you and Morton today, and I really think that you two are going to be thanking me at the end of our time together here."

Eve lifted her index finger on her left hand like she was going to start counting. She cleared her throat loudly.

"Hunter, you have till the count of three to start talking or Morton and I are going to walk straight out of here. And I cannot promise that we won't call the police on you for this experience. In essence, you..."

"Kidnapped you two? Hardly, Eve-baby. No self-respecting cop or judge is going to see what's transpired today as anything akin to that. Be my guest if you want to embarrass yourself with that charade. But before you do, let's be utterly and completely honest with one another, shall we? What I'm proposing today is more than just giving you the tools to save your marriage and inspire you both in the bedroom. It's really offering you the opportunity to see my most valued treasure in the world, the keystone to my museum. Hopefully, after you hear what I have to say and see what I want you to see, you'll help me get my hands on something else that rightfully belongs to me."

"One."

It was now clear to Hunter that he was about to lose his audience, so he hastened over to the card table and lifted the sheet off it with the flourish of a magician performing a grand trick. On the table was a small orange, black, and white rectangular box with a photo of what looked like a glass vacuum tube from an old radio attached to a rubber bulb of a sphygmomanometer from a blood pressure cuff. In bold white letters across the box, it said "Harmony Vacuum Developer." There were some obvious and interconnected gender symbols of male and female emblazoned below this.

"Hunter, what in the hell is that?"

"Well, Morty-baby, that's a penis pump. I bought it for you. I've never told you before, but I took a correspondence course last year to become a licensed sex therapist. So, I'm offering my services in a private session in the reserved honeymoon suite at the Kum Back Inn to help you two learn how to use this device and fix your marriage."

Morton Richardson blanched noticeably. He looked down at the box on the table and then over at his wife – who seemed completely perplexed by everything at the moment – and he saw that the turning and rumbling gears inside her head were nearly visible on her forehead. He then glanced back at Hunter Cooper. It felt to him as if the house around him was collapsing upon him, and he gasped with the realization of what was about to be revealed.

"Morton, what kind of pump did he just say that is? And why does he think our marriage needs saving?"

Morton could not get his mouth to work. He was so overwhelmed by the situation, he inhaled his words and sounded like he was attempting to suck the air out of a balloon.

"I think your husband is too touched by my offering to speak effectively at the moment, Eve. But let me see if I can attempt to condense everything into a presentable nugget for you, okay? You see, Morton has confided in me that you think that his penis is too small. What I'm suggesting today is that I can help fix the problem with his boy part *and* I can take a hands-on role in assisting you two in rediscovering your wedded bliss again. In the privacy of our shared motel room, I think that the three of us can work together to get your marriage back on its feet again."

"I think that I *do* need to sit down," Morton said.

He lowered his body into a vintage armchair with the same speed and consistency as that of a coffin being lowered into the grave. When his buttocks gently settled onto the cushion of the chair, it appeared as if his legs were going to continue to retract into him, as if he were preparing to assume the fetal position. He averted his eyes from everyone in the room and kept them focused instead on the carpeted floor before him.

The oppressive silence in the room was only encroached upon by the distant ticking of an old Seth Thomas mantle clock somewhere in the house and the rumbling of the westbound CSX sorghum tanker train on its way to St. Louis. Otherwise, except for the stretch of moments that spanned themselves into a vast chasm of time, all three individuals remained stationary and silent.

"Is he telling the truth, Morton? Did you talk with him about private details about *our* marriage?"

"Yes."

When no further argument or explanation seemed forthcoming, Eve continued, her voice as taut as tendons.

"Why on god's green earth would you do that?"

Morton was still staring down at the patterns in the carpet at his feet as he replied weakly, "I dunno, Eve." His voice trailed off, but then he suddenly looked up and his face went from dubious to defiant. "I guess, for the same reason that you tell all your intimate secrets to your friends in those dark dens at all of those social gatherings."

"What are you talking about? Oh my, Morton, have you been eavesdropping on me and my circle of..."

"Slutty friends," Hunter interjected. "And that's the problem."

Eve Richardson spun around and her body looked like the hooded shroud of an Indian cobra (*Naja naja*) turning to face Hunter Cooper as if he were the snake charmer in their little act. When she started to speak, her voice even started out as a hiss.

"You shut your damn mouth, you evil little twerp! Shut it now and keep it shut, or you're not gonna have a tongue to speak anymore. Got it?

When Hunter gave her a quick nod of acquiescence, she spun her body back around to face her husband once more. But now, when she spoke, her words came out kindly, almost soothingly.

"Oh, no, Morton. How many times have you listened to us? You didn't overhear *all* of what we said, did you?"

"I didn't mean to listen to any of it, Eve, but when I came to get you one night, you were talking in a very honest manner about one of your ex-lovers. I couldn't help but hear what you had to say about the guy. You were talking so glowingly about him, and I kept listening in. Then it became a habit at the end of each of those cocktail parties to overhear what you had to say about all of your former boyfriends."

Eve continued to look at him calmly and kindly as she spoke.

"There wasn't any new information to be shared, Morton. You and I have been totally honest with one another about our pasts. Why would you take what I was saying and come to the conclusion that I was unhappy in any way with you? Did that dwarfish shithead over there put these ideas into your head?"

"No, it wasn't Hunter. You see, you've been pretty consistent, Eve. As in, you'd presented this information – which you're right in saying that we've already shared with one an-other – but you'd done so in a new and noticeable pattern. You've disclosed that all of your former boyfriends have had bigger than normal wieners and yet you haven't ever even mentioned me once in the conversation. Not once. And, well, it doesn't take a genius to connect those dots."

"No, I'd imagine," Eve said and twisted her upper torso to look over at Hunter Cooper again, "it would take an absolute moron to do that."

"I didn't do anything of the sort. Morty-baby came to those conclusions all on his own. I merely listened to him and shared his pain. Then I set about to help him with his feelings of inadequacy and improve the intimacy between the two of you. And look what we've accomplished today. Imagine what I can do with more time in a motel room."

"Morton and I are not spending a second more with you, you little twerp!"

"But I went and bought this penis pump and I have reserved..."

"Oh, no. No more talk. I'm going to grab my idiotic hus-band and we are going to march ourselves out of this dun-geon of horrors and never look back. Good day."

Eve reached over for Morton's hand, and he smiled tim-idly, took it, and stood up. She gripped him tighter than was normal, and as she leaned in, she whispered harshly, "Don't think this means I'm not still absolutely furious with you, Morton Richardson. You might not be going to the Kum Back Inn, but you've got the best room at the *chateau d' bow-wow*! While it's obvious that we have some clearing of the air to do, we're sure as shit not gonna be doing that here with that tiny freak watching us. Come on. Let's go home."

Like a small tugboat towing a larger ship behind it, Eve started churning her legs to begin dragging her husband toward the front door."Please, don't go," Hunter whined. "I really do need your help."

"Too bad. We're leaving...right now. Don't interfere or I will injure you. I'll walk right over you and keep going. And don't contact my husband again, you ridiculous dwarfish man."

"I need your help, Morty-baby!"

Hunter had yelled this so loudly that the shrillness of his voice echoed off each wall as it worked its way down through the hallways of the large mansion. The vocal demonstration was so powerful that Eve stopped pulling Morton, and the two of them turned to look at the little man, who was slumped over in dejection.

"How so, Hunter?" she asked.

"Come back and take a look at the item I was telling you about the other day at the Poor Farm, Morty-baby. I think that, once you see it, you will hear me out and want to help me."

Eve resumed pulling her husband toward the exit, but he now resisted her, and he whispered at her, "Perhaps we should look at it, Eve. Remember I was telling you that, whatever it is, it's gonna be the main attraction of his whole museum concept. Seeing it would help me assess its value for the insurance estimate."

"Where is this damned object? And don't lie or I'll take my husband home and you won't get anyone else to hear you out."

"Why, it's right over here. Look!"

Hunter Cooper moved fluidly over to another sheet-covered shape on a side table that had, up to now, gone unnoticed by either Eve or Morton. Without any hesitation he pulled the sheet off and revealed a bejeweled golden dagger inside a well-built glass display case. The weapon looked ancient and was incredibly beautiful.

Both Eve and Morton gasped at seeing it, and they started walking back toward the newly revealed case.

Hunter's voice took on a devote reverence as he spoke. "According to my grandfather, it's a Bronze Age dagger. It's a bit crude in design – I mean, you can see the not-too-far-distant relationship between it and a jailhouse shank – but this blade here is pure magic. You can *feel* it calling to you through the glass as it speaks words of encouragement to you. I swear, it's got a heartbeat. Come closer, spend some time with it, and I swear that it will converse with you."

Eve and Morton made their way slowly over to the glass case and stood and stared at it.

"What kind of gems are those on the sides of it?" Eve asked.

"Ah, you've got an eye for the details, don't you, Eve-ba-by? Those stones are unlike any that I have ever seen before. I've tried to research them, but they are not in any of the gemology books I've been able to get my hands on. Actually, there's only one book on this planet that will have that information – and even more – about this dagger, and that's the copy of my grandfather's book in the antiquities collection at Vincennes University. That's what I'm begging you two to help me do today...get my hands on that book."

"Why do you need our help? Why can't you just go over there and look at it yourself?"

"Well, it's complicated. You see, the university and I have a slightly contentious relationship due to some...improprieties that I may or may not have committed in the past. Those academics hiding in their ivory towers have chosen to interpret my actions as being malicious in nature, but, of course, they were not. I've just grown so darn desperate to have a look at my grandfather's book that I may have crossed a line or two in their regular decorum, but they really shouldn't have kept my own family member's book hostage. To be honest, I'm banned from stepping foot on the campus. That's why I need you guys to help me. I *need* to look at that book, more so now than ever."

Eve was ready to gather up her husband and continue their evacuation from this dreary house and the odd little man, but she'd taken notice that Morton's vision was defiantly glued onto the knife. She put her hand tenderly on his shoulder and attempted to make eye contact with him as she purred, "What do you think, Morton? Isn't it time to leave now?"

"I don't think so, Eve. You see, I know this knife intimately. I've not only seen it before, I've held it."

"How is that even possible, Morton?"

"Come on, Morty-baby, stop kidding around."

"When I attended the Great Fair here in Vincennes on Sunday, October 27, 1929, it literally fell into my hands. It might've been taken from me later by some experts from the university, but my memories of that momentous day and that specific golden blade in there have been haunting me for the last fifty years."

It's Not Rocket Science, Wernher von Braun!

Harvey's rather odd behavior at the Kum Back Inn had not gone unnoticed by Buchanan Sanderborn. Aside from vomiting outside the main office – and the billionaire was surprisingly understanding about blowing chunks in public like his personal assistant just had – he could not get past the subtle and not-so-subtle changes he'd begun to perceive in the young man as of late. And like all good business executives, he decided that there needed to be a rather radical restructuring of their relationship without putting too many of his own cards onto the table – the old "tell 'em what's what, but keep 'em guessing" as to what comes next, that is the common meat and potatoes strategy of the capitalist world.

Once they'd unpacked and settled into their separate rooms at the Kum Back Inn – Sanderborn in the overly ornate presidential suite and Harvey in one of the nicer but plainer nearby rooms – they held a somewhat contentious meeting with the motel staff in the parking lot. This uneasy gathering centered upon Buchanan Sanderborn describing his vast vision for the transformation of the motel into a place that would be sought out by the rich and famous the world over.

Some of the employees found themselves very excited to be a part of such a potentially magnificent rebuild, but most of these people understood quite clearly that they were soon going to be out of a job.

It was this latter group who listened half-heartedly to the pompous rich guy from back east while they scoped out items that they could bring home with them whenever they got their pink slips. Since the place was such a shithole, there wasn't going to be a great windfall from this potential criminal act, but it'd make them feel better about being canned.

Right afterward, Harvey was a bit surprised when Sanderborn announced that it was time for them to go to the new office downtown. For starters, he had no idea that there was a new office downtown, and it unsettled him that his boss was continuing to move with such stealth and impressive energy without alerting him or apparently anyone else of his actions. Also, Harvey was under the impression that they were scheduled to go straight to the university to take a look at the book about Stonehenge and get a bearing on where the all-important golden dagger was located. The blatant disregarding of this planned event made Harvey's already unsettled stomach writhe like a massive mealworm (larval form of the yellow mealworm beetle, *Tenebrio molitor*), and he found himself on his back foot in regards to what they were really doing in Vincennes, Indiana.

The limo ride toward downtown started out as an unpleasant event. The two men rode in absolute silence, and Harvey could not figure out why his boss looked so stern, but he correctly determined that this was not the moment to attempt to talk. It was clear that Buchanan Sanderborn preferred to be undisturbed deep within his thoughts, so both of them pretended to be supremely fascinated by the banal scenery unfolding outside their windows instead of conversing. With no words being exchanged, the back of the limo became akin to a stove with two simmering pots atop it.

Sanderborn broke the terseness of the situation by addressing the driver through the still open rear compartment divider.

"Hey, Jerry?"

"Yes, Mr. Sanderborn?"

"Could you please continue to drive the route that I prescribed and close the divider again so that I can talk frankly with my assistant now?"

"You got it, boss."

The metal screen rose mechanically, cutting off the riding area of the limo from the driver's section. Harvey Ferguson inhaled quietly and awaited whatever heaviness was going to be exchanged.

"So, Harvey, we need to have a heart-to-heart, son, but as we do, I want you to continue to look out the window as we drive around Vincennes. Much of what I'm going to tell you needs to be processed with the sights and sounds of this place fresh in your head.

"First off, I've been a bit worried about you for the last couple of months. You haven't seemed like yourself. I can't place my finger on it totally, but you've just been a little... off. I've noticed the slightest of differences from you since you came back from your first trip to London to open the back-channel negotiations about purchasing Stonehenge. Somehow you've changed, Harvey, but not all in a bad way.

"Before you went to London, you weren't so thrilled about my idea about buying Stonehenge and rebuilding it here in this country. But from the moment that you returned, your new attitude on this matter has been like chalk and cheese to your older one. You've become so *gung-ho*. First you became really, really interested about some golden dagger that you found out about and wanted me to take a look at, then you decided I needed to peek at an obscure book by a total crackpot. I'm not going to lie. It's been a bit unnerving to hear you express your newfound enthusiasm on all of this without any prompting or encouragement from me. I may be a healthy anglophile and want to buy and relocate Stonehenge, but your sudden prattling on and on about some inane book and this stupid dagger has perplexed me a bit. No, if I'm being totally honest, I would say that..."

"Well, you see, sir, this was all because..."

"Shut it, Harvey! This is my time to talk *at* you, not with you. We will have time to talk with one another in a moment or two, but for now, I need to be the one talking. Please don't interrupt me again."

"Yes, sir."

"As you are well aware, my portfolio is extremely diversified. I try to dabble in the many economic sectors that are availed to me, but my Achilles' heel is that I enjoy possessing things. My critics would say that this passion extends to people too, but that's absurd because, as everyone knows, I'm totally against slavery, of course. My interest in owning Stonehenge is different. It stems from a growing desire to leave an indelible mark on this planet as my legacy. I'm getting to the age where my inescapable demise is growing heavy on my mind, and I've begun to question if anyone will remember me after I'm dead and gone. I literally have nightmares of being totally forgotten by this world.

"So I've become a little obsessed with finding ways I can fight that inevitability. I know that I've embarked on some madcap behaviors before that have had even my staunchest supporters questioning my sanity, but each one has been an attempt to force the world to acknowledge that I was here. Being the person responsible for bringing the magnificent Edificio de Erik Weisz into existence will definitely ensure my place in the history books for the foreseeable future, but I came to the big conclusion that the individual who actually owned Stonehenge would be carving their initials right into the walls of the human experience. If I could pull that off, I'd be remembered forever.

"Then the trip to London happened. Not only did you not succeed in your mission of helping me acquire Stonehenge, but you came back suggesting the strange plan of building a new monument, finding an odd ancient dagger, and directing me to get my hands on a book that you've apparently become obsessed with – all in Vincennes, Indiana, for god's sake. I'll admit that I was hesitant to accept defeat when it came to buying the original British monument, but some of this plan of yours started to catch my ear. I must admit that I began to get a little excited. However, I felt the need to make sure that I wasn't being swindled, and to be sure that you were on the level, so I did a deep dive into the researching of this remote, obscure Midwestern town you'd become so hot to trot for.

"Well, I gotta tell you, this quickly revealed that you were really onto something, Harvey. The more I looked into Vincennes, the more I recognized it as the absolutely *perfect* site of my *magnum opus*. If I cannot own the real Stonehenge and gain eternal recognition that way, then I'm going to build a replica of it here and reshape Vincennes to be the center of the Universe, literally and figuratively."

"How, sir?"

Harvey had blurted out his question before he could curb himself. From what he was looking at outside his window, he only saw evidence of a decaying small city, not the location for something eternal or memorable.

"I know it might be rather blunt to say this aloud to you, but you really don't need to know all the details, Harvey. Truthfully, I'm not one hundred percent sure I can entirely trust you. So, I'm going to keep you on a short leash. But suffice it to say, I see nothing but a blank canvas when I look at this town, and I plan to create the most exclusive, the richest, and the most advanced settlement on this planet by quietly purchasing every aspect of Vincennes. I envision establishing this place as something that will be so enticing to the social and economic elite of New York City, the rest of the country, and the entire world, they'll trip over one another trying to get here. Since I know what excites this exclusive segment of the population, I know how to get them to come here. Safely ensconced upon the banks of the nurturing Wabash River, this new, modern version of Vincennes – complete with an updated version of Stonehenge – will become the place that the rest of the world looks to for inspiration. *Then* the name of Buchanan Sander-born will be etched onto the annals of human history forever.

"That's the *why* of things, but the *how* is to understand that the real key to a massive redevelopment like this is to use speed and innuendo to lure your targeted audience closer. You see, rich people love both the picture of a sure thing and the thrill of hunting something that's unattainable. So I will quickly set up those two aspects. When they look at Vincennes, they'll see the sure value of this area – the transportation, the enter-tainment, the lodging, the housing, and the like – and their fear of missing out will combine with the overall potential of this place. They will sniff out the chance to make some more money and to gain some much sought attention and accept-ance, and my interest in the development will cause a domino effect in them. I will settle here, and then I will be followed by more and more of them – until it becomes a mass migration – everyone wanting a piece of the pie that Buchanan Sander-born has deemed as necessary. We've already triggered an incredible level of interest without even trying.

"Oh, and before you think that I've gone completely off my rocker, did you know that about seventy-five miles downstream from here is the location of another, similar uto-pian plan? That's right. New Harmony, Indiana, was the site of three such attempts at creating a perfect community. They might've failed, but I'm going to succeed here. In this case, the fourth time's the charm."

"In Vincennes?"

"Oh, I know. It's not much to look at right now. But im-agine what we could do here. Also, did you know that the name of this place has roots in the medieval words meaning 'victor' or 'conqueror'? If that doesn't indicate that we're fat-ed to succeed, I'm not sure what does, Harvey.

"Now, I know that this is a lot to absorb, but I think you can agree that it's going to be an amazing experience to be a part of, even if it's from the sidelines."

"The sidelines, sir? You're benching me?"

Harvey wasn't able to resist interrupting his boss yet again, and he cringed with the fear of retribution from an-other such misstep.

"I am not. I actually like you, Harvey. I just need to be able to do some freewheeling on my own right now, and that means you're going to be left out of many of the decisions and the planning that go into the main event. But I want you to manage something big, and something directly connected to your obsession with a new Stonehenge, the dagger, and the book."

"Are we going to look at the book, sir? I do think that it will have some necessary..."

"Oh, Harvey. As soon as you first mentioned that obscure book, I flew my experts here and had them go over it with a fine-toothed comb. Turns out, it's mostly gibberish from an apparently mentally unstable man. However, they could not completely discount the very detailed directions for rebuilding Stonehenge in its original form to empower the monument to be some kind of a beacon to an alien race. While these self-proclaimed prophecies are entirely laughable, my academics are intrigued enough to encourage me to build a facsimile of Stonehenge here in Vincennes on some land that I recently purchased in the western part of town to see what will happen. And I'm putting you in charge of *that* project, Harvey."

Sanderborn stopped talking and let the scene outside their windows speed past. When enough time had gone by to indicate that he was supposed to respond, Harvey, who was now smiling contentedly, tapped his hand against the glass window and nodded to no one in particular.

"Thank you, sir. I'm extremely honored by the responsibility that you're bestowing upon me. And I appreciate your honesty. In regards to my role in this whole undertaking, I'll do my best to stay out of the way and yet jump in whenever you need me."

"I knew I could count on you, Harvey."

The limousine, which had clearly been taking the most indirect route to their location, stopped its serpentine passage through the downtown blocks and slowed next to the curb. The metal barrier between the driver and the riders sank down slowly and was replaced by Jerry the driver's face.

"So, boss, you still want me to pull into that spot between them wrecked cars?"

"Yes, Jerry, as we talked about, it might be a little snug, but it'll provide us enough cover to avoid unwanted attention. Just leave enough space that we don't hit our doors on the other cars when we get out."

"You got it, boss."

Harvey looked out his window for the location of Sanderborn's new office, but there wasn't anything around that seemed a likely location for that. Other than the impressively large brick, twin-spired St. John's Catholic Church, the only other nearby building of interest appeared to be a uniquely shaped old garage. As the limo began its wide turn and started to head onto the concrete apron around the odd edifice with vehicles in various stages of disrepair outside it, he realized that this was the destination after all.

The building was made up of three connected components – what appeared to be a one-car garage, a low connecting wing, and an octagonal guardhouse-looking main building. The brick of all three had been painted white, but the slender chimney, the terra-cotta roof tiles, the external trim around all the windows, the front door, and the one garage door were all painted the tone of aquamarine that the George Kirby Jr. Paint Company from New Bedford, Massachusetts, classifies as #07 C Green. The ornateness of the pagoda's roof and what looked like fortified gun loops to repel an enemy gave the little utilitarian building an exotic feel, but the sea of disabled vehicles surrounding it made it disappear from view as much as if these vehicular corpses were devouring it.

The limousine pulled into the prescribed spot between two parked derelict cars, came to a stop, and the engine shut off. Jerry Moniz got out and walked back to Sanderborn's door and opened it up for him.

"Here we are, boss."

Harvey realized that the driver wasn't going to come over to his side, so he took care of opening his own door. He scanned the surrounding neighborhood again and took another look at the building. Close up, it still didn't look like much. But the young man knew enough to withhold judgment until he was inside and had a good look around.

"Ya know, Mr. Sanderborn, the limo blends right in here. It's got some great company. I mean, that's a 1978 AMC Pacer beside the limo, a 1971 Ford LTD Custom right here, a 1972 International pickup over there, a 1975 Chevy Chevette right next to us, a 1977 Ford Pinto up on blocks next to the building, a 1970 Gremlin next to the Pinto, and a 1946 Nash Ambassador on the other side of the limo. If anyone looks over here, no one's gonna think there's anything out of the ordinary happening. They'll have no idea that you guys are even here."

"Well, Jerry, very astute observations. And you really know your cars. We're gonna be inside the office for about forty-five minutes. Please wait in the car for us."

"You got it, boss."

Just then a man came shuffling down the street. It turned out to be Felix Simmons, Vincennes' notorious hobo. The man lived on the streets and acted like he was ready to catch every train heading through town to go elsewhere, but he never went anywhere. He stayed under some of the underpasses and camped in some of the park areas, and the churches all took turns feeding and helping the homeless man. He was not only considered as harmless as a kitten, but he had a position in the social fabric of the town – much akin to a mascot.

Felix was headed straight toward them now, muttering to himself as he walked. Jerry Moniz saw him coming and swelled up like a guard dog spotting an intruder. He even took a step forward in what looked like the preamble to charge at the intruder.

"Oh, hey, boss, it's Felix. You want me to go rough him up a bit and move him along so he don't bother you guys none?"

"No, Jerry, that's fine. Let's let sleeping dogs lie on this one. He seems to not even notice that we're here. Better not to cause a scene that might alert more attention."

"Okey-dokey, boss. Hey, did you hear about the body they found out by Egan Zumquist's cornfield?"

"No, Jerry, I can't say that I have."

"Well, the way I heard it, they found this wacko dressed in some kind of tan coverall with the strangest emblems on it. Not only that, but the guy – who was as bald as a cue ball, by the way – had had some strange plastic surgery on his nose. No one's ever seen nothing like it, boss. The authorities were all stumped until someone suggested that he was probably from California. Everyone knows that they do some pretty weird stuff out there. I mean, that place is like a bowl of granola, right? Once you've gotten rid of the fruits and the nuts, all you're left with is the flakes."

Sanderborn ignored his driver's last comment and stared at the approaching, harmless vagabond. He gestured with his head toward the garage.

"Come on, Harvey, let's get inside quickly. I don't want to attract too much attention, and there might be some prying eyes in these houses who are watching that homeless man."

Once inside, Sanderborn was careful to lock the door behind them. When he turned on the overhead lights, Harvey could see that, although the space had not undergone any radical modernization or even gotten any basic improvements other than a good cleaning, it was filled with several large, top-notch architectural models. In the center of this first room, a completely intact Stonehenge sat proudly on display. It had all of the original rings of ceremonial rocks, lintels, mounds, and the strands of copper cables going around the top of the inner circle. Despite Sanderborn's attempt to herd the young man along further to see the massive model in the garage showing all of the proposed changes to Vincennes, Harvey was unable to tear his eyes away from the Stonehenge model.

"Geez, this one's incredible, sir. This looks just like it did after it was constructed."

"Well, no one's seen it in that condition for over a few thousand years, Harvey. But yes, the model is an impressive reconstruction. My architects used the details extracted from the book by my experts just like a recipe, so it looks exactly how that wing-nut Professor Cooper said it should. If that mealy brained 'scientist' was correct, then the monument that we're building here in Vincennes – and that you'll be overseeing – will be the real deal. Course, that's a really big 'if.' After all, if the guy ends up having been nothing but a stark raving lunatic, then we'll be building nothing but a bogus monument to our own stupidity, right?"

"What *if* we get it right?"

"Like I just said, Harvey, we don't know for sure that we will. But the kook scientist was quite certain he was correct in the dimensions and descriptions of the monument. One thing you could say about the guy, he sure didn't lack any self-confidence. In his book, he's absolutely confident about his details. He claims that he found some kind of ancient message on a ceremonial dagger that he was studying which directed him to dig a hole near Stonehenge. So, he traveled there in the mid-1940s and got permission to do some kind of minor academic excavation at the site. He claims in his writings that he retrieved some kind of stone box with an ancient deer hide that had the precise measurements and the original layout of Stonehenge carefully inscribed onto it along with a small leather pouch containing a piece of sculpture. The present whereabouts of either of these artifacts is currently unknown, and most now question their authenticity."

Harvey leaned in toward the model until his nose was almost touching it. He made a noise that sounded akin to the clicks used in echolocation, but he made them to show how impressed he was.

"It's uncanny, sir."

"Well, the actual monument is currently still unfinished, Harvey. And you know how impatient I can be under the best of circumstances. I am well beyond those normal feelings of discontent right now. I want this new Stonehenge completed...soon. After I'm done showing you some of the models of the other improvements we've planned for this town, your job is to have Jerry take you immediately over to the site and get a lay of the land. I want you to really understand the scope of the project and survey the overall layout of the place. Over the next few days, I need you to go over there as the new supervisor and seriously rattle some chains to get those workers off their asses so you can jump-start this thing."

"Yes, sir."

"As for me, I'm gonna stay here to make some phone calls to encourage some more high-level investors to buy into this little Vincennes development of mine. Oh, before you go, let me show you where the monorail is going to be built. That thing is going to be so cool."

Harvey knew it was risky to keep ogling the Stonehenge model as he was, but he could not break away from it quite yet. When his boss loudly cleared his throat to get his attention, he reluctantly walked away from this exhibit and joined Sanderborn inside the garage portion of the building, where a sprawling model of the entire city covered the large space. The lighting of the intricately designed modernistic city came from a series of naked light bulbs temporarily hanging over the model, each one creating an unnatural glare over the faux scenery like it was under a supernova.

Upon seeing this, Harvey sniggered to himself. He could not help from thinking that if the light was going to be this bright in the new Vincennes, everyone would surely have to wear some ridiculous-looking sunglasses all the time to not be blinded.

The image of that amused him greatly.

You're Between a Rock and a Hard Place, James Hutton!

The next time the Mkultrans made an egregious mistake with an unknown world, it would have truly dire consequences for their species. This time, the error was due to the opposite emotions that had caused the mishap on Earth and it had to do more with their arrogant attitude toward planets that they deemed as sterile. Even though they usually were fastidiously determined to make sure a new planet's life forms were protected before they descended to explore the surface in person, they were almost cavalier in their approach when all the results came back that a sphere was lifeless. In such instances, they immediately took these harsh and potentially unwelcoming conditions as a challenge that only Mkultrans could conquer. A pronouncement of planetary deadness only opened the door for their attempting to create an unlikely settlement there.

It must be pointed out that most of these endeavors were actually free from overt imperialism. Instead of looking at these dead planets as a chance for some kind of territorial gain, the Mkultrans took on their colonization as a purely scientific advancement that defied all of the odds – a practical application of one of the main tenets of the highly academic Mkultran culture.

Their advanced intellect should have warned them about this dubious practice. After all, everyone knows that there may be only one truth in the Universe: life happens. Even when it seems obvious that a place is unconducive to encouraging any life forms in a Goldilocks-like way – it's too harsh, too poisonous, too cold, too hot, too liquid, too gaseous, etc. – things might not be as they seem. After all, those inhospitable conditions could either stretch the normal parameters of understanding and support some unknown specimen that could be, somehow, thriving there undisturbed as either a single-celled or a multi-celled entity *or* those inhospitable planetary characteristics could switch at the drop of a hat into the perfect broth needed to promote life in the near future.

In other words, the impossible *can* happen.

The Mkultrans had forgotten that no mere mortals have the ability to determine if a planet is actually full of life, dead, dormant, or going to sprout life someday. And it was a colossal fuck-up for them to assume that they somehow could.

The inconsequential seventh planet of their own solar system proved to be where this questionable assumption finally bit them on the ass. The tiny icy planet of Gherrard was assumed to be nothing more than a dead floating ice cube orbiting in the shadows of the other life-rich planets. Initial scans came back with the prognosis that it was far too harsh to maintain any form of life. Those drones that were sent down to conduct geological surveys and managed to survive the trip and come back in one piece usually provided more questions than definitive answers. The tumultuous and icy climate and the unusual rock of the planet made all scans and samplings inconclusive, at best.

As a result, the Mkultran scientific community made the faulty conclusion that, with such an obviously unfavorable environment, there wasn't anything alive down there. A movement to begin settling the planet started immediately, and vigorous efforts were thrown at solving the problem that was Gherrard.

The frozen planet did not go quietly into the night. It presented some of the worst weather ever encountered by Mkultran colony makers. Rather than be daunted, these persistent settlers wanted nothing more than to prove their brains could overcome anything that the planet had to offer. Originally, small outposts made up of specialized living quarters were set up to allow further scientific research to learn how to live comfortably in such a deadly environment. However, as they continued to overcome each obstacle presented, bigger and bigger settlements were designed and built on the planet. These, in turn, started to thrive and grow. Soon, other Mkultrans began to come to Gherrard seeking a fresh start in the newly constructed colony.

One Mkultran scientist saw the threat of an impending disaster. She'd had the wherewithal to persevere with running an old-fashioned deep manual coring mission, and when her drill tip broke through a substantially thick ice coating under the outer rock layer and then into nothing but breathable atmosphere, she'd realized the true depth of the Mkultran error. There might not have been anything alive on the *surface* of the planet, but she'd discovered that there was no question that the *interior* of the planet was quite capable of sustaining living things. The only conclusion she could come to was that the Mkultrans had just built a colony right atop a ticking time bomb.

Unfortunately, instead of taking her findings straight to her colleagues or the colonial government and preventing an impending disaster, she went for a quick swim in her settlement's public pool. By the time she stepped out after completing her usual fifty laps, the Gherrardians, who'd now become agitated by the apparent invasion of their subterranean world, had already burrowed up from within their hidden hives and were swarming over the Mkultran colonists in a bloodthirsty frenzy of killing.

As it turned out, the unique geology of the planet of Gherrard – the hollow center encapsulated by an incredibly thick rock crust sandwiched between an inner and outer sheet of ice – had made all of the earlier Mkultran scans useless. Blind to the fact that there actually was a savage species living undisturbed beneath them and within this planet, the very activity of the Mkultran colonists had agitated the rugged inhabitants. So, when they came streaming out of their underground colony, they were just like fire ants (*Solenopsis saevissima*) responding to an intruder. Not only were the Gherrardians on the warpath, they were quite pissed off.

The inside of the frozen planet had protected these creatures from the extreme elements and from any previous visitors, but the interior of the small planet was a rather tight space that could only contain so many of the creatures. Packed in like sardines (*Sardina pilchardus*), the Gherrardians were more than a little eager to burst out of their cramped quarters and unleash their intrinsic anger about being confined together against their wills for far too long on whomever they could find. They streamed into these newly constructed Mkultran colonies and slaughtered the inhabitants with glee.

A Gherrardian looks just like a blue crab (*Callinectes sapidus*), except much bigger. Actually, each individual is about the size of a white rhinoceros (*Ceratotherium simum*). Their natural shell armor is strong enough to repel almost any lightweight weapons that they're likely to encounter, and their claws are very effective killing tools. The right claw is large and is sharp enough to quickly decapitate almost any opponent with one swipe, while the left claw is a bio-battery capable of shooting highly lethal electric pulses in very effective and damaging bursts. They are a well-armored, well-armed relentless fighting machine, and the sight of an advancing horde of them might be particularly terrifying to a kabourophobe, but it is certainly nothing anyone in their right mind wants to see.

To make matters worse, these creatures are surprisingly intelligent. Once they quickly reduced those Mkultran colonists to nothing but Kibbles 'n Bits in their horrible mass orgy of destruction, they happily discovered a small fleet of Mkultran transport ships. The Gherrardians, in fact, had lacked the technology to design spaceships, so they were tickled pink that the Mkultrans had provided them with a ride to get off their dead planet and go anywhere they wanted.

As quick as a wink, the Gherrardian scientists keenly gleaned all the information they could from the Mkultran computers, loaded up some of their warriors onto the Mkultran space cruisers, which were all fueled up and ready to carry large loads of cargo and personnel throughout the solar system, and got the duck out of Fodge. As the rockets ascended, these new space travelers all squirmed as their gonopods swelled with excitement.

Part of their exuberance was due to the fact that the Gherrardians now knew everything that the Mkultran colonists knew. They now held in their barbarous claws an extremely good roadmap of the neighboring planets and solar systems, and even though their understanding of interstellar space travel using wormholes was rudimentary, they were suddenly well aware that the rest of the pertinent information on all of those topics was waiting for them to tap into on the home planet of Mkultra. Inspired by the promise of getting all of this knowledge for themselves, they quickly learned how to pilot the Mkultran spacecraft and they prepared themselves to play a devastating game of hopscotch as they made their way toward Mkultra.

The first stop was the very next planet. It had a much nicer atmosphere and a small population of unarmed residents. The Gherrardians made quick mincemeat of the unsuspecting inhabitants there. The crab-like marauders continued to send the pirated ships back to Gherrardia to ferry the rest of the cast to this planet to amass their forces for the next assault. Soon, with all the members of their species now on the new planet, their home world was actually left as lifeless as the Mkultrans had incorrectly assumed it was in the first place.

The Gherrardians were on the move now and, like a wave of viciousness and violence, they were ready to hop on and off the next planets in their quest of destruction. They were drunk on the promise of eradicating any species who had the misfortune of getting in their way and of plundering all available riches and technology in their path, and they were ready to repeat this cycle untold more times.

But they really only had eyes for one planet. Mkultra.

[Paranthetical Aside from the Quasi-Omniscient Narrator Morgen an Spyrys]

Pythia and I've known one another for over three millennia now, and, truthfully, she's been nothing but a thorn in my side since the first day that we met. Back then, I was an up-and-coming royal seer for King Danu, the powerful chieftain of a tribe ruling in the area near modern-day Dover, England. Meanwhile, Pythia was a rising soothsayer for King Erc, the leader of a warlike tribe from present day Wales who had eyes on the lands to the east. The ambitions of these two power-hungry chieftains had brought them to a direct confrontation with one another. The resulting stalemate between them had been forecasted to have an unpleasant outcome – by none other than Pythia and myself – so they both decided to meet at Stonehenge for a détente of sorts to avoid this unnecessary bloodshed.

Neither leader was overly troubled about spilling the blood of their people, but they could not stomach the fact that they'd been told by their psychic advisors that the imminent war between the two tribes was going to lead to their own deaths. In another bit of bad news, they were informed that their deaths would leave a dangerous power vacuum in the region that would be filled by another king who would become legendary in history. All this information did not sit well with either one of them. So, in a naked act of self-preservation, not to mention self-promotion, both of these weak men made an attempt to avoid the inevitable conflict at all costs.

Things started out well. Both King Erc and King Danu opted to leave their armies behind and travel with only their spiritual consultants – which included Pythia and me – to the most magical of sites, Stonehenge. There they hoped to let calmer minds engineer a compromise that would prevent a disastrous war without completely sabotaging their own personal lusts for land and power. With a peace treaty in place, they figured that they could stay very much alive and continue their aggressive acquisition of territory in a quieter way until they received a less dire prediction about their demises from an armed conflict with the other.

Pythia and I were both mere preteen girls at the time. Being children born with the gift – the uncanny ability to talk with dead people, read some minds, and see into the future – we'd both been drafted into the service of our leaders rather than taking our rightful place as their sexual concubines. I'm not being arrogant when I say that both of us were stunningly beautiful, so we had been spared some unspeakable physical hardships by our psychic skills.

Actually, being able to prognosticate not only provided us with a foolproof way to work our way into the inner circle of the leadership by continuing to correctly predict what was going to happen, but it also allowed us to be in a position to quietly take possession of the reins of the whole show without the foolish kings having any idea that we were doing so.

These were the times before most people understood anything about most everything, so even though we hadn't had our first period yet, both Pythia and I were highly esteemed by our kings and our people as soon as we'd nailed a few perfect predictions together into a string of successful prophecies. It might sound self-aggrandizing, but we each had achieved the status of a minor deity, and this position of power gave us carte blanche. And like all psychics through the ages, we understood how – once we'd hooked our audience – we needed to play them out before we boated them.

This very important gathering at Stonehenge between King Danu and King Erc proved to be a peaceful one. The tribe of caretakers of the venerable stone monument had supernatural skills that were heralded throughout the entire region, and they went out of their way to accommodate the two tribal representatives and their psychic guides. Everyone involved performed admirably as we all danced in our silly performance to avert a bloodletting between these two moronic chieftains which was actually unavoidable.

All the while, however, the Stonehenge guardians used every trick in the book to get Pythia and me alone long enough to recruit us. We were the real big prize.

King Erc and King Danu finally came to an oral agreement. The terms of the treaty sought to create a lasting peace by avoiding any head-to-head conflicts that might jeopardize that fragile peace as the two tribes coexisted in the same area. By the time the idiots had finally committed to pretending to play nice, Pythia and I had been wooed away from our handlers. Truth was, they hadn't had to work too hard on either of us. We both agreed to join their ranks and be tutored by the most powerful witch of the surrounding woods, the legendary Haggur, almost before the question was out of their mouths.

After the two concerned parties had returned to their homelands, Pythia and I cleverly snuck away from our respective caravans to hightail it back to Stonehenge to begin our training. Other than our interactions at the peace summit, Pythia did not know me and I did not know her, but we both could see our futures, so we understood that we were about to embark together on the opportunity of a lifetime. We were both giddy as little girls to become Haggur's apprentices.

Unfortunately, our departures away from our kings were to have dire consequences. Both King Erc and King Danu quickly lost faith in the tentative truce once they'd learned that their young mediums – Pythia and I – had taken their leave, and believing our disappearance revealed some kind of conspiracy with Haggur and so became an invalidation of our previous visions, the two imbeciles amassed their armies and attacked one another in a huge and devastating battle. As forecasted, each leader ended up dead as a doornail and their lack of any living heirs opened the door for a new third party, a lowly tribe to the south led by a king with great ambitions named Arthur, who swooped in and took control of both leaderless kingdoms. As Sir Isaac Newton pointed out, it's easy to calculate the motion of heavenly bodies; it's impossible to calculate the madness of men.

From the git-go, our tutelage with Haggur was a rocky affair. Both of us being psychics certainly didn't help matters, nor did our immaturity. While Pythia and I both could clearly see that we were fated to fight one another for the rest of our lives, we were far too young at that moment to understand that we could change our futures with some minor acceptances and a few compromises. Instead, Pythia and I put our defenses up and prepared ourselves to best the other. With nothing ahead of us but a lifetime of sabotaging one another, apparently, it was extremely hard – quite impossible, actually – to build any kind of team spirit between us. Everything we did, we did only to get a leg up on our competition.

Haggur made it abundantly clear that, while all indications pointed to the likelihood that the two of us would become each other's nemesis and we would foolishly spend the countless millennia needlessly fighting one another, we needed to put aside our baby games long enough to prepare ourselves for the important roles we were also to play in the unfurling fate of the human race over the course of time. When Haggur gave any kind of command like this, there was little doubt that it needed to be followed wholeheartedly, so Pythia and I called our own truce and began to concentrate on honing our talents.

However, this alliance was not built out of philanthropy or for the common good of our species. No, we did so with the primal understanding that we each needed to be just as strong and skilled as the other. When you're training and practicing with the one person you know you will have to fight against for the rest of your existence, you develop a uniquely intense regimen to get better, stronger, and more powerful than the other.

Well, there was one other reason for our apparent eagerness. Haggur had made it known to us that she was going to retire soon, and she was training us to be her replacements. After leapfrogging her way through the eras since time immemorial, Haggur was tired. Using a simple soul-transference spell to jump from one host to the next had taken its toll on the old witch over time. She'd seen enough, experienced enough, and fought enough, and she said that she wanted nothing more than a little peace and quiet for the conceivable future. The physical body she was currently occupying was going to expire soon, and instead of choosing a new one to inhabit, she was opting to get off the bus at the next stop and take five.

There are only vague legends in the mystical world about mediums who have selected this pathway before, but there aren't, for obvious reasons, any real testimonials about what actually happens. Haggur said she trusted in the theory that her soul would just become one with Nature to drift around the ether for the rest of time, and she looked forward to the transition into a more peaceful existence/non-existence. Before any of this happened, however, she needed to be sure that she had some capable successors to leave this world. So she threw herself into turning Pythia and me into the most powerful duet of psychic entities the world had ever seen.

Haggur was downright maniacal when it came to teaching us everything. All of the spells, stories, potions, spiritual advice, and shape-shifting knowledge that she'd acquired in her lifetimes needed to be absorbed by her pupils as quickly as we could properly soak it all in. Such a comprehensive learning experience was demanding and exhaustive, but Pythia and I wanted to pass all of our tests with flying colors. We both desired to make our teacher happy with us, and so we learned everything she had to teach us, pushing ourselves to be the best at all the skills Haggur was trying to hone in us with her relentless training.

And in the meantime, we secretly looked to become proficient in other ways to best each other or even banish one another to the Void.

One of the most memorable stories Haggur told us then was about the first contact between the humans and a visiting bunch of space aliens called the Mkultrans. At the time, our young brains were not advanced enough to fully understand any of what our teacher was telling us. The fact that our world had been visited by space travelers who had left behind their gift of a stone circle beacon was much too much for us to comprehend, and we stored it with all the vast parcels of information our teacher was dispensing to us at that time, but we could not access it or use it.

I cannot speak for Pythia, but only later did I begin to understand that Haggur had been spreading seeds onto our fertile ground when she'd told us this specific tale. To be blunt, she was practicing a little psychic onanism when she told us all about the aliens and our role in calling them back some day. Little did Pythia or I have any clue that we were about to embark upon a long-term journey toward our ultimate fate.

I guess we know it now.

As was prophesied, Haggur's last earthly body eventually started to give out. Although the death of an elderly woman during these times was usually considered a non-event, this one had a somewhat higher level of observation. Her coterie of priests and priestesses brought Pythia and me to gather around her deathbed to witness her passing. But as she was laboring for breath, she suddenly called out to speak to her chief priest. He leaned over the old hag as she whispered something into his ear. When she was finished, Haggur lay back, exhaled one last time, and died.

Without a word, this high priest headed off immediately to secretly bury Haggur's sacred bejeweled golden dagger for safekeeping. He came back a little later and told us that her last words were that that very special item needed to be safeguarded until there was someone around who was actually trustworthy and mature enough to wield it. As he said this, he gave Pythia and me a withering look of discontent. He felt the need to point out further that Haggur didn't trust us enough to let either of us get our hands on something so powerful and valuable, so she'd hidden it from us.

Pythia and I were far too overwhelmed by all that we needed to do to finalize Haggur's death rites to squabble about the dagger. The truth was, we were too busy to be interested in it at that moment. We'd been handed the role of being the head witches of Stonehenge, and that responsibility required us to place Haggur's lifeless shell within a secret bog and complete a series of elaborate spells to help set her soul free.

By the time all of these duties were over, we were exhausted to the point of collapse, and I think we simply forgot all about the dagger...well, for the moment we did.

Pythia and I were then officially named as co-chief witches of the Stonehenge area. This position had never been a cooperative one before, but our holy attendants were hopeful that there might be strength in numbers. After all, two of something is usually better than just one. However, this isn't true when it comes to positions of power – especially high priestesses, ship captains, or head chefs – so our previously peaceful little duet was not to be long-lived.

With Haggur no longer around to referee, Pythia and I were now entirely free to contemplate how we were going to get rid of one another. If the glass between two Siamese fighting fish (*Betta splendens*) is suddenly removed, those two fish are going to immediately duke it out – it's just in their natures. So when our powerful mentor popped out of the picture, Pythia and I both set about trying to take care of the competition. And the gloves came off.

Looking back upon this now, I can clearly see that we were nothing but two bratty, ambitious little girls who'd been given too much power too quickly. I guess that it's understandable that we acted like a pair of immature, catty bitches, but it still causes me to wince with shame.

However, shadow boxing in front of a mirror is a lot harder than it looks. Haggur had succeeded far too well in training us to be equals in the mystical arena, and Pythia and I were too evenly matched for either of us to actually win any kind of a head-to-head confrontation. No matter what spell, incantation, or evil deed that we tried, we were unable to best the other since there was the perfect defense already in place. All of our skirmishes kept ending up in frustrating stalemates.

At this point, another reality about the relationship between Pythia and me reared its head. A new and powerful psychic repulsion was developing between us. We both felt very sick whenever we were in close proximity. We tested this hypothesis by moving closer and farther away from one another, but the results were painfully clear. We were prone to waves of headaches, general emotional agitation, nausea, and hot flashes whenever we were too close. Somehow Haggur had been able to buffer all of this to make our training together possible, but her death had removed this and left us each with an opponent we couldn't beat and one we couldn't stand to be around either. We were in a real no-win situation.

The solution finally presented itself. The truth was, while being the head co-priestesses at Stonehenge was a great gig, it certainly wasn't the only show in town. The position might have had one of the highest levels of prestige during those dark days of the human experience, but there were plenty of other, similar soothsayer positions around that could provide both power and great economic reward for any ambitious medium with the right skill set. So, under another temporary flag of truce, Pythia and I met together to discuss all of our options.

Surprisingly, we were both actually able to stay fairly civil while we openly discussed what we needed to do to get ourselves out of the mess we currently found ourselves in. We came to a pretty quick agreement that it'd be best for the two of us to separate. If no town was ever going to be big enough for the two of us, one of us would have to leave and set out to find a place far away to put down her own tent stakes, while the other would stay and play the high priestess role at Stonehenge.

Pythia was actually the one who rationally pointed out that I should stay, since I was really what amounted to being a local. She, on the other hand, had her eyes on something farther in the west...Ireland. By using a simple soul-transference spell, she hoped to hop from her current body into one of our low-ranking older male priests and head over to the mystical lands with some gold traders who consistently sailed to Eire. She'd heard of a venerable monument where she was convinced she could take over as head priestess.

In a rare moment of solidarity, we actually came to an agreement on this plan, shook hands, and kept the peace while Pythia made the preparations for her journey. With her soul transferred into a better traveling vessel, we waved good-bye to one another as Pythia walked away from Stonehenge.

Her departure revealed yet another unknown connection between us. Before Pythia had even reached the coast to make contact with the traders, I suddenly felt the first mild inkling that I should follow after her. It turns out that we have an equal magnitude of repulsion *and* attraction between us. To our disdain, we discovered that we are, in fact, like two big, walking, talking magnets when it comes to our relationship. Whenever we're too close, we repulse one another. But when we're too far apart, there's a natural attraction so strong that we feel compelled to follow.

As luck would have it, however, on this first separation, things worked out in our favor. Once Pythia had settled into her new gig at the ancient monument at Newgrange, the geographic distance between our two holy sites turned out to be ideal for balancing the push-pull of our dysfunctional connection. While I could sense that Pythia was out there somewhere and felt the slightest of impulses to head her way, the faint attraction was neutralized by the weak repulsion I felt from her being close. And since I was more than content with my role at Stonehenge, I was happy to stay put and carry on with my duties. Little did we know that this harmonic stasis was going to last for nearly five hundred years of peaceful bliss.

Now, back to the rest of the story...

Don't Get Bent Out of Shape, Adonis Ames!

Morton Richardson had ceased staring at the golden dagger in the display case and then focused on something about halfway up the wall which was only visible to him. Without any prompting, he began to talk, but his face now had a blank expression and his voice was a robotic monotone.

Both Eve and Hunter Cooper understood that the man was about to recite something memorable, and he wished to do so without any interruption. They quietly sat down in two chairs that were nearby and listened intently to whatever was going to be shared.

"I was seven years old. Vincennes was abuzz with the excitement that a Grand Fair was going to be held on the land down on the riverfront where the infamous Fort Sackville once stood. This immense gala was to celebrate the sesquicentennial anniversary of George Rogers Clark's expedition *and* raise the necessary local funds needed to start the construction of the national monument.

"Word had gone out, far and wide, about this special gathering, and the world-famous Cole Brothers Circus was scheduled to come to perform. Every small circus troupe, freak show, and entertainment venue within a thousand miles was also signing up to be involved. Even the great evangelist Reverend Billy Sunday had committed to have a massive revival at the event. The people of Vincennes were over the moon about all of this. It was all that anyone could think about, talk about.

"As the date of the Great Fair approached, our little town appeared to become the center of the Universe. I can still remember watching the endless trains coming in loaded with the exotic animals, tents, circus performers, and amusement rides. The roads, in all directions, were full of caravans of trucks, tractors, buses, cars, and horse-drawn carriages carrying and towing attractions to take part in this once-in-a-lifetime event. The growing anticipation of it all held us – adult and child alike – like a fever.

"My friends and I rode our bikes on a daily basis down to the site to watch the hustle-bustle of the crews as they erected the giant canvas tents, set up the rides and attractions, stockaded the animals, built the avenues of entertainment on the fairgrounds, and arranged the various trailers of the eccentric cast of performers and acts. To this very day, the palpable excitement we all felt still makes the hair on my arms stand up.

"On opening night, my mother, my father, my older brother Henry, and I – my whole family – got ready to go to the fair. My mother had insisted that we all bathe and put on our Sunday finest, which took some of the fun out of the experience, but it was a small price to pay. While we started walking there, the usually quiet sidewalks of our neighborhood became bustling tributaries of humanity, flowing with every inhabitant of Vincennes and every visitor to our fair city as we all made our way toward the fairgrounds.

"With each footstep, a building symphony of the senses grew. The sustained, excited murmurs of the crowd joined the far off sounds of calliopes, the performed music of various bands, the organ music coming from the revival tent, and the shrill voices of the hawkers shouting out their promises about their attractions. These sounds mingled with the ever-present smells of the livestock, circus animals, wood smoke, and aromas of cooking food to create an inebriating ambrosia that was as irresistible as a siren's song, drawing everyone in helplessly, closer and closer, to its core.

"Inside the gates the absurd energy only gained more intensity. Even my parents struggled to stay calm. But, because Reverend Billy Sunday's sermon that day was going to be about sexual infidelities, divorce, and the evils of drinking, they'd decided that Henry and I could skip the revival and instead head off to explore on our own at the fair while they were inside the tent. Drunk from this sudden freedom and overstimulated by what was going on around us, my brother and I ran everywhere we went, like we were frantically searching for some kind of lost treasure.

"Only much later did I understand the layers of this new world that my brother and I found ourselves in as we headed out on our own adventures that day. Even though there was a real circus set up there, the two of us found ourselves in the very midst of another, much wider metaphorical three ring circus, and this one was going to have immense impacts on our lives.

"For starters, the crowds of the religious pilgrims who were there for Reverend Billy Sunday were looking for piety, salvation, and redemption. The civic leaders of Vincennes, on the other hand, were there because they were overly eager to sell their souls to create something that would put our town back on the map again. And, most importantly, there were the throngs of hedonistic thrill-seekers who wanted – no, needed – nothing more than to have a good time. These three independent forces were not complementary to one another. Actually, when these three groups came into contact and stood shoulder to shoulder at the fair, they were one wee spark away from producing a violent and scorching immolation.

"Disregarding our parents' strict warnings to stay away from the tawdry sideshows, we were drawn directly to them. Without meaning to, we found ourselves standing in the middle of a virtual village of mystery-filled tents, campers, and sheds, each flying countless colorful canvas banners and hand-painted signs portraying the almost unbelievable sights within. Here, the spittle-rich bellowing of the hawkers rained down like sleet upon the engorged crowd as it grunted anxiously while making its way through this area and sounding very much like cattle headed to the slaughterhouse.

"We were about to buy tickets to go into the exhibit that promised us to be able to view the mummified body of Myrtle Corbin, the four-legged woman who had been a sideshow legend since she was thirteen years old. She'd died the year before, and the sing-song shouts of the slimy ticket seller claimed that the poor woman's body had been secretly extracted from her grave so that she could continue touring. Henry and I were intrigued to see the macabre exhibit and were ready to plunk our coins down, but a pair of bony hands suddenly grabbed us by the arms and yanked us away and back into the current of milling spectators.

"'You kids don't wanna go in there. It's a fraud. I know for a fact that Myrtle Corbin's family poured fresh cement onto her coffin to keep the grave robbers from getting to her. Whatever they've got in there, it ain't Myrtle. Naw, boys, if you wanna see the real McCoy of entertainment, we got it over there in our tent. Truth be told, all the performers in our act are headed right out to Hollywood after this fair to be in a motion picture called *Freaks*. When we've become big movie stars, ain't nobody gonna be able to afford gawkin' at us then, I can tell you that much.'

"As the man continued to pull us through the crowd toward another attraction tent, we were able to make out that he was nothing but skin and bones. He was so slight in stature, there was a chance that my brother and I might have outweighed this man who was forcibly maneuvering us toward his show. We did not resist him because his grip was so tight as to be nearly painful.

"'Please, mister,' my brother Henry implored, 'we don't want any trouble.'

"'Trouble? You two ain't in any trouble, kids. My name is Peter Robinson, and I'm known as "The Living Skeleton." I'm taking you two to an attraction that will change your lives. I'm tellin' ya, you're in for a real treat when we get there!'

"At the ticket stand outside the canvas tent, the skinny man arranged a deal so that we'd only have to pay for one admission. Henry put down our money and the gaunt man escorted us inside. He took us right over to the fat lady, a Ms. Helen 'Bunny' Smith, and introduced us to her. This immense woman was wearing a baby doll dress and was sitting on a substantial red leather love seat that was made for two people, but barely fit her.

"'Where ya been, Pete?'

"'Went to check up on Koo Koo over at Pythia's trailer. She's gonna stay there and keep an eye on things.'

"'Whatcha doing with those two kids?'

"'Oh, they were about to head into that distasteful Myrtle Corbin scam, so I steered them in here instead.'

"'Well, Pete, they look downright terrified. I think you're scaring them. Why don't you let go of them before they piss their pants?'

"'Oh, sorry, boys. I didn't mean to scare you none.'

"The fat lady moved her head forward and smiled warmly at us.

"'Pete tends to get a tad bit passionate about things. That's why we've been married for as long as we have. He didn't mean no harm, boys. But he's right. You two are in for a treat inside these walls. Take your time and enjoy the show.'

"The woman's voice was calming, and any fear from the apparent abduction by the skeletal man now dissipated as we turned to survey the scene inside the tent. I can still see all the sights and hear all the sounds of that freak show today as clearly as I did back when I was seven – now, fifty years later. I haven't forgotten a single detail about anything.

"We saw Olga Roderick, the 'Bearded Lady,' as she combed her beard with a thick bristled Fuller hairbrush. We were awed by the legless Johnny Eck, the 'Half Boy,' as he performed his one-handed handstands atop a Hack & Simon beer barrel. We stood silent and still as the caterpillar-looking, limbless Prince Randian, 'The Human Torso,' rolled his own cigarette and then lit it with a match, all using only his mouth. We marveled at the dwarfish Angelo Rossitto as he danced atop a dinner table in a miniature tuxedo. We gasped in amazement as the armless Frances O'Connor, 'The Living Venus de Milo,' used her feet to aim and shoot a rifle, flawlessly hitting the spots on the playing cards suspended in the air. And lastly, we stared speechlessly as the pinheads, the Snow Twins – Zip and Pip – and Schlitzie all danced together to music performed by the Siamese twins named the Hilton Sisters.

"At the exit, the half-man, half-woman hermaphrodite Josephine Joseph was stationed to send all the visitors off with a hand-blown kiss and to act as a bouncer to prevent people from sneaking into the attraction through the exit. As my brother and I passed, he/she leaned down and harshly whispered at us in a deeper male voice.

"'Go outside and then over two rows of avenues, until you get to Pythia the Magnificent's trailer. She's a fortune teller, and she's expecting you.'

"He/she then said in a higher feminine voice, 'When you get there, just walk right in, you two little darlings.'

"Henry and I were understandably more than a little bit overwhelmed. After the life-changing and magical experience of seeing all the exotic performers in the exhibits, we wanted to get some food and then go on a few rides before the service finished up at the revival tent and we needed to return to our parents. But the command to go to Pythia's trailer had been so stern, we knew we couldn't refuse it. After all, we figured that if a psychic was expecting us, we couldn't make her angry, since there'd be no way to escape her wrath.

"Just like Josephine Joseph had told us, Pythia the Magnificent's trailer was a short walk from the freak show. It was nothing more than a glorified gypsy caravan with big wagon wheels and an ornately painted wainscoting siding, with hand-carved ornamentation on the corners and around the doorway. We could see through the windows that there were people inside, but my brother and I kept losing our nerve as we repeatedly went up and down the trailer's stairs, just looking for a way to escape something we knew in our guts was inescapable.

"The door to the trailer swung open, and there stood a bald woman wearing a feathered outfit. She had a huge fore-head and very large circular glasses. Her beak-like nose was thrust at us in an accusatory and slightly threatening way. She was not very tall, but her figure took up the entire door-way. From our vantage point at the bottom of the stairs, she loomed very large and seemed ready to pounce on us.

"A voice called out from inside the trailer, 'No, Koo Koo, that's not her. Those two little boys do play a major role in it all, so bring them inside and show them where they can sit and wait.'

"The way that the bald woman nodded made her resemble a chicken" (*Gallus gallus*) "even more than when she was confronting us. She brusquely pushed my brother and me inside, spun the sign to show that the trailer was now closed for business, and then slammed the door shut. Henry and I were forcibly placed onto a battered and uncomfortable horsehair sofa in the main parlor and instructed to not say a word, no matter what happened.

"Pythia was sitting at a table and wearing a gypsy cos-tume. She was seated across from an older black couple, a man and a woman, and she was handling what looked like a tattered family cookbook. From time to time, the psychic brought the opened book up to her face and chanted some kind of incantation into its pages.

"'You want me to look for any ghosts, is that right, Mrs. Bishop?'

"'Yes, ma'am. That very cookbook's been in my family for generations. We've been thinkin' that there's some kind of magic in it.'

191

"'Well, there's definitely something spiritually powerful to this book, that's for sure. Do you feel comfortable leaving it with me? I need to reopen for business and keep reading the futures of the crowds at this fair – I have to pay the bills, after all – but I want to take my time with your cookbook and give it my full attention so that I can give you a proper reading about it.'

"'Yes, ma'am. I s'pose we can leave it here with you. We can come back tomorrow and get it, if that's alright with you.'

"'Certainly. I'll take good care of it. Once we're fully closed down for the night, I'll spend some time going through it, and I'll have a definitive answer for you tomorrow.'

"The couple answered in unison, 'Thank you, Miss Pythia.'

"'No, thank you, Mr. and Mrs. Bishop. This is the first interesting thing I've had my hands on all day. It wouldn't be an understatement to say that most of the hayseeds living around these parts do not live the most thrilling of lives. Except for the occasional pronouncements of, "The pig is going to give birth soon," "Your husband is having sex with your neighbor in the corn crib every Thursday afternoon," or "Your Auntie Gertrude is hiding her money in the floorboards of the living room," there hasn't been anything overly exciting to divine from these people. It's been enough to put any psychic to sleep, honestly. But this cookbook is very different, very interesting.'

"She said goodbye and the elderly couple left the trailer, escorted out by the odd bird woman. Henry and I sat very still on the couch, not speaking, and watched as Pythia hummed to herself and continued to peruse the pages of the cookbook. Finally she looked up at us and smiled.

"'You two are among the best behaved lads I've ever seen. Seriously, how many little boys your age would just sit there and wait for whatever's going to happen next? Not many. Fewer adults, actually. I cannot imagine this particular future being in better hands, Henry and Morton.'

"I remember looking down at my hands. They were too small to be holding much of anything, and I doubted that the woman was being honest with us.

"'How do you know our names?'

"Henry's question was rife with the swirling emotions inside him, but it took a moment for the full impact of his inquiry to hit me. The fortune teller had just uttered our names, even though we hadn't said them aloud to her!

"'Oh, my dears, I'm a psychic. That literally means that I can see into the future. So I knew you two – Henry and Morton Richardson – would be sitting right here in my trailer with me tonight. Well, that's not entirely true. I've seen enough to know that we humans have an unlimited number of choices at our disposal to choose from at every instant of our lives, so any prediction about what is going to happen or what is not going to happen is certainly not ironclad.

"'You two were faced with many decisive moments that led you to come inside this trailer and sit down on that sofa on this very night, but anywhere along the way, you could have chosen to take your leave from this timeline's main channel. From the time you left your house and entered the fairgrounds to the moment of your arrival here, there was an almost unlimited menu of decisions that could have possibly altered this present. You could have resisted Pete's strong-arm tactics of getting you into their tent, disregarded Josephine's direction to come to this trailer, or then run away before Koo Koo let you in. Even now, you're both free to escape. However, I'm betting that you're going to stay and watch this whole thing play itself out.

"'So listen up, Henry and Morton. The next few theatrical moments are going to be somewhat scary, but I need you two to sit right here and do one and only one thing. Whatever happens, whatever you witness, you must save this here cookbook and that golden dagger over there on the table when it falls onto the floor later. I want you to snatch them both up, run right out of this fair, and don't ever tell anyone about what happened here tonight. I'll come find you to retrieve both items. Got it?'

"Henry and I nodded and stayed silent. We snuggled closer to protect each other from whatever was going to take place.

"Just then, firecrackers went off outside of the trailer. They sounded like gunshots. Koo Koo the bird lady charged to the front door like an angry goose." (*Anser anser domesticus*) "When she opened the door, the outside fair-going world was in a panicked pandemonium from the perceived gunplay.

"If I weren't staring straight at Pythia, I would never have noticed the trailer window slightly behind her open silently and the small midget dressed all in black stealthily climb into the trailer, grab the golden dagger in his hand, and approach Pythia with clearly murderous intentions. I nudged my brother and he turned to warn her, but we both remembered the admonishment we'd just received from her to stay silent no matter what, so we held our tongues.

"Pythia seemed preoccupied with the clamor coming from outside the front door, and the dwarfish assassin came up closer behind her with the blade poised to slit her throat. I started to avert my eyes, but Koo Koo somehow spied what was happening and came running straight at the attacker, squawking with alarm. She tackled the little man and the dagger went clattering across the floor.

"Their ruckus knocked over some candles and a kerosene lamp that were lighting the space, and these broke out into flames that caught quickly and spread unnaturally fast throughout the trailer. Koo Koo's feathered suit ignited, forcing her to run out through the front door and down the steps to roll onto the ground to extinguish the flames. While our attention was focused on this, the little man in black came flying out of the smoke like he was shot out from a cannon. We would learn later that he was a miniature acrobat from a nearby trapeze act, but when we saw him spring through the embers, his movements seemed almost superhuman.

"In midair, the man twisted his body and grabbed the cookbook that Pythia had in her hands to keep it off of the now fiery table, and using his impressive momentum, he shoved this directly into Pythia's larynx. The woman fell like a clump of bricks to the floor of the trailer as the tiny ninja landed on his feet and turned around to face my brother and me. We were hugging one another because we were sure that the little man was going to hurt us next.

"Just then, however, Koo Koo, her outfit singed and smoking, burst through the doorway and grabbed the man. He dropped the cookbook onto the floor as he attempted to ward her off. They wrestled furiously with one another and then tumbled back out the door and into the chaos reigning outside.

"The trailer was now nearly fully engulfed in flames and was completely filled with a smothering smoke. Pythia remained a lifeless shape on the floor, so my brother nudged me and yelled that we needed to get the hell out of there.

Remembering Pythia's commands, I jumped off the sofa and ran over to the dagger and the cookbook on the floor and grabbed them both. Henry took the dagger from me and shoved it deep inside his pocket as he forcibly ushered me out of the trailer.

"That old expression 'out of the frying pan and into the fire' applied to what we found as we reached what we'd assumed was going to be safety outside the trailer. While Koo Koo had extinguished the flames on her costume by rolling on the ground, she had inadvertently ignited the straw and sawdust that had been spread to make the avenues of the fair, and the flames that were now engulfing Pythia's trailer were spreading to the other nearby trailers and concessions. At the same time the members of the midget's trapeze act had come looking for him, and when they saw him and Koo Koo engaged in their brawl, they joined the fray. That's when Koo Koo's friends from the freak show tent came over to see the disturbance and the fire, and as they saw one of their own being attacked, they came to her rescue. The ensuing rumble escalated and spread.

"My brother and I darted out of the trailer and headed toward the exit of the fairgrounds just as we'd been commanded to by Pythia. I was holding the cookbook against my chest like it was a life preserver, and we ran blindly through the crowd. As we did, the waves of discord, panic, and fire seemed to follow us. When the righteous revival attendees – by now all whipped into a fervor by Reverend Billy Sunday to fight the demons of Hell – rushed headlong into the mass of frantic spectators running away from the fire and then into the violent melee of carnival workers embroiled in their fist-fight, it looked like three massive armies colliding in the middle of some kind of fiery battlefield.

"As luck would have it, Henry and I ran right into our parents. Seeing that all hell was breaking loose, they instinctively scooped us up as they hurried to exit the fairgrounds. The sound of shouts, screams, curses, and cracklings from the fire behind us was deafening as we made our way toward home. The expanding orange light from the raging fires made the black nighttime skies look like an early dawn was rising on the area.

"Unfortunately, the entire world was plunged into darkness with another event of the next few days when the calamitous events of the stock market crash of 1929 took place. So, the repercussions from the Great Fair Debacle were slightly muted. As soon as the financial institutions of this country took their dive and plunged the world into a seemingly bottomless abyss of hopelessness, the fiery failures – albeit disastrous – of a local fair in rural Indiana gone terribly bad kind of paled in comparison.

"That being said, with all the tents burned to the ground, with the scores of trailers and vehicles nothing but charred piles, and with the fairgrounds blackened into a nightmarish scene, the organizers had no other choice but to declare the Great Fair as an unmitigated disaster. What funds had been raised for the memorial were going to be spent trying to recoup almost unfathomable losses from it all. And someone was going to be responsible for paying the troops who had to be called in to quell the pockets of continued violence and subdue the escaped and roaming circus animals.

"Incredibly, the fiery riot had only produced one known fatality. That turned out to be the carnival psychic known as Pythia the Magnificent. The grisly discovery of her grilled corpse in the remnants of her trailer, which investigators later identified as the epicenter of both the fire and disturbance, was the only confirmed death from the whole horrible fiasco. While there were still many people unaccounted for, it was assumed that they were either part of the flood of injured patients currently clogging the region's hospitals or the wave of stragglers who'd hit the road to flee from any retribution, legal or otherwise.

"The next day, my brother and I hopped onto our bikes and rode down to the ruined fairgrounds to see the devastation for ourselves. We couldn't get too close, but the smells and smoky sights of the ravaged area were repulsive enough to send us immediately on our way out to the Bishops' farm to return their cookbook to them. They were completely surprised that it had survived, since they'd figured the cherished family item had been consumed by the great fire, so they were incredibly appreciative. Upon inspection of the book, however, they were somewhat dismayed to find a fresh new entry on the last page. They confronted us as to why we'd write something in their possession, but my brother and I were so staunch in our denials that they eventually came to the conclusion that maybe Pythia had left that message for them.

"It said, 'I will be right back.'

"My family never spoke again about the events of that night. The Great Fair Fire and the Great Depression proved to be a debilitating one-two combination punch to our lives. The latter laid a financial shadow over all of us which we would never really get out from underneath, and the former had been an absolute financial disaster for my father's insurance company. Wheatfield Insurance had issued some large policies to cover the event, and the payouts from those nearly destroyed the company. It survived, barely, but my father was never the same again. He resisted the urge to take his own life, but the man was broken so badly that he couldn't ever be fixed.

"Henry and I kept the golden dagger our secret. We took turns hiding it among our clothing drawers, and we resisted the urge to take it out and admire it. There were some moments when we could not stop ourselves, however, and we would stare at the artifact like it was something divine. Even more, although we didn't know why, we took an oath to keep it safe, no matter what. With the publicized death of Pythia, we knew that she wasn't going to be coming back for it like she'd said she would, so we figured it was ours to protect forever.

"Unfortunately, all of our possessions had to be inventoried and catalogued when my father filed for bankruptcy. This humiliating experience was made worse when a very keen auditor found the dagger hidden among our clothing. He alerted his superiors that we had something of great value, and they made the decision that a charitable donation of this magnitude to the University of Vincennes would go a long way to helping us pay off our family's debts. A school archivist wearing white gloves came over immediately to our house, carefully wrapped the artifact in tissue paper, and put it in a box, and then quickly drove away. That was the last time I ever saw the golden dagger...until this very moment."

Morton Richardson turned his head to look at his wife and Hunter Cooper, and he exhaled deeply, as if he'd just run a marathon.

"So, now you two know how I'm connected to this dagger, but there's something even weirder that I need to report. It turns out that there's a new player in town these days – some kind of billionaire from back east – who has big plans for Vincennes. He approached me to take out some humongous policies to protect a few of the outlandish projects that he's already started and intends to implement here in our town. I happened to mention to him your museum project, Hunter, and he's very, very interested in meeting you. I've set up a meeting for you guys to talk tomorrow."

"Oh, that's great, Morty-baby! I'm so tickled, I could kiss you right now I'm so..."

"No, Hunter, there's more. He says that he currently has his hands on the very book you're looking for – your grand-father's book on Stonehenge. And, in a surprising twist, he also really wants to find this very magical dagger to make it his own possession."

They all went silent after this and stared mutely at one another.

Only the sounds of the CSX train with a load of grain headed south to Evansville could be heard somewhere in the distance.

You Had Me Running in Circles, Archimedes!

Meanwhile, Shaniqua and Pythia were having a come-to-Jesus moment in their motel room at the Kum Back Inn. The psychic was beginning to recognize just how extraordinary the young black woman she was residing within actually was. Instead of the usual pushback from most hosts she possessed, Shaniqua not only seemed willing to accept that she now had a psychic medium from the Bronze Age living inside her, but she was absolutely fine with the developing plan to get their collective hands on some kind of sacred dagger that was connected to Stonehenge.

Conversely, Shaniqua was currently digging in her heels a bit more to get an honest explanation from her spiritual stowaway about the *real* reasons behind her now having to dry heave into the dirty motel toilet.

Normally, such a psychic medium like Pythia operating within a host's body would have been tempted to give the old speech about how such information was on a need-to-know basis, and since there was no need for Shaniqua to know, there was no need to tell her anything. But Pythia was still in a weakened state from both the recent escaping from her imprisonment in the cookbook and the sudden detection that Morgen was nearby, so she felt more inclined to address the young woman's ultimatum. The truth was, she liked Shaniqua. And she had a hunch that the young woman might actually be able to understand the madness of the past and yet still be willing to help her with getting through the zany present into the predicted future.

Without using "Once upon a time...," Pythia started at the beginning. She talked about her birth in the countryside of what is now modern-day Wales and the emergence of her "gift." Her psychic ability had instantly made her become a local celebrity among her people and, more to the point, caught the eye of the local chieftain. This led invariably to her involuntary service to King Erc, and as one of his psychic advisors, the visions coming to her arrived in nonstop strings. She'd seen the threat of war, the peace accord at Stonehenge, the meeting of fellow soothsayers Morgen and Haggur for the first time, her recruitment into the Stonehenge people, training with the mythical witch, King Erc's death, Haggur's passing, the resulting feud with Morgen, and even her eventual departure to become the head priestess at Newgrange.

She stopped the historical recounting to start a lengthy sidebar to explain the details about the soul-transference spell. She called this surprisingly simple magical ritual the "bread and butter" of any time-traveling psychic medium, but she freely admitted that "time-traveling" wasn't really a realistic term. The soul-transference spell only enabled a clairvoyant to be able to ride time, like a surfer carving a barrel, not really travel into the past or into the future. In actuality, this spell allowed the psychic to hang ten on the temporal wave for as long as they can. She went on to relay how her mentor Haggur had been insistent on teaching her students how to do it so well that they could cast it all with their eyes closed. Understanding this was the key to understanding the past that Pythia was going to disclose to Shaniqua.

What made the spell so special, she said, was that it did three things at once. It simultaneously prepared the exiting souls for becoming loosened up enough to exit the body, readied the new host – animate or inanimate – for possession by a foreign spiritual energy, and set the entire process into motion as soon as it started. It truly was one-stop shopping.

The key was for the spell's caster to do some proper planning to ensure that things went smoothly. Because the spell had a trinity of impacts, all of the psychic avenues needed to be made completely clear for transport. That being said, Haggur had instructed her two young prodigies that, in some special and necessary situations, the spell could be done on-the-fly to react to a particularly tricky and dangerous moment. When it came to a fight or flight situation, Haggur went so far as to say, "When in doubt, cast it out!"

However, the one requirement that should not be overlooked was that the targeted entity for a possession must be incapacitated at the *very* moment before an exchange. When done right, the medium inside the old host who now desired to get into another body just needed to begin the incantation as they came up to the mark of their choice, knock them out cold, and make the jump inside. The psychic's soul would end up inside the new vessel while the old body-supplier was left with the basic knowledge that their former ride-along was now gone. Depending on the relationship between the two – possessor and host – this either came as a relief, a moment of depression, or a sustained period of deep confusion.

Hearing all of this did not upset Shaniqua too much. Everything Pythia'd said so far made complete sense to her, but she did ask for some clarification about the role of the vessel. Up to this point, the presence of Pythia within her was much like suddenly having a stranger sharing her thoughts and someone suggesting that her body do certain actions. While it was clear that Pythia was strongly urging Shaniqua to do the things she asked, there hadn't been the sense that she'd been turned into an unwilling zombie puppet in this pursuit. Pythia had encouraged a shared responsibility within their partnership, and Shaniqua was very grateful for the medium's acknowledgement that she played a role in this. But she had to wonder if this would always be the case.

Pythia was so deeply touched by the young woman's understanding and her complimentary language toward her in all of these inquiries that she set about attempting to explain this part of the process as honestly as she could. After a moment to gather her thoughts, she told Shaniqua that the soul-transference spell was best understood if compared with an example involving a pilot, a co-pilot, or a passenger in an airplane.

During those specific times when the goals of the medium require absolute control, the body and brain of the host were both entirely taken over. All actions, words, and deeds became those of the pilot now flying the craft. Pythia freely admitted that these types of arrangements were not her favorite, but they had been sometimes necessary. Sadly, the hosts in this technique were pushed out of the limelight and into the shadows of their own being. If these types of relationships lasted up to the end of their natural-born lives, their original personality was lost forever.

However, in the shorter hop-on-hop-off arrangements of these take-the-controls scenarios, most people were left behind confused, but usually unharmed. Once their time together was over, the vessels were in control of themselves again, and just thought that they'd endured a classic "I've been possessed by the Devil" type of situation.

Clearly, Pythia and Shaniqua were involved in the more give-and-take type of relationship, when the medium comes in and shares the controls like a co-pilot. While this seemed a kinder type of circumstance, it was also fraught with dangers. Not all hosts were as mentally capable to understand their new situation as Shaniqua. Some reacted to the attempts of the foreign co-pilot as if they were the haunting voices in their heads associated with schizophrenia, multiple personality disorder, and other forms of madness. When this happened, the spiraling down of their mental state became yet another metaphorical similarity to the airplane model, for the medium was frequently required to bail out of the fiery wreckage before it crashed into the ground. And since it was impossible to know for sure if the host who they'd targeted could actually handle the transfer or not until *after* the medium was ensconced into the cockpit, it was usually too late to do anything about it until after things started to go south.

Being a passenger was a far easier way for mediums to transport themselves quickly and, especially during modern times, for great distances. But it required a great deal of patience – something Pythia did not always have – for it relinquished control completely over to the host. But if there was a need to get away from sudden trouble, it was better to just enter a person like a passenger boarding a jet plane and hitch a ride with them, *incognito*. That way, sitting in the safety of their seats within the virtual smoking section of the vessel, they could puff on some cigarettes, enjoy the in-flight movie and meals, and just wait for the flight to reach its destination, wherever that turns out to be. Once there, the medium could then work on transferring to a new body, far away from the personal danger where the trip had started. This technique had the benefit of complete anonymity, since the hosts rarely even knew that anyone else had been inside them, and there were no residual feelings of violation, which were so profound with the two other ways.

Inserting a soul into an inanimate object was a whole different kettle of fish, Pythia pointed out. It was usually seen as a psychic medium's last resort since it provided such a different set of pros and cons. Obviously, there was no damage that could be done to an inert object's mental health. One could slip into a lifeless item and not have to have conversations with it or witness the mental destruction that such a ride-along could cause. And nonliving things could provide a far more secure transit through time than something that could die or be killed at any moment.

The down side of it all was the total powerlessness that resulted from being inside a shell where movements and travel cannot be controlled or altered. An established emergency exit strategy was essential, since if there wasn't a prescribed way out of the inanimate soul chamber at some point, it could become far too easy to develop into a form of eternal self-imprisonment.

Shaniqua interrupted Pythia at this point. Politely, she asked why any psychic worth their salt would ever choose this form of possession, since the risks were so apparently overwhelming.

Pythia appreciated the practicality of the young woman she was currently engaged within. Her question was apt and showed a deep understanding of the topic. She proffered the case of a psychic Pythia had known who inserted himself inside of Leonardo DaVinci's *Mona Lisa* in 1939 to avoid the oncoming war. As a soothsayer, he could see the devastation that was going to take place in the next six years, and he had hopped into one of the people who was responsible for the priceless artwork. When he was able to discern the plan for protecting the painting, though, he transferred his soul into it with several clear exit strategies in place.

After six years, he popped out of the painting and into an expat from Buenos Aires who had fainted from an unknown pregnancy in the newly reopened Louvre – just like he'd foreseen was going to happen. By doing all of this, he had avoided the unpleasantness of the war, defied recruitment from the Nazi paranormal squads, and came out the other side of everything entirely unscathed – showing, once again, that the 6 Ps Rule (Proper Planning Prevents Piss-Poor Performance) is actually quite true. It was at this point in her explanation that Pythia became overly aware of Shaniqua's keen intellect. The young woman had begun to quietly connect some major dots in her mind, and the psychic medium saw that she needed to take an even more honest tack with her. Like the old adage states, a good offense is sometimes the best defense.

Yes, Pythia admitted freely, she had indeed been imprisoned inside the Bishop family cookbook by her nemesis Morgen in Vincennes, Indiana, during the Great Fair of 1929. She'd explain all of the essential details of this event later to her, but right now, it was important for Shaniqua to understand that the falling hickory branch that had knocked her out and freed Pythia's soul to enter Shaniqua's body had been a random event. However, this moment had set the two of them onto the unified course that they were now engaged in – to get their hands on that damn golden dagger. The possession of this item was the sole goal for the two of them now.

Here, again, Shaniqua surprised Pythia. She didn't put the kibosh on going after the dagger. She merely wanted to know why it was *so* damn important.

There wasn't an easy answer to this. But Pythia realized that if Shaniqua was ever to get a handle on it all, she needed to know about what happened after Morgen and Pythia had gone on their separate ways. For those first five hundred years, Pythia and Morgen had maintained a fragile peace with one another, and although it would be foolhardy to describe any of those dark days as being anywhere near blissful, they both had been quite contented and fulfilled during that time.

For Pythia, she'd been busy at Newgrange. This exceptionally impressive passage tomb was particularly active during the winter solstice season, but the place had a year-round complement of rites and rituals, holy festivals and holy days, and countless ceremonies. There wasn't much downtime as head priestess of the site.

To carry on being the mystical commander of such an incredibly important religious site, Pythia had used the soul-transference spell as need be to move from one volunteer and into another. She was a little guilty to admit that all of these relationships had been as undisputed pilots, but all of the hosts had been fanatical to become martyrs in something bigger than themselves. Pythia'd done some great things as the head priestess there, and the spiritual power of the holy place had been successfully maintained, sustaining a peaceful link to the Fourth Dimension, uninterrupted and true, for all of those five hundred years.

But then new, odd, and powerful sensations began within her. She wasn't proud to admit that they may have origi- nated in her woman parts, down in her loins. A throbbing had developed there, and its constant rhythm grew to the point where it refused to be ignored. It spread throughout her body, until she found it difficult to concentrate enough to do her religious rituals or even have a moment of peace to think. She'd put up a good resistance to it, but she was eventually worn down enough to decide that she needed to answer the call and swim with the psychic current that, for some unknown reason, wanted to carry her right back to Stonehenge.

It was Haggur's buried golden dagger calling her, and it demanded that Pythia come and get it. She was well aware that if she left Newgrange and headed to Stonehenge she'd be upsetting the balanced relationship with Morgen, but she calmly accepted that she really didn't have any choice in the matter. The power of that dagger was just too much to ig- nore for too long.

Just how does one psychic sneak up on another psychic? The answer to this was probably the most important lesson that Haggur taught her underlings, and it is pivotal to under- standing the rest of Pythia's and Morgen's story. It turned out to be pretty simple. Since the main connection between two mediums was on the mental and spiritual plane, there was a long list of psychological manipulations, distractions, decep- tions, sleights of hand (mind), and misdirection that could be employed to confuse an opponent to get close enough to strike. And, depending on their readiness, almost any opportunity could be utilized to enact a successful assault. On this first foray against Morgen, the truth is that Pythia used this lesson from Haggur to catch her with her metaphorical pants around her ankles.

Pythia abruptly abandoned her position at Newgrange and, utilizing a series of quick soul transfers, began to retrace her steps back to her homeland. She became quite adept at the quick change – popping into one person and then another as it suited her needs – until she'd become akin to some kind of skipping rock as she made her way to the coast, crossed the Irish Sea, and proceeded toward Stonehenge.

It was while she was in her native Welsh lands that she'd shown a flash of ingenuity. She transferred her soul into a falconer's goshawk *(Accipiter gentilis)* to fly very quickly and undetected toward Stonehenge. Because she was approaching Morgen in such an unorthodox manner, she could literally swoop in undetected. After a little overhead reconnaissance, Pythia crashed the bird into a highly skilled thief and injected herself into that person who was so well versed in infiltrating guarded locations and stealing things.

Her timing for this all was providential. There was about to be a very large and very important holy festival held at Stonehenge, and Morgen – who'd become nauseous enough to suspect that Pythia was nearby – was far too distracted by her vast responsibilities for the upcoming and vital sacred rituals to commence a proper search for her. Undiscovered, Pythia used the thief to instigate some trouble amid the throngs of people coming to the celebration, and this resulted in what amounted to a small riot. As unchecked bouts of violence and mayhem broke out among the pilgrims, the nimble thief had the distraction necessary to approach the dagger buried in the middle of Stonehenge. All he had to do was follow Pythia's commands as she picked up the pulsations that were now radiating off the buried metallic knife right into her psyche.

In the midst of the commotion, the thief dug the artifact up, tucked it away into his tunic pocket, and he and Pythia quickly made their way north. The chaos had been the perfect camouflage, and they departed unnoticed. No one, including Morgen, even knew that any crime had been committed.

After Morgen had put out all the fires, literally and figuratively, from the civil unrest to ensure that the much-anticipated religious festival was able to take place, she began to feel better. With the ultimately successful ceremony then complete, she'd turned her attention to the source of her feelings of sickness. They'd come and gone so quickly, but Morgen ascertained that Pythia had, for some unknown reason, come close enough to cause the dis-ease and then had gone far enough away to allow those sensations to abate. Unaware yet that the dagger was missing, Morgen wasn't sure why Pythia would have risked their mutual peace to come near, and she just chalked it up to a juvenile prank.

However, it wasn't too long before the retreating Pythia had traveled far enough away to make Morgen suddenly feel like she needed to leave Stonehenge and go after her. To add fuel to that fire, the dagger itself had begun to call out to Morgen, alerting her to the fact that not only was it missing and now on the move, it wanted her to give chase.

Possession of this artifact was now becoming an all-consuming obsession for both Pythia and Morgen. This set into motion an endless cycle, a twisted and ridiculous game that most closely resembled a combination of leapfrog, counting coup, and tag-you're-it. Pythia and Morgen were forced to play this contest against one another from that very moment all the way down to the present day. Their whole existence became nothing more than a repetitive series of the same steps of pursuing and locating the dagger, repossessing it, incapacitating the opponent, and then fleeing once more. Over and over, a ceaseless tit for tat arose between Pythia and Morgen as they kept switching their roles in this absurd struggle. For the next several centuries, the trophy of the game was the dagger and their playing field was the host of holy sites throughout what we now know as the United Kingdom.

These were days before easy travel, so getting far enough away from one another was not a very quick or graceful affair. And, lacking the electronic accuracy of modern technology, tracking down the signals coming from the fleeing medium and from the stolen dagger was more akin to wandering aimlessly through the countryside using a dowsing rod to find water. Both Pythia and Morgen found themselves staggering around very wild and dangerous lands in pursuit of that elusive and invisible target. Their searches were full of dead ends, sidetracks, and unforeseen divergences. It was not uncommon for these chases to take decades before having any success. The two became like balls in a vintage pachinko game, bouncing randomly between the holy sites and attempting to blend in as priests and priestesses in order to hide in plain sight – all the while tumbling toward the dagger's location.

Pythia had laid the groundwork for how to orchestrate a successful dagger transition. By using somewhat random and unusual human vessels to get close enough to strike the other, while, at the same exact time, inciting some kind of distraction to blind the opponent, it became possible to slip in, incapacitate the holder of the dagger, and take off safely with it in hand. Both Pythia and Morgen got very creative in their employment of their ruses and their diversions. However, often times, even the best strategies didn't work, and then the chase was back on once more.

It was Morgen who finally changed the game. In a small coastal port town in the region that is currently called Devon, she double-backed and lured Pythia into an inescapable trap. There, she blindsided her opponent with a surprise soul-transference spell which shuffled Pythia into the wooden staff of a local shepherd. With her opponent imprisoned within this crook, Morgen confidently sailed for mainland Europe and opened up the scope of the game in ways that the two mediums hadn't thought of doing before.

Up to this point there had been an element of playfulness to this whole chase-and-be-chased game between Pythia and Morgen. There hadn't been any real animosity between the two and no permanent damage had been caused to either by the reclaiming of the dagger. A fair descriptor would have been "silly" for the whole thing. But Morgen had upped the ante by successfully figuring out a way to actually end – or at least suspend – the game by putting the other psychic in an enclosure she couldn't get out of and, at the same time, enlarging the geographical scope of the whole shindig. There was an endless list of holy sites throughout what we call Europe, the Middle East, Africa, and even parts of Asia which required some kind of acting psychic leader. With an unlimited amount of holy destinations to choose from, Morgen virtually disappeared from sight with the dagger.

Meanwhile, Pythia was stuck helplessly within the shepherd's crook. With no way to force the issue, all she could do was sit around and hope for the unlikely event that the object that served as her enclosure would be used to knock someone unconscious so that she could get out. But with each passing day, week, month, and year, it became quite obvious that a shepherd's implement such as this was not usually fielded to render another person unconscious. And with every moment that she was unable to free herself, the distance between the two mediums grew. For the longest of times, it totally appeared as if Morgen had won the whole enchilada, leaving Pythia behind in the dust.

But you can't keep a good woman down. Pythia did eventually escape. When the shepherd's crook was broken over the head of a marauding rogue wolf (*Canis lupus*) by the shepherd's grandson, it freed her soul. She instantly transferred into the unconscious animal, woke it up, escaped further beatings, and took off into the dark woods. Through a series of slightly embarrassing body jumps, Pythia was once again able to get on the trail of Morgen. The chase for the dagger was back on.

With the impressive result now revealed from Morgen's performing an involuntary imprisonment of Pythia into an inanimate object, the rules of engagement – not to mention the overall feelings of the two mediums about each other and their conflict – changed forever. What had begun as a somewhat childish game now turned into a blood feud between two vengeful and overly competitive individuals. And what was once a rather inane affair limited to the confines of a relatively small geography now became extended campaigns that covered continents and generations. It'd been a prime example of a loss of innocence, actually, as Pythia and Morgen became determined to raise the stakes higher and higher. There was no basement to the depravity and no ceiling to the animosity.

Drawn to the psychic hotspots throughout the world like members of the order *Lepidoptera* to a flame, this eternal clash between Pythia and Morgen crisscrossed these regions for the next two and a half millennia. Wherever there was the need for a soothsayer, an oracle, a diviner, prophet, sage, fortune teller, wise woman, forecaster, visionary, medium, prognosticator, clairvoyant, or augur throughout the histories of the great cultures of Mesopotamia, Egypt, Rome, Greece, the Norse, the Celts, the Germanic tribes, the Huns, the Magyars and Persia – to name a few – there's a good chance one of these two might have had a finger in that pie. Truthfully, these two souls built up some of the most impressive psychic resumes of all time.

This game of pursuit – with its goals and emotions elevated to unhealthy levels of hatred and contempt – continued on and on, until neither Morgen nor Pythia was capable of stopping herself from playing the game, even if she so wholeheartedly wanted to do so.

At this point in her story, Pythia stopped her ridiculously lengthy and in-depth explanation to see if Shaniqua was still awake. She was. She'd been quietly digesting every important fact in the tale, and she was now caught up in it. She calmly stated in as loud a psychic voice as she could that it was time to make that bitch Morgen pay and get their hands back on that dagger again.

Let's Make Amends, James Madison!

As soon as Harvey Ferguson stepped onto the construction site on the grounds of the former Blackford Window Glass factory, it was like he'd just cannonballed into a wet surrealistic painting. Still stunned by seeing the model of Stonehenge and by hearing for the first time the big plan of Buchanan Sanderborn, he was neither fully mentally nor emotionally prepared for the ridiculously busy scene that he was seeing. His boss may have complained of too much inactivity and the need for cracking the whip, but it seemed as if there was too much motion, too much chaos, too much entropy going on around him in this place. It all was quite unhealthy.

Large trucks carrying huge limestone blocks lumbered into the area and empty ones left, heavy equipment rumbled by as they moved these stones hither and yon, workmen pranced around while surveying the ground and barked directions about the placement of these stones, and the skilled Italian stone carvers yelled loudly to one another in their native tongue with measurements and engaged in highly animated debates at their carving stations. There was a circus-like atmosphere to the place that belied a dangerous current of energy flowing beneath the surface.

Harvey was uncertain of where to go to take up his role as supervisor of the project, and he had little understanding of what was expected of him. His momentary and all-apparent air of uncertainty did not escape the eye of those men who were in their fevered battle to erect the modern version of Stonehenge as quickly as was humanly possible. To be blunt, after their boss Mr. Sanderborn had made it clear that failure was not going to be tolerated and that all inactivity was to be rooted out and excised like an unwanted skin tag, the sight of some idle loafer on the grounds caused hackles to get raised and tempers to flare. A particularly rough-looking foreman diverted his purposeful stalking around and swooped over to intercept Harvey.

"Hey, buddy, can I help ya find something?"

"Uh, yeah, I'm Harvey Ferguson. Mr. Sanderborn put me in charge of this project as supervisor."

The gruff man seemed to deflate, and he took on a more appreciative and friendly air. He exhaled so strongly that it seemed he was trying to blow out some invisible birthday candles in front of him.

"Ah, thank the damn lord! You're here to rein *him* in, right?"

"Who?"

"The little faggot in the shower cap over there in the office trailer by the porta-potties. Ever since he stepped onto this site to take charge, he's been doing nothing but shrieking out orders that have been near gibberish as far as I can tell. Please tell me that Mr. Sanderborn has sent you over to bring some sanity to this project."

Trying to convey more confidence than he currently felt, Harvey nodded strongly and pointed at the trailer the foreman had just identified.

"Yes, that's right. I will head over there right now and start bringing some sanity back. What's your name?"

"I'm Tip Montgomery, but most people call me Jocko."

"Alright, Jocko, I'll head right over to that trailer and start figuring out what's going on. If you have any further issues, don't hesitate to come over and check in with me, okay."

"Okay, sir. Will do."

Harvey strode confidently toward the white construction office trailer as if he was prepared to dive right through the aluminum siding of the structure, but then he noticed how all the workmen seemed to be avoiding it like it was a quarantine area. He stopped and gathered himself before ascending the half dozen steps and opening the door. Right in front of him was a man standing near one of the two desks, and he was issuing orders into a walkie-talkie in a high-pitched shriek. Harvey did a double take. The man was the very spitting image of the author Truman Capote, but he was wearing a mauve shower cap which matched his mauve tie. He continued to shout orders into the two-way radio in his hand as he watched Harvey close the trailer door and walk over to him.

When he stopped his commands to the unseen workman he was berating, the little man rubbed his nose like it itched terribly and closed his eyes as he spoke. "And who might you be? And why are you in *my* trailer?"

"My name is Harvey Ferguson, and Mr. Sanderborn put me in charge as the head supervisor of this project. So I guess that fact makes this trailer mine more than yours, wouldn't you say, Mr....?"

The little man's eyes opened wide in surprise and then narrowed into slicing slits. He brought his hands up to his hips like he was ready to dish out a sassy rebuttal.

"Mr. Hunter Cooper, at your service. And Mr. Buchanan Sanderborn actually put *me* in charge of this whole project. He did this the other day when he found out that it was my grandfather who wrote this book" – he pointed at the thick volume on the desk near him – "with the exact dimensions for rebuilding Stonehenge. I guess he thought I would be more useful than his other so-called experts because I can decipher my grandfather's...unique way of speaking and thinking. So here I am."

Harvey no longer felt as confused or overwhelmed. He was still fighting the strong feelings of oppressive nausea he'd been dealing with since landing in this town, but getting away from the hectic environment outside had allowed him to recover his calm resolve again. He looked over at this diminutive and ridiculous-looking man in front of him, and he smiled like someone satisfied when meeting their attractive blind date for the first time.

"Well, Mr. Cooper, he put me in charge because I'm his right-hand man and he knows that I've become quite knowledgeable about Stonehenge in my own right. I've made multiple trips to England and have met repeatedly with historians and British cultural ambassadors about this monument. As I've toured it with them, I've even touched the stones with my very own hands. So, you see, I know it intimately."

"Intimately?" Hunter shrieked, throwing his arms up in alarm, "This book, my grandfather's book, definitively gives every single detail on how to rebuild this holy site to its original status. There's no one alive on this planet, Mr. Ferguson, no one, who actually knows how to make it work again. My grandfather was the last human who had this information. When he unearthed an ancient blueprint written by the acting high priestess during one of his archaeological digs at Stonehenge, he knew that he'd found what amounts to the one-and-only instruction sheet on what those stones can really do. He took all that info and put it into his book, this book. So, I don't know how you could possibly think that you have a more *intimate* relationship than that, good sir."

Harvey turned his head robotically to look down on the book which Hunter Cooper now had in front of him. For the first time during this whole interaction with this silly little dwarf of a man, his interest was piqued enough to neutralize his mounting resentment.

"Did your grandfather happen to jot down the name of that high priestess by any chance?"

"Hmm, lemme see. I remember some name. Let's see, where did I read that? Ah, yes, here it is. Her name was Haggur."

Harvey gasped audibly. He'd known there was something fishy about Carter Cooper's book when he'd first heard of it, but he wasn't entirely sure just how piscine. If Haggur had created some kind of a diagram to show how to reset Stone-henge, it most definitely wasn't some kind of fluke or a coincidence. She was a lot of things, but Haggur never exhibited any behaviors which could be misconstrued as coinciden-tal. Harvey had to wonder what the old hag had been up to when she decided to leave some kind of how-to-rebuild-it diagram behind. She was on the way out, after all, and yet leaving some kind of an artifact to be found later on seemed somehow to be setting something up for the future.

This new information both turned on the hot tap of ex-citement and the cold tap of dread in the emotional bathtub inside of Harvey. He realized that his whole being, his whole strategy, was going to have to be reviewed and renewed on the fly.

"Ah, Mr. Ferguson, I could not help notice that you had a strong reaction when I read that name. Does it mean something to you?"

"Yes, it certainly does, Mr. Cooper."

"Hunter."

"Okay, Hunter. I know for a fact, from my own personal research, that Haggur was *indeed* an important high priestess of Stonehenge, and if she was your grandfather's source, that changes everything about how I view that book...and you. It's now obvious that you and I need to work together to get the placement of the mounds, the pathways, the various stones, the lintels, and, well, the entire orientation of the site totally correct, but it's the pattern for the weaving of the copper cabling that's going to be absolutely crucial. If we don't get that right, we'll never be able to call the Mkultrans, right?"

It was a major risk to mention the name of the alien visitors, but the effect it had was exactly what Harvey was going for. Hunter Cooper looked too dumbfounded to talk. Eventually he was able to regain his wits enough to speak.

"And how do you know about the copper cables and the Mkultrans? Those two details are not well known or recognized as important, Mr. Ferguson."

"Harvey."

"Okay, Harvey. As I was saying, they are not widely held in the most favorable of light by the rest of the scholastic world."

"Well, let's just say that your grandfather's book may end up being the main source of details for this project, but I have plenty of other information that you may not even be privy to – and I will be glad to share it all with you as we work together on this."

Harvey's olive branch reduced the level of tension inside the trailer to a basic distrust, but both men eyed the other differently. A similar ambivalent expression had been on the faces of those who'd been present during the negotiations between the Montagnard people and the Central Intelligence Agency in the early days of the Vietnam War. In both instances, it was a real mixture of sweet hopefulness, bitter self-preservation, and salty realism. If it were to be given a cocktail name, it would be called a frenemy.

It was at this moment that Harvey caught a whiff of something in the aura of Hunter Cooper, and he lifted his nose up and sniffed in the odd little man's direction. Like the incriminating aroma from the perfume of an extramarital affair, the scent was revealing something unknown and secret. It would be hard to ever say that a metal dagger has a certain smell, but Harvey became immediately aware that Hunter Cooper not only knew where the sought-after sacred artifact was currently located, he had spent a great deal of time around it. Without a doubt, Harvey now knew that he'd found a crucial missing piece to the puzzle.

Everything You're Saying Is Falling on Deaf Ears, Ludwig van Beethoven!

As the Gherrardian swarm closed in on the Mkultran home world with the unwavering goal of wiping out every living member of the species and stealing their wormhole knowledge, there was one question that must be posed: How could a highly advanced composite species ever be threatened by a much more primitive, albeit aggressive, enemy? After all, the situation seemed akin to a bunch of gigantic land crabs (*Cardisoma guanhumi*) attempting to invade the Union of Soviet Socialist Republics. One would think that a highly developed brain, the vast knowledge gained from extensive space travel and contact with other life forms, and the ridiculously high level of technological advancement would have kept the Mkultrans completely safe from this kind of threat.

However, the reactions of a couple Mkultran characters to stressful situations which were seen earlier in this story reveal the real problem that the Mkultrans now faced. First, Xandrus merely shrugged after seeing the scenes of the decimation of the colony on Noosbit on his computer screen. Then the Mkultran scientist on Planet Gherrard made the rather unusual choice to go for an extended swim just after she'd discovered that the colony was not built upon a truly lifeless planet, but atop a container filled with a hidden menace.

Were both these reactions examples of some kind of psychosis occurring within the species? No, the fatal flaw that the modern Mkultrans were facing was a paralyzing level of apathy.

If an earthling had had a similarly unimpressive reaction to the sight of a massacre of his own people by an oncoming army of murderers hell-bent on wiping out his entire species, or had decided to do some laps rather than alerting the authorities about the imminent attack, one might be inclined to call them psychopaths or, worse, governmental workers on the fast track toward retirement. But the real reason behind both of these tepid Mkultran responses actually lies in the very earthling concept of evolution.

While the scientist Charles Darwin is called the "father of evolution," he only used the term "evolution" once in the very last paragraph of his *Origin of Species*. He actually preferred the term, "descent by modification." While a matter of semantics only – since Darwin believed that his theory illustrated how species change over time, give rise to new species, and share a common ancestor – the topic of this process in the Mkultran species must be discussed to further understand their situation as the bloodthirsty Gherrardians approached and there didn't seem to be a healthy Mkultran response to their bloody invasion.

The evolution – or descent by modification – of a complex composite entity is an exponentially more complicated pathway than for a creature with merely a singular origin, since the development of both species' components that make up the whole must be considered as well. Therefore, whenever talking about the advancement of a composite species, one must actually view the changes in the *three* parts of the deal, each species individually and their combo-pack result. Instead of some kind of a vertical family tree, the give and take of such a process actually creates a kind of insane Punnett square with an exponentially widening list of evolutionary possibilities – or descents (plural) with modifications. Even the AAA would agree that this TripTik of the resulting three-dimensional road map of the development of those involved would be overly full of unforeseen consequences and negative impacts.

As soon as Oxus climbed aboard Chyggan all those many moons ago, both creatures – the Milbrookian and its Gottliebian host – voluntarily entered into a relationship with such intrinsically clear and overarching benefits for both species that there was no need, at the time, to establish a singular, dominant leader. Since both species instantly became nourished – and abundantly content – from their new arrangement, there was no impetus to debate about who was in charge. Things had just gotten better for both of them, so why rock the boat and question "Who's the captain?"

Because of their greater physical size and mobility, the Gottliebians assumed that their role in the composite species was to be the main act. As for the Milbrookians, they seemed to be fine with getting a free ride for their free food. Their mutual acquiescence toward this central assumption removed any potential early dissent between the two components. Chyggan was thrilled to be large and in charge, and Oxus seemed keen to let him do so. And every partnership between the two species henceforth appeared to contain the same harmony.

However, a highly complex, three-prong evolutionary – or descent with modifications – pathway for the Mkultrans, the Milbrookians, *and* the Gottliebians was set into motion. Even though Dr. BZit's startling research project many generations after the initial combining had clearly demonstrated that the two parts of the Mkultran whole had already reached an intricate level of reliance in which each species required the other to stay alive, there were several unseen, yet vitally important, independent developments that were to become divergent in nature for the whole Mkultran entity...namely that the Milbrookian's incessant hunger for the energy from the passionate emotions of their Gottliebian hosts was growing with each passing generation while, at the same time, the Gottliebians were actually becoming so appreciative of their resulting clear mind and higher intellect that they were purging all of their emotions in a fire sale of epic proportions.

The result was that, despite all appearances to the contrary, the Mkultrans were heading toward a major crisis. By the time the Gherrardians were threatening complete devastation of the Mkultrans, the truth was that the Gottliebian component of the union no longer had *any* emotions to give to the partnership, while the Milbrookian part was too intent on getting enough to eat that they didn't seem to care either.

To state it bluntly, they both had undergone an evolution – or descent with modifications – that had turned them into something that resembled the inhabitants of an illicit opium den in Cambodia. While the Gottliebians – and hence the apparent controlling force of the Mkultrans – weren't just indifferent, they were stoned out of their minds...constantly, and the Milbrookians were blinded by looking for their next fix.

The Mkultran species had become a giant taffy-pulling machine of incongruous elements that produced an emotionless, overly contented creature that appeared to no longer care about much of anything. Actually, these modern Mkultrans did not really want to learn as much, had less impetus to explore or experiment, and sadly, barely even wanted to mate these days. They'd all become shells of their former selves.

The Milbrookians now found themselves looking like rugged, action-hungry, bronco-breaking cowboys who were sitting atop nags on their way to the glue factory. This would have been slightly comical, in a way, if the oppositional needs of these two organisms were not the ingredients of the recipe for the destruction of the overall composite entity.

As the Mkultrans watched the Gherrardians bearing down on them like a buzz saw ready to cut them to shreds, the Gottliebian component of the species was now faced with something they had never encountered before – a situation to which they needed to react to survive. But they were not only physically unable to do this, whatever strong emotions that they were still capable of generating were immediately sucked in by the starving Milbrookians, who were so hungry that they could have eaten a whole cow (*Bos taurus taurus*).

None of this mattered to the Gherrardians, of course. They were locked onto their target and progressing toward their goal. They really did not give a rat's (*Rattus norvegicus*) ass if their enemy wallowed helplessly in front of them or put up a rugged defense – they were creatures who just enjoyed kicking some ass as they scuttled their way toward what they saw as their destiny. Oh, and they loved a good fight...and the taste of blood.

Don't Let It All Go Down in Flames, Max Pruss!

Morton and Eve Richardson were both in foul moods as they checked into the honeymoon suite of the Kum Back Inn. Overnight, it seemed, the traffic in and around Vincennes had amped up to such unthinkably high levels, it was a major challenge to get anywhere. The couple had become deeply irked at having to circumnavigate around stifling traffic jams as they made their way through their once sleepy little town to get to the old motel. Inexplicably, there were fleets of large trucks carrying massive limestone blocks, a surprisingly large number of limousines and other fancy town cars with tinted windows suddenly plying the city's streets, an endless stream of construction crew trucks filing in from out of town, and several unscheduled freight trains arriving at the railyards to unload their loads. Morton and Eve had even seen several huge modular houses and other massive structures on semi-truck trailers making their way in a snail-like fashion to their new locations within the Vincennes city limits, and they'd clucked their tongues and shook their heads like two grandparents disapproving of their progeny.

Ever since their uncomfortable meeting with Hunter Cooper at his house, the Richardsons had been engaged in the gentle process of mending the broken fences of their marriage. And while Eve felt like she needed to assuage her husband's hurt feelings about the perceived slights from her comments at the social gatherings, she also sought some answers from Morton as to why, after years of a happy marriage, he felt like he could sneak around and eavesdrop on his wife and then get as angry as a toddler, like he had – all without even talking with her first. She knew that, as a member of the weaker sex, her husband needed more coddling to make his wounded pride recover, but she also silently hoped that he could address his wrongdoings in the process as well. She realized that currently, as a couple, they probably more resembled someone trying to tap cotton caulking in between the seams of a wooden boat while standing atop the ice of a frozen pond.

However, although it pained them to admit that Hunter Cooper had been correct in any way, they also were in agreement that some kind of physical healing between them should be attempted – that they should, *at the very least,* try to save their marriage. And since the room at the Kum Back Inn was already reserved in their name, they decided that perhaps a romantic weekend – without Hunter Cooper around – actually might serve them well. Unfortunately, their traumatic drive over to the motel had clouded any of their initial building sexual tension from the much-anticipated tryst, and they now sat in their room looking at one another like they'd just made a terrible mistake.

"Morton, what the hell is going on with Vincennes these days? That traffic was absolutely ridiculous. And we seem to be in the middle of a sandstorm of activity here at the old sleepy Kum Back Inn. What is *happening* to our small town?"

Morton shrugged his shoulders and looked around the motel room slowly. He shook his head to show that he was pondering the same thing.

"I think it's all because of Buchanan Sanderborn. He's swooped in with his billions, and it is clear as mud that he wants to turn Vincennes into a new version of New York City. Overnight, he's become my biggest customer. So I cannot complain too much and still take the man's money, which he's heaving at me."

"But he seems to be changing *everything* about Vincennes."

"He certainly does, Eve. You know how I said that he called me because he wanted to insure the book by Hunter Cooper's grandfather and that I had then arranged a meeting here between the two of them?"

"Yes."

"Well, it looks like they hit it off really well. So well, in fact, that Sanderborn gave Hunter complete access to the book *and* he even offered him a job. If I didn't know any better, I'd swear that the two are becoming *friendly*!"

"You're kidding me."

"No, Eve, I'm not. Did you see those huge stones on the backs of all of those trucks?"

"Hard to miss them."

"Hunter swore me to secrecy, but he says he's now in charge of that project. He says that they're trying to reconstruct Stonehenge here in Vincennes over at the former Blackford Window Glass factory."

"Why would they do that?"

"Dunno. Hunter wouldn't tell me, even though I tried to pry the information out of him. He just said that it was going to change everything. He also warned me that Sanderborn seems to want to own our whole little village. And, like a bunch of seagulls," (*Larus argentatus smithsonianus*) "other mega-rich people from all corners of the world are actually swarming here to get a piece of the pie. It's like some kind of moneybags feeding frenzy. None of this makes any sense to me, but I cannot really complain since the company's never been busier, and the money is pouring in faster than we can count it."

"But how will any of us normal people afford to live here when they're done with the place? I mean, look at what they have planned for the Kum Back Inn. This has always been an affordable motel, but now it sure seems like they want to turn it into the Waldorf-Astoria, complete with French chefs and triple-digit room rates!"

Morton looked around their room. He and Eve had been in such a foul mood when they'd entered it, they hadn't even had a chance to check it out. Now, as he glanced around, he could see that the room's motif was in the red and white of Valentine's Day. The walls were lined with a faux white brick layer that went halfway up them and a rich red velveteen wallpaper topping this up to the ceiling. The floors were covered by red shag carpeting, and there was a prominent heart-shaped hot tub in the bathroom, which was the size of a garage for a small car.

The star of the room, however, was the most unique bed that Morton had ever seen. It was a large king-sized bed that had a plush white bedcover with two wine-red stripes running its length. At the head, there was a red padded backrest with inset buttons, and at the foot was a sturdy red and white bench that was long enough for someone to lie atop. But the most surprising feature was the white dome which loomed above the headboard and half of the bed. Due to its rounded shape and the large half-globe at its top, it curiously resembled a sectioned woman's breast. In this overhead structure, facing down toward the inhabitants in the bed, a complement of entertainment features, including a pair of large mirrored panels, a TV screen, an AM/FM radio, and a cassette player, all resided in a very modern layout.

Morton was overwhelmed by what he was looking at and his mind began to race. He was trying to imagine exactly what kind of changes anyone but the original Kum Back Inn owner could make to a room set up like this. Not that it was ideal in any way, but it was unapologetically designed to elicit a tawdry sexual feel. Although it was too old and dingy these days to get anyone in the mood for loving, Morton had to admit that it got an A for effort.

Slightly irked by her husband's momentary distraction in the middle of such a deep conversation, Eve suddenly spoke loud enough to bring him out of his own thoughts. "Morton, I will repeat myself – how will any of us normal people afford to live here when they're done with the place?"

"It's more than a little troubling to me, Eve, but I don't have any good answers for you. And truthfully, we're caught right in the middle of everything now. Because of Sanderborn, we're making money hand over fist with the insurance company. A prudent man would ride that wave for as long as he can. That being said, I'm wondering if we need to start looking to move somewhere else."

"Leave Vincennes? This little village is our home, Morton."

"Without a doubt, Eve. But isn't a home wherever you set up your tent? The kids are all moved out, it's just you and me in that house, and we don't have to be *here* anymore. Theoretically, we could reap all of the benefits of whatever is going on in Vincennes these days, sell our place, and then head off together to somewhere new with a wallet full of cash."

"Are you suggesting that we leave this town, leave all of our friends, and discard all of the memories we've made here to go to some newer, greener pastures together?"

Morton scratched his chin with the apprehension that he was going to ruin the moment with his wife by stating something too honest. He blew some air through his lips, letting them flap like a loose tarp in a hurricane.

"Yes, I suppose I am suggesting that, Eve. I'm no economic guru, but it sure seems like some kind of gigantic bubble is expanding daily here in Vincennes. But all bubbles pop eventually. And I think we need to plan what to do whenever that happens."

Eve Richardson had begun to unbutton her blouse. She was aware of doing this, of course, but she was stunned that her husband's surprising comment about moving away together had triggered such a flood of sudden amorous feelings. He had undeniably just gotten her in the mood again. Unbeknownst to him, she'd been waiting for her husband to say that he wanted to leave Vincennes and go somewhere, anywhere, with her for some time. His affirmation of this desire now seemed to bypass her ears and go directly into her body's nether regions instead, and she found herself wanting to commence their love-making immediately.

Regrettably, there was a knock on the door.

Both Eve, with her fingers still on her buttons, and Morton, who had picked up the unspoken invitation for sex from his wife and was wrestling to remove his tie along with the rest of his suit, looked over at the source of the noise and held their breath.

"Don't answer it, Morton!"

There was such a breathless, erotic quality to Eve's plea that Morton closed his eyes as he hoped and prayed that whoever had disturbed them would move on without needing to receive an answer from them.

"Morty-baby, open this door immediately! Don't make me use this master key I got from the office to let myself in. I will count to five, and then I'm coming right in."

There was no mistaking that voice – it sounded like the author of *Breakfast at Tiffany's* issuing a threat to commit some kind of home invasion. It was the one and only Hunter Cooper. Under normal circumstances, if the person knocking was anyone but this man, Morton would have felt comfortable responding that the occupants of the room were not decent enough to open the door. However, he knew that such an admission would not be a deterrent but an encouragement for his odd friend. Both Eve and Morton let out a lamenting mewl and began to get re-dressed.

"Be right there, Hunter."

"One."

"I'll be right there, Hunter."

"Two."

Morton whipped open the door. Hunter Cooper stood at the threshold wearing a dark suit and a very large and floppy herringbone newsboy cap atop his head, but he barged through the opening like he was a running back rushing through the tackles toward the end zone. He came to a stop in front of Eve, surveyed her, and then slowly took in the whole motel room. As he returned his gaze to Morton, he had a knowing look of appreciation on his face.

"You know, the word *erection* is one of my favorite in the entire English language. It's almost onomatopoeic to me. Whether it be penile, nipple, or even piloerection, I cannot help but feel a bit aroused whenever I say the word aloud."

The sound of his creepy voice speaking about sexual – not to mention slightly judgmental, terms – and the fact that he'd just barged in and ruined their romantic moment were enough to get Morton angry enough to point at Hunter threateningly and growl. It took a moment for the words to work themselves out of his mouth.

"Hunter, what the hell are you doing here? And why are you wearing Barbara Streisand's hat?"

"Firstly, Morty-baby, I'm here to assist you and your wife in our session of sexual therapy to save your marriage. Secondly, you continue to mock my fashion sense, but all I ever see when I look at you is a middle-aged man who's slowly losing the war to his ultimate balding. Now, let's all just agree to get naked and let the chips fall where they may, hmm?"

Now it was Eve Richardson's time to move with a surprising quickness. Like an Olympic ice hockey goalie sliding to cover the net, she slid over to the rotary phone next to the bed, picked up the receiver, and put her finger in the position to dial.

"Now, listen to me, Hunter Cooper. I'm going to do my own counting down before I dial the police to report a deviant entering my room, and, unlike you, I'm not going to tell you what the target number is before I do so."

Hunter put his hands up as if he were being held up at gunpoint. He backed away from her to seem nonthreatening.

"I'm sorry, I'm sorry. Eve, please just put that phone down. The police do not need to be called. I just assumed that, if you two were in the room that I reserved for our session together, you'd want to continue with what we agreed upon earlier. My mistake."

"We did not agree on any such thing, Hunter. And we *certainly* did not commit to engaging in any kind of 'therapy' with you. After some thought and discussion – inspired by our time with you, by the way – we came to the conclusion that we should use this room..."

"That I reserved, Morty-baby!"

"Yes, Hunter, you did make the reservation, but Eve and I decided that we want to use it – just the two of us. Don't worry, we're going to pay for it."

"That's not what's at issue here, Morty-baby! You went behind my back. I feel *betrayed*."

Morton was about to say something to assuage his friend, but he noticed that the man's face had taken on a more confident aura as he placed a worn Army-green rucksack on the floor in front of him. When he spoke, his words dripped with a tantalizing syrup.

"Well, let's let that all be water under the dam. No, I also came here for another reason altogether. I've brought the dagger here to let you two touch it. Perhaps in the heightened sexual state that you're currently in, it might be able to channel some of its power out into your love-making."

"That is totally preposterous, you toad of a little man. Get out of our room, right now!"

Eve's rebuke was cut off by the movement of her husband, who seemed drawn to the backpack. His mindless steps startled her, but Eve moved away from the phone on a course to intercept him before he got there.

"Come on, Eve, what harm could there be in feeling the power of that ancient piece one more time? I don't believe in its aphrodisiac qualities, but it *is* powerful. Can't you feel it, calling from inside that backpack?"

"Come on, Morton. Let's not get all fluttery in the eyes again. It's just an old knife."

Hunter Cooper seemed to purr with satisfaction as he took the bejeweled golden dagger out of the backpack and then uttered his next declaration. "Oh, it's so much more than that, Eve. Come on, I'll let you hold it first."

With her husband behaving like some kind of a love-sick zombie and the little creep Hunter Cooper acting like a drug dealer, Eve snatched the golden dagger out of his hands. She wanted to quickly dispel any significance to the item, expel the "little faggot" from their room, and attempt to get back to bedding her husband to save their marriage. Once Morton saw how silly he was acting, Eve hoped that he'd want to resume what the little puke Hunter Cooper had just interrupted.

With it in her hands, however, she had to admit that the weapon had an unnerving energy rushing through it. Eve Richardson brought the metal dagger up in front of the bridge of her nose for a closer inspection, and even she could tell that it was truly a special artifact. The gems on the sheath seemed to catch the light from the lamps of the room and filter them into a mist of different colors that flowed over the metal of the object in a magical display.

She was by then too distracted to notice that Hunter Cooper was suddenly resembling a coiled black mamba

(*Dendroaspis polylepis*) ready to strike. When he lunged toward her and pushed the side of the dagger's scabbard directly into the front of her skull, the collision between bone and metal made a sickening sound.

Eve dropped to the floor unconscious.

For Morton, it was like watching a movie scene in which one character gets attacked. It did not seem real, and it did not seem to have any personal consequences for him. He was still in the middle of a disabling haze caused by the turgidity of their interrupted sexual lead-in and the reintroduction of the magical dagger, so by the time his brain had finally recognized the fact that his wife had just been attacked by Hunter Cooper, she already lay on the floor like a discarded comforter.

It might have been a delayed reaction, but now Morton's all-consuming rage was building, and when he turned toward Hunter, he only saw red. He leapt at the little man like a mountain lion, cougar, panther, or catamount (*Puma concolor*), hands and feet aiming to make contact and hurt his former friend.

Hunter Cooper responded like someone in a slapstick silent film. He turned tail and ran frantically out of the motel room before his assailant had a chance to get too close. He continued his screaming as he headed away, and Morton Richardson could not resist giving chase, leaving the poor unconscious Eve on the floor for several minutes.

When Morton finally returned to the room to check on his wife, he was far more concerned with her wellbeing than his failure to catch Hunter Cooper. He quickly saw that she was breathing, and he started to crouch down to comfort her and help her regain consciousness. He was holding her head in his hands as she stirred and awoke. He gasped aloud as she opened her eyes. This was partly because she now had a golden nimbus around the pupils of her eyes and partly because her left hand was currently cupping his scrotum through the woolen trouser material of his pants, and her grip was getting firmer by the moment.

Look Before You Leap, Sonora Webster Carver!

Hunter Cooper had been chased by hostile pursuers enough in his life to know that he was not going to get caught by Morton Richardson. He'd correctly assumed that the man was going to be more motivated to go back and check on his stricken wife than to keep running after her attacker once he'd fully acknowledged the futility of the chase.

As soon as he felt safe enough to slow himself down, Hunter stopped his sprinting and broke into a brisk walk through the hallways of the Kum Back Inn. However, as he turned a corner and headed toward the parking lot, he was seriously surprised by the activity going on outside the building. An ambulance, a Vincennes Fire Department pumper truck, and a police car were all haphazardly parked, their lights incessantly flashing and their sirens wailing their fatigued and ineffective calls. Ever the improviser, Hunter straightened his clothing and joined the parade of uniformed personnel headed toward the presidential suite like he was supposed to be there.

Upon entering the room, he saw Harvey Ferguson lying prone on the floor, being attended by a paramedic. The young assistant was propping himself up on his elbows, but his face had the most unusual appearance. It kept changing from satisfied to angry to confused and looked like a young child who had just drunk his first cup of Aztecan *Xocolatl.*

Buchanan Sanderborn was standing nearby, watching the attending of his assistant with a look of concern. He glanced over at Hunter. "What are you doing here, Mr. Hunter?"

"Good day to you, Mr. Sanderborn. What's happening here?"

"I'm not rightly sure. One minute Harvey was sharing his update about the impressive progress on our project and the next he was convulsing on the ground and making the oddest sounds."

"Oh, my. He had a seizure?"

The paramedic looked up at them.

"It's too early to say that he suffered a seizure. My partner was called off to another room to deal with someone who was supposedly having the very same experience. Highly un-usual, I must say. Might be a gas leak."

Hunter rolled his eyes and straightened his cap on his head. When he spoke, his tone was as if he were delivering the keynote address at a very important symposium.

"One must admit that there have been some highly unu-sual occurrences happening around our fair city these days. For a sleepy place, we certainly now find ourselves in the middle of some infectious hustle-bustle, don't we? For some, this can be a tad...overwhelming."

This comment seemed to bring Harvey out of his stupor, and he swatted at the paramedics hands as he struggled to stand up. As he did, he glared at Hunter. However, he ad-dressed the paramedic as he got to his feet.

"I'm fine. Thank you for coming, but I am fine. Whatever happened, it's over. Thank you for your quick response and thorough care."

"When Mr. Sanderborn calls with an emergency of this nature, we come a-running. It sounded like it was a life or death situation, and..."

"You know which side of your bread is buttered by this man, aren't I right?"

The paramedic now also glared at Hunter so hard that it looked like he was about to punch him. This potential hostility was curtailed when the other paramedic returned to the room.

"You're not going to believe this, Sam, but there's a black chick over there in one of the cheap rooms who had the same thing happen to her and seemingly at the very same time that it happened to Mr. Sanderborn's assistant."

"His name, my good sir, is Harvey Ferguson...you boob."

Hunter's comment not only added a glare from the newly arrived paramedic, it enhanced the already existing ones from both Harvey and the other paramedic.

"She...uh, she said it was kinda like...gosh, this is embarrassing...uh, a mental climax."

"What?"

"Yeah, she said it was like her brain had just had an... orgasm."

Hunter clapped his little hands and scrunched up his shoulders. "Ooh, I want one of those!"

"Sure, whatever. Anyway, she said she was fine, and then she chalked it up to it being that time of the month."

Harvey's face shifted quickly again. It went from one of sustained anger aimed at Hunter to an expression of deep shock, and then to one of complete mortification.

"It sounds like we're both fine. I don't want to take up more of your precious time. Again, thanks for coming...arriving so quickly."

Sanderborn nodded at them, and the paramedics quickly gathered their medical bags and backpacks and hastened out of the room. As the suite door swung shut, Harvey, Hunter, and Sanderborn could hear them relaying the embarrassing information about the call as a humorous anecdote to be shared and laughed at. This was all silenced with the closing of the door, and the three men stood in silence for a prolonged second or two.

"What the hell is he doing here?"

The ferocity of Harvey's snarl made his boss gaze over at Hunter Cooper, who seemed entirely unfazed by anything that had been said or had happened so far.

"Yes, Mr. Cooper, to what do we owe the pleasure of this..."

"Visit? Well, an immensely good thought hit me just the other day, and I just *had* to share it with you. I know that, once you hear me out, you'll see the genius of it too, and set about to making it happen."

"Make an appointment like everyone else. Let me get Mr. Sanderborn's appointment book and I'm sure we can set something up for when he's..."

"Available? Well, he seems to be very available right now, don't you think, Harvey-baby? I mean, your little cranial cumjob has apparently opened up his schedule, wouldn't you say?"

Sanderborn snickered, but when he saw the building agitation of his assistant, he stepped toward Hunter Cooper in a protective gesture.

"Mr. Cooper, you have my attention. I'd love to hear your idea. But make it quick."

"Well, I've been thinking. If we're going to actually turn on this beacon to signal an alien race to come to our planet, we need to assemble a proper audience."

"Audience?"

"Of course. If we're calling back a space people who visited once and decided not to come back for some reason, we cannot now invite them to our planet, to Vincennes, and not prepare the proper reception. I'm of the belief that if we were to do that, we'd be risking offending them or worse. It could be *déjà vu* all over again."

"This is preposterous..."

Sanderborn waved off Harvey's comment like he was shaking water from his fingertips.

"What do you propose, Mr. Cooper?"

"First off, we must exclude the press. We cannot let a story like this one get away from us and be spun negatively by those media whores. Above all else, we need to be the main dispensaries of the information about all of this."

"Okay, I can certainly see the value of that."

"And secondly, we need to assemble the leaders of our planet here in Vincennes. We can't just request the presence of these aliens, expect them to travel the huge expanse of space to get here, and then greet them with any Tom, Dick, or Harry. No, no, no, we need to show them that we mean *business*. We bring the goddamn UN here to Vincennes and really impress them with our seriousness. Undoubtedly you have the connections to make this happen, Mr. Sander-born-baby. And just think about what this would say to our extraterrestrial visitors to see the most powerful leaders of the entire globe gathered here and ready to negotiate. They won't be stepping out of their spaceships asking to meet our leaders. No, no, we'll be the ones saying, 'Hello, guests! Here are all of our leaders!'"

"But we don't even know if this thing will work," Harvey interrupted. "We'd have the biggest egg on our face in all of known history if it doesn't."

Sanderborn turned his body abruptly to face his assistant. His face looked stony and cutting.

"What the hell did you just say, Harvey? *You've* been pushing for all of this. Go to Vincennes. Find the dagger. Find the book. Build a new Stonehenge. From the get-go you've been haranguing me to do this and that – to do all of what we're currently undertaking. So, failure, my young man, at this point, is not an option. If you had second thoughts, you should've brought those up a long, long time ago. No, it *will* work – it has to! – and Mr. Cooper is absolutely right – when it does, we should have every leader worth a damn here to partake in whatever happens next."

"But, sir..."

"No buts, Harvey. I need you to get on the phone and get Ted Kennedy and Kissinger working on this task immediately. If they need me to make personal phone calls to help facilitate anything, I can do that. From this moment on, this becomes your new and most pressing task. I'm taking you off the Stonehenge crew and putting you on this. Now, chop-chop, get going. I need to pick Mr. Cooper's brain a little more about his vision and how we need to get things started at the building site to accommodate this..."

"...most impressive occasion ever in the history of the world," Hunter asserted.

Harvey reluctantly headed out of the room to start the necessary phone calls, and as he walked by Hunter Cooper, he noticed that the tiny man not only looked like he was the cat (*Felis catus*) who'd eaten the canary (*Serinus canaria domestica*), he looked like the cat who'd eaten the entire aviary of the Bronx Zoo.

Okay, Ghandi, Keep the Peace!

"What the hell was that?"

Shaniqua had shouted this question into the empty motel room like she was calling down to some stranded miners in a coal mine.

Truthfully, Pythia had not a clue. Between her bouts of nausea and the most recent debilitating psychic episode, the medium, despite her vast existence on the planet, had never experienced anything like this in her entire life. She was not only battered and bewildered to a point of being useless, she now could not even sense the presence of the dagger. It'd just vanished off her psychic radar, and nothing made any sense at the moment.

Sensing the lingering discombobulation of her co-pilot, Shaniqua sought to provide her some respite by offering a trip to a local diner for a slice of pie and a cup of Joe – two things which had usually given the young black woman a chance for some recuperation whenever grad school or life had gotten too harsh. Pythia was still too weakened by the episode to be able to put up much of a resistance to the idea, so Shaniqua headed to the main desk to ask for directions to a diner far enough away from the motel to see if that helped her stowaway recover.

As Shaniqua walked past the honeymoon suite, she found herself forced against the door like it was magnetic and she was a piece of magnetite. Unable to keep her body away, her ears were buffeted by the erotic sounds coming from within the room. Not only was this embarrassing and awkward, but she could not help feel a spark of electricity coming from the fissures of her groin. Not accustomed to being sexually stimulated by the sounds of love-making at a roadside motel, she pushed against the door like it was crushing her. From the sudden absolute silence from Pythia within her, Shaniqua had to figure that the medium was just as startled by the powerful attraction of the room and frightened by the arousal resulting from hearing the intimacy within it. It was natural to have those kinds of sounds coming from a honeymoon suite, but the force pushing her body against the door and the power of the sensations resulting from the room were of the most wholly unnatural sources.

Shaniqua was suddenly shoved back away from the door as if it had opened outward and bashed her away. Free from the odd situation, she did not hesitate a second before breaking into a quick trot to continue on her way. She refrained from looking back, partially because she was scared that whatever was manifesting itself within that room would reach out like a steely hand, grab her, and force her back.

The main office of the Kum Back Inn had changed so dramatically that it was hard to remember how it had been when she'd first checked in. There was no longer a pimply faced young man behind the protective glass in the midst of a drab lobby of a squalid motel. Now, a sharply dressed, professional young woman stood purposefully behind a hand-carved walnut podium, and new, expensive, and exotic chandeliers hung from the frescoed ceiling. These gave the freshly carpeted floor and the ornately painted walls a shining quality that was almost blinding.

Shaniqua was so startled by all of this that she walked toward the registration podium like a drunken sailor as she took in the details. For some unknown reason, she was almost giddy with excitement over the banal task.

"Excuse me, can you recommend a place to get a decent piece of pie and cup of coffee?"

The coiffed and suited young woman gave Shaniqua a warm smile and pointed over to another area of the lobby occupied by a fancy wooden desk and a young man in a very expensive-looking suit.

"Yes, ma'am. I think you want to ask the concierge about that."

"Concierge?"

"Yes, ma'am. Alfonse would be glad to help you in your search. Have a wonderful day."

Shaniqua walked toward where the young woman was pointing. The motel that she'd checked into certainly did not have a concierge, and she felt the turbulence from the winds of change that were now gusting through the lobby.

"Yes, ma'am, can I help you?"

The young man, who looked just like a young Clint Eastwood, seemed eager and happy to help – almost to a fault.

"I'm looking for a good slice of pie and a cup of coffee in the area."

"Definitely, you need to go to The White Kitchen."

Shaniqua snorted contemptuously and put her hands on her hips. She'd been the victim of racism in the form of humor enough to know that this handsome white guy was insulting her to her face.

"For real? You're suggesting that a sister like myself goes to a place called The *White* Kitchen? Hardy-har-har, young man."

"No, ma'am. I wasn't making any funny business with my recommendation. There's just no doubt in my mind that the best pie and coffee in town would come from there. The name is not any kind of insult. It refers to the white tiles of the kitchen, which the owner, Gustav Gulet, keeps immaculately clean. The place should be judged on the content of its character, not the color of its tiles."

"Really?"

"My attempt at lightening the mood, ma'am."

Shaniqua looked at the young man and slowly smiled. His voice was deadpan enough to show that he was actually attempting some form of humor.

"Well, it sounds like a good recommendation, Alfonse. Can you give me directions?"

"Certainly, ma'am."

Half an hour later, after having to navigate through some very heavy traffic and then circle the downtown blocks several times to find an available parking spot, Shaniqua walked under the large red sign with the white lettering and a bright neon arrow indicating the location of The White Kitchen. In the doorway a large man barred her way.

"Sorry, lady, but we're having a pretty important meeting in there. Go somewhere else."

"I'm just trying to get some pie and coffee."

"Try the Frostop. It serves your kind."

"Excuse me?"

From inside the restaurant a voice boomed out from a middle-aged white man standing there in a very stained white apron that was accentuated by the roundness of his paunch. In his hands was a dishrag that had once been white but now resembled the coloring of a battleship hull.

"For goodness sake, Herman, let the young woman in. She just wants pie and a cup of coffee. Let her in. I'm still trying to make a living serving food to folks, you know, not operating a gathering place for insurrection which gives away free coffee. My accountant says that I cannot let you all turn my restaurant into Vincennes' version of the Bürgerbräukeller, for god's sake."

The large man gave way and let Shaniqua pass. As she walked into the crowded restaurant, she noticed that there was only one seat available. The rest were filled with men and women of various ages, sizes, social status, and dress, who all went stony and silent as she went to the one available place to sit. She was the only black person in the restaurant, but she was used to that in this world.

As she had been doing from the moment of leaving their motel room, Shaniqua continued to reach out to Pythia to check on her, but she was only receiving what could be called psychic static in response. Much like when a car radio cannot pick up any signals strong enough to come in, her passenger was only emitting a steady white noise. Shaniqua had to admit that she'd grown accustomed to having someone to bounce ideas off and engage in mental conversations, and the sudden disappearance of her co-pilot added to her growing sense of unease. A loud comment by someone in the restaurant brought her out of her moment of thoughtfulness.

"I saw her at the monument the other day. She's just a harmless tourist."

This gruff announcement was made by none other than the ranger Annie Bliss. The muscular woman was out of her park ranger uniform, but she was still quite recognizable.

The man in the apron came over to Shaniqua. As he introduced himself to her, he poured her a cup of coffee.

"My name is Gustav and I own this diner. What kind of pie do you want?

"What do you have?"

"We got the regulars like apple, cherry, pumpkin, strawberry-rhubarb, shoofly, and chocolate cream, but I would recommend the pawpaw cream pie. My cousin Roberta makes it, and I gotta say it's not only divine, but you can only get a slice here."

The offering of a pie made with the fruit she'd been searching for jolted her into letting her guard down a little. In circumstances like these, she usually felt like keeping her head down and staying invisible was the best strategy for staying out of danger due to her skin color. But she could not help herself.

"I will take a slice of the pawpaw cream pie then. It's funny, I came here to Vincennes to look for a grove of pawpaws over on the old Bishop property. I didn't find them, and now I'm caught up in the developments happening around here."

"Oh, jeepers creepers, you're lucky ol' Egan didn't shoot you! He's a mean old bastard. I'll get you an extra big slice of pie, young lady."

Shaniqua didn't know it, but her comment about the changes in Vincennes had been akin to prodding a large skin boil with a very sharp syringe. The group of people surrounding her in this restaurant had been uncertain of how to resume the conversation that they'd been heatedly engaged in before her entrance, but now they squirmed in their seats as if they all had a case of chiggers (*Eutrombicula alfreddugesi*) in their underwear. A very meek-looking older woman broke their silence when she spoke in a near whisper to the group.

"Perhaps she knows someone in the Black Panthers."

"Geez, Arlene, what a crazy thing to say! You gotta be smarter than that to just blurt things out like that."

Annie Bliss made no motion after barking this out, but her head slowly kept shaking in a way that showed her deep displeasure. She stopped the motion suddenly and looked earnestly at Shaniqua.

"I mean, you aren't in the Black Panthers, are you?"

"Well, my brother *just* happens to be Huey P. Newton."

"Really?"

"Naw, I'm just joshing with you all. My skin is black, but I'm not a member of the Black Panthers, nor do I know anyone who is. I'm just a graduate student from Boston who came here to make some connection between Native American and black cultures here in the area, that's all."

Annie Bliss took a sip of coffee from her mug and muttered, "That's too bad. Nope, she's useless to us and our cause."

Shaniqua glanced around the group assembled in the diner. They seemed to be, quite literally, a cross-section of a sleepy Midwestern town. She was startled that such a collection of milquetoast-looking people would ever be caught allowing such a radical conversation to happen, but she now felt empowered to ask why.

"Why in the hell would you all want the Black Panthers *here*?"

An older man wearing worn overalls and appearing much like a farmer, complete with deeply tanned and leathery skin, looked up and over at Shaniqua. It seemed like he was pondering something deep, and then the words came out of his mouth as if he were spitting watermelon seeds.

"Well, you said it when you first sat down. Things are changing here in Vincennes, but not in a good way. You seen it on your way over here, I'm sure. Traffic like we've never had. And super rich outsiders are coming in and buying everything up. Buildings long vacant are now suddenly being fixed up and turned into places too expensive for any of us to afford to go into. Something evil's afoot, and we locals are gettin' tired of it."

A spinsterish-looking lady scanned the group with her rheumy eyes. She pursed her lips and spoke in a voice tinged with venom.

"An Arab came to my door the other day. An Arab! He offered me a million dollars for my house. One million dollars! My family has lived in this same dwelling for generations, so I told him firmly that I wouldn't be selling any time soon...or ever. He had the *gall* to shrug his shoulders at me, then he proceeded to head off without another word and go to my neighbor Margaret Cohens. I saw him make the same offer and that crazy bitch – pardon my French – hugged the man! Hugged the man!

"It turns out that she not only accepted his offer, but allowed him to send a private moving company over immediately to move her stuff out and take ownership of the house. Within a few days the entire property was under construction with an outlandish renovation project to make what had been a semi-acceptable place even bigger, and much more luxurious.

"And since that all happened, there's someone new on my doorstep on a daily basis. Arabs, Chinks, rich people with accents I can't understand – all offering to buy my house, doubling the previous offers."

"Mildred, how high was the latest offer?"

"Does that even *matter*! You cannot put a price on the land and structures that are stained with the blood, sweat, and tears of your people, your ancestors. You just cannot!"

A well-dressed business man stood up. His face was flushed with anger.

"Well, you know what happened to me the other day? I had a doctor's appointment for something very important, and I headed out with plenty of time to make it punctually. But when I got close to the office I ran into a huge traffic jam caused by giant semi trucks carrying a cut-up house on their trailers. Get this! Someone purchased the Miller House – the infamous Eero Saarinen-designed structure in Columbus – and cut it up into transportable pieces to bring it here! Can you imagine?"

Gustav brought Shaniqua her piece of pie. It resembled a coconut cream pie with some meringue on the top. He winked at her as he pushed the small plate towards her and then he turned to face the group.

"You know what I heard? That's the Saudi royal family who's doing all that. And supposedly, they're digging up all that house's gardens and transporting them here too once the building is reassembled."

The businessman cleared his throat forcefully and continued.

"I wasn't done. I was stuck in that traffic jam for a whole *hour*! So, by the time I got to my doctor's office, the receptionist informed me that not only had I missed my appointment, but my doctor has decided to retire from his practice so a new plastic surgeon from California could set up shop in his office. What about me? I asked. And she just shrugged at me, like that gesture answered the question suitably."

"Speaking of plastic surgery," a mild and meek elderly woman seated in one of the booths suddenly uttered, "I was talking with Dr. Samuels about that dead stranger found out by Egan's farm, and he said that the autopsy resulted in far more questions than answers. As far as Doc Samuel could figure, the person must have had plastic surgery on the *inside* of his body as well as on the outside. There was no other explanation for what the doctor found when he went in to determine the cause of death. The stranger must have paid someone in California to *rearrange* his organs and change the color of his blood! Just when you think you've seen everything, aren't I right?"

A skinny man in the corner slouched down as he started speaking in a hissing voice and his eyes flitted from side to side behind his half-closed eyelids.

"You didn't hear this from me, but I have it on good authority that Mayor Gandy is starting to evoke his usage of eminent domain."

The chorus of gasps was followed with members of the assembled group interjecting their own outbursts.

"He wouldn't."

"He couldn't."

"He has no legal authority."

Here, the skinny man held up his hand as he started to hiss another oration.

"He would. He could. And he has been helped by a very powerful outside legal authority to discover some loopholes in the city charter of Vincennes which are justifications for seizing private property to be used for the 'public good.' In this case, the loose interpretation of what's good for the public of Vincennes has opened up the doors to all kinds of acts that benefit the city and the city officials more than the individual residents. Again, you didn't hear it from me, but it's happening, and I'm tellin' you all, the legality of it is air-tight."

The pawpaw cream pie was as good as advertised. It was such an unusual mixture of banana, pineapple (*Ananas comosus*), and mango that Shaniqua's taste buds struggled to identify the delicious flavors bombarding them. The meringue added a nice cover to the culinary fireworks currently happening in her mouth, and the shots of the bitter black coffee only seemed to enhance the sensation of pure joy that the simple slice of pie evoked.

The pawpaw pie and its complex impact had also touched Pythia. She was not only suddenly awake and communicating with her host again, but she seemed to have a renewed sense of urgency. The discontent of the citizens inside the diner, the swirling jet streams of change which seemed to emanate directly from the motel, and the recent strange psychic maladies that'd hit her like punches from Muhammad Ali – including the autoerotic cranial stasis, as she now referred to it – these all pointed to the indisputable fact that the out-of-town billionaire staying in the Kum Back Inn was the key to everything. If so, she commanded Shaniqua to cram the rest of the delicious pie into her mouth, pay the bill, and get going. They had a lot to do.

As Shaniqua settled her bill, however, the continued sharing of travesties happening in ever-changing Vincennes continued to flow from the mouths of the men and women at The White Kitchen. Their long list of litanies was interrupted by Annie Bliss standing up with so much force that her chair was catapulted backwards.

"Blah-blah! I'm so sick and tired of hearing y'all whine about all of the bad things that are happening. What I want to know is, what the hell are you planning to *do* about it? We've all had it up to our ears with this stupid stuff and all the suspicious changes taking place here, but now we gotta act. Listening to grievances in this diner all day isn't going to change a damn thing. Something has to actually happen to force the change we're demanding."

The intensity in the room was reaching a ceiling, and Shaniqua thought the timing was perfect to take her leave. She thanked Gustav, nodded at the gathered people, who were still so focused on answering the gruff ranger's challenge that they barely noticed her departure, and headed purposefully towards the front door.

As Pythia urged her to make haste to get back to the motel, Shaniqua heard a soft voice rising from the diner crowd. "We need a leader. We need someone passionate, well-connected, and *well-liked* by all of us to help us figure out what to do next."

Annie Bliss's voice boomed out of the resulting silence.

"Yuh, no shit, Sherlock.

Olly Olly Oxen Free, D.B. Cooper!

As pointed out earlier, the atmospheric and geological conditions of the planets Mkultra and Earth are eerily similar to one another. Obviously, due to the vastly different chemical properties of their rocks and stones and their air and water, however, the overall layout of each place is vastly different. Interestingly, both planets have what the inhabitants call a Grand Canyon. However, whereas the Earth's version lies open and exposed like a field-dressed deer (*Odocoileus virginianus*), the Mkultran canyon much more closely resembles the honeycomb of a honey bee (*Apis mellifera*).

This is due to differing formation stories. While an ancient river carved out the softer rock on Earth, eroding the limestone of the Arizona and Colorado deserts to create an open and massive gorge, the waters of Mkultra possessed an acid-like ability to seek out and destroy that planet's softer rocks as they leached out and then drained the minerals in a downward fashion. What resulted was a gigantic subterranean labyrinth of endless tunnels, weaving in and out of massive underground chambers that were full of magnificently protective overhangs and hidden pockets.

Indeed, to go down into the Earth's canyon, one needs either a good mule (*Equus mulus*) or the stamina to descend the trails down to the river. A Mkultran planning to go down into their canyon would need some kind of technologically superior, automated spelunking gear and a genetically modified nocturnal pack creature.

Truthfully, however, most Mkultrans did not choose to explore their canyon. Those great minds, known throughout the Universe as the most skilled space travelers, were far more seduced by the sexy aspects of learning only what was out there, far away, and beyond their ability to grasp, than their exploring anything in their own, seemingly mundane, backyard. And, just like Rodin's statue *The Thinker*, most of the Mkultran intellectuals were more focused about what was out there in the depths of the unknown than where the rock met their own ass.

There were ageless legends about the shadowy creatures who inhabited the nooks and crannies of the place, but these were always discounted as the ridiculous and idle speculations of their overly emotional ancestors. There was only one Mkultran scientist who had ventured down into the canyon to map it out, but the much-anticipated cultural exchange with another planet in their solar system eclipsed the fact that this singular scientist had never returned from that expedition. The headlines at the time were far more devoted to discerning whether the newly contacted Kukulcans actually spoke through their genitals or not, so the whereabouts of the missing scientist were never followed up. One could say that that story was buried by the lede.

So, ostensibly, the Mkultran Grand Canyon sat wholly undiscovered and ignored by nearly everyone. If any other scientists had been brave enough to attempt a second venture into the caves, they'd have been immediately blown away by the hidden world which lay in this protected underground tomb. Much like Madagascar, Australia, or the Galapagos Islands on Earth, the remote features of the place had provided enough geographic isolation to allow those creatures living down there the privacy to develop any which damn way they pleased. And develop they did!

The tunnels and chambers may not have been the most hospitable of places on the planet, but the inhabitants of this space found ways to make them work for their population. Where there's a will, there's a way. When survival depends upon adapting, most organisms will opt to do whatever it takes to get it done, and these life forms of the canyon, ignored completely by the above-ground residents and free to do as they wished, achieved a mastery of their unique underground ecosystem which was pretty incredible.

These were not the benign kind of underground critters found on Earth, like the cave-dwelling Benton County crawfish (*Cambarus aculabrum)* or the Ozark cave fish (*Amblyopsis rosae*). Nope, these creatures were not only much more advanced than these Earth examples, but they were also quite eager to play a role in their planet's story. To be totally honest, one specific species of those living in the Mkultran Grand Canyon was getting ready to be the big cheese in the club sandwich that this tale is becoming.

To fully understand this, one must head back to that insightful Mkultran discourse about the history of the original union between Gottliebians and Milbrookians. If one were to closely peruse the wording, they would discover back there in this very story that the terms "nearly all" and "most" were not just casually thrown around when describing the participation of these two species in the original pairing-up process that created the Mkultrans. Clearly, the vagueness of those specific terms was no mistake.

On that day when Oxus and Chyggan decided to bond and began encouraging their species to merge into their super-union, there were a number of Gottliebians as well as Milbrookians who did not want to have anything to do with forming a new composite entity, regardless of the reported benefits. So they took their act underground. No, literally. They went down deep into the Mkultran Grand Canyon to escape this shotgun marriage, and they disappeared from view. And in the excitement over the feel-good results of the brand-new Mkultran species, their absence went completely unnoticed by anyone. Over time their very existence was completely forgotten.

But one must ask how two organisms that were engaged in such a strong predator and prey relationship could ever make the unified decision to disappear into a harsh environment *together*? Well, it turns out that, as both of these populations of defiant Gottliebians and Milbrookians watched what was happening on the surface of the planet, their shared moment of resistance over this arrangement actually allowed them to engage in some sort a dialogue. The outcome of this was the shocking discovery that they were actually amenable to accepting a momentary truce between themselves for long enough to allow each other to establish a new life down in this underground world. So, as the white flags of armistice were waving for the mass coupling up above, both of these more rebellious components of the equation were helping one another to push the down button on the elevator and disappear from view.

This agreed-upon time of nonviolence between these refugee populations of Gottliebians and Milbrookians turned out to be more than enough for them to begin to adapt to their new underground world and to identify new food sources independent of one another. In fact, when the timeout was over, neither one needed or wanted much to do with the other. They'd established territories far enough away from one another in the cavernously vast subterranean world to prevent much contact, and they were happy to go on with lives free from almost any relationship whatsoever.

The Milbrookians were amazed to find that the magnetic ores that they'd fed off before were actually embedded in the geologic layers of the canyon in greater concentrations. The eight-legged creatures suddenly had it made in the shade. With more than enough magnetic ore to consume in the privacy and safety of their new isolated realm, the species was free to feed and reproduce without limitations. In truth, the Milbrookians never gave another thought about the Mkultrans or the world that they'd left behind. They didn't need either one of them, and they got busy living their best lives down in their new home.

Even better for the Milbrookians, their ore deposits were far away from the tunnels that the Gottliebians had adopted as their turf. The Gottliebians had discovered that the seemingly harsh canyon environment was actually a surprisingly lush ecosystem. The tunnels and chambers of the underground canyons spouted life not found on the surface – including a bioluminescent algae-based creature which generated enough light to see, even in the deepest abysses. And there were also vast populations of a giant mite-like creature infesting the tunnels of the canyon, and these tasted absolutely delicious and were totally nutritious. With a solution to the impermeable darkness and a plentiful and delicious food source to eat, the underground world was actually easier to survive in than the above-ground world ever was, and the canyon became an incubator of sorts for them.

Shockingly, these populations of un-partnered Milbrookians and the Gottliebians ended up taking an evolutionary – or descent by modification – pathway that was probably the one that they would have followed if the meteor shower had never happened in the first place. Content to be left alone and allowed to eat, sleep, and fuck to their heart's content, these underground creatures both developed into peaceful and introspective species. Whereas the Milbrookians remained as passive and meek as they seemingly had been before going down into the canyon, the Gottliebians, who had initially brought their overly aggressive nature underground with them, had softened over the generations as the prosperity of their new underground domain smoothed their rougher edges.

Both of these species, Gottliebians and Milbrookians, developed such a strong sense of self-pride about their freedom-filled lives underground that they began educating their young about the value of their own cultures, the devastating impacts of the forced pairings above, and the untold horrors that existed "up there." The foolish idea of leaving their protective womb of a canyon to go up to such a perilous world above became the topic of many cautionary tales told around their bioluminescent algae-lit gathering spaces.

That's not to say it was all milk and honey for those underground-dwelling Gottliebians. Before they fully shed their aggressive natures, they continued to be a very power-hungry bunch with violent tendencies. Those early years in their dim- ly lit dens within the canyon were chock-full of insurrections, mild rebellions, and even a few fairly bloody battles against one another down there in the tunnels. But as they matured, things started to settle down. Eventually, they were actually able to create a peacefully structured hierarchy among the diverse marauding clans of the differing tunnels and cham- ber zones. As most anthropologists – or, in this case, Got- tliebianologists – might describe, these creatures were tak- ing the natural steps that ultimately led to the development of a singular, powerful leader, a chieftain, who could unify the multiple clans and tribes and rule authoritatively over the entire underground population.

A stable governing body was an important step for the species as a whole, to start the Gottliebians on the pathway to serenity. They continued to discard many of their overly emotional and violent characteristics and thereby to estab- lish more secure and fair forms of government, and they even began to utilize technology to create better tools that only further promoted their advancement. Oh, yes, everything certainly was going along swimmingly for the Gottliebians.

Well, until Mooghaag began her meteoric rise through their ranks, that is. That's when things took a drastic turn.

There seems to come a time for nearly every form of life in the innumerable corners of the vast Universe when, as their development appears to be progressing exactly like it should, it somehow finds a hidden flask of grain alcohol hidden somewhere in its ever-changing tunic, and this pro- duces a total shake-up. In the process, new chapters are spawned, completely different tracks are taken, and new norms are formed. And in this case for these canyon-dwelling

Gottliebians, Mooghaag was that shake-up...or – probably more fittingly for her style – the pelvic thrust for a lasting change. Her birth did not attract much attention. As a red-haired female born into an average family, Mooghaag seemed to be slated to be forgotten by all those around her. And as she grew, she faced no unusual hardships, endured no extreme abuses, and suffered no excruciating losses. She was loved by her parents, and she was neither afforded any special luxuries nor denied any of the usual essentials. As a healthy young preteen, she appeared to be average, nondescript, and even slightly boring. None of her family members, teachers, or friends saw – until it was too late – that the girl was wired totally differently than almost all of her fellow Gottliebians.

Only Mooghaag herself knew that she was destined for greater things, and she seemed patient enough to wait to prove this point.

As she approached the age when most Gottliebians become sexually mature, some latent element of dissension began to bubble up within Mooghaag. Not only did she start to vocalize her refusal to accept the current cultural norm of the subterranean, male-dominated Gottliebian society which said that all females were secondary citizens who supposedly were nothing more than child producers, but she spoke out on her intense belief that it was she who was going to be the one to guide her people back upstairs to reclaim what she believed they were due.

Since *neither* of these expressed opinions was very popular – especially with the male leadership – a whopping large target was suddenly sewed onto the young lady's back. Her low social status, as a female with humble origins, meant that she was as good as dead if she kept working her mouth as she'd been doing.

So, how did little Mooghaag escape this quandary? Well, to be blunt, she used sex to advance herself. After all, her opponents had already claimed that she was a nymphomaniac. This is a moniker that's a complete misnomer on the grandest of scales, since most nymphs throughout history have been afflicted with unibrows, uncontrolled armpit hair, and untrimmed pubic regions, all of which, combined or taken alone and individually, must be viewed as questionable in terms of being sexually attractive in human beings.

While Mooghaag did not suffer from any unusual, physically unattractive hairy qualities, she definitely had rampant sexual desires, which, unlike the rest of the female Gottliebians at the time, she neither attempted to hide, distort, nor curtail in the least. In fact, she fanned those flames and used them just like a flamethrower to burn her way up the chain of command.

Mooghaag was a deadly combination. She had quietly grown into a staggeringly beautiful and physically strong specimen, but she also had an unparalleled intellect. She could out-fight, out-fuck, and out-fleece all of her people. Not only that, Mooghaag's personality was like looking at the album cover of the Pink Floyd's *Dark Side of the Moon* in a mirror, because she was able to channel the multiple beams of her overt sexuality, her limitless ambition, her broiling emotions, and her vision of her people reclaiming the exterior of the planet as their natural-born right into a focused laser that was able to cut its way upwards and through the thick layers of her culture. So, as she used the familiar trick of offering illicit sex to either enthrall or blackmail the male leaders and their female partners along the way to gain higher levels of status in the hierarchy, she actually incited the average folks of the canyon-dwelling Gottliebians, who had all begun to admire her, into becoming feverish to join her in her mission to retake what she believed was their long-lost possession: the surface.

In a relatively short amount of time, Mooghaag had successfully worked her way into the role as *the* head chieftain of all the clans of the Gottliebians. Through the time-tested method of purging and culling, she surrounded herself with individuals, male and female, who she could trust, and who shared her intense belief that it was now time to head up and kick the current surface residents out of the way. In spite of the Gottliebians having created a very comfortable life for themselves in the tunnels and caverns of the Grand Canyon, they were all now beginning to become completely blinded by the thrill of opening a can of whoop-ass on their composite cousins.

And of course, although it never makes any sense, a potential universal truth is that the lust for war is as strong for most creatures as is the lust for sex.

That's not to say that the first Gottliebian invasion of the above-ground world of Mkultra went smoothly. In their whipped-up state, Mooghaag's forces were still not fully prepared to leave the dark safety of their underground world. The bioluminescent algae of their caves had always produced enough light to see, but the Gottliebian eyes hadn't experienced a blast of full sunlight in so many generations that they had evolved – or descended in modification – into having eyes that functioned better in the dark than in the light. So, as Mooghaag and her warriors burst free from their earthen hive on their first excursion, they happened to emerge on a typically sunny Mkultran day. Upon hitting the intense sunlight, they all simultaneously collapsed to the ground in excruciating pain from the overwhelming brightness.

If the Mkultrans had had any form of surveillance around the Grand Canyon or enough interest in preventing a possible invasion from within their own planet, they would have witnessed the helpless mass of writhing Gottliebian warriors, all wailing and groaning in ocular pain on the ground. If a military force, even armed with rubber bands and spitball straws, had arrived at that moment, they would have squashed this rebellion, once and for all.

Luckily for the Gottliebians and for Mooghaag, no one found them in this pathetic state, and they were afforded the opportunity to slink back safely into the darkness of their caves and regroup. Mooghaag was able to prevent any chaos or finger-pointing resulting from this failed military campaign by giving a rousing speech that pointed out that being so light-sensitive was a mere obstacle, not a deterrent to reclaiming what was theirs. She encouraged her generals to train her warriors for primarily nocturnal warfare, and she incentivized her scientists to develop some kind of eye protection to keep her soldiers from being incapacitated by the harsh daylight of Mkultra.

Mooghaag was still growing as a leader. After using the strength of her beliefs to fuel her rapid ascendance into her destined role, she now recognized that she needed to be patient enough to take her hands off the throttle, just a little. This first, aborted assault was definitely a small failure, but the lessons learned from it would assure the next foray would be successful. First off, she and her soldiers would be more prepared for the challenges truly facing them, and they'd be outfitted to use strategies that played to their strengths. Secondly, she had learned something about her enemy – the Mkultrans – and that was that they were a hopelessly disinterested and apathetic foe.

A formidable opponent would have swooped in and literally erased Mooghaag and her warriors while in their pathetic state, but it was now clear to her that the Mkultrans were entirely unaware of the Gottliebian presence...or the threat of any kind of rebellion. This lack of response told her all that she needed to know about the black-hearted thieves of her people's destiny – they weren't only utterly ignorant of the existence of what lurked right below their feet, they were too feeble to do anything about it.

Immediately, she set about to use this newly identified weakness to develop some innovative tactics. She organized, outfitted, and sent out specially trained recon units at nighttime to get a lay of the land and to work close to the enemy so they could spy on them. By doing this, she not only gained the necessary intelligence about the terrain and the infrastructure of the Mkultran society needed for the final assault, she developed a three-pronged trident strategy for keeping the peace within her own people in the meantime. She kept her soldiers too busy to think about that first gut-wrenching defeat or contemplate the benefits of any coup against her. She focused her intellectuals on the invention of some kind of vision protection to keep them from stirring up any trouble. Finally, she made sure that her people would be inundated with only the most positive of reports from these surface scouts about the wonders of a world up there and therefore not become too restless. This artful use of misdirection established Mooghaag as the incredible leader she had been developing into, and solidified her place among her people.

When her full Gottliebian force finally came out of their caves for the big attack, they were prepped and fully ready for the takeover of their planet. Mooghaag had decided that if she was going to snatch back the whole Mkultran pie, everyone had to take part in the cutting of it into slices. So, on the fated day, each and every member of her people came rushing out of the caves. While the spearhead of the attack was to be led by her professional soldiers, Mooghaag's army was going to be made up of everyone – including women, children, and the elderly. One hundred percent participation was fully expected, and this was accomplished with some subtle death threats and her catchy slogan "The army won't be winning back the planet for the populace, the populace will be taking it back for themselves."

As they came out into the cool air of the Mkultran night, every Gottliebian wore a clear black onyx-like crystal visor shielding their eyes from the harming rays of the soon-to-be-rising sun. This ingenious innovation allowed Mooghaag and her troops to fight comfortably in the fully lit world above, but it did make them appear more like patrons of a 3-D movie theatre emptying out into the parking lot due to a fire alarm, rather than an organized army of conquerors. But no one cared. They were protected against any incapacitating eye pain, and they had a straight shot at the gleaming and proud prize of the capital city of Glaxopolis.

As her people gathered outside the canyon and awaited the inspirational speech from their leader before heading on their way, Mooghaag chose to make it as clear as snot to her people about the crucial importance of their dedication.

As she dramatically surveyed their impressive numbers, she gave her engineers the signal to blow up the sole entrance back to their realm. The explosion was massive, and the ground shuddered as the rock face slid like sand to effectively bury their world.

The echoes of the explosion and the reverberations of the resulting avalanches continued in the channels of the canyon like the rumblings of a distant thunderstorm. A vast cloud of dust slowly ascended in the sky. Mooghaag's people were astounded as they silently watched the debris rise higher and higher. Then they looked at her with murderous eyes, demanding some kind of explanation for what seemed to them like a foolishly rash action.

As cool as the other side of the pillow, the woman warrior yelled out in an even-keeled voice to the massive gathering of her people this message: "Now there's no home to run back to, no haven to retreat to. We only move forward!"

Her intention was clear. Everyone understood one hundred percent that this Gottliebian attack on the Mkultrans was an all-or-nothing affair.

The strategic plan of the whole assault was pretty straightforward. Even though they had no real idea of the numbers or even the weapons of their foes, Mooghaag's army believed they would storm the sprawling city like some kind of a murderous tsunami and wash away all of the Mkultrans residing there. And once the city was under their control, they'd figure out what to do next. No one was sure what that was, but they'd cross that bridge whenever they came to it.

Don't Add Fuel to the Fire, Edwin Drake!

While Eve was in the bathroom taking another shower, Morton Richardson surveyed the current state of their honeymoon suite. He imagined that his childhood hero, Solomon Meredith, the brigadier general of the famous 19th Indiana Regiment, also known as the Iron Brigade, probably had had a similar response right after the Battle of Gettysburg. Morton stood there in the center of the tawdry red room and felt he was experiencing the range of emotions that man must have felt in that particular moment. After all, the battle had been a hard-fought victory for the Union Army, but as many as fifty thousand soldiers from both the Northern and Southern armies had been killed, wounded, captured, or missing in the three days of fighting.

Two thirds of the Hoosiers under Meredith's own command had become casualties from the action. On top of that, his own skull had been fractured by stray pieces of shrapnel, and his back and lower body had been squashed when his horse was shot out from underneath him. With the battlefield still strewn with the countless dead and dying, Morton Richardson figured that Solomon Meredith, like most survivors of such an epic and bloody ordeal, had probably experienced some genuinely mixed feelings.

Now, as Morton looked around at the carnage of the ravaged motel room, with the sheets torn from the mattress and, in some places, ripped to shreds or still tied into makeshift restraints, and the curtain rod and curtains lying on the floor where they'd landed during a particularly feisty and combative interaction with his wife, he felt the scratches, bruises, bite marks, pulled muscles, and possibly a broken nose resulting from their intense love-making session, and he had to admit that he currently also had some mixed feelings from his sexy time with Eve.

He groaned as he sat up from his position on the bare mattress, and he tousled his rumpled hair with his hands. He had never experienced anything like what had just taken place. He hadn't ever engaged in rough, passionate sex like this before, not with any girlfriend, and certainly not with Eve.

As he tried to recount exactly what had transpired, he found himself wondering if he maybe was remembering a porno movie he'd seen in his youth rather than what had actually happened to him. The mental images of his wife's activities, outbursts, climaxes, and, well... ferocity during their time together were so out of character and so foreign to him that he'd begun to doubt the veracity of his own recollections.

Morton got up and walked over to the full mirror that was askew on the wall because it had been the site of some particularly kinky and downright violent events between Eve and himself. He looked at his reflection and took note of the black eye, the bloodied nose, and the other visible scars of the physical and violent sex play that he'd just experienced, and he saw the proof that many of his memories – as semi-fictional as they seemed – were the accurate remembrances of what had, in fact, *actually* occurred.

His wife had been beyond passionate. Even though Eve and Morton enjoyed a rather healthy and satisfying sex life – especially for an older married couple – during this time together in the honeymoon suite she'd acted like a starving person at an all-you-can-eat buffet. She had greedily grabbed, smashed, masticated, fondled, clawed, bucked, sucked, and devoured so fervently that she'd repeatedly scared her husband. Several times, right after climaxing, she didn't even wait to restart the proceedings until he'd had enough time to recover from the last session, and she often began in again without his help or involvement. She'd even made such unrestrained sounds of encouragement, direction, and satisfaction that he was certain that there might have been some people in faraway Indianapolis who'd heard her overly loud vocalizations.

The mishmash of conflicting emotions he was feeling made him now move sluggishly and caused his thoughts to be like those of a man sobering up. He was simultaneously tired, sore, sated, afraid, proud, embarrassed, energized, stunned, intrigued, empowered, and uncertain. He wanted more, yet he was secretly happy it was all over.

All of these confusing and ambivalent states instantly evaporated when a fully clothed Eve came out of the bathroom and prepared to put on her shoes and leave the room.

"Well, that was the most fun that I've had in years."

Morton croaked out a shocked response. "Years?"

"More like millennia, right? Whoof! I sure had to clear out some cobwebs from down there. I feel as good as new."

"Where are you going, Eve?"

"Well, that was fun and all, but I've got some really important things I need to take care of now. Don't wait up for me. I'll see you when I see you."

Her glib succinctness had blown the haziness out of Morton's mind as effectively as a large portable drum blower fan. He now started to add a new emotion to the mix: anger.

"You can't possibly do what we just did together, Eve, and then walk off like nothing happened. I mean, we need to sit down and chat about some of this...or at least savor it, for god's sake."

Eve sighed heavily. She continued to put on her shoes as if she hadn't heard her husband speak. Then she looked up at the ceiling like she was spying something of importance. In what looked like a moment of sudden understanding, she turned toward Morton with an expression that showed she was miffed.

"Oh, I get it now. You're still worried that I think that your little pee-pee is too small. I mean, is that what this is all about?"

Morton sputtered like he'd been gut-punched. "No, of course...but you said you didn't feel that way."

"Oh, women lie, Morton. We lie all the time. We say whatever it will take to appease any of the men around us. You strut around like you think you're so superior, but we know that we're better than you. That means we often have to sometimes utter things that we don't really believe, but we know will assuage your masculine fragility."

"What? You *really* think I have a small penis?"

"I really do not have time to squabble over something this inconsequential. I've got much bigger fish to fry. You know what, Morton? I wish you men spent as much time thinking about how you could be better, kinder, and more thoughtful as you do about your little wing-wongs. Why are you all *so* obsessed with the size of your genitalia?"

"It's sort of central to our being..."

"No, it's not. Some men are big and some men are smaller, but it's all part of the package. Are you asking if I've ever had bigger than you? Of course I have. You're pretty average sized, which is a good compliment. And, to give you some more encouragement, you're pretty good at using what you've got. So, overall, I give you high marks, Morton Richardson. Take the victory, enjoy the moment. Your wife has been pretty satisfied with you. Don't get so caught up in the measurement of that little flap of skin in between your legs. In the grand scheme of things, it's all small potatoes in regards to the bigger stuff. Well, I'm glad that we've had this chat, but I gotta go."

"You're not leaving, Eve! As your husband, I command you to stay here with me."

Eve paused in mid-motion. When she revolved her body awkwardly to confront her husband, those golden bands around the pupils of her eyes shimmered so brightly that they gave off heat.

"Did you just say you *command* me, Morton Richardson? Is that what just came out of your mouth? I'm going to give you the benefit of the doubt and say that you were not insinuating that you are the master and I am the dog. That's right, isn't it? Think carefully before answering, little man."

"I'm just asking you to not leave, Eve. I need you to stay."

"Oh, you *need* me to stay. Well, there are things at play here in Vincennes that are way beyond the ability of your tiny brain to comprehend. I've got to weave some immense destinies and fates together like some kind of a cosmic Irish sweater, so I'm going to completely disregard your direction to stay here with you and share our feelings about what happened or how we made each other feel. You see, I'm going to head right out to take on this world, and others, in this vast Universe. So – and I hope you do see – I have some important things to attend to at the moment. So, ta-ta, Morton Richardson, thanks for the fun time."

She went over to the ancient dagger that was still lying on the floor where it had landed after Hunter had hit her with it, and she put this back into the rucksack he'd brought it in. Then she pivoted and exited as quickly as a sliding shadow.

Morton was left looking at the battered rack rate placard on the back of the motel door. It seemed illuminated by a spotlight from a lamp that had been knocked over in their intense romp. And it was while he was staring at that specific sight, and trying to make some sense of it all, that his confusion and his disbelief congealed and morphed into something much more complicated and complex – the need for pure, unadulterated vengeance.

In that very instant Morton Richardson had the most negative enlightenment of his life. All of those deep-seated feelings of inadequacy which had been exposed when he'd overheard the final piece to his wife's ex-lover genitalia puzzle had been like some kind of pigmy-barf that he'd been attempting to stymie ever since. Yet, instead of sour bile that he had to fight to swallow, it was his pride and his wounded feelings.

The recent conversations with Eve might have originally mollified him enough to let bygones be bygones, but the mean bluntness she'd just expressed before her departure had freed those suppressed caustic contents within him and allowed them to spew out of him like molten lava from an active volcano.

He began moving around the room with a newly animated purpose. He gathered up his clothing, got dressed, and headed out of the motel room with conviction. He needed to do something to vent all of his pent-up rage before he exploded. Morton Richardson wasn't sure exactly what that was going to be quite yet, but he had become a man on a mission – the mission to burn the whole motherfucking house down.

I Spy With My Little Eye, Nathan Hale!

Buchanan Sanderborn looked like a treed raccoon (*Procyon lotor*) as he was forcibly backed up against his writing desk by the movements of the aggressively advancing Hunter Cooper. And much like any trapped animal, his face had a mixture of slight trepidation, growing annoyance, and a twinge of desperation on it. However, when he spoke it was mainly annoyance that came out.

"I have had my room's privacy assaulted twice in a short period of time, Mr. Cooper, and for someone with a reclusive nature like myself, such frequency does put me on edge. Perhaps you could back up a bit and explain your unexpected presence here."

Hunter Cooper straightened his zoot suit, readjusted the outrageously large porkpie hat atop his head, and pushed his magenta-lensed sunglasses further onto the bridge of his nose. He coughed shallowly and took three steps back.

"I apologize, Mr. Sanderborn-baby. My enthusiasm got the better of me. I just came over from the worksite with the most exciting news, and I forgot my manners. I have something *incredible* to report."

"You could've called."

"Such information cannot and should not be reported over the phone, Mr. Sanderborn-baby. You need to hear this firsthand. I guarantee, it's gonna knock your socks off!"

Just then there was a rap on the door, which hadn't closed fully after Hunter had barged in, and Harvey looked in tentatively and grimaced when he saw the body language between his boss and the Truman Capote lookalike confronting him.

"Excuse me, sir, but I have some news to share."

"Oh, thank goodness, Harvey, come right in. You're just in time to hear Mr. Cooper divulge some news that he seems unable to contain within himself. Let's listen to him first. Then we can send him on his way and you can tell me yours. But please, close that damn door behind you."

"Yes, sir."

But his assistant was so excited he merely swung the door with what he thought was enough force to close it. However, his effort hadn't actually accomplished the task, and the door remained slightly agape.

"Okay, Mr. Cooper, what is this *big* news?"

Hunter Cooper put his hand on his chest and then made a grand gesture of spreading his arms wide, either resembling a crucifixion victim or a cast member from an off-Broadway production of *Oklahoma!*

"Stonehenge is finished."

"How's that?"

"It's done. Finito. Completo. All finished."

"How is that possible? I thought it was going to take weeks more."

"Oh, come on, Mr. Sanderborn-baby, the men you hired for this task were very motivated to get it done...and get away from me, I fear. All the stones are in position, the lintels are hung, and, using my grandfather's book, the copper wire has been woven into the correct pattern. We left off the final connection so as not to inadvertently start the thing up too prematurely, but the landmark is sitting there like a brand new DeLorean, just waiting for the battery to be connected and the key to be turned. We are, at this point, just waiting on you to give the word to start this baby up."

"That *is* incredible news, Mr. Cooper. I find myself dumbfounded by it, actually, and that is not something that a person in my position ever feels. I mean, we aren't really ready for it to be..."

"Completed, but it is. It's one hundred percent done, Mr. Sanderborn-baby. Well...close enough. It's ready!"

"I'm at a loss for words here. There's so much still to plan and so much to set into place, I'm not sure how we can catch up to your amazing accomplishment, Mr. Cooper."

Harvey stood a little more erect and took a step forward from where he'd been standing with the enthusiasm of a veteran high-school debater getting a chance to finally deliver his rebuttal.

"Excuse me, sir, but I also have some earthshaking news of my own to give you today, and I think it will be the icing on the cake for what Mr. Cooper just delivered."

"Ah, Harvey, bring it on. I don't know how you can top Mr. Cooper's news, but give it a whirl."

"Ted Kennedy and Kissinger have worked some diplomatic magic, and nearly all the world leaders that they contacted are committed to coming here to Vincennes for the moment when the aliens are to arrive."

"That's great news!"

"Kennedy is such a shrewd negotiator and old man Kissinger still seems to lace his words with laudanum. They had everyone in the palms of their hands within minutes. I mean, they're all ready to come here at the drop of a hat, and everyone is sworn to secrecy and they are keeping all of this out of the press. The recruitment of the President of the United States went off without a hitch. That man was eager to say 'yes' to something, anything, really."

"Who else are we talking about then, Harvey-baby?"

Both Harvey and Sanderborn turned to look with some outrage at Hunter Cooper. He'd asked this question with his usual flamboyant flair, his eyes closed and his hands contorted against his chest like sleeping pigeons (*Columba livia*). Harvey fought the impulse to punch the annoying little man in the face, but then turned back toward his boss like he was getting ready to recite a poem.

"All of the A-list, sir, and even some from the lesser important countries. From Europe, let's see, Margaret Thatcher from England, Willy Brandt from Germany, Valery Giscard d'Estaing from France, Felipe Gonzalez Marquez from Spain, Charles Haughey from Ireland, Leonid Brezhnev from the USSR, not to mention most of the leaders from the Soviet Bloc, as well as all of our NATO allies. From Asia, we have Masayoshi Ohira from Japan, Charan Singh from India, Hua Guofeng from China, Choi Kyu-Hah from South Korea, Kim Il Sung from North Korea, Pol Pot from Cambodia, and even Ton Duc Thang from Vietnam, sir. From the Middle East, we have commitments from Menachem Begin from Israel, the Ayatollah Ruhollah Khomeini from Iran, Saddam Hussein from Iraq, Hafez al-Assad from Syria, King Hussein from Jordan, Muhammad Anwar el-Sadat from Egypt, and King Khalid of Saudi Arabia."

"Golly, that's *quite* a list of who's who you've got there, Harvey!"

"I am not even done, sir. Kennedy and Kissinger reached out and got Francois Duvalier from Haiti, Augusto Pinochet from Chile, Yusufu Lule from Uganda *and* the deposed dictator Idi Amin, Julius Nyerere from Tanzania, Jose Daniel Ortega from Nicaragua, and even...Fidel Castro from Cuba."

"No! That's incredible."

"He took some convincing, sir, but your guys hooked him and reeled him in like pro anglers."

"What about our neighbors, Harvey? Did the leaders of Canada and Mexico say yes?"

"Yes sir. Pierre Trudeau from Canada and Jose Lopez Portillo from Mexico are in, and they are offering their assistance in getting our distinguished guests to us."

"Who said no, Harvey?"

"Well, some seemed less convinced of the need to come, but only Malcolm Fraser from Australia said absolutely no to the invitation. On the bright side, he did say that if everything went well with the first meeting, he'd look into re-evaluating his position. Nonetheless, we are poised, sir, to assemble the most diverse and powerful contingency of world leaders here in Vincennes to greet the alien visitors – an accomplishment that has never been even attempted in human history before. We have the opportunity to affect immense change on a global stage here."

Buchanan Sanderborn began to pace. Even though both Harvey and Hunter were standing there looking at him, he shook his head and muttered things as he walked absentmindedly in front of them. The man was obviously consumed with his own thoughts.

"Are you all right, sir?"

"Yes, yes, I am. However, the logistics behind what we need to do before we turn on the beacon to the aliens seem suddenly overly daunting. We have a finished Stonehenge and a committed group of our planet's leaders to be in attendance when we turn it on, but we now find ourselves with a rather large headache on how to pull this all off, don't we? We have some *major* logistics to wrestle with, and time is ticking, time is ticking."

"Well, sir, I do have some more good news on that matter, too."

"Let's hear it, Harvey. Maybe you already have the answers to all of our problems."

"Yes and no, sir. Ted Kennedy and Kissinger are going to keep working on some things from Washington while we continue to address the issues here. When it looks like we're headed toward the actual turning on of Stonehenge, those two are going to come to Vincennes and help us with any remaining issues. You're probably thinking about how we are going to get all of those leaders here safely and house them comfortably. After all, given some of their currently rocky relationships with our own country – not to mention some very deep and long-standing running discords between each other – two details, transportation and lodging, will be kind of tricky to handle."

"Yes, Harvey, I'm very worried about those insurmountable issues that that list of leaders that you just recited brings up. I mean, we can't just put them all on a Pan Am plane and fly them here to Vincennes to get a room at the Kum Back Inn, can we? Some of them are going to fight like cats and dogs if we put them next to one another. No, we're going to need to..."

"Do something special to prevent any bloodshed. And I think I can really help you here, Mr. Sanderborn-baby, by…"

"Hold your thought there, Mr. Cooper," Harvey interrupted. "I think we've got this handled. You see, sir, some of the world leaders who have access to their governmental planes and who can fly directly here without incident are going to do so. The enlargement projects on the runway and tarmac at the Lawrenceville-Vincennes International Airport are now completed, so there is plenty of room for even the largest airplanes to land and park for this event. For those leaders with the most potentially frosty relationships with the US right now, Canada and Mexico have pledged to allow their airspaces to be used to let anyone who might not be welcomed directly into the United States to land there. From those two countries, they will get on armed and secure buses to drive them across the border and right to Vincennes. Another solution will be sending our own private jets to pick up some of the leaders and bring them here, since, as you know, the requirements of traveling that way are much looser than commercial flights."

"So we're going to get everyone here by plane or bus, huh?"

"Yes sir, except Kim Il Sung. He won't fly. However, he's agreed to board his armored train and head to the Russian port of Vladivostok, where he will be transferred to a Soviet train transport ship that will secretly bring him to Homer, Alaska. There, his carriage will be part of a faux freight train that will make its way down from Alaska to Vincennes."

"That certainly seems like a convoluted route. How on earth are we going to coordinate his travels with the timing of the arrival of the aliens?"

"Oh, he's already left on the trip, sir. He seemed ready to embark on any kind of adventure."

"Okay, maybe transportation is set, but what about housing?"

"Mayor Gandy is helping us there, sir. Your brilliant idea to find the loopholes in the city charter about eminent domain was definitely a good one. He's made it his personal crusade to claim the nicest houses in the Vincennes area. Once we get the displaced owners settled down – to the point that they won't report these actions to the local press – then we will set about assigning the world leaders to these houses, carefully placing natural enemies and historical foes in distinctly different areas of the city to avoid any unnecessary bad blood. Mayor Gandy has acquired enough well-suited structures to house these heads of state in differing neighborhoods, so I'm starting to feel confident that we can avert any trouble."

"Well, Harvey-baby, that plan certainly relies on everyone staying calm and playing nice. I mean, if they can do that, everything should go just fine, right? Of course, a betting man with a penny to his name would place a wager that that ain't likely to happen."

Hunter's comment was ill-received by both Sanderborn and Harvey, and they looked at him like they wished that he wasn't in the room. Harvey inhaled deeply before beginning anew.

"Also, sir, your friend over at *Forbes* magazine came up with the list you asked him for. He said that he never considered that anyone might want to read a list of the richest people on the planet, but he's definitely going to push it through to become an annual part of the magazine. The collection of names that he compiled – which you're on, of course, sir – has become our team's source for recruiting people of substance to come to Vincennes. They are, as you forecasted, *quite* interested in investing, buying, and helping turn this city into a hub of economic fecundity. Many of them have offered to be here when the aliens arrive, so they are going to be part of this once-in-a-lifetime collection of greeters when the beacon is answered."

Buchanan Sanderborn clapped his hands together and did a little dance in celebration. His joyous actions were completely out of character for the usually somber billionaire, and Harvey regretted the way his boss had just resembled Adolf Hitler's supposed victory dance after the surrender of France in World War Two. Harvey knew personally that that dance had never happened. The Nazis, acting thoroughly German, had searched high and low to locate the very same train carriage that they'd been so deeply humiliated by some twenty years earlier when they were forced to sign the Armistice in the Forest of Compiegne to end the Great War. Hitler had gotten off that specific railcar and merely had taken an awkward, knee-lifting step while the cameras were rolling, and an English propagandist took the footage to create a mythic jig of elation. The fact that it was a fake did not become common knowledge until long after the war, but the image was permanently stuck in the western world's consciousness as another piece of evidence of what a monster Hitler was.

Adolf Hitler *was* undeniably a monster, and Harvey thought it disrespectful for Buchanan Sanderborn to do any movement which mimicked the man. Even though he knew it was not the time or place to challenge his boss, he was about to speak his mind on the matter.

It was at this very moment, though, that Pythia – who'd overheard everything after she'd positioned Shaniqua outside the still-ajar motel room door – decided wholeheartedly that it was time to insert herself into whatever huge undertakings were now underfoot in this Indiana town. She saw that everything was no doubt now filtering straight through the visiting billionaire whose presence had stirred up so much activity on the physical, emotional, and psychic planes, and she decided that a frontal assault on Buchanan Sanderborn was the best tactic. She instructed Shaniqua to use her ample birthing hips to power open the door the rest of the way into the Presidential Suite and charge inside.

The young black woman forcibly entered the room and confronted Sanderborn like a member of the paparazzi ready to capture a bombastic photo shot. However, before she could utter her well-rehearsed warning that the disharmonious locals were gathering and preparing some kind of upheaval, her body involuntarily revolved to face Harvey. She issued an exhalation similar to the one Curly had made famous in The Three Stooges films of long ago, and when this was finished, she spoke in a croak.

"You goddamn bitch!"

Buchanan Sanderborn, who was clearly agitated that his suite had now been invaded yet a third time by an uninvited guest, turned to his assistant to issue an order for the squad of Pinkertons he'd hired to guard his room to now come to their rescue, but Harvey was making a similar sound to the exhalation the young black woman had just made. When the assistant's mirror reaction finally ceased, he spoke in a ghostly voice.

"You fucking twat."

Harvey grabbed a stapler from Sanderborn's desk and began issuing forth an auctioneer's voice to invoke the soul-transference spell as quickly as he could while he hurled himself toward Shaniqua in hopes of knocking her out and trapping her inside the piece of office equipment.

Shaniqua then snatched up the Vincennes phonebook lying there as a form of protection against his assault.

For the briefest of moments, the two were like two ninjas in a martial arts film as they thrusted, deflected, and parried with their absurd weapons of choice at one another. They were too engrossed in their fracas to hear the multiple outbursts for them to stop and desist being issued from both Buchanan Sanderborn and Hunter Cooper.

The thunderous sound of a gun going off snapped Shaniqua and Harvey out of their bellicose trance, and they stared over at Hunter, who held an outrageously large Smith & Wesson Model 29 .44 Magnum pistol in his hands, pointed up at the ceiling, smoke still issuing out of its ebony barrel. Where the undersized man had stored the impressive weapon on his body was uncertain, but the conviction of the words which he issued next in an uncharacteristically restrained monotone was definitely clear.

"You two must stop this madness this instant. We are *so* close to accomplishing everything that we so desire – so near to wrapping up this whole gargantuan plan – and I will not tolerate this kind of behavior. If either one of you cannot stay on task, I swear I'll shoot you in your pretty little noggins. Got it?"

Harvey and Shaniqua both nodded and retreated from one another. They returned the items they were using as weapons to the writing desk and warily took another step apart as Hunter put the huge pistol into his belt.

Sanderborn, who seemed to be quite shaken by all of these events, looked up at the impressive damage from the bullet in the ceiling. When he looked down and saw that the manager of the motel was at his door, accompanied by two Pinkertons, he straightened his shoulders and took on a calmer countenance to speak to them all.

"We're fine. Thank you for your quick response. Mr. Cooper was just demonstrating the weakness of the ceilings and the lack of soundproofing of this motel, and upon reflection, I do believe we need to contact a construction company to fix the damage in this room and begin evaluating the rest of the structure for deficiencies. Please close my door firmly as you leave."

The billionaire's stark command cleared the assembly at the doorway and returned the four inhabitants of the Presidential Suite to their stony silence.

"Well, I'm entirely confused here. What in the *hell* just happened, Harvey?"

"There's some very bad blood between us, sir."

"You've met this woman before?"

"Yes sir, a long, long time ago. And it didn't go well."

"It didn't go well *at all*!" Shaniqua concurred.

Sanderborn rubbed his face like he was kneading pizza dough. He stopped and then looked sternly at Shaniqua.

"And who are you, young lady? Why have you barged into my room like this?"

"My name is Shaniqua Bishop, and I came here today to warn you about a dangerous group of dissenters assembling here in Vincennes."

Sanderborn looked over at Harvey to see if he could lend any further explanation, but he was still glaring at Shaniqua.

"And why would you think that this is any of your business?"

"That's a *very* good question, sir," Harvey offered.

"Shut up, you bitch!"

"Go to hell, cunny."

Hunter Cooper cleared his throat and reached for the handle of the pistol protruding from his pants. The threat hinted at reached both recipients, and Shaniqua unclenched her fists and addressed Sanderborn directly.

"You see, initially, I came to Vincennes to find a grove of pawpaw trees on some ancestral lands to complete my research for my doctorate thesis. But I quickly got caught up in the frantic pursuit of an ancient dagger. You could even say that I'm feeling possessed by it. In the search for this artifact, however, I inadvertently stepped right into the major undertakings happening in this little city. My research's been completely overwhelmed by it all. The dagger and now the building rebellion in this backwater Indiana town have my full attention."

"I had the dagger," Hunter Cooper admitted matter-of-factly.

Both Harvey and Shaniqua broke off their angry staring contest to let out a sound that was akin to Charlie Brown's scream of anguish whenever Lucy pulls the football away from him in the Peanuts cartoon. Sanderborn remained more stoic, but his expression was that of a parent who had just learned that the must-have Christmas gift – the Kenner's Star Wars figures and spacecraft – were gone from the shelves on the final Christmas Eve shopping trip. He cocked his chin to imply authority.

"What do you mean 'had,' Mr. Cooper?"

Hunter Cooper reviewed the looks of intensity now coming from those around him, and he chuckled rudely at them.

"I mean, I had it, but I gave it to a friend for safekeeping. I'm a little prone to lose things – if my head wasn't attached to my body, I'd probably misplace it – so I made sure that someone more reliable had the most important and integral component of this whole production. That dagger needs to make its reappearance to this world at just the right moment, and my friend will assure that this happens."

Harvey actually stepped in front of his boss and put his hands out like a quarterback ready to receive a football hiked from the center.

"Hunter, Hunter, that dagger's extremely important to me. Why don't you contact this friend of yours and tell them that it would be a lot safer with me."

Shaniqua wagged her finger at Harvey. Then she set her hips and spoke directly at Hunter.

"Uh-uh, Mr. Cooper. Tell your friend that *I'm* someone they can trust. That dagger would be a ton more safe with me than with this dirty whore."

"You're nothing but a dried up shrew who needs someone to kick..."

"Uh, hey, Harvey. Mr. Cooper appears to be reaching for his gun again. Perhaps we need to let the issue of the dagger go...for right now. Why don't you let Ms. Bishop continue on with her explanation as to why she's here?"

"Certainly, sir. I'm sorry. No more outbursts from me."

Shaniqua sneered at Harvey's compliance, and she began speaking again to Sanderborn.

"I was just at the diner The White Kitchen for pawpaw pie and coffee, and there was a hostile gathering of local people there who sounded as if they were getting ready to rise up and cause some trouble for you. I thought you might want to know."

"Yes, Ms. Bishop, that is helpful information. I'm still not exactly sure, though, how any of this concerns you enough for you to barge into my room uninvited and cause such a ruckus here."

"I think you would agree, Mr. Sanderborn, that the impressive activities happening in Vincennes these days are at a very fragile tipping point. An armed insurrection would topple everything you're working so hard to create here. When I heard their anger and their desire to find someone to lead them into battle with you, I felt enough concern to come straight here and tell you."

"Oh, she's a total quack, sir."

"Shut your trap, you filthy mongrel!"

"Enough! Harvey, you must refrain from insults or I'm going to send you out of here."

"Sorry, sir."

"As for you, Ms. Bishop, thank you for thinking about our plight. Now you can go away."

Looking just like Truman Capote answering Dick Cavett's question about why he'd started writing in the first place, Hunter Cooper began an oration aimed solely at Buchanan Sanderborn.

"Whoa, Mr. Sanderborn-baby, don't send her away just yet. She's right with her assessment. We've worked so hard on the completion of these things as part of a bigger plan, and the appearance of an armed mob could cause this house of cards to fall quicker than my underpants when I am headed to the loo after a particularly fiery meal at Wong's Chinese restaurant.

Perhaps this young woman could serve an important role for us. Those people who were grousing over at that appalling diner obviously felt comfortable expressing themselves in front of her. We could use that to our advantage. She should infiltrate the uprising and report directly back to you. That way you could be prepared for any trouble, and head it off."

"You want me to be a spy? A *snitch*?"

"It wouldn't be the first time, you sniveling tart!"

"Harvey!"

"Sorry, sir."

Sanderborn started nodding to himself. He pointed at Shaniqua like he was picking her for the big Capture the Flag game.

"Yes, I think Mr. Cooper is right. We need an ear in the midst of all of this agitation, and you could be just that, Ms. Bishop. If such a task hurts your feelings of sensibility, feel free to leave and head on your merry way. Your message of warning has been delivered and we've heard it, loud and clear. If you don't want to take us up on our offer to play a role in these future undertakings, then there's absolutely no reason for you to be involved with anything we're doing anymore."

"Naw, I can go back and insert myself with those people and report to you if I hear anything new. I'm intrigued now to see what's going to happen, and being your inside source gives me a front-row seat to that."

"Excellent. Why don't you head back downtown and see what's going on."

The young black woman gave Sanderborn a mock salute and she turned to leave. As she headed toward the door, she twisted her head to look over at Harvey.

"Just watch your back, white boy. I'm coming for you."

"Bring it, sister."

"Harvey!"

This Is Going to Cost You an Arm and a Leg, General Dan Sickles and General Thomas "Stonewall" Jackson!

Morton Richardson, now so blinded by rage that the world around him was nothing but an amalgamation of blurred funhouse mirror images and shapes, marched up to the front door of his house with the force ($F = ma$)) and momentum ($P = mv$) of the infamous Light Brigade. Just as he was about to open the door and storm inside, however, the piece of paper taped to the door stopped him in his tracks as effectively as if the vaunted British cavalry had run into an enclosed and locked paddock instead of into heavily armed Russian troops. He actually found himself pressed against the entranceway with a slightly unnerving pelvic thrust from stopping so short to read the notice.

The white paper with the vivid red printing stated quite clearly that the City of Vincennes had taken possession of the Richardsons' house and property through eminent domain. Morton's eyes refocused to take in the wording, the legal arguments put forth, the authorizing signatures, and the dire and final consequence of the message. His reaction was to clench his teeth so tightly that there was an audible cracking and crunching from the extreme mandibular pressure being put on the calcium hydroxyapatite, dentin, cementum, and dental pulp gnashers in his mouth.

Morton's momentary hesitation took only long enough for his brain to process that he was going to, indeed, follow through with the harsh thoughts he'd had as he'd left the ravaged motel room at the Kum Back Inn. With this final acceptance absorbed into his being, he proceeded to the garage, where he gathered a gas can, his case of empty vintage Indianapolis Brewing Company bottles, and a clear plastic bag full of rags made from his shredded old T-shirts.

Atop his worktable, he carefully assembled twenty-four Molotov cocktails and then found the lighter that he kept hidden in a pair of old sneakers for those secret late-night cigar-smoking sessions whenever he was feeling mischievously rebellious. Toting his arsenal of crude incendiary devices in the wooden brewery crate, he walked out of his garage and around toward the front door of the house.

Without sentimentality, Morton lit three bottles and threw them through the two windows on the first floor and into the second-story window of his son's vacant bedroom. The crashing sound of glass and the inhalation sound of the gasoline catching fire within made a sneeze-like katzenjammer that Morton did not stand around to listen to any more.

As soon as he'd launched his flaming projectiles successfully, he grabbed the case of beer bottles to head off to his next target, Mayor Gandy's office at City Hall. He had a vicious sneer on his face as he stomped away because he was happy to have just stuck it to Eve and these goddamn projects of improvement going on in Vincennes. Plus, he knew firsthand that their house was insured for the maximum amount.

Luckily for Morton Richardson, his path for continuing to commit blatant acts of arson brought him into direct contact with Shaniqua Bishop. Literally. He was concentrating so hard on creating a long list of targets for his beer bombs that he didn't see her approaching until he ran smack-dab into her. This collision didn't cause any lasting damage to his flammable payload, Shaniqua, or himself, but it did create a situation in which two separate, undefined agendas were directed through the same lens, creating a refracted image that served all individuals involved. Pythia, inside of Shaniqua, was still stewing in her own psychic juices because having been sent on a mission to overhear the pathetic rabble rousers of Vincennes was not what she felt she needed to be doing. Her only goal was to figure out a way to sneak up on that Harvey character, surprise Morgen within him enough to incapacitate her with something inanimate, and entrap that horrific witch for another sentence of indefinite imprisonment. Then she could track down the dagger and get the hell out of this cow town. She needed only to find some kind of massive distraction to pull it all off.

Morton, even with his frenzied vengeance-filled brain continuing to churn out irrational thoughts and plans, recognized with some clarity that he wasn't going to actually accomplish much storming around with his twenty-one remaining Molotov cocktails and cherry-picking those specific targets causing him the most angst. No, with the heightened security, the recently enhanced firefighting capabilities, and the frenetic activities of this new Vincennes, he knew that it was only a matter of time before he was stopped by some form of lethal force without inflicting any real or lasting damage on anything. He needed an army to lead into battle to bring about the most permanent change.

Their chance collision served all of their needs. Shaniqua, sensing the dangerous rage fuming off the man, informed him that she was just on her way back to a spot where a growing uprising was taking shape. Morton, hearing that there were other residents angry enough at the changes to strike back, altered his course from City Hall to The White Kitchen. They headed off together, a white man with a renewed aim of getting real revenge, a black woman who was currently bodysurfing through the rogue waves of these tormented times, and an ageless psychic as a familiar agent of necessary upheaval.

The White Kitchen had devolved into a seething melee of shouting and yelling. With the disorganized mob within its walls working itself into the fevered pitch of a religious revival meeting, regurgitating their complaints and grievances without any resolution until they were almost talking in tongues with their charges of discontent, there seemed to be nothing which could silence them, or unify them.

However, the entrance of the disheveled Morton Richardson holding a case of petrol bombs did just that. As the once-respected businessman walked into their group, looking more like a partisan leader of *La Résistance*, all of their squabbling stopped immediately to hear what he had to say.

"I'm prepared to do whatever it takes to drive these foreign invaders out of our beloved Vincennes, but I cannot do it alone. I'm gonna need some help."

The brevity and lack of eloquence of Morton's attempt at a pep talk did not help his cause. Sure, the group had been looking for someone to take the reins, but the succinct comment just made by the obviously frazzled president of the local insurance company had failed to inspire. If he'd just lobbed a metaphorical Molotov cocktail at them, he would have incited the group to follow him. However, Morton's verbal projectiles had been more filled with Dr. Wells "pepper-style" soft drink, not gasoline, and his words had landed with only a thud.

Pythia, sensing that they were about to lose this perfect opportunity, got Shaniqua to yell out that she knew what was really going on in Vincennes. The young black woman proceeded to tell them everything. No detail of what she'd overheard at Sanderborn's motel room was left out, and by the time she was finished talking about the new Stonehenge being a beacon for the aliens to come back to Earth, the gathering of the world's leaders to greet the extraterrestrial visitors, and Sanderborn's aim to turn Vincennes into a destination for the mega-rich and powerful, the assembly inside the diner was stunned into a simmering and angry silence.

Morton had listened to Shaniqua, and his intense negative emotions that had been directed at Eve and Mayor Gandy were channeled in such a way as to give him back his powers of reason and rhetoric. Like a subject being brought out of hypnosis, he took on the new demeanor and posture of the leader they were all searching for.

"I'm looking around this room and I see almost every aspect of our city. I see the business sector, the legal circle, the industrial complex, the social world, the agriculturalists, the young, the older, the more mature, and even a few veterans – we all need to leave this diner and go out and organize. If we were all to approach our respective groups and tell them what Ms. Bishop has just shared with us, we'd have the *whole* city behind us. If we could create some kind of a massive, unified movement and go to that Stonehenge meeting to let Sanderborn and all his followers know that we are not going to go down without a fight, we could show them that we're willing to stand up for our city."

There was a general murmuring of growing support within the diner. Excited whispers of how to gather their forces were beginning to be issued. Then Helen Montgomery, the head librarian of the Vincennes Public Library, slowly stood up and looked around the room as if she was about to silence noisy teenagers in the reference section. Everyone immediately stopped talking.

"Mr. Richardson, are you suggesting that we engage in a physical confrontation of some sort? I don't think that a seventy-two-year-old woman like myself, or any of the various book group ladies I could organize, are up to engaging in any type of fisticuffs or open warfare. Are you really declaring war on Buchanan Sanderborn, his rich and power allies, and these supposed visiting aliens?"

"Hell, yeah, he is. We're going to kick their fucking asses!"

The group gave Ranger Bliss looks full of doubt, but then they turned their attention back over to Morton, who had his hands out in front of him in a plea to keep the peace and to hear him out.

"No, no, Ms. Montgomery. I am *not* asking you or anyone else here to take up arms. What I *am* saying is that we can form a huge phalanx to confront that gathering at Stonehenge to show Sanderborn and the others that we, the people of Vincennes, are unified enough to put up an organized resistance. For some of us, that may involve acts of physical violence. It appears that Ranger Bliss could lead those forces. But what if Mayor Gandy suddenly understood that his voting constituency was now against him? What if there was a component of us that was armed with the law? Imagine, if you will, all of the lawyers of this town coming to the gathering using the legal system as their weapon – that would certainly put them all on their heels. What would happen if the business and industrial executives and labor union members, arm in arm, confronted all of those world leaders and rich people gathered there with some negative financial news – strikes, boycotts and embargoes and the likes? What if the farmers and railroad men all said that their food and transportation was now a bargaining chip? Having all the cops and firemen on our side would be paramount to an impressive assault on the ne'er-do-wells. We could hit our opponent high and low at the same time, just like the defense of our Lincoln High School football team did against those Jasper High School Wildcats in the Wabash Football Classic last year."

The mention of this proud moment in Vincennes' sports history caused a buzz of excitement as everyone in the diner replayed the exciting conclusion of that football game one more time. Their hubbub was then broken by the reptilian voice of the skinny man in the corner again.

"It's going to take some time – not to mention a huge effort – to pull off what you're asking, Richardson."

The way that the hush fell in the room indicated that this factual statement could be more correctly viewed as a deep personal challenge to Morton's plan. All eyes turned to the man to see if he was going to be able to fend off this real challenger.

With a calm demeanor, Morton paused a little before answering, but his head was like an orbiter sprinkler as he addressed each member of the gathered group.

"From what Ms. Bishop just told us, we have some time. The arrival of both the world leaders and the aliens is not going to happen tomorrow or the next day, so we can be patient and persistent. I truly think we'll have ample time to drum up enough support to create an impressive army of people who love Vincennes enough to resist this hostile takeover by outside forces. I cannot guarantee our victory, but I know that I need to give it the old college try."

His answer was the lynchpin, and it was agreed that they would all immediately go out to recruit the people of Vincennes to join forces to prevent the takeover of their city by crashing the "outsiders'" little party at the new Stonehenge. The proposal to use the Richardson household as the headquarters to this movement was quickly dispelled by the news that that edifice had been destroyed recently by fire. This obstacle was overcome when someone suggested that The White Kitchen become the nerve center for the movement. Despite the loud protests from Gustav, they agreed that the diner made the most sense as the place for them to be so that all of their future communications and decisions could be made together there.

Almost immediately the assembly broke up and all its members left to start the process.

Morton and Shaniqua were now alone. Gustav was still grumbling about the takeover of his diner, and he used the push broom as if he were pushing demons back down to their hellish domains. It was not the right time to ask the man for more, but Morton suddenly realized that he himself needed a place to stay since he had no home to go back to anymore.

"Hey, Gustav, can I stay here for the next few nights? I'll pay both room and board. Can't go home and I can't afford to stay at the Kum Back Inn."

Gustav reared back at the suggestion, but then the financial wheels began turning in his head. Renting to Morton Richardson and preparing food for his future Vincennes freedom fighters might make up for any lost business from shutting down the diner. He nodded tentatively at Morton.

"Thanks, Gustav."

"You know, I need somewhere to crash, too. I cannot stay at the Kum Back Inn anymore. Gustav, can I stay here? Same idea, room and board?" Shaniqua asked.

"Sure. Yeah, that works. From respected diner to cheap flophouse – how did that happen to me?"

"Hey, Gustav?"

"Yeah?"

"Could my old friend Morton and I have a slice of pawpaw pie and a cup of coffee? We've got some planning to do, and that pie is scrumptious."

"You got it. Two slices of pawpaw pie and two cups of coffee coming right up."

He decided to not mention the instant mark-up in price of both, but he figured that they wouldn't care as long as they remained caught up in the cause. He grinned mischievously at how things truly work out when you let them.

Here's Mud in Your Eye, Bartimaeus!

Buchanan Sanderborn had insisted that the first viewing of his new Stonehenge would happen at sunrise. So the three men – Harvey, looking tidy and professional as ever; Hunter Cooper, wearing a particularly preppy outfit of an Icelandic sweater with another sweater tied around his neck, tan corduroy pants, and an oversized knit beanie atop his head; and Sanderborn, attired in an Italian business suit – were the only living souls at the deserted construction site. They made their way toward the stone circle in utter silence and looked like travelers on a pilgrimage who were almost reaching their long-sought destination.

An odd fog had settled on the area during the night, and now that the sun was rising, everything was covered in a soft, wet coating like the sweat of a tropical lover. The stones and wires of the Stonehenge monument dripped suggestively, while a trio of white-throated sparrows (*Zonotrichia albicollis*) sang out to a world just awakening. The sounds of far-off train activity and traffic on the highway provided the background chorus to the avian overture.

Although there were enough aspects to make the scene mysterious and beautiful on this misty morning, it was still, in fact, a construction site. The ground had been churned up by the equipment and foot traffic and was exposed and raw-looking. No landscaping or lawn sodding had yet occurred, so the land looked as barren and harsh as the terrain of an imagined alien planet. Also, the heavy machinery involved in the assembling of the stone circle – the bulldozers, the front loaders, the cranes, the construction trailers, and the boom trucks – all slumbered like dinosaurs off to the sides of the site.

Having not worn the proper footwear, all three men approached the freshly carved sarsen stones, lintels, and central trilithons as if they were playing a slow, dyssynchronous game of hopscotch to avoid the mud puddles. Their clumsy movements were accompanied by the sounds of their disgust whenever their fancy shoe-clad feet made unexpected contact with muck.

Their progression stopped suddenly as the three reached the outer rings of the monument. They each froze in place, and a silence that was almost oppressive dropped upon them. There seemed to be no words to convey the depth of the emotions they were all feeling.

Sanderborn shattered the moment by taking another step forward and then turning to face his two subordinates.

"Oh, Mr. Cooper, you were so right – it's *magnificent!*"

"My grandfather's plans were very detailed, so this is exactly how it looked when it was first created. Just like you asked, Mr. Sanderborn-baby."

"The world owes you and your grandfather a huge debt. You will be rewarded in kind."

"If it weren't for my research, sir, we would never have known about Vincennes, the book, or the dagger," Harvey offered.

Sanderborn looked over at his assistant and frowned. Something was *way* off with the young man, there was no doubt. The changes in Harvey had been slight at first in New York City, but they'd become more and more apparent in Vincennes, and blatantly obvious as of late. To stoop so low as to brag about his effort right now, during such an intimate occasion, merely to usurp the praise of the odd little man who'd been so instrumental in getting the whole project completed, well, that seemed very, very out of character for him. And Sanderborn was no fool. Whenever he had any doubts about those in his inner circle, these became major indictments with the most immense of consequences.

"Indeed, Harvey. You're a good boy, too. But when it comes to an accomplishment as grand as this magnificent monument, and what we are attempting to do here in this city, one cannot attempt to steal the spotlight – it was a group effort, wouldn't you say?"

The verbal glue trap just laid on the ground before him gave Harvey pause. His boss was clearly giving him a warning that if he couldn't get himself put together, it was going to cost him in ways that were unthinkable. He swallowed his pride and pretended to be subservient once more.

"Oh, we are all just cogs on the wheel, sir. I know that, and I appreciate my place on that wheel. We have all moved mountains to have this splendid replica of Stonehenge here in front of us, just ready to be started up to be the beacon that will call the aliens back to Earth."

Because Sanderborn was in a particularly suspicious mood, his assistant's slice of humble pie seemed spiced with a dusting of ghost pepper (*Capsicum chinense*) powder or a sprinkling of arsenic, and he raised an eyebrow to indicate that future changes might have to occur if this uncharacteristic behavior continued.

"Yet here it is! Stonehenge is rebuilt, and it is one wire connection away from being able to do what it is supposed to do, huh? Harvey, go find a ladder so we can put that hanging wire where it needs to go."

"Me, sir?"

"Yes, you. You're taller than Mr. Cooper. He'd need a boost, even with a ladder."

As Harvey carefully trod over to the nearest construction trailer, where an aluminum ladder rested, Sanderborn addressed Hunter Cooper directly.

"And your grandfather's book does not give any account on how to start this thing up? Or how long before the aliens supposedly are going to show up?"

"No, he doesn't. He seems to spend all his time on the arrangement of the stones and the wiring at the top. It is a construction blueprint, not an operational manual, Mr. Sanderborn-baby."

"Well, we'll plug this thing in and see what happens."

Harvey was lugging the aluminum ladder past them to the loose wire. He'd heard enough of the conversation while on his task to have some serious concerns.

"What if nothing happens, sir?"

"We'll never know unless we give it a try, right?"

"Guess so, sir. But..."

"It's gonna work. I just know it."

Hunter's comment was laced with so much confidence that it dripped as blatantly as the stones of the monument did with the morning's dew. Harvey whistled loudly with frustration. He stopped his movements completely and spoke directly at his boss.

"Should I get some rubber gloves, sir? I mean, what if there's electrical current running through this thing when I connect the wire?"

"It's not connected to a power source, for goodness sake, Harvey-baby. Just wrap it onto that spot there where it's supposed to be. Don't be such a sissy."

Harvey fought the urge to come down the ladder and attack the little dimwit, but he had a feeling that Sanderborn was now watching his every move. He sighed aloud and then spoke to his boss.

"Clearly this creates a circuit of some kind, or else the monument would've been calling the aliens all these centuries, right, sir? Maybe I should go and find some electricity-proof gloves to protect myself."

"No, we don't have time for that. I think it's going to be safe enough to connect it, Harvey. It's my belief that you're going to be just fine."

"Okay, sir. I trust you. But are you sure that you want to start this thing up today?"

"I think we have to. I haven't heard anything from that black chick spy of ours. Have either of you heard anything from her?"

"Nothing, sir. If I had, I would have put a baseball bat to her head, that's for sure."

"Your anger with that young woman is very concerning to me, Harvey."

"Well, Mr. Sanderborn-baby, I haven't heard a peep either. I mean, she just disappeared when we sent her away on her mission."

Sanderborn made his neck more erect to get a better view of the entire construction site.

"That uprising of the locals worries me the most of anything facing us, gentlemen. If they organize and sabotage the monument or throw a wrench into the works in any way, this whole kit and caboodle we've been working so hard on and investing so heavily in could come to a sudden screeching halt. No, we all need to take some risks and proceed like we're on borrowed time, which we may well be. So, just connect the damn wire without wasting another goddamn moment, if you please."

Harvey moved as if he were suddenly holding an electric eel (*Electrophorus electricus*) in his hands rather than a large copper wire. When he prepared to put the loop of wire onto the stone nub where it was supposed to go, he did so with a split concentration. He needed to get it there, but he also was prepping his body for jumping for its life off the ladder and into the mud below if there was any kind of spark.

Nothing happened as the wire was connected. There were audible sounds of relief from each of the men, but especially from Harvey, who scampered down the ladder and then leaped onto the ground like he'd escaped death itself.

"What now, sir?"

"I dunno, Harvey. Maybe it is like one of those plug-in heaters and we just need to let it warm up."

"How long should we wait, sir?"

"That's not a thing that we could possibly know, Harvey, so we'll just wait for a little bit. We can't stay here all day staring at it, though. We've got lots of other things we need to get done."

"But how do we know when the aliens will get here, sir? That makes it very hard to know when to officially send out all the invitations to our important guests to come here and meet the visitors. If we mess this up, we are either going to have an impatient gaggle of impossible personalities to deal with *or* we will have no guests here to receive the aliens and we lose the ability to make a good first impression."

"You're stating the obvious here, Harvey. We just started Stonehenge up again, so I think we put caution to the side and just send out the invitations as soon as is possible. It's better to have all our dignitaries here early. That way we can wine and dine them, and maybe they will all want to invest in the Vincennes Project. Hell, we can babysit them for as long as it takes, if need be. I mean, it's better to have them all here rather than the alternative. The way I see it, the fundamental concept of Business 101 is that people don't really know what they need or want, so it's up to the salesman to convince them of all that. I say get our guests here, then we'll sell them the whole concept."

"Right on, Mr. Sanderborn-baby."

It was then that all three men realized that they were not alone anymore, and they all turned their bodies slowly to face the source of the mud-sloppy footsteps approaching them. It was Eve Richardson. She was barefoot and striding toward them with what should be called a purposeful gait, almost like a female tango dancer approaching her partner. Her hair was disheveled seductively and, from the movement and sightings of her cleavage, it was clear that the woman had removed her bra when she'd untucked her dress shirt. She was casually carrying an Army-green rucksack on her shoulder, and there was a purplish aura around her body. Her golden-rimmed eyes shone like headlights in the mist.

"Eve-baby, what on earth are you doing here?"

Hunter's question lacked enough sincerity that Harvey tilted his head to better hear what the woman said in response. When she answered, her voice seemed to be coming from somewhere other than her voice box – more like from the ground, the woods, and the sky.

"I'm here because you men are such idiots."

"Well, madam, I certainly do not know who you are, but I'm going to ask you to stop right there and come no closer. You're trespassing on private property, and I have security forces on call. They're ready to move in and dish out some physical force. Please leave before I'm forced to alert them."

"Get out of my way, puny mortal man. I am here to turn the monument on and signal the Mkultrans. I don't have time to ignore any more of your ridiculously idle threats."

When Eve began to speak in the ancient language of the Stonehenge people – something unheard for the last three thousand years – Harvey felt as if his whole body had been immersed in ice water. His lungs compressed and his muscles twitched involuntarily. He knew that Haggur had somehow returned in human form, and that she was casting one of her spells.

As she concluded her ancient conjuration, she reached into the rucksack and pulled the ancient dagger out of it. She then invoked another spell directly at the metal object in her hands. The gems on the sheath immediately popped off, hovered for a second, and then shot to their locations on the lintels as if they were bullets sprayed from a Gatling gun.

The new Stonehenge instantly rumbled to life like a Detroit Diesel v12 truck engine. After a short delay, the wiring around the top glowed brightly with a red-hot intensity. Then a pure alabaster beam shot out of the center of the monument and pulsed straight up into the sky, cutting the fog and the clouds, and disappeared from sight. With this tumultuous moment over, the monument went silent and appeared to the onlookers to be entering a post-coital moment of satisfied bliss.

"What the hell just happened?"

Sanderborn's question was aimed at no one in particular, and his voice was tainted with a healthy dose of panic.

"I have sent a message to the Mkultrans that we are ready for their visit."

Eve Richardson looked at the three men with a faint smile on her face, but when she looked back up at the sky where the bolt had disappeared, Hunter, Harvey, and Sanderborn all gazed up there too. They all looked like that silly trick when one person looks up and makes everyone else look up for an imaginary object in the sky. No one spoke.

A magenta-colored beam shot back to Stonehenge, creating a cloud of pink smoke that was laced with a series of symbols floating in it. This swirled in front of them and then dissipated. Eve's countenance took on a look of supreme happiness.

"And what the hell was that?"

Again, Sanderborn's question was tinged with far too much apprehensiveness to be taken seriously. Eve looked over at him as if he were a black-tailed prairie dog (*Cynomys ludovicianus*) chirping out a call of warning. She sighed heavily.

"They just replied that they will be here in seven of our Earth days."

"Seven days? That seems oddly specific, madam."

"Ah, little man, as you will find out, the Mkultrans are an extremely precise species. When they say that they will be right here in seven days, you can set your timepieces for that moment."

"Mkultrans? You keep saying Mkultrans. Who are these Mkultrans?"

"Little man, no more inane questions. It is not the time for lengthy explanations. It is the time to call that mini-army you threatened me with just a moment ago to set up some kind of protection for this site. Although our guests now have a bearing to take to reach us, it is important for their punctuality to maintain this signal until their arrival. Nothing can stop that, if you want things to go as planned."

Eve Richardson started walking away without a word. Such insubordination as this could not be taken lightly, even by Sanderborn.

"And where do you think you're going, madam?"

Eve turned slowly and looked at Sanderborn, and the golden rings around her eyes turned the dark purple color of a deep bruise. When she spoke again, her voice sounded like thunder. "Little man, I've been asleep for far, far too long. I still have some catching up to do. And only a week left to keep doing that. I'll be back when it is time."

Her words were as powerful and direct as the beam of light just sent up into the atmosphere, and two of the three men were silenced. Harvey, though, took a meek step forward and then put one knee onto the mucky ground.

"Haggur..."

The woman in front of them seemed to grow taller and her aura blazed like neon. Her voice came out sharply and she uttered something akin to a record being played backwards. Hearing this, Harvey gasped and stood again, and the damp stain on his fancy suit which now covered his knee looked like a pee patch.

Loosely translated, the words the age-old medium had just spoken to Harvey meant, "Shut the fuck up, you worthless wench. Your day of reckoning is coming in one week. Ta-ta."

I Am Going to Throw the Book at You, Bi Sheng!

It should be noted that Mooghaag's plan for reclaiming Mkultra was not too dissimilar to the early promises made about the enhanced-radiation weapon (ERW), the neutron bomb. This small hydrogen bomb of the 1950s, designed by Samuel T. Cohen *of the Lawrence Livermore National Laboratory,* claimed to use neutrons to kill the humans inhabiting the target city without damaging all of the edifices. However, once the weapon was detonated in a test, it was discovered that it actually produced a massive, fiery, and destructive atomic explosion that would blow to smithereens any people, vehicles, and buildings anywhere nearby. Not that any of this mattered to the US military in the least. Any way to erase the enemy was good enough for them. False advertising notwithstanding, all of the major armies of the Earth put the neutron bomb on their holiday shopping list.

Mooghaag had ordered her troops to just focus on the killing of the Mkultrans and to completely avoid the destruction of any property, possessions, or structures that they came upon during their advancement. This was not a popular decree at first, but the Gottliebians' fearless leader explained it all as clearly as she could in her final pep rally before their first attack on a Mkultran outpost when she spoke the words, "We're going to evict the tenants and keep all of their belongings as ours."

When Mooghaag's massive force descended upon some isolated and unarmed technological labs set in the wilderness to increase the Mkultran academic accomplishments, they slaughtered the mostly apathetic scientists residing within, but they left their labs and experiments wholly untouched. This assault turned out to be the perfect dress rehearsal for the big show in the capital city.

The killing of these scientists by the Gottliebian warriors also revealed the need to develop a new method for the killing of a Mkultran. Unlike with the usual Gottliebian-cide – when a single slash, stab, or even beheading worked like a charm – with the Mkultrans their usual methods did not cut the mustard. They were a bit disillusioned to discover that, when it came to dispatching a composite creature, there really needed to be two death blows. The hapless Mkultran scientists proved that if their main body was fatally wounded, the Milbrookian component atop it was still very much alive. And these usually jumped off the dead or dying host and tiptoed around on their eight tentacles as they frantically looked for a new host.

Seeing this caused even some of the bravest of Mooghaag's fighters to scream like washerwomen, so it was decreed that, after this unsavory scene had played out a few times, the eight-legged symbionts also required a quick smiting.

A new fighting technique was designed on the fly. Delivering a vicious blow that cleaved the Mkultrans from atop the head down killed both the Milbrookian sitting atop and the host Gottliebian down below. This move quickly became the way to kill their enemy, and many of Mooghaag's troops began referring to it as the "Hassan Chop."

Leaving the structures standing and untouched paid dividends, as the marauding Gottliebians discovered a dust-covered armory in the basement of these labs which was full of Mkultran laser blasters. These weapons were simple enough for a child to use, and it became clear that any Gottliebian holding such an armament had a much easier way to eradicate the enemy than swinging what amounted to a broadsword down from top to bottom of their foes.

With these new weapons, Mooghaag's generals issued another order to always aim for a headshot with the lasers, since that would took care of both the Milbrookian and Gottliebian at the same time.

Mooghaag and her advisors had been apprehensive after the massacre at the labs. Since they were still under the impression that their first bloody act of aggression would cause a quick, powerful, and armed reaction from the Mkultrans, they pushed ahead with the idea that they were about to be set upon at any moment. But with each unopposed step as the Gottliebian army continued on its way toward Glaxopolis, there came the understanding that there was to be no retribution-filled counteroffensive, no interception by defensive forces...in fact, no opposition whatsoever. Eventually, the scope of the Mkultran lethargy began to take hold inside Mooghaag's mind, and most of her caution was thrown right out the window. When her forces reached the edge of the forest and nothing but an open plain lay between them and their desired destination of Glaxopolis, she gathered her troops one more time to share with them a final rallying speech before their assault.

Mooghaag was a straight-shooting kind of gal, and she usually let her actions speak for themselves. But on the topic of reclaiming their world from their former cousins – a pathetic species who was too indifferent these days to lift a finger to keep control over their own lands – she was able to become quite eloquent and passionate. Within a matter of moments she had her people whipped into such a frenzy and so full of piss and vinegar that they were primed to race across this exposed terrain with a devil-may-care attitude. Many didn't wait until their leader's final words before turning and running, screaming mightily, toward the shimmering, towering skyscrapers of Glaxopolis.

Simultaneous to all of this, the armada of Mkultran transport ships carrying the Gherrardians was preparing to land upon the planet of Mkultra on the opposite side of the capital city from where the Gottliebians were advancing. As soon as they had set down and their spacecraft doors had opened up, the swarming mass of the crab-like warriors exited and immediately headed straight for the city. Assuming that this was where the main computer was located, with all the knowledge about navigating through space using wormholes in it, the Gherrardians only had ommatidia for Glaxopolis.

A truly bizarre scene resulted. The Mkultran capital city was smack-dab in the middle of two opposing forces. From one direction, the crudely clothed army of Mooghaag was currently rushing on foot like a bat out of hell and looking just like the charging, rebellious army of Kirk Douglas in the golden age of Hollywood classical movie *Spartacus*. From the opposite direction, the advancing Gherrardians appeared to be giant versions of the subjects of a National Geographic documentary about the Cuban red crab's (*Gecarcinus rurico-la*) migration to the sea near Havana. These two massive and malicious forces were on a collision course, and the gleaming city of Glaxopolis lay right in the intersection of them like a concord grape (*Vitis labrusca* 'Concord') about to be squeezed by two powerful pinchers.

However, just as this collision was about to occur, the engines of a hidden fleet of immensely large space transporters simultaneously ignited and an almost uncountable number of these craft went airborne. Like lustrous arrows aimed skyward into the atmosphere, the spacecraft lifted off with a deafening roar and a bombastic cloud of fire and ash.

That impressively loud scene stopped the two invading forces in their tracks. In their sudden stupefaction, the Gherrardians and Gottliebians watched as the gigantic spaceships flew above the clouds and disappeared from view. Neither force seemed able to move a muscle until the mighty thundering of these departing Mkultran ships grew fainter and the ambient noises of the stunned surroundings finally repossessed the now vacant city.

Unable to fully process what they had just witnessed, the two armies pressed ahead again and made their way forward through what was now clearly an abandoned place until they were face to face with one another. As these two mobs both suddenly came to the conclusion that the Mkultrans – their shared enemy – were no longer around, the two opposing forces now turned their hostilities on each another. After all, the prize that was Glaxopolis was still ripe for the taking. The earthling Stephen Stills may have written a song with the title "Love the One You're With," but if he'd known the

Gherrardians and the Gottliebians, he might have entitled his song "Fight the One You're With."

And fight they did. The earthling physicist Newton stated in his Third Law of Motion, "For every action, there is an equal and opposite reaction." While most physics teachers will go on and on about cute pairings of little colliders like pool balls, butts, seats, and other nonviolent interactions, the collision that day between Mooghaag's forces and the Gherrardians was more akin to two trains hitting head-on. The long string of train cars behind the leading and halted locomotives continued their forward motion and continued to smoosh into one another...all the way to the little red cabooses at the end. Those two trains – one Gottliebian and one Gherrardian – were instantly transformed into one giant concertina accordion, with the rear ends collapsing upon the middle sections as they crumpled into one another like the bellows between the handheld ends of that wind instrument.

Their swelling momentums were so great that when they slammed into one another in opposition, row after row of soldiers in their waves crashed into one another and continued coming until the two sides had ground one another to paste. There's no other way to say it...the armies of the Gottliebians and the Gherrardians began to beat the living shit out of each other.

Nothing was off the table in terms of violence in the hand-to-hand combat, close-quarter fighting, urban guerrilla tactics, and the generally furious free-for-all of killing that took place. Combatants died at such an alarming rate that soon the fighting was taking place atop the mounds of the corpses of the fallen. And as if this weren't bad enough, they were all so intent on continuing their bellicose activities that not a single one of them heard the amplified beeping that had started coming from all of the untouched edifices of Glaxopolis. That sound usually only ever indicates some kind of countdown on a self-destruct timer, but none of the waging troops took time out of their busy bloodbath to take notice, or to heed the warning.

Not that it would have mattered. The entire city was wired to blow. Whoever had booby-trapped the metropolis had aimed for the utter destruction of anything and anyone in or near to the city limits. Unfortunately for Mooghaag, her army of Gottliebians, and all of the Gherrardians, they were all well within this intended blast zone. So, regardless of anything that they thought to do or didn't know to do, they were going to go up in smoke as soon as the timer reached zero. And when it did, and the beeping stopped, the resultant cosmic sneeze of the planet-rattling explosion left not a single organism alive in the area that had once been the capital city of the Mkultran Empire.

KA-BOOM!!

Have You Lost Your Marbles, Lord Elgin?

Harvey Ferguson had returned to the Kum Back Inn in the car he'd commandeered, and he now sat in the silent vehicle to collect his thoughts. His decision to go directly to the diner to meet with Shaniqua and to have a *tête-à-tête* with Pythia had not gone as planned. He had hoped that, even with all the swirling mayhem of the uprising of the Vincennes rebels beginning to sweep the downtown area, the two mediums could have a civil conversation about the reappearance of Haggur. Knowing how, not to mention why, this had happened, at this very moment in time and place, were mind-bogglingly ineffable questions that seemed to require answers from the two entities so intimately connected to the old witch. He had high hopes that they could help one another somehow come to grips with the impact of the news of their dead mentor's sudden arrival.

However, as Harvey approached the restaurant and made his way through what looked like the common people of Vincennes arming themselves for a major battle against Sanderborn's personnel in their planned attack on Stonehenge, he saw the young black woman he sought sitting right next to the revolutionary leader Morton Richardson and acting as the man's aide-de-camp.

This sight caused the same reaction deep within him as a faulty septic effluent pump – the foul fecal waste products buried down within the psychic medium which had been catching a ride inside of him started to suddenly flood him, and he was overwhelmed by the rising disgust, rage, and blind need for vengeance. Any hope for a peaceful discourse went right into the hamper, and taking its place was Morgen's plan to use the entropic situation at the nerve center of the uprising as the distraction she needed to sneak up on Pythia and use a soul-transference spell to imprison her one more time.

Despite Shaniqua's unwavering focus on the planning of the attack now being unfurled by *el jefe*, Morton Richardson, Pythia was not only aware of Harvey's approach, she was prepared to launch her own counteroffensive. Sadly, the resulting scrap was more a moment of pure embarrassment, especially since the people in the diner knew nothing about the battle between psychics taking place in front of them. No, to them it all looked like the nice black lady who they were starting to like and trust had surprisingly started hurling silverware at a dressed-up dandy who'd just come into the diner. This fancily dressed young man had responded ineffectually in return, and with both of them now flinging cutlery while seemingly talking in tongues, the townsfolk in the diner saw only a most surprising and utterly ridiculous scene. It didn't help that neither Shaniqua nor Harvey seemed able to hit the broadside of a barn.

One soup spoon did hit Harvey, and although it was not sufficient to knock him out and complete the spell, he realized that he was currently more vulnerable than he wanted to be. Plus, it hurt like hell. A small goose egg appeared on its contact spot with his forehead, and that was all he needed to turn tail and run out of the diner as fast as his Foot-So-Port wingtips could get traction on the slick diner floor and propel him away from the situation. He did not stop running until he had reached his car.

Now, as he watched a similar militant energy at the Kum Back Inn to that brewing at the downtown diner, Harvey moped silently about the utter failure of his trip. It all weighed heavy on his heart. He had not been able to talk with Pythia about Haggur's appearance, so he still had no idea where she'd come from or why she was here at this very moment. He also could not explain why the dagger no longer held any power over him or why he didn't care if it was close or not. On top of all that, he had made a regrettable scene with Shaniqua at the diner and had probably kicked over a nest of bald-faced hornets (*Dolichovespula maculata*) there.

He was sure that Pythia would now attempt to sneak up on him in the chaos that was going to undoubtedly soon be taking place on the shores of the Wabash River in her own attempt to imprison Morgen. The damn tit-for-tat chase was back on.

It was a forceful rapping on the car window which brought Harvey out of his funk. One of the defensive linemen from the Lincoln High School varsity football team, which Sanderborn had hired as extra security, was peering down at Harvey as he continued to tap his meaty knuckles on the glass window.

Harvey rolled the window down and looked up at the young man. The huge athlete had a vacancy in his eyes which made him seem either possessed or incredibly dumb. Either way, the large individual confronting Harvey no doubt required his respect.

"Yes, what is it you need?"

"Mr. Sanderborn sent me out to find you. He said to go to his room ASAP. He's kinda pissed that you disappeared at such an important time. He didn't say it directly, but he sorta implied that I'm to throw your ass out if you take off again like this."

"I don't think that will be necessary, my fine young man. Au revoir, crétin."

"What did you just say to me?"

"Just how happy I am for your hard work."

"Yuh, whatever. Just get to Mr. Sanderborn's room, pronto!"

Harvey did not look back at the juvenile behemoth as he made his way to the Presidential Suite. He had a good, well-prepared excuse for leaving, and he thought that his boss might accept it without worry.

Another impressively large man was standing at the door to Sanderborn's room, and he gave off much more dangerous vibes than the high-school kid had. After he'd frisked Harvey with an unnerving intensity, the huge man knocked on the door and announced him to the people inside the motel room.

"Where the hell did you go off to, Harvey?"

Sanderborn's question was half accusation and half indictment. His expression was so impassive it made Harvey shudder, and the way that little pissant, Hunter Cooper, was standing so casually next to his boss gave rise to enough emotion in Harvey to force his reply.

"I went off to talk with our spy, Shaniqua, sir. She reports that the locals are arming themselves and preparing for some kind of action."

"No crap, Columbo. If you'd just stayed here and had been paying attention, dumb-dumb, you'd be able to see quite clearly that the peasants are revolting. You didn't need to leave your post to figure that one out, Harvey-baby."

Harvey gave Hunter the stink eye. Even though the little man was wearing a casual outfit and some kind of ridiculous slouchy, baggy, oversized knit beanie on his head – looking like Dopey from the Seven Dwarfs – Harvey now fought the temptation to physically attack him.

"Mr. Cooper is right, Harvey. If you'd been here, you would have known that those bastards firebombed my in-town office and burned it to the ground. They're out of control! I've had to hire armed mercenaries to come in and cordon the rebels off in the downtown area, and keep them away from the new Stonehenge. I'm still floating offers of unlimited funds to those who we think we can turn, but the rebels have built up some impressive numbers of people, many of whom are resisting being bought off. They threaten the very success of this whole venture, and I need you to be here with me and Mr. Cooper to help us get to the finish line. We're so close to a truly memorable accomplishment. We cannot take our eyes off the prize and head away willy-nilly to waste time."

"I am sorry, sir. It won't happen again."

"No, it won't."

"But I did see their leader, a man named Morton Richardson."

"Oh, Morty-baby? He's haunted by the belief that he has a small penis."

Harvey held his arms up in the air as he gave Hunter a fiery look of displeasure.

"What does that have to do with what we're trying to do here?"

"Morty-baby is paralyzed by this particular thought. If we ever come into a direct confrontation with the man, we all need to start yelling, 'A little dick does not do the trick!'"

"You're serious?"

"It'll wound him very badly."

"Enough senseless babble!" Sanderborn's voice boomed like an explosion. "We need to make sure that everything is in place for the arrival of the aliens in three days. I need a report from both of you about the tasks you were to undertake."

"Let's start with the totally good news, shall we, Mr. Sanderborn-baby? The landscaping at Stonehenge and at the George Rogers Clark Monument is complete. The entire area is a secure, good-looking venue for the Mkultrans to meet the dignitaries from Earth. What was once an ugly and muddy construction site now resembles a pampered lawn, complete with bathrooms and chairs for all of our guests."

"Well, that *is* good news."

"Oh, yes, it is, Mr. Sanderborn-baby. You are going to be amazed at what we have done. Plus, we now have half a dozen milliners set up to start making hats here in Vincennes in some of the industrial buildings around the city."

Sanderborn's eyes, which had been wide open and expressive, suddenly tightened into slits, looking more like horizontal embrasures in an old stone fort.

"And, pray tell, Mr. Cooper, why is that important to what we're talking about here today?"

"Oh, I thought that was as obvious as the nose on your face, Mr. Sanderborn-baby. Not only do all the greatest cities of the world have the ability to make fancy hats for their wealthy, but this is yet another pledge of economic improvement we can offer the people of Vincennes to calm them down. The promise of new jobs and careers always soothes the savage beast, dontcha think?"

"Sure, I suppose so. Okay, that's more good news. But more importantly, you're sure, Mr. Cooper, that the area around Stonehenge is secure enough to avoid any kind of embarrassing attack from the rebels?"

"It's tighter than Fort Knox, Mr. Sanderborn-baby. Nothing is going to impinge on the important undertakings going on there when it's showtime."

"Marvelous. Stay on top of it, Mr. Cooper. And Harvey, how are all of your efforts going? Hopefully as well as what Mr. Cooper just reported."

"Well, sir, let's be honest. Our two tasks weren't actually equal. I'm doing a little more heavy lifting than he had to undertake. He's had to deal with sod and hats. I've had to deal with Israelis and Palestinians. But that's neither here nor there. We're ahead of schedule on most of the aspects of the gathering of the world leaders, uber-rich, and economic captains here in Vincennes. The airport has been turned into a virtual aircraft boneyard of the most important planes of the world leaders and the squadrons of luxurious private jets. We've had a steady flow of our special guests crossing the Canadian and the Mexican borders to be transported here. Ted Kennedy and Kissinger have been working tirelessly to get the leaders to Vincennes safely and without incident, and the settling-in of everyone into the appropriate housing has gone well, too. There've been no problems between anyone yet, and we've worked tirelessly to keep opponents and enemies as far from one another as possible.

"Arafat's a bit of a pain, since he wants to be sleeping in a new bed each night, but we figured on that when we came up with a housing plan. So we've kept moving him, which makes him happy. Kim Il Sung may not make it here in time, but taking a train from North Korea to Vincennes is not a feat that is timely or predictable. We will do everything we can to get him here for the aliens, but we're going to need a few things to go our way for that to happen.

"So, it's mostly good news, sir. There's so much excitement about meeting the aliens that most simmering conflicts or open hatreds have taken a back seat to everybody behaving properly. Mr. Cooper and I have worked hard together to come up with a seating chart to ensure that no one will be seated too close to someone they don't get along with during our introduction to the aliens. We got the actual layout of the UN from Kurt Waldheim, so we have our fingers crossed that we'll be able to keep things from boiling over before, during, and after the big event."

"What about that odd woman?"

Hunter Cooper looked at Harvey Ferguson, who returned his expression of uncertainty. They both shrugged simultaneously.

"I haven't heard anything about the woman directly, sir. Just hearsay and rumors mostly."

"My contacts are just saying that ol' Eve is wandering around town without attracting too much attention, other than seemingly doing whatever she wants to do to excess. She comes around, enjoys herself, Mr. Sanderborn-baby, and then she disappears again. She's only caught the eye of the locals because she's a well-known personality who's acting strangely. But these days, it's harder and harder to differentiate between normal and abnormal behavior, isn't it?"

"Right. Well, let's hope that no one interferes with her too much in this shitstorm. I think we might need her to make the first inroads with the aliens when they finally get here. Dammit all to hell, I just wish we could quell this anarchy just a little! All we need is to make a good first impression with the aliens and then this town has the real chance of going on to become a renaissance center of economic and cultural growth. We're so close, but it certainly could blow up in our faces."

Harvey had the audacity to reach out and put his hand on his boss's shoulder. It was totally out of character for the assistant to proffer any kind of physical display of affection with Sanderborn, and the billionaire looked down at the hand on his shoulder as if it was a recently spewed glob of baby vomit.

"Sir, I think we're at a standstill when it comes to the uprising of the locals. It is my belief that, once they see the aliens and understand the vision of what you have in store for their city, they'll get in line. They'll see that it will all benefit them too."

Sanderborn moved to shed his second's hand. He then looked down at the spot to make sure that nothing had stained the area. He scowled at Harvey.

"I appreciate your optimism. In spite of what seems obviously a situation one spark away from total upheaval, I also know that if this does blow up, it will be more on my face than either yours or Mr. Cooper's. So, I don't mean to sound unappreciative, but maybe you should keep your useless rays of sunshine inside their absurd little box. We need to focus on the reality going on around us."

"Yes, sir."

Hunter Cooper suddenly became very animated and took a step forward and gestured his arms as if he were about to sing a show tune.

"Hey! Why doesn't Harvey-baby attempt to make contact with our ebony spy again to set up a meet with Morton Richardson? The man is...was...a friend of mine, and maybe if we got him here, one on one, he'd see the reasonable path to take in regards to help relieving the unrest of the area. We could talk some sanity back into the man's mind."

Sanderborn shook his head silently and looked like an audio-animatronic doll on the Walt Disney ride "It's a Small World."

"Ah, Mr. Cooper, I've already tried that, repeatedly. And each time the only reply I get from Richardson is, 'N-U-T-S.'"

"Nuts?"

"It's a historical reference, I guess."

"Well, we still could have Harvey-baby go and try to convince our inside girl to attempt to derail the actions of the insurrection.

"No, sir, I cannot do that."

"Really? And why not, Harvey?"

"Well, sir, the last attempt to make contact with her did not go well. Not only did the others in the diner identify me as one of the enemy, but Shaniqua attacked me. I'm afraid she's gone over to the dark side. Such an effort would be a fool's errand."

"That doesn't mean he shouldn't *try*, does it, Mr. Sanderborn-baby."

"It wouldn't do any good, you ridiculous clown! It most definitely would not do any good. I should stay here and organize the event to make sure that it goes off without a hitch. That's the best course of action, you twit!"

Sanderborn took a step to get closer to Hunter and Harvey. He actually appeared to want to run them down, forcefully.

"Let me clarify something I just said to the both of you. If this all goes well, we all will reap the benefits. But if this goes badly, I will be looking hard for some healthy scapegoats to heap the ball of bodily waste upon, and you two are looking perfect for the parts. As a matter of fact, to me, you both have horns, a beard, four cloven hooves, and sound like you are making a 'baa, baa' with all this bickering. I don't need excuses, apologies, or bullshit optimism. I need the two of you to be motivated to make this whole fucking endeavor succeed, no matter what.

"For now, the press is totally in the dark about what's taking place here, and we need to keep it that way. You two should keep prepping for the big day, including making sure that our guests continue to be happy and content. I'll work on ensuring that those rabble-rousers are kept far away from us. All we've got to do is keep everything glued together until that woman can make her grand entrance and get the show rolling. Got it?"

"Yes, sir."

"Of course, Mr. Sanderborn-baby. But I also want to offer my services for helping you pick out the perfect outfit for the big day. I'm thinking of putting you in a seersucker suit just like the one that Atticus Finch was wearing at the end of the movie *To Kill a Mockingbird*. You need to look like you're keeping your cool in the middle of a tempestuous event, just like he did. And to top it all off, you need a lovely Panama hat in the colonial style that he wore with the outfit. Remember, 'clothes makes the man.'"

"For the love of Pete! Could you two leave immediately? I need time to collect my thoughts and make some private phone calls. And when it's time to meet up again, don't call me, I'll call you."

That Ship Has Sailed, Captain Edward Smith!

The morning of the big day dawned as a lovely Indiana day. Buchanan Sanderborn had been "given" a copy of the book *Hoosier Poet* by James Whitcomb Riley from the Vincennes University's rare book collection, and he had enjoyed his nightly readings of the man's sentimental poems. The book now lay on his bedside table, and as the billionaire opened his curtains and looked out at the perfect daybreak outside, he remembered the multiple references the poet had made about such ideal days in the Hoosier State, and he thought how exquisite such a backdrop would be for the first meeting with the aliens. He inhaled deeply to acknowledge that his dream was going to come true as the idyllic sunrise, the blue sky, and the sounds of a world waking up proved that.

Despite his initial outraged protests, he had acquiesced to the ridiculous pleas of Hunter Cooper to wear the tailored seersucker suit and the Panama hat, and after donning them, he looked at his reflection in the large mirror in front of him. He had to admit that that little poofter had nailed the outfit. It really was perfect for such an important occasion as this.

This thought stopped him in his tracks. With this important day so heavily on his mind, he'd had a restless night of sleep, and now, as he prepared to leave the relatively quiet room and enter the hustle-bustle of the goings-on at the Kum Back Inn, where his staff continued to scurry here and there to pull off one of the most important events ever, he took a moment to acknowledge that he was actually as giddy as he'd ever been. His present mood even surpassed the happiness he'd felt at the unveiling of the Edificio de Erik Weisz.

He loved his life, but he had to be honest and say that true happiness was harder and harder to come by, as of late. Like an adrenaline junkie who can no longer get enough excitement from anything risky or life-threatening, a man with Sanderborn's bank accounts and clout felt like the bar to true contentment had been raised so high by his normal undertakings that the so sought-after emotion was almost impossible to attain anymore. This new version of Stonehenge, a rebuilt Vincennes, and the one-in-a-lifetime chance to meet space aliens – well, that went way over any ridiculously high-set bar very, very easily. Because of that, Buchanan Sanderborn felt very much alive today.

Outside the motel room was the pandemonium he'd expected. Waves of people were busy escorting dignitaries staying at the motel to the Stonehenge site, security was vetting the situation and keeping order, and Harvey and Hunter Cooper were busy barking commands to their underlings. Part the pre-show preparations to a Broadway production, part the lead-up to the big Super Bowl football game, and part the frantically precise buildup of a military invasion, the scene was electrifying, and Sanderborn, once he nodded his good morning greetings to Harvey and Hunter, made his way to the parking lot with some pep in his step.

He found Jerry Moniz standing beside a black stretch limousine that Sanderborn did not recognize.

"Morning, Jerry."

"What a good morning it is, too, boss."

"Is this a new limo?"

"Yes and no. It's the Lincoln Continental SS-100-X that Nixon used while in the White House. I had a buddy who owed me a *big* favor, and...ta-da! Here it is."

"Is it armored?"

"Yep, boss, just in case."

"Huh, hopefully we won't need that. Hey, you look different too, Jerry."

"Yeah, I'm wearing a flak jacket, just in case."

"Harumph. I wasn't offered one."

"Mr. Cooper said that kevlar and seersucker conflict, fashion-wise, sir."

"Well, I suppose so. I just think that lead and skin conflict a little more."

"Ha! I think you'll be as snug as a bug in a rug in this limo, boss."

As they drove toward Stonehenge, Sanderborn noticed that they were going a new route. He strained to get a better look at something that would cement his bearings.

"Why are you going this way, Jerry?"

"Those upstart rebels. They've been active and have caused some damage to the other routes to the site, boss. Your defenses have bent, but they haven't broken. I just thought that we should err on the side of caution and take the safest way."

"Good idea. Are you excited by the possibilities of today, Jerry?"

"Incredibly, boss. I truly think that all our lives are going to be forever changed by what happens here today. My taxis and limos are going to be busy as bees with all of the transporting of the dignitaries, and it's my deepest hope that, when the aliens do land, they'll want to ride in style, too. After today, I'm sure as shit that none of us is gonna be the same, I can tell you that."

"Well said, Jerry, well said."

The scene at the new Stonehenge defied even Sanderborn's greatest expectations. The grounds were beautiful and perfectly landscaped, and the row after row of folding chairs set up in symmetrical sections around the stone circle were already filled with the recognizable world leaders and their entourages, their translators, and their security forces. Other people of great importance were also in the chairs, and Sanderborn noticed some familiar faces in the vast group and some who were new to him. It was a sea of people who had extensive wealth intermixed with the most powerful men on earth – all in one area. Everyone seemed to be very excited and happy, as was the constant babble of their conversations.

At the four corners of the vast area that comprised the now-connected Stonehenge circle and the George Roger Clark Monument were four concert stages with performers on them. Bruce Springsteen played on a stage in the northeast for a younger audience. Meanwhile, on the northwest stage, Arthur Fiedler and the Boston Pops performed a concert of the familiar classical numbers. To the south, Johnny Cash strummed his top country hits on one stage, while on the other platform Miles Davis blew his iconic trumpet and produced some groovy jazz. Hunter Cooper had been right in suggesting live entertainment, and Sanderborn was now glad that he had pulled the necessary strings to get these classy acts here. The sound of the music and the appreciative audience gave the gathering a feel of a concert or a festival.

Sanderborn looked around, supremely satisfied, and he took a deep breath of air into his lungs. There were the smells of a fresh morning, of cigarette smoke mixed with some essence of marijuana, and of a sophisticated mixture of expensive perfumes and colognes...and burning rubber. This last scent gave Sanderborn some panicky feelings, and he looked around for someone to ask about it. Harvey and Hunter had just arrived, and they sidled up to their boss with apprehensive expressions on their faces.

"What is that smell?"

"The locals have set piles of tires afire around the town, sir."

"Yes, they've certainly stunk up the joint, if I do say so, Mr. Sanderborn-baby."

"Are we going to be able to pull this off without incident, gentlemen?"

The concern in Sanderborn's voice was palpable. Harvey knew enough not to sugarcoat the answer. His boss needed to know the truth.

"Your security forces have them contained at the moment, sir. The mob is literally nothing but a group of people who are no match for the professionally trained soldiers you hired. Imagine angry townsfolk with pitchforks and torches running into a unit from the Special Forces. They're trying to find the soft spots in our defenses to make it in here, but they've been turned away each time. Unless something changes, I really don't foresee them becoming much of a major disturbance to this event."

"I concur, Mr. Sanderborn-baby. They're being held in place. I don't think they have either the fortitude or the desire to incur enough violence to make a successful uninvited appearance. I think that they'll just be watching from the sidelines. Too bad...so sad."

"Thank god. Let's make our way to the grandstand. I need to address this crowd right away, so send word to the performers that I need them to stop after their last number so people can hear me. Let's get this show on the road!"

Once they had found their seats, which were in front of all the local, state, and national leaders – including Mayor Gandy, Governor Otis Bowen, Secretary of State Henry Kissinger, Vice-President Ted Kennedy, and the President of the United States – the music coming from the four stages ceased. In the ensuing void of silence, the immense murmurs of the gathered multitude replaced those notes with a sound that was somewhere between expectant whispers and an agitated buzz.

Buchanan Sanderborn stood up and took a step toward the vintage Ear Trumpet Labs Myrtle microphone on the tall stand, and he spoke into it. Upon hearing the volume and pitch of his voice uttering the first sounds and words as they bounced off the cold granite of Stonehenge and the polished marble of the nearby George Rogers Clark Monument off in the distance, he adjusted the timbre.

"Hello, gathered guests. We are here today in Vincennes, Indiana, to celebrate a truly momentous occasion. Not only are we going to turn this humble little city into a universally acclaimed center of culture and commerce, we have the unique opportunity to be the first to meet an alien species. We don't know when they're going to make their entrance *exactly*, so we might all have to be patient and just enjoy the moment. In that regard, the fabulous entertainers will continue to serenade you from the stages in the corners. And for food, we have none other than the world famous James Beard, Julia Childs, Ettore Boiardi – better known as Chef Boyardee – and the king of hamburgers, Dave Thomas, to provide us with their scrumptious dishes. We have something for everyone. So sit back and enjoy the sights and sounds of this momentous event. My friends, we're going to make history today."

The applause was sustained and heartfelt. Sanderborn's short speech had apparently soothed any concerns and anxieties of the large crowd and had perfectly set the stage for the ultimate arrival of the aliens. He was about to turn around and return to his seat to confer with Harvey and Hunter when he suddenly spied the woman walking directly toward him through the main aisle. His frozen gaze seemed to signal the crowd that someone of great importance was approaching, and they strained to see who it was.

Eve Richardson's hair looked even more tangled than before and her clothes were stained and ripped. Yet there was something noble about the woman, something regal and powerful, and the hushed people watching her entry were mystified with her presence.

As she made her way slowly to the end of the platform, Sanderborn motioned for her to come up to the microphone to speak. Instead, she turned toward the crowd and, in a voice that seemed magically enhanced and projected, addressed the massive gathering. They all could hear her.

"I am Haggur. The Mkultrans will be here soon."

Almost on cue, a bolt of light blazed down upon Stone-henge and created a pink cloud of smoke with swirling symbols in it. The massive crowd gasped and swelled in disbelief at the display, many of them craning their necks to look up into the heavens from where the ray of light had originated.

"The Mkultrans are ready to come down. You must pre-pare yourselves for this meeting."

Unfortunately, this was the exact moment when the pro-verbial shit hit the fan and the sounds of incoming cannon shells and their subsequent explosions rocked the ground under everyone's feet. Chaos suddenly reigned supreme. The audience either rose to take flight or take up arms against their perceived aggressors. Those world leaders who were on edge for being so close to their natural enemies assumed that the whole event was nothing but a trap set for them by their foes, and since no metal detectors had been put into place, they all began pulling out their pistols and rifles to fight off what they thought was an inevitable assassination attempt. What had just been a scene of serenity, pacifism and unity immediately dissolved into one of screaming, up-heaval, and sporadic gunfire.

When Sanderborn then saw the advancement of some American tanks coming toward them all, he twirled quickly and hissed at Harvey and Hunter. "I thought you said that the locals were *unarmed*?"

Hunter Cooper took a timid step forward and said softly, "Well, there were rumors that they had reached out to the National Guard to get reinforcements, Mr. Sanderborn-baby. But I didn't think those held any sand. My bad."

"That's outrageous! I begged the US Army to come to town and help out with everything, and I could not get them on my side. How did those people do it? Harvey? Harvey? Do you have any ideas?"

Alas, Harvey Ferguson was unable to answer at the moment. After those initial explosions, he had looked up and seen Shaniqua rushing at him with a golf club in her hands. If it hadn't been for some pretty good reflexes, Harvey would have had a crushed skull and Morgen would've been imprisoned inside of a vintage Ted Ray 3 Tone Brassie Wood driver.

He'd moved in time to avoid the next swing as well, and he grabbed his metal folding chair as a shield and pressed forward to try to hit Shaniqua in the chest and head with it. Pythia had used the upheaval as a distraction for Shaniqua to sneak up on Harvey, and he now sought to regain the advantage with his own attempt to knock her out and imprison her in the chair.

Sanderborn surveyed the riot that had broken out in front of him. The international delegations had converged to take up arms against one another. The Israelis were fighting Palestinians, the Americans were duking it out with the Russians, the North Koreans were brawling with South Koreans, the African leaders were in a melee against one another, the Iraqis and the Iranians were at each other's throats. When he saw Morton Richardson leading the forces of the Vincennes locals into the midst of the assembled audience, Sanderborn let out a sob of sadness at the sight of the unadulterated violence and at the fact that his vision of a better future was now being erased by it all.

"Behold, you pathetic humans, the Mkultrans are here," Haggur's voice, coming out of Eve Richardson's body, bellowed with an unnatural loudness. Her words cut like a scalpel through the screaming and the mayhem, immediately stopping all of the violence and silencing the entire area. Once again, everyone present looked up to see what the woman was staring at up in the sky.

The fleet of Mkultran ships appeared first like a massive flock of starlings (*Sturnus vulgaris*) in the Indiana sky, but as they came closer and closer, they began to resemble drops of mercury falling from a toxic rainstorm. As these giant silver airborne obelisks lowered themselves to land, picking the open spaces available to them, Sanderborn tried to count just how many alien ships were actually landing. When he reached sixty, he knelt on the front edge of the stage and harshly attempted to get Haggur's attention.

"Psst. Psst. Just how *many* of the Mkultrans are coming?"

"Your mind is limited, little man. You cannot truly conceive what you are experiencing right now. Just remain silent and take it all in."

When all of the silver spaceships were firmly on the ground and their engines were shutting down, an amplified message came out from all of them simultaneously. "EARTHLINGS, WE ARE VERY, VERY EXCITED TO MEET YOU!"

The giant crowd was now literally surrounded by a wall of the silver alien ships, far too many to count, and everyone was staring in befuddlement at what they were witnessing. The violent undertakings that they had been engaged in just moments before had instantly stopped, and they all waited to see what miraculous event was going to happen next.

Doors on all of the spacecraft opened and walkways spread to the ground. These ramps were suddenly filled with Mkultrans as they disembarked from their spacecraft and entered the Stonehenge site. From the crowd's first glimpse it appeared as if the aliens looked pretty much like normal people, except that they all wore tan coveralls and had some kind of octopus atop their heads. They walked wordlessly and their ranks soon surrounded the collection of world leaders, economic high-rollers, entertainers, Vincennes rebels, and National Guard soldiers.

When the last alien had gotten off a ship, the utter silence of the moment was chilling. The earthlings stared at the throngs of Mkultrans, and the Mkultrans stared back at the gathered earthlings. Haggur broke the uneasy silence.

"Ah, Mkultrans, I've waited an *awfully* long time to see you all again. What took you so long?"

Everything then changed in an instant.

That is not an understatement. Quite literally, the next thing to happen took place in the blink of an eye and was over just like *that,* and nothing was ever the same again.

The Milbrookians atop the Mkultrans disengaged themselves from their perches and skittered faster than could be believed to the nearest humans. While the lifeless Gottliebians then all slumped to the ground like marionettes with their strings cut, the mass of shocked earthlings had no chance to avoid having the octopus-like creatures take their place on the top of their skulls. Like particles in a wave, the Milbrookians swept over the crowd and covered every one of the earthlings.

The painful boring of their talons into the earthlings' skulls took only a second or two, and then every single person in attendance there in Vincennes had a new alien headpiece in place. After what seemed like half a minute, the only people in the massive crowd who were not wearing a Milbrookian were Harvey, Shaniqua, Eve Richardson, and Hunter Cooper.

When the last scream from the quick alien attachments had ended, there was a new soundless serenity that hugged the ground of the site like a morning fog. Shaniqua, who had dropped the golf club, and Harvey, who'd shed the folding chair, both slid closer to Eve Richardson. Shaniqua spoke first.

"Haggur, is that you?"

"Yes, my child Pythia. It is I."

"How is this possible? We saw you die. We saw to your final wishes."

"Ah-ha-ha, you've been a pawn in a much bigger plot. You and Morgen, you've been nothing but a means to an end."

Shaniqua turned on Harvey.

"How could you not tell me that Haggur was back?"

"I tried, but things went sideways. After that, I didn't have time to try again," Harvey responded sheepishly.

Hunter Cooper then strode to the front of the platform and took position behind the microphone. He removed his jaunty French beret to reveal the Milbrookian already attached to his head. He spoke into the mike.

"Welcome, my brothers and sisters. Ever since this rather ridiculous earthling I'm currently riding on pushed that artichoke button and sent out a secret beacon for me to come to this planet to prepare the way for your invasion…er, visit…I've had to endure a lot waiting for you all to arrive. But I am so glad that you're all here now. Welcome to our new home."

An ear-splitting roar came up from the mass of individuals – now united earthlings and Milbrookians – who were standing there facing him. He heard the pure elation and joy in their voices and he waited patiently for their happy outburst to die down.

Next, Haggur's voice boomed out magically from Eve Richardson's mouth.

"But our deal is still good, right? You're gonna get me off this godforsaken planet and take me to a superior place, aren't you?"

When Hunter replied to Haggur, he sounded just like Truman Capote telling his life story as a guest on the David Susskind Show. He closed his eyes and moved his hands in random orbits.

"Well, we're not an inherently deceptive species, Haggur-baby, but let's just say that our plans have changed in the last few thousand of your Earth years. Today is the first of many such transferrals planned for our people with yours. All of these world leaders and economic bigwigs who are under our control now are going to go back to their homelands and make their own Stonehenge monuments to create more beacons to get the rest of our species here for their new beginning. The total population of Milbrookians and of earthlings alike is surprisingly close in overall numbers, so we'll all be finally able to ditch those pathetic Gottliebians and hop onto your species. We'll all feel like the earthling I heard recently who said, 'Hey, man. We've got ourselves a new ride.'

"As for you and your cohorts, Haggur-baby, you did just as you promised you would in that long-ago meeting between you and our special agent in the woods outside the original Stonehenge. By inciting the conflicts between your underlings and inserting your soul into that dagger, you three have been circling this globe to psychically find the perfect location for the recreation of the first Stonehenge beacon and to make the ideal preparation for this life-changing event to take place. We owe you a great deal. But we also see what dangers you three pose to our plan. People with your skills are *dangerous* to everything we want to accomplish here. So, you will be leaving this planet, but not in the way you might have imagined."

"Wait!" Harvey Ferguson implored. "Pythia and I were not part of any plan. Why don't you leave us two out of it? We could be your allies. We aren't dangerous, we're just kinda silly."

"Attempting to save your skin even at the last moment, huh? Sorry, lamb chop, a little too late for that. As my ol' auntie Clover Cooper used to say, 'Well, you've made your own bed and now you have to lie in it.'"

Three Milbrookian-earthlings standing near Hunter grabbed Eve Richardson, Shaniqua Bishop, and Harvey Ferguson and roughly held them in place. As someone in the mob uttered the unmistakable words of the soul-transference spell, three others carrying the bizarre, sitting stuffed fox, a taxidermied common loon (*Gavia immer*), and an extremely rare mounting of a dodo bird (*Raphus cucullatus*), all from Hunter Cooper's house, came menacingly toward the restrained three.

The wooden base of the dodo bird was then thumped against Eve Richardson's head, knocking her out. The same thing happened to Shaniqua Bishop as she was hit with the base of the loon. Both women were lowered to the ground and a free Milbrookian scrambled atop them and burrowed its talons into their heads.

The fox was positioned in front of Harvey's face. He yelled out, "Stop! Let's talk about this. Now that you've gotten rid of the other two, maybe we could negotiate something. I could help you guys. I could definitely be an asset!"

Hunter Cooper leaned forward as if he were listening to something far off in the distance. The crowd grew even more silent than they had been.

"Oh, your species certainly isn't lacking in ego, that's for sure. But that's been your undoing, hasn't it? You've been so cocksure...well, except for ol' Morty-baby over there, he was a bit cock-unsure...but that feeble belief that you're all that and a bag of potato chips was both the beginning and the end of your kind. Ta-ta."

"Come on, maybe you need some confident guidance right now. I mean, what is going to happen now? What's your next move? Who's going to help you figure that out?"

"Certainly not *you*! Don't you see that it was your arrogance that got you into this place?

Well, the bottom line is this, earthling – you simpletons lost sight of everything as you willingly and enthusiastically handed control over to your overinflated egos. Then, you inserted a gigantic stick of TNT up your anuses, let its fuse be lit by powerful influences from outside your own galaxy, and everything ended up blowing up in your faces. It's been nice to meet you, but it's time to exit stage left."

The wooden base of the fox was viciously bashed into Harvey Ferguson's forehead, and his lifeless body slumped down onto the ground. A free Milbrookian skittered over and assumed it place on the top of the unconscious man's head.

Th-Th-Th-Th-That's All, Porky Pig!

Well, this is certainly not the way I thought things were going to end up.

The preposterousness of a psychic ever uttering a statement like this isn't lost on me, and there certainly is not enough balm in the world that we left nor the ones that we're traveling past to soothe the wounds created by this admission. But the facts are the facts, and one must submit to eating crow (*Corvus brachyrhynchos*) whenever forced to do so.

The taxidermied fox in which I'm trapped in for eternity has two glass orbs for eyes, and these allow me to peer out at our surroundings. Of course, due to their shape and material, a distorted, convex world full of inverted details has been created for me to look out upon, much like the vision of a walleye (*Sander vitreus*). But at least I can see out.

Well, that's bittersweet, I guess. I can watch what's happening out there, but I'm impotent to effect any change. If seeing is believing, this might be a time when I wish I could not see...just to prolong my disbelief at my current status.

Cruelly, those little fuckers, the Milbrookians, positioned the three stuffed vessels that contain Pythia, Haggur, and me in the seats of the captain, first mate, and second mate of a Mkultran ship before they sent our craft off into the hallows of space. Because of this, I'm fairly certain that, like me, my two cohorts can also gaze out of their stuffed-animal glass eyes, but we are all powerless to communicate with one another or to change our situation. We're all facing the cockpit's viewing screen showing the emptiness of the cosmos in front of us and reminding us constantly how unlikely it is that our freedom will ever be returned to us. Unless a random asteroid or an alien boarding party from some space pirates ever encounter us, we're assured of our unending prison sentence for the rest of time.

Just in case you were wondering, the Milbrookians put Haggur in the captain's chair. I'm assuming that was their way of pointing out that this whole fucking shitshow was hers to own. Pythia and I were only incidentals to the bigger plan, so we were given positions of a lower rank. The curve of my vision allows me to see the others, and sometimes when the light is just right, I can spy our reflection in the viewing screen in front of us. We look ridiculous – a dodo bird in the middle chair with a common loon on one side and the asininely posed fox that's my cell on the other, all staring blankly and unendingly at the screen in front of us like comatose viewers at a drive-in movie.

There's been nothing to do but think about how we all got here. Just when I was extracted from my body and imprisoned in this vessel, there was a moment of universal clarity that gave me all of the necessary clues to figure out why things went down the way they did. The truth of this matter is something that's tough to digest, but it's something that I'll have to keep on consuming repeatedly until the end of time. It's nothing I'm looking forward to, actually.

Obviously, it all starts and ends with the Milbrookians. They are certainly a far more patient and cunning species than anyone gave them credit for, and they're the ones who have actually been pulling everyone's strings. I'm still in complete awe of how they played everyone around them so well, and for so long. They may have seemed like the passive entities in the merger that created the Mkultrans all those eons ago, but somewhere along the line – perhaps even at that instant – they not only secretly started to drive the whole damn bus, but they took each egotistical entity that they encountered on a crazy ride with only the destination of their own choosing in mind.

Nope, no way around it, those Milbrookians are nothing but eight-legged puppet-masters.

From all of what I can see now, the real bosses of the Mkultran species have always been none other than those meek octopus-looking creatures atop their heads. Using Pythia's explanation to Shaniqua of the relationships between psychic mediums and their possessed vessels, I'd have to say that the Milbrookians have been the chief pilot during the whole supposedly symbiotic affair. They've been somehow steering the Gottliebians in the direction they've wanted right from the git-go, and inexplicably, they've been able to do so without ever alerting their hosts to this fact. The Gottliebians actually believed that they had free will, but this has been absolutely untrue – the Milbrookians have been the ones running the show.

And what's worse, they've known, from day one, that their symbiotic relationship with the Gottliebians was doomed to fail. Somehow they figured out that their consuming all of the emotional energy of their hosts was ultimately going to lead to a debilitating level of apathy within the composite creature, and so they've been on a search for alternative food sources since the very beginning. They actually used Dr. BZit's findings to convince the Gottliebians that their union was essential for their survival, all the while knowing full well that they themselves could survive almost indefinitely without their hosts. That was a pretty cheeky usage of misinformation to ensure that no one left anybody until they were ready to cut ties.

Nothing inspires complete loyalty and unconditional love like codependency, am I right?

The Milbrookian quest for an alternative food source took a long time. When they finally encountered the earthlings during the Mkultran scientific visit, they realized that they had found exactly what they were looking for in the bipedal creatures of that planet. But like a vintner who comes across a vineyard that's too small, and with grapes that aren't quite ripe, they decided the primitive people of Earth needed some time to ferment and grow in population to serve the role the Milbrookians had set for them to fulfill.

Then they met Haggur. She gave them a path to ensure that things went their way, and they immediately came up with a plan to use her like some kind of utensil at a fine meal. That Milbrookian-led secret agent appealed to her overwhelming desire to get away from the simpletons around her and easily recruited her into his service. In that meeting in the holy woods, Haggur was given both the instructions on how to rebuild the beacon when it was finally time for the Milbrookians to come back to Earth, as well as an emergency signal to set off beforehand to alert the Milbrookian special operations agent that it was clear for them to come to the planet and set up things properly for the following "invasion" of their species.

She was also instructed to pick out two mentees who could be pitted against one another, once she feigned her own death and deposited her spirit into the ceremonial dagger, to create a psychic storm that would rage over the planet like the Great Red Spot of Jupiter. The maelstrom of competition for the dagger between Pythia and me cloaked and changed the paranormal environment of the landscape long enough that a proper site for the invasion could be discovered. And that site, as it turned out, was Vincennes, Indiana.

I would never say this to her – even if I could – but I feel really badly for Haggur. All she desperately wanted was to go somewhere better than Earth, and she let that desire blind her to what the Milbrookians were actually doing. This powerful witch, a wise soothsayer and a timelessly sage entity, was bamboozled like some kind of a wet-behind-the-ears rookie, and it cannot feel too good for her to now know that she sacrificed thousands of years inside a knife to only end up trapped inside a stuffed dodo bird for the rest of eternity. I feel bad for my situation, but I have a deep pang of pity for hers.

Anyway, the Milbrookians guided those Mkultran scientists home and made sure that the information about Earth got buried and forgotten, but not, of course, by them. Each move after that was only another line in their script, with the final act being them getting back to Earth and shedding the useless Gottliebians for the cornucopia of the ripe, overly emotional, modern earthlings awaiting them.

Their pitting the Gherrardians against the Mooghaag-led rebellion of the uncoupled Gottliebians was pure art. Even the American CIA could learn some lessons from the Milbrookians. Their management of the minutiae required to manipulate two different populations into war-lusting frenzies, their use of the perfectly precise timing required to pull off their plan without getting their hands (talons) dirty, and their patience to allow everything to evolve as it needed to were a symposium in how a successful coup should be pulled off. A true piece of intelligence artwork.

The placement of the singular Milbrookian agent on Earth at the very place that Pythia and I were getting ready to confront one another again was another stroke of genius. When that little Truman Capote doppelganger set off the emergency signal on the prescribed date and alerted the Milbrookian special operations that an advance force was needed in Vincennes to prepare the way for the bigger invasion, they sent their best agent. They somehow knew that a local would be useful and, in this case, that turned out to be Hunter Cooper, and in him they had the perfect host to start pulling the strings from behind the scenes. The result was like spraying gasoline on the fires that were already beginning to ignite.

I must admit that, although my current status leaves a lot to be desired, I'm grateful that I'm not around to see what's currently happening back on Earth. It doesn't take a rocket scientist to understand that the planet's leaders and wealthiest individuals are now all being controlled by the Milbrookians atop their heads. It's my guess that they've all headed home, riled up their populations for an upcoming war, and set out to build more beacons in the most populous locations to make sure that all the future Mkultrans coming to the planet in the transport ships sent back to Mkultra and the far reaches of space will have a ready roadmap to the new feeding trough. And when those ships get there, the Milbrookian passengers will find a host of overly emotional humans at their disposal. With such a healthy selection to choose from, it won't be long before the slogan for Earth will become "Billions and billions of Milbrookians served."

Before I sign off and contemplate nothing important for eternity, let me state one thing that strikes me as ironic. For all intents and purposes, the Milbrookians have opted to go from a symbiotic organism to becoming a parasitic one. Maybe it will develop over time, but humans and Milbrookians don't have the same synchronized natures as the Mkultran complex organism had. The emotions of the earthlings will be there for the taking by the Milbrookians, but there's likely nothing that the humans are going to get in return that's usable. In fact, it's likely that they'll be as hungry and thirsty as they were before the union, but now all of their thoughts and actions and futures will be controlled by the alien parasites sitting on top of their heads.

This whole story turned out to be a tale of two species. The Milbrookians – now that they have successfully demonstrated that they can jump between hosts without any negative consequences – will exploit the human race until they use them up and decide to leave to go to the next food source. In essence, they can write their own ticket to being happy and well-fed wherever they go. For the humans, however, they've been sentenced at the very same time to nothing but a life of eternal slavery.

That's it. This story is over. Well, my part in it is, I guess.

I am left with such a feeling of profound sadness from having this collection of raw observations and conclusions about the follies of the Universe ending up on such a futile *cul de sac* of a lifeless spacecraft drifting aimlessly through-out the cold and dark regions of space, but I have remem-bered a little trick I picked up over the millennia of possess-ing people. Even though it appears as if the relationship ends as soon as I transfer my soul into a new vessel, there seems to be an unbreakable psychic connection between my hosts and me that exists after our time together ends. No matter how far away I am from them, I can send messages to them and ask for updates about them and their lives. I like to call them psychic postcards. In a lifetime of endless squatting in-side of strangers' bodies, it is the closest I've come to getting any closure.

There's a troubled, half-crazy Vietnam War veteran and budding science-fiction author chap that I once inhabited, and I'm sending him this whole narrative tale wrapped up with a little bow. I figure that if there's anyone left on Earth who isn't paired up with a Milbrookian yet, this guy is prob-ably it. He's alone and safe in his house, writing stories non-stop, so he's the perfect recipient of the lessons that have come from this whole situation. He'll know just what to do with it all. Perhaps it's too late for any kind of real resistance, but I'm thinking that having more people read about how things went down will make them more aware of how to stop it from continuing to happen.

Wishful thinking, I know.

Well, there's nothing more for me to do now. I should re-ally sign off by saying something profound. Hmm... it's been nice knowing you.

The End

About the Author

The facts about Sam Sumac are hazy, at best. Any details we have about his life come from his own handwritten autobiographical sketch, "Please, Don't Forget to Pay the Debt." According to it, he was born in Buffalo, New York, exactly ten months after V-J Day, to an unwed Polish woman by the name of Ewa. While he never knew his father's identity, Sam describes his childhood as a happy one spent with his mother in a home in North Buffalo. He claims to have attended various local elementary, junior high, and high schools throughout his youth before enrolling in the State University College of Education at Buffalo for one year, where he majored in physics. He dropped out to enlist in the United States Army.

Sam contends he was conscripted as a tunnel rat during the Vietnam War due to being just over five feet in height. While those early days of his military training brought him some moments of happiness, his deployment to the combat of the war only damaged him. Although unsubstantiated, Sam alleges that he was a member of one of many of the companies of subterranean soldiers in the Củ Chi district who were given a cocktail of hallucinogenic drugs before heading into the tunnels to do battle with their North Vietnamese enemies. He believes that these induced narcotic highs led him to have many out-of-body experiences, which he repeatedly calls "his enlightenments" in his writings.

Sam attributed the combination of the violence of the war and these unauthorized military experiments as cause for his nervous breakdown. According to him, the stress of the tunnel warfare and the impact from the unstable narcotics caused him to be briefly institutionalized in a military psych ward in Phoenixville, Pennsylvania. Prone to fantastical hallucinations during this time – most involving alien invasions, time travel, the apocalypse, the oil crisis, psychic mediums, the Middle East, and the gruesome punishments of many of the people he held responsible for his ordeals (especially a Bill Buchanan from Kenmore, Washington, allegedly a special operative with the CIA who Sam blamed for the administering of narcotics to Sam's unit) – he spouted a nonstop string of prophetic stories and sagas. He says his mental health gradually improved with care until, ultimately, he was well enough to be discharged from the Army.

When he returned to Buffalo, he found out his mother had passed away some time during his hospitalization. Devastated, he decided to settle in his former hometown. He rented a house in the same neighborhood of his childhood and began working as a salesman at a local shoe store. While this job might not seem too exciting to most, Sam reported he "had a thing for feet" and the work appealed to him deeply. During this time, while living alone and working full-time, his compulsion to write down the stories inside his head hit him. Sam spent every spare moment writing late every night and putting onto paper the bizarre delusions from his time in the tunnels and in the military mental hospital, and in the process, he created a series of science fiction stories.

He vividly describes not being able to contain the flow of creativity coming out of him. During these writing frenzies, he wrote without purpose or order. He merely transcribed all the imagery and characters as they came out. These manic periods never left him enough time to edit or to prepare a manuscript for publication before the next story needing to be penned demanded his attention. He aptly recounts how he felt like a faucet of stories which was unable to be shut off.

Then, one day, Sam Sumac disappeared. When his landlord went to check on him after not receiving his rent payment, there was no trace whatsoever left behind of the man. The police were called, but they quickly decided there was no evidence of foul play so no further official investigation was needed. However, it is still unclear – even at this point in time – what actually happened to Sam. He simply vanished.

Some would like to think he changed his identity and moved to another city to resume his writing in a new locale. Others have a darker interpretation. Regardless, whatever happened to him is just part of the mystery of Sam Sumac.

The world would have likely forgotten all about the man if it were not for several boxes belonging to him being discovered in a storage unit a year after his inexplicable disappearance. Due to the lack of an annual payment for the storage and the absence of any next of kin on his rental application paperwork, these unclaimed items were given to his ex-landlord, who, in turn, gave them to a fellow employee at the same shoe store where Sam had worked. When this individual opened the boxes and saw the chaotic state of their contents, he resealed them and put them in his garage, where they remained undisturbed for nearly twenty-five years.

Finally these boxes landed in the hands of a retired Episcopal priest who was asked to claim the possessions of his former parishioner who'd recently passed away. It was only then, when the boxes were re-opened, that the writings of Sam Sumac were once again exposed to this world.

Sort of.

These boxes were brimming with intermixed and disarrayed heaps of handwritten pages on different types of paper and were done with various writing implements. With no organization or order, the process of collating and transcribing them has been a maddeningly complicated and time-consuming endeavor.

Who Drew the Short Straw? was apparently written in the late 1970s or early 1980s, and this is the third attempt to get a Sam Sumac story into a completed format. *Piss & Vinegar* and *Ain't Nobody Here But Us Chickens* were the first two. It is hoped that, over time, more of his novels might eventually get reassembled and come out in print sometime in the future, but the Herculean effort needed to accomplish this makes the task an incredibly slow process.

So, sit back and savor these words from an unknown genius, Sam Sumac.

P. B. – February, 2015

Author Profile

The facts about Sam Sumac are hazy, at best. Many details of his life have not been corroborated. Supposedly, he was born in Buffalo, New York in 1946, where he lived with his mother until he joined the U.S. Army and fought in Vietnam as a tunnel rat. After the war, he suffered mental breakdowns, sold shoes, and wrote sci-fi novels, and then vanished without a trace. *Piss & Vinegar* and *Ain't Nobody Here But Us Chickens* were his first two transcribed novels. The Sam Sumac Association has been tasked with preserving this mysterious author's works for the future generations.

Website: www.samsumacass.com

Instagram: @samsumacass

Facebook: @samsumacass

Publisher Information

Rowanvale Books provides publishing services to independent authors, writers and poets all over the globe. We deliver a personal, honest and efficient service that allows authors to see their work published, while remaining in control of the process and retaining their creativity. By making publishing services available to authors in a cost-effective and ethical way, we at Rowanvale Books hope to ensure that the local, national and international community benefits from a steady stream of good quality literature.

For more information about us, our authors or our publications, please get in touch.

www.rowanvalebooks.com
info@rowanvalebooks.com

www.ingramcontent.com/pod-product-compliance
Lightning Source LLC
Chambersburg PA
CBHW030633020726
47493CB00006B/1685